# KATIE AND ROLAND ROBERTS
## AND
# The Warlock's Revenge

# LARRY L RHOTON

ISBN-13: 9781514299180
ISBN-10: 1514299186
Library of Congress Control Number: 2015909490
CreateSpace Independent Publishing Platform
North Charleston, South Carolina

# Dedication Page

I dedicate this book to my Lord and Savior, Jesus Christ.
May he protect us from the evils of this world.

\*\*\*

In appreciation to my friends, family, and wife Marsha,
who constantly inspires me to write.

# Preface

This is the second novel in a series of three. Within the pages of these novels, the reader accompanies Katie and Roland Roberts on a magical, but dangerous journey, into the ghostly-unknown world of the supernatural. Grounded in their beliefs that magic and the dark side of our world doesn't exist, they soon realize just how wrong they were.

In the belly of the earth, there is a place known as Terra Demorte, or the Land of the Dead, this is home for all types of evil, and the creatures in this place are cryptic, horrifying, and, oh, so wicked.

Trespassing in and out of our world, they rain down on the innocence people on the surface. They wreak havoc, death, and destruction, at will. They are the author of chaos and the reaper of death.

Battling these dark creatures is no easy task for Katie and Roland; their lives become filled with the realistic thoughts of witches, vampires, warlocks, assassins, and many other creatures that go bump in the dark, all which live in Terra Demorte.

\*\*\*

In the first novel, ***Katie and Roland Roberts and The Ghost of Sarah Wheeler***, the Roberts, a normal family, with no magical powers, find they must move to Johnston, South Carolina when Roland's job changes locations. Once the Roberts purchases their home, they find they are not the only inhabitants living in the old 1890's house.

For Katie and Roland Roberts, moving into a haunted house was exciting...at first. Upon encountering the ghost of a small girl, the couple immediately fell in love with the harmless, beautiful apparition. However, what began as a harmless encounter quickly turns dangerous when a bumbling old witch, by the name of Wisteria, befriends the couple. She tells them that Sarah's ghost isn't the only spirit in their house.

With a vicious warlock seeking Sarah's spirit to complete an ancient and evil ritual, Katie and Roland must endure hell to fight for Sarah's spirit and their own lives.

As the story unfolds, a devious spirit, by the name of Notor, is hiding in the Roberts' house. A lowly spy, for two vicious warlocks, Notor keeps his masters, Creed and Olin informed of the movements of Wisteria, Katie, and Roland. This, of course, is only second to his primary mission, which is to persuade Sarah, to come out of hiding and join the dark side. Thus far, he has been unable to convert the small girl. He realizes he will have to pay a terrible price for his failures. His master has sworn to sell him to the trolls.

Through a magical spell, the old witch soon discovers that Notor isn't alone in the old house, there are other spirits dwelling there, as well.

The warlocks Creed and Olin hire an assassin from Terra Demorte, to kill the good witch, Wisteria. She and the Roberts have interfered, once too many times, in their affairs. A fierce battle unfolds, the dark assassin fails, and the powerful witch kills the assassin. Before she beheads him, she offers him a deal: *work with us, or die.*

The assassin, out of pride and loyalty to the assassin clan, choose death. Knowing that his resurrection would be eminent once his body disintegrates and returns to the Land of the Dead. However, Morto, the assassin, hadn't anticipated the old witch keeping his medallion, and without his medallion, he could never return to the surface. A medallion is the one magical possession that all inhabitants of Terra Demorte have, the one thing that allows an evil being to pass between their world and the surface world. Without his medallion, one couldn't pass through the portal.

For the dark beings of Terra Demorte, it was more humiliating to lose ones medallion, than it was to be killed in a surface battle, as the body could be resurrected, but the medallion couldn't be replaced.

***

While Wisteria, Katie, and Roland prepare to fight Creed and Olin, another assassin comes to the surface to kill Wisteria and regain Motor's medallion. His name is Thor, a very proud and experience killer.

He, as well, underestimates the old witch and she allows her gold snake's head dagger to bite Thor. In minutes, the assassin would be dead, only she has the antidote. She offers him the same deal she offered Morto: *Work with us, or die.* The assassin, agreed to help the witch, Katie, and Roland. He is now a rogue assassin, and all of Terra Demorte, turn their backs on the traitor, Thor.

Thor stays on the surface and he, Wisteria, Katie, and Roland attempt to kill the two evil warlocks when they raid his mansion, but they failed. The two warlocks retaliates, but they, as well, fail to kill the warriors. The good witch Wisteria and her companions realize that time is of the essences and if they are to save Sarah, her nanny, and her father, they must act immediately.

In a last minute effort, Wisteria holds a dangerous triangular séance. Once started, it cannot be cancelled, and if it fails within the given allotted time, the spirits of Sarah, her nanny, and her father, will automatically, convert to the dark side and all will be lost forever.

Doubled crossing, lies, and deception infiltrates the characters as the séance fails. Are Sarah, her nanny, and her father lost to the dark side forever? Will the dark warlock, Creed get the spirits he needs to complete his ancient ritual to transform his spirit body into a body of flesh-and-blood-and the dark magic that comes with his return to life? Your questions are answered in the first novel, ***Katie and Roland Roberts and the Ghost of Sarah Wheeler.***

\*\*\*

In the second novel, ***Katie and Roland Roberts and the Warlock's Revenge,*** the story continues where the first novel ended.

Katie and Roland Roberts have made powerful enemies since saving the spirit of Sarah Wheeler. The warlock Creed, trapped between the spiritual and mortal worlds, continues his quest to attain a flesh-and-blood body—and the dark magic that comes with his return to life.

Joined in his quest by his brother Olin, a powerful warlock in his own right, Creed seeks a mysterious artifact known as the Secret of Life, but finds his every move countered by Katie, Roland, and their magical allies.

In anger and desperation, Olin and Creed gamble on a dangerous plan: abducting the Roberts' son Josh and hiding the boy in Terra Demorte—the Land of the Dead. If the other residents of the evil land discover their plan, the warlocks will be executed—along with the Roberts' bloodline.

Now the Roberts, the good witch Wisteria, and the dark assassin Thor find themselves in a race to rescue Josh before the boy's presence in Terra Demorte is discovered. To save his son, Roland will do anything—even make deals with the inhabitants of the Land of the Dead. Of course, such deals have a way of coming back to haunt a person.

The second in the Katie and Roland Roberts series, ***Katie and Roland Roberts and the Warlock's Revenge*** hurls the non-magical family into ever-greater supernatural peril. To retrieve their son, Katie and Roland will risk the wrath of the Land of the Dead's many clans.

They'll need every ally they can muster: the good witch Wisteria, the assassin Thor, and a shadowy figure in Terra Demorte itself—a figure with her own dark agenda.

\*\*\*

The third novel, **Katie and Roland Roberts and the Great Dark Witch**, will be completed in 2016. This novel will tie all three novels together and complete this series.

Although this doesn't end their adventures, Katie and Roland Roberts will continue to fight the dark magic of Terra Demorte, and save innocent people, from its evil wrath.

# One

## A Dark Night

Roland stared out of the dark alley; he was standing but kept his movements to a minimum, ensuring he made no noise. He placed his back against the rock wall, allowing the dark shadows to consume him. Somehow, in the middle of the night, the cold wall made him feel at ease, or at least a little safer. He knew why he was in such a ghostly, gloomy place, but he was at a loss as to what he should do next.

As he watched the entrance of the alley, all he could see were the two dimly lit streetlamps across the narrow cobblestone street and a two-story building. The fog, threatening in nature, consumed everything in its path, and although the tall streetlamps struggled to keep it at bay, they were losing an endless battle.

The building, dancing in and out of the menacing fog, looked to be packed with people. They were loud, very loud, laughing and making all kinds of happy noises, but tonight, there was no joy in Roland's life. There was just darkness and the unhappy thoughts of why he was there. If he strained his eyes, he could make out silhouettes through the large glass window that fronted the building. At times, he could hear parts of different conversations coming from the cheery people within.

*Men and women,* he thought, studying the building.

1

He pressed his back harder against the wall. It did take some of the pressure off his feet and legs, and he could feel the coolness of the rocks. It felt good. The night air wasn't moving, but there was a chill in the mist and fog that settled in around him. It slowly engulfed everything, and the things Roland could see far down the alley started disappearing as the fog crept slowly toward him. He pulled his cloak tighter around his face and arms.

"This is how Creed must see the world," he said softly, "always staring out from under his cloak." He slowly pushed his hands beneath the long black garment; he could feel the cold grips of the two nine-millimeter pistols tucked neatly under each arm. He knew they were there and if needed would answer his call and perform their task of delivering excruciating pain and death. Somehow, just touching the two death machines calmed his nerves and made the lump in his throat smaller.

Roland looked up into the blackness; there were no stars, no moon, just pitch black. *Nothing but a dark, empty hole*, he thought. It was scary to be in such a gloomy place, but then again the darkness would help conceal his presence, and at this time, he certainly didn't need to be seen. From where he stood, he could watch the building across the street and part of the alley behind the buildings where he stood. He stared intensely out of the alley, and then his eyes would wander down the alley in the back. From this vantage point, he felt no one could catch him off guard.

Roland's thoughts quickly evaporated. He snapped to attention. He'd heard something, a noise of some kind; it was different from the noise coming from the building across the street. This noise was…

*Yes*, he thought, *the noise is coming from down the street in front of the alley.* It sounded like someone walking on the cobblestones with wooden shoes. He strained to hear or see which way the intruder was coming.

"Whatever it is, it's in front of me!" he whispered to himself. He pushed his hands back under his cloak and slid down the wall into a crouching position. *Less to see!* he thought. He felt the cold metal of the guns and wrapped each hand around the grips. He sat with his back to the wall and waited.

Roland listened with anticipation. Whatever was making the noise was unquestionably coming down the street toward the busy tavern, or at least what resembled a tavern—he wasn't sure. He waited with the expectation that if it came to an altercation, he had to be ready. *There, something moved.* Were his eyes playing tricks on him? He closed them to clear his mind and quickly reopened them again, focusing on the objects across the street. It was strange, but the streetlamps began to move toward the approaching sound.

"No way that's happening!" Roland whispered. "This can't be real." The streetlamp was changing its position and bending toward the noise, as if wanting to light the path of the intruder. "There's no way that can be happening!" he repeated. He closed his eyes again, but only for a few moments before focusing them once more on the eerie streetlamp. He watched, and indeed the streetlamp was changing positions. It bent slightly to his left and then continued until its light disappeared past the edge of the alley where he sat.

Minutes later, a man came into view, walking casually down the street, heading toward the tavern. With each step he took, his shoe made a clacking noise. The lamps light was directly over him, lighting his path and adjusting itself with each step. The man didn't notice or care about the moving lamp, but suddenly, and for no reason known to Roland, he stopped his steady stride. He turned slightly, looking directly into the alley where Roland was crouching. The man stared for a few moments as if searching for something.

*Does he see me?* Roland thought. *Did I make some kind of noise?*

He watched the man carefully. His hands were gripping his pistols, he could feel his heart pumping faster, and could feel the sweat on his palms. *Please, God!* he thought. *Please let him continue on his way!*

The man readjusted his posture and walked once again toward the tavern. The noise was loud and becoming louder as the inhabitants of the building celebrated the evening. As the man approached the door of the tavern, he stopped and turned once more to face the alley. He was slow to turn, but all the time, his eyes never left the entrance of the black alley.

Once again, he stared into the darkness where Roland crouched. He leisurely lit a cigarette, and as he released the smoke from his lungs, it rose gently over his head. It circled his head and floated effortlessly, forming a halo before vanishing. Roland remained frozen; he peered from under his cloak, returning the stranger's stare. The walker took another draw from the cigarette and turned back toward the tavern; he started to enter the building but changed his mind and continued on his slow, casual walk down the cobblestone street.

The first streetlamp had bent to the right to provide light for the man but couldn't do so any longer. The second streetlamp bent left gently, toward the walker, and placed it's light directly over him while he slowly strolled past the tavern. The first light went back to its original position and stood erect, shining its light downward.

Roland watched the man make his way down the street until the building at the edge of the alley blocked his view. He sat for a few moments before standing up. He questioned what he had just witnessed. How could it be that the streetlamps bent to shine for people walking? What kind of strange place was this? He had never seen this before.

Once again, the thoughts running in Roland's head were interrupted. Although, from time to time, his mind would stray on the strange surroundings, he had to focus on where he was and how dangerous it was to be there. Now he listened closely to a different kind of noise. "I've got to stay alert!" he said softly, scolding himself. "Stay alert, Roland."

He listened for a moment, and this time the unexplained noise was in the alley behind him. *He must have seen me and is trying to slip around the back!* Roland thought as he turned slightly to watch the alley behind him. *If he is, he's making way too much noise!*

Roland stood frozen against the wall as he watched down the dimly lit alley. Suddenly he saw something, something moving, and when the object came into full view, he saw straight away, what was making the noise. It was a man; a rather large man dragging two sacks—or what appeared to be sacks—across the alley. There were no buildings on the other side of the alley, nothing but darkness and a small railing about

4

three feet high. There was a huge dark void beyond the railing, and no matter how hard the small lamps tried, their lights couldn't penetrate the darkness on that side of the alley.

Roland assumed that behind the blackness was rock, the same as he was leaning against, but he had no way of knowing how high or how deep into the darkness the rocks went. The man picked up the mysterious sacks and threw them over the railing, and lazily strolled back toward the building, puffing on a smoke. Roland watched the man until he disappeared out of sight. He heard a door open and then shut. Moments later, there were two soft thuds, as the bags that had been thrown over the rail hit the bottom of the pit.

Several minutes passed and Roland refocused his attention back to the cobblestone street, the tavern, and the odd streetlamps. When suddenly, as before, he heard the same noise coming from down the alley. He heard a door open and then slam, and once again, a large, loosely clothed man came into view. He watched as the man dragged two more sacks across the alley and, with one continuous motion, repeated his actions as before and hurled the bags over the small railing. He crossed the alley, and Roland heard the door open and sharply slam once more. He heard the bags make two soft thuds, the same as the ones before had done, and it occurred to him that the pit was deep, very deep. He whispered softly to himself, "That's a bloody deep hole. Very deep."

Roland's thoughts returned to the reason he was in such a gloomy place. He thought of his son. He knew Josh was somewhere in this strange place, but where? He turned toward the tavern once more. He was getting tired, but there was no time to sleep. He needed some kind of sign or signal, anything that would help him or give him some kind of clue as to where his son might be, but what? Maybe he would know when he saw it, but for now, he was staying put until he saw something or until someone saw him.

A loud growling sound came forth from deep within the thick fog. "What was that?" whispered Roland, staring down the alley into the fog. Moments passed and Roland heard nothing. He started to believe he was hearing things, after all; this was such a strange place. He released the grips on the pistols and let his hands drop slowly to his sides. "For a moment there, I thought I heard something growl," he said softly with a sigh of relief. The words had barely escaped his lips when chills cut him deep to the bone. He froze, and for a second time, Roland didn't think he could move, even if necessary. He strained his eyes to see down the alley, but the small lights on the posts only lit up a small area. They flickered, as if having a hard time staying lit, but nonetheless, they continued to put forth small glimmers of lights and past that, the alley was dark and consumed with fog.

It was as if the small lights kept the fog at bay, and with each moment that passed, the fog inched forward only to be chased away with another flicker of the lamps.

There was another loud growl. This time Roland didn't question the noise. It was a growl, and he knew it. His hands went beneath his cloak, and propelled by instinct, the pistols were out of their holsters and held tightly in his hands. He turned his head to see better, but there was nothing to see.

There was a slight noise and then a loud clash, as if someone had kicked something, something large and made of metal. Now, another type of noise reverberated up the alley, like someone dragging something, and Roland could tell it was metal by the sound it made on the cobblestones.

"Whatever that is," he said, "its heavy." Roland took a quick glimpse out of the alley toward the tavern, but there was nothing to see in that direction, so he refocused back on the noise and problem at hand. He heard the dragging noise again, and this time it was drawing closer to the edge of the fog. He strained his eyes to see, and he did see something moving, but what?

Whatever it was, moved closer to the light. Roland could just barely make out a silhouette, but he was sure it was that of a man. It was moving slowly and dragging something heavy. This wasn't the same man that he had seen earlier dragging sacks across the alley; this man was much larger and taller in stature. He couldn't see what he was dragging, but its metallic clanging on the cobblestones continued.

Then, once again, he heard a loud growl and no doubt about it this time—it was a growl. Roland froze again. The noise had sent chills up and down his spine, and he could feel the alley grow colder. His body shook violently as he tried relentlessly to regain his strength. He knew now wasn't the time to be scared. He had promised himself that, no matter what he had to face in this place, he wouldn't let it frighten him. He was on a mission, a mission to locate and save his son; he couldn't afford the luxury of being frightened or scared.

The growl came once more, but this time a very large beast followed it. It hung in the shadows with the man, but Roland could see it well enough to realize it was some kind of dog or wolf. "No," he said softly, "it's much too large to be either." He flipped the safety off his guns as the beast stepped a little closer to the light. Roland could see its monstrous eyes, and they were glowing. They were bright green, and they were staring directly at him. The beast growled once more, and Roland saw the enormous man bend down and unsnap the chain from its collar.

"Kill," the man whispered to the beast.

# Two

## Work Day

Roland sat up in bed and rubbed his face then gently slid his hands through his thick, dark hair. He was wet with sweat and shaking slightly.

"Another bad dream, sweetie?" asked Katie.

"Yeah, same one!"

"I'm sorry!" Katie said. "Are you getting up?"

"Yeah, I'm going to check on Josh. Do you want him in here with you?"

"That would be good!" she said, turning over to face Roland.

"I wonder why I'm having these dreams," Roland said. "They feel so real, and they're getting worse. Do you think it has something to do with Creed? It's been almost a week, and we haven't heard anything from him or Olin. I wonder when they're coming to collect Sarah and the rest of them. Do you think he's already back?"

"I don't know, sweetie, but don't worry about it. It's your first day back to work, and you've got enough to worry about besides Creed and his group of thugs."

Roland turned toward her, and a faint smile crossed his face. He knew she could see the worry on his face.

9

"It's not Creed that I worry about, baby," he said. "It's you. I really hate to leave you all alone today. Are you sure you'll be all right?"

"Yes, honey. Don't worry about me. Josh and I'll be fine. Wisteria wants us to come by the café this morning for breakfast. We'll be fine, honey." Katie tried to sound confident, but she and Roland knew that Creed was coming back to his mansion, and when he did, he would be coming for Sarah, Horace, and the nanny...but when?

* * *

Roland stood in the doorway and watched Josh sleeping in the center of the bed. The bed was large and the little boy so small in comparison, but Josh had chosen this room, and by all appearances, it was just right for him. Roland walked over and slowly bent over and kissed him on the head. With a smooth motion, he gently scooped up the curly-headed little boy. "Want to sleep with Mommy?"

Josh replied with only a moan as Roland placed him in bed with his mother.

"If you need me for anything—anything—give me a call at the office," he insisted. "You do have the number, don't you?"

Katie smiled at Roland and gave him a quick wink. "Yes, honey. Don't worry about us. We'll be fine." As convincing as she was, there was still a small quiver of doubt in her voice. Then she sent Roland a thought, *I promise, sweetie.*

Roland did worry about leaving Katie alone in Number 12, and he had his reasons. This would be the first time he had left her and Josh by themselves since the clash with Creed and Olin—the night of the triangular séance. Katie and Roland wondered if Creed or Olin had been killed in the skirmish. They had been wounded in that horrible fight, and no one from the dark side had been seen since that night.

Creed or Olin being dead was only wishful thinking for Katie and Roland, and—what's more—they knew it. The probability of the two warlocks being dead was slim, and they knew it was just a matter of time before they reappeared. Then the battle between good and evil would continue, but neither knew to what extent or what level the battles would ascend to next.

Creed would find his precious spirits gone, along with his servant Notor, and his transformation delayed yet again. He would be furious and would seek revenge. He had been humiliated and defeated the night of the séance, and one thing they knew: Creed and his demons would want retribution.

Roland bent forward and kissed Katie on the forehead; he smiled at her and then kissed his son on the cheek. "If anything happened to either one of you, I don't know what I would do."

"Don't worry, sweetie. We'll be all right. Scoot off to work and don't worry about us. We love you, Roland. We always will!"

Josh stirred slightly and softly muttered. "Love you, Daddy!"

Roland left the bedroom and walked down the stairs to the first landing. He knew how blessed he was to have such a wonderful family. No matter what was to come, he wouldn't let anything happen to Katie or Josh. He wasn't afraid of Creed or Olin anymore, and if they came for him or his family, he would give them a war they couldn't survive.

For a moment, Roland glanced down the lonely stairs; he noticed how empty they looked. "No Sarah, no Notor, nothing but steps," he said quietly. "That's good, really good!"

\*\*\*

Roland started out of his drive when he saw his neighbor Jim step out onto his porch, heading for his pickup. "Seven o'clock, right on time! Good morning, Jim!" he called out the window.

"Howdy, Roland. Going to work?"

"Yeah, first day at the new office!"

"Have a good one!" Jim said, opening his door and getting into his truck.

*Neither rain nor sleet nor snow stops the mail; I wonder what it would take to stop Jim from his early-morning ritual.* Roland laughed and waved at his neighbor. He pulled out of his drive and headed to work. He knew that Jim met a group of retired friends every morning at Hardees. "Those biscuits must be really good," he said, laughing.

# Three

## The Protection Spell

Katie and Josh met Wisteria for a late breakfast. The old woman looked surprising youthful in spite of her age. Her black hair streaked with gray surrounded her oversized body. It moved as if it were alive flowing around her arms, shoulders, and waist. Some parts were long, others shorter, but each, and every strand, flowed and clung to the old woman's body as if it was protecting her from something-but what?

Feeling concerned about Roland, Katie gently laid her hand on Wisteria's and spoke softly. "Wisteria, Roland's been having these dreams—dreams about Josh. He's afraid that something may happen to him. Do you have any idea what this could mean? Do you think Creed would come back and try to hurt Josh?"

"I don't know, dear, they're warlocks, you never know what they'll do. If hurting Josh hurts you and Roland, then they are certainly capable of doing just that. Did he tell you about the dreams, or what he sees in them?"

"No, he doesn't discuss them in detail with me, trying to keep me from worrying, I suppose. It's always the same dream and it has something to do with Josh. He doesn't like to talk about them, but he said the one he had last night was more intense."

"Well, we haven't heard a peep from Creed or Olin. Hopefully and if we're lucky, wherever they're at, they'll stay!" Wisteria paused for a second and then took a sip of her coffee. "But"—she paused again—"we know better than that, don't we, dear?"

"Yes!" Katie said sympathetically. "I'm afraid we do, I just wonder when—you know, when will they return. I just wish we knew."

"Well, don't worry, dear. We'll be ready for them, but we really need to talk. The fight last week was just another battle, although a major one. I'm sorry to say just another battle against good and evil. The war will continue until..." Wisteria paused. Katie wondered if she would continue but Wisteria did not.

"Until we kill Creed and Olin!" Thor pulled up a chair and sat down in front of the booth. "Good morning, Josh. How's my little buddy doing?" Thor reached over and rubbed the small boy's soft curly hair. He had come to love the small boy. It wasn't in an assassin's nature to like children—let alone love something so small and innocent—but Thor had made a special bond with Josh.

"I'm OK. I saw a red bird this morning, Thor, and it was sitting outside of my window in a tree. Mommy said it was a Cardin," Josh said, looking up at Thor.

"No, sweetie. It was a car-di-nal, but you were close," Katie said.

"I like redbirds, no matter what they're called. Don't you, Josh?" Thor laughed and rubbed the small boy's curly hair once more.

Agreeing with Thor, Josh lowered his head and said "Yes!" He then went back to coloring on the place mat.

Thor patted Josh on the hand and turned his attention back to the two women sitting in the booth. "I went by Creed's mansion this morning. I crossed the wall and went in the back door, scanned the place, and left. There wasn't anyone there, no dark spirits, no Creed and no Olin. The place was empty."

"Thor wasn't that dangerous for you?" asked Katie.

"To a point, but I scanned the place as soon as I entered the kitchen. Since no demon guardians came to the gate when I rattled it, I assumed no one was home and went around to the back. The placed is totally empty. They haven't returned."

"Katie, Thor and I need to come by the house this afternoon," Wisteria said. "I need to cast a spell so we will know if any evil spirits enter your home. It will only take a minute, but we agreed that we would feel better if we knew you had some kind of protection while Roland was at work." The old woman placed her hand on top of Katie's. "It's just a little extra precaution, dear."

"You can do that?" Katie said, looking at Wisteria and then at Thor. "I mean cast a spell so that you will know if a dark spirit enters my home?"

"Are you kidding? This witch"—Thor looked around to ensure no one else was listening—"this witch can do all sorts of things, including beating an assassin at what he does best." Thor laughed and gently slapped the table. "Don't ever, and I mean ever, underestimate our frail little old witch, Wisteria."

Wisteria looked at Thor. "You flatter me, Thor! When you speak like that, I assume you want something. What is it, dear?"

Thor dropped his head for a moment, and then lifting it to make certain no one saw the change in his facial expression, he said softly, "I don't need a thing." He looked across the table and elevated his voice to a more teasing tone. "Just bragging on you, Granny!"

"Granny, my foot. Stop calling me that before I cast a simple little irritating spell on you. How'd you like hair growing on the bottom of your feet, or an itch somewhere you can't scratch?" Wisteria snapped at the assassin. He knew she wasn't fond of being called anything except Wisteria, and calling her Granny, rubbed a nerve.

"Oh, easy now. Just joking a bit. Besides, you're not old enough to be a granny!" Thor smiled as he reached over and patted the old woman's hand. "Just joking!"

Wisteria smiled at Thor and said kindheartedly, "Gotcha!" She bent forward. "I saw your expression change, dear. What do you want, Thor? You've not been yourself the last few days. Come on. I know something is bothering you, dear. You might as well tell me."

Thor smiled. "Nothing you can help me with, Wisteria. Just thinking about home. Just trying to accept the fact that I can never go back. It's hard you know, you know, knowing you can't go home, ever." Thor straightened his shoulders and smiled. "Besides, my work here isn't finished. We still have business to conclude with Creed and Olin, right?"

"Thor," Wisteria said softly, "our bargain was for you to steal Creed's gold. You've fulfilled your bargain to me, and you owe me nothing else, dear."

"Yes, I fulfilled my contract with you, but not with Roland and his family. You know, Roland and Katie saved my life when I stole Creed's gold. Now I must stay until their problem is eliminated." Thor smiled and patted the table once more. "In other words, until Creed and Olin are dead and gone from their lives forever." Thor smiled at Katie. "An assassin never forgets a debt, nor do we forget the people we care about! That's what brought me to this miserable world in the first place—no offense intended. Morto was my friend."

"None taken, Thor," Katie responded. "But you don't owe us anything either. You helped us save Sarah; and if you were indebted to us, it has been paid in full. Roland and I thank you for helping us. You went way beyond your call of duty, and it's my family that owes you the debt." Katie smiled at Thor. "Besides"—she reached over and picked up Thor's hand—"we Roberts's don't ever forget our friends and especially the ones we love! You always have a home with us."

Thor smiled. "Well, the feeling is mutual!" His face became more serious, and he quickly changed the subject. "Now for more pressing business. What are we going to do about Creed and Olin? They're coming back—you realize this—and probably very soon. They won't be so passive this time—I mean when they return and find Sarah, Horace, Notor, and the nanny gone. I suppose Creed will unleash Olin on you and Roland." Thor paused as his mind switched gears. "Then again, he might wait; I mean he may wait to settle things with you and Roland. He might want that pleasure himself. He doesn't want to draw attention to himself from outsiders, so he might hold off until his transformation is completed, which thanks to us, may take some time.

"Think about it; now that Sarah is out of your house, he might think that you and Roland are out of his life, as well. Yes, he just might keep a low profile until his transformation is completed. Wisteria, what do you think?"

"It doesn't really matter, dear," the old woman answered. "If you're right and he decides not to unleash Olin on Katie and Roland—or all of us, as far as that goes—it will be just a matter of time until he retaliates himself. However, you may be right. If he decides to wait, it would give us more time to dispatch him and Olin." Wisteria looked at Katie and continued in a low whisper. "We will have to kill both of them if we are to save Johnston. You realize that, don't you, dear?"

"Maybe he'll just stay away and not come back to Johnston," Katie said. "Maybe he'll complete his transformation somewhere else. Why should he come back here to Johnston? There's nothing for him here. Sarah is gone, and once he finds this out, maybe he'll just leave. He could go anywhere." Katie looked at Wisteria and then at Thor. "Maybe we can put this whole thing behind us."

Katie knew she was wrong, but there's always a ray of hope around the corner, and where there's hope, there's always a small, small chance that things just might go in another direction. The words she heard next confirmed her worst fears.

Wisteria took a deep breath. "No, dear, Creed will be coming home. This is his lot, and he won't leave it for anything or anyone. His roots are here, and so is his home. He'll return to complete his transformation and to rule Johnston from the dark side. He wants this little town for some reason, dear. No, he'll return. And when he does, we must be ready for him. Thor and I will come by Number 12 this afternoon to cast the protection spell. We'll start with that, and then we'll all need to sit down with Roland and discuss our next move."

\*\*\*

Katie and Josh spent the rest of the morning playing in the yard of Number 12. The day was warm and becoming warmer, and the sun had dried the dew from the trees, grass, and flowers. Josh played in the thick green grass, stopping every once in a while to play with the neighbor's dog, who would wander over to see what all of the commotion was. Katie had put the conversation with Wisteria and Thor out of her mind while she played with her son. She knew things would heat up again with Creed and Olin, but for the time being, she was enjoying the moment with her son and her wonderful old house.

Josh finally became tired, and he and Katie entered the house through the large green door. Once inside the door, Katie noticed the enormous amount of light flooding the rooms and cascading over everything in its way, as if the sun had a mission to fulfill and wouldn't let anything hinder its task of filling the room with its magical radiance.

Although the large panes had imperfections, the hand-blown glass welcomed the light and allowed it to pass through them unobstructed. They cast small shades of greens and blues here and there, reflecting yet again from vases and other items of glass that sent sparkles of light cascading all over the room. Katie stood in the center of the room in amazement; she hadn't seen Number 12 this way before, and it struck her how beautiful it was. It was at that very moment she knew why the Wheeler sisters had loved their old house so much and why she, as well, loved her new home.

\*\*\*

It was about twenty after one when Wisteria and Thor came calling. The grandfather clock had struck its four single tones and was waiting patiently for the chance to sound them again. Katie had put Josh to bed and had dozed off on the sofa when the doorbell rang.

"Wisteria, Thor, please come in!" she said opening the door wider.

"I hope we aren't disturbing you, dear." Said Wisteria.

"No, not at all. Please come in. Why would you think that?"

Wisteria stepped into the house and, when she passed Katie, reached over and pulled a pair of panties from Katie's shoulder. "This is why," she said, smiling.

Katie laughed and grabbed for the underwear. "I was folding clothes on the sofa. I'd been playing in the yard with Josh, and I was so tired I took a little nap...static cling."

"You don't have to explain, dear. We all wear underwear on our shoulders from time to time!" Wisteria chuckled and headed toward the den.

"Don't worry, Katie; your secret's safe with me. Besides, if Wisteria wore her underwear on her shoulders, it would serve quite well as a cape!" Thor whispered softly.

"I heard that!" said a voice from the den. "Come on in here, and let's get started. I didn't come here to discuss my undergarments!" Katie and Thor heard her chuckle and watched the old witch make herself comfortable on the sofa.

Wisteria didn't say a word while Katie and Thor found seats in the den; she sat very still and quiet. Then, ever so softly, she spoke. "Katie, would you get me the crystal ball and cradle that I gave you and Roland?"

"Sure!" said Katie as she headed for the kitchen. Moments later, she returned with the crystal in her hand. "We used this to watch Notor. I'm glad he's happy now."

"It has many uses, dear—more than you will ever know. Just put it there on the table, dear!"

Katie placed the ball in its cradle. It was clear and hadn't been cloudy since the night Notor had passed over into the light. Katie sat and watched the old witch.

Wisteria placed her hand in one of the large pockets of her dress and produced another crystal identical to the one on the table; she placed another cradle on the table and gently placed the second ball in it.

"By the powers I possess I remove the spell from this crystal." Wisteria gently reached over and touched the ball that Katie had produced. "Now that that's done, let's continue." Wisteria paused for a moment. "Thor, do you see anything on your scanners?"

"No, the house is clear."

"Let's continue." Wisteria started muttering softly under her breath. She closed her eyes and sat quietly for a moment, then softly spoke. "I'm calling on the ancient witches of old to come forth and protect this house with your power and magic. Guard this place against the forces of evil and the dark side. I cast this spell and invoke the magic and power that I possess combined with the powers of my ancestors to enter into these crystals and watch over this house and family, warning each crystal when dark spirits enter into this dwelling." She settled back into the soft cushion of the sofa. "There, it's done. Katie, if a dark spirit enters this house, the crystals will turn red. I'll take one with me, and you will keep the other. I also have one for Thor. If you enter the house and the crystal is red, leave immediately. Do you understand, dear?"

"Yes."

"Good. Well, Thor, we must be going. Have a nice evening, dear," Wisteria said, turning back to Katie. "I know you and Roland will. We'll see you later."

Wisteria and Thor left the house, and Katie sat alone watching the crystal. Her thoughts ran back to what Thor had said earlier at the café, that Creed's house was empty.

"That's good, good news!" she said. "So, I'm not going to think about that today. I'll worry about that tomorrow." She sat for a moment and wondered what Wisteria meant by her and Roland having a nice evening. She shrugged and smiled.

*** 

Katie had fallen asleep on the sofa again when the doorbell made its gentle calling. She sat up, shook her soft blond hair, and headed for the door. When she opened it, she looked at the pretty middle-aged lady standing at her door. It was Pat, their next-door neighbor.

20

"I hope I'm not disturbing you, Katie, but Jim and I would like to take Josh to Edgefield this afternoon for an ice cream. They have a small petting zoo there, and we thought Josh might like to see it."

"Really?" Katie asked. Over the past few days, Pat had visited with Katie and Roland several times; and she and Jim had grown quiet fond of Josh. Josh, also, had fallen in love with Pat and Jim. Katie and Roland thought it might be their soothing spirits or the way they spoke, so soft and caring, and of course, having a dog and a cat didn't hurt either. Katie and Roland really liked the couple next door, they were great neighbors and they could see why Josh had fallen in love with them the moment he met them.

"We know its Roland's first day at work, and we thought it might be nice if he came home and had an hour or so to relax, you know, a bit before dinner." Pat smiled at Katie. "If it's all right, we'll pick Josh up around five."

"That's so sweet of you guys. He'll be delighted!"

"Oh, think nothing of it. Glad to do it, and besides, Jim and I want to spend some time with Josh and get to know him a little better."

"Thank you. When he wakes up, I'll let him know. He loves animals, not to mention the ice cream." Katie smiled at the adorable little woman standing at her threshold.

"Well, he certainly can't like ice cream any better than Jim does." Pat laughed, turning to leave. "See you at five, sweetie!"

21

# Four

## A Special Evening

Katie spent the rest of the afternoon getting ready for Roland's arrival while Josh slept. His afternoon naps were becoming longer, and this gave Katie some time to herself. When he awoke, he was excited with the news that he was going on an adventure with Pat and Jim. As the seconds ticked by, the little boy's fortitude was tested. "Is it five o'clock yet, Mommy?"

"No, sweetie, but it's getting closer," answered Katie.

As predicted, Pat rang the doorbell promptly at five. She and Jim picked up the anxious little boy that lived in Number 12, and all three of them set off, heading toward the small town of Edgefield and, of course, ice cream.

\*\*\*

It was a little before six when Roland arrived at the house. He stared at the back door. There was a note attached to it: *Darling, please come in the front door!* Roland laughed and walked up the drive toward the front of the house. "I wonder what she's up to?" he said with a grin.

He opened the door and, not to his surprise, there was a chair sitting inside the doorway. Taped to the chair was another note. When Roland touched it, a slight aroma of perfume rose and an exotic fragrance filled his nostrils. He had enjoyed that smell so many times before, and instantly his thoughts went to Katie. He read the note. *Please take your shower downstairs and put these on, then come to our bedroom.* He looked in the chair and saw his silk boxers and nightshirt. He picked them up and, as instructed, headed for the bathroom.

The shower felt good after a busy day at the office. He splashed on some cologne and combed his thick hair back. He slowly walked up the stairs until he reached the hall outside of his bedroom. Katie was waiting for him there; she was wearing a short skirt with fishnet hose, and her bronze legs looked stunning as the net clung tightly to them. They conformed to every muscle and highlighted her tight thighs. Roland gazed at her in silence. Her top was short and barely covered her breasts. The soft cotton fabric pressed against her hardened nipples, and he could see the impression of each one. Her breasts pushed the thin fabric away from her stomach, and Roland thought he could see a small portion of the bottom of her swollen breasts.

He stared at her as she walked slowly toward him. "God, you're beautiful!" he said, watching her move. Her breasts bounced ever so lightly with every step and the soft cotton of her top rose slightly. Roland strained to catch a slight glimpse of what the soft material was covering. He reached out to touch her.

Katie wrapped her arms around her handsome prince and gave him an intimate kiss. Roland's strong arms wrapped around her waist, and he returned the kiss.

\*\*\*

The night air slowly engulfed Roland and Katie as they lay in bed. Josh had been returned and was tucked into his bed, at least for now. Both knew that sometime in the night, most likely, they would hear soft footprints on the hardwood floor and then the words, "Daddy, help me." This, of course, was when Josh would hold up his hands and Roland would pitch him over into the middle of the bed with him and Katie.

But for now, the huge windows in the bedroom were open and the breeze felt relaxing as they lay in their bed. The night air stirred as if some huge unseen machine was mixing an invisible concoction. It was intoxicating. It took them to the edge of unconsciousness and then brought them back to reality as the warm summer breeze explored their bodies. The crickets sang their songs, but tonight their songs were soft and relaxing, and every once in a while an owl would join in and give his hoot. All was right and good at Number 12, at least for the moment, and in Roland's mind, the evening couldn't have been more beautiful.

He loved Katie more than anything, and no one, not even Katie, would ever know how much he really loved her. There were no words to describe his love, but he knew in his mind that there would never be another Katie. Of course he loved his son, but that was a different kind of love—exactly like the love he had for Katie, but exactly different. He thought about how beautiful Katie looked as she had stood in front of him earlier in the evening. But then again, just being with her always please him beyond words.

As the night air teased them, both slipped into an endless sleep that could only be interrupted by an annoying alarm clock or soft footprints in the early morning hours.

# Five

## Creeds Return

The next few days were great at Number 12, for Katie and Roland, and the hot summer days in South Carolina seemed to drift by slowly. They'd met with Wisteria and Thor to discuss what actions to take if Creed should come back. They knew if he did return, they would have no alternative but to kill him, but there was always the chance that Creed and Olin wouldn't return. This was what Katie hoped, prayed, and wished for every evening as the sun vanished from the sky and the moon and stars began to appear: "Star light, star bright, I wish upon the first star I see tonight. I wish I may, I wish I might have the wish I wish tonight...I wish Creed and Olin would never return to Johnston."

The crystals were in place, and if anyone or anything from the dark side showed up at Number 12, they would certainly send out the alarm. Wisteria had cast her spell and, as usual, done a splendid job of it. However, it was a waiting game now, nothing to do but wait until something happened or until Thor picked up something on his scanners. He went by the mansion several times a day and rattled the gates, and each time, when no demon guardian showed up; he would creep around to the back of the estate, cross over the wall, and enter the mansion through the back door.

Seconds later, he would complete his task and be heading back over the wall. No one had asked him to do this, and if Creed or Olin caught him, it would be a fight to the death, but for Thor the risk was worth taking because the only family he had now was a small boy, an old witch, and Katie and Roland.

\*\*\*

The morning air was warm as it gently flowed across Katie and Roland's bed. The large windows were open, and the breezed flowed like a slow-moving river, going somewhere but taking its sweet time getting there. Roland dozed in and out of sleep as he waited for the clock to sound. It was relaxing as he pulled the sheet around his neck; it was the first night since the battle with Creed and the dark side that he hadn't had the terrible dream about Josh. Earlier that evening, he had fallen into a deep, restful sleep and had slept soundly. When the alarm went off, he would be ready to begin another day at work, away from the two people he worried about the most.

Katie, as well, had slept peacefully and for her, it would be another busy day with Josh, playing in the yard and going shopping in the small town of Johnston. This is what she and Roland had wanted, for her to be home with their son and to spend quality time with him while he was still small.

\*\*\*

Katie had gotten her beach bike out of the garage and inspected it with care, and the child's seat that was attached to the rear, as well. She was happy that the bike had managed to come through the move unscathed.

Each day, she would load Josh onto the bike and they would take a leisurely ride through the sleepy little town of Johnston. Some days it was to do the banking or pay the electric or water bill, but then other days it was just for the fun of it. And it did offer up a good excuse to get an ice cream at the pharmacy. Katie and Josh loved their time together and loved the ambiance that the small town of Johnston offered. It was nice there, and everyone who met Katie and Josh on their daily jaunts would speak and wave as they pedaled by.

Every day she fell more and more in love with the friendly people in the small town of Johnston as well as the town itself. She had managed to put the thoughts of Creed and Olin out of her mind. They were gone—in her mind, gone for good.

She and Josh would go to the park on the other side of the street to eat their ice cream; Josh would play on the brick pavers that serpentined around the daylilies and benches. It looked like the yellow brick road in *The Wizard of Oz*. Though the pavers weren't yellow, they nonetheless wound endlessly throughout the park.

The crape myrtle trees provided plenty of shade for all, and Katie would sit, watch Josh play, and enjoy the other people who wandered into the park.

There was something in the park, which called to Katie. Something that captivate her attention, but not in admiration or appreciation. It was the large mural painted on the old warehouse wall, at the end of town. She would sit in the park and stare at the mural with a fixation that she couldn't explain. It was of local farmers, sitting and waiting on the train to sell or load their wares, but there was something about the mural, that scared Katie—something hidden in the painting that no one could see, not even Katie. But she knew it was there. She would sit and study the mural when she was in the park, trying to figure out what was so suspicious and mistrustful about the huge painting. She was skeptical of it and feared it was more than just an artist's rendering of old local life. "Something evil dwells there," she would whisper softly.

*** 

The door made a soft creaking sound as Creed pushed it open; he stepped quietly into the cool dark room. "I need a light!" he hissed.

Instantly, the small lamp on the dusty night table glowed. It sent an eerie light around the room that chased away the shadows.

"I'm sorry, Master!" it said.

"Olin, how are you doing today?" Creed said, ignoring the lamp. "Are you feeling better? How are your wounds?" Creed bent over the body lying in the bed. He pulled back the blanket to inspect Olin's wounds. "Ah!" Creed smiled. "Much better. You'll be completely healed in a few more days, and then we can go home."

"My wounds are healed, and they're not life threatening anymore." Olin paused and looked at the bandages on his ribs, arm, and shoulder. He looked at the assortment of potions and poultices sitting beside the lamp. He lifted his eyes toward his brother. "We need to go home, Brother, today. We need to complete your transformation and then..." Olin paused once again; a slight smirk crossed his face. "We need to take care of a few things in that one-horse town you like so well. And that"—he paused once more and looked up at Creed—"will be my job. I'm going to kill that meddlesome old witch and then that cute little blonde. I'm going to make her suffer for shooting me, not once, but twice." Olin flung his arm and struck the lamp. Its light went out as it bounced against the wall and tumbled onto the table before falling to the floor, sending potions and poultices flying in all directions.

"Light!" hissed Creed. The lamp straightened itself up and stood erect once again. Floating up to the table, it cast forward its eerie light. "Sorry, Master!"

Once again, Creed ignored the lamp. "We won't leave until you are completely healed. I won't take that chance!"

"It's not a chance. I'm fine!" snapped Olin. "I'm tired of this dark, dreary place, and I'm going home!" Olin sat up in the small bed. "Either you help me or I'll go alone, but one way or another, I'm going home today!"

Olin stood up and smiled at Creed. "We'll get Sarah and the rest of them as soon as we get home, and tomorrow we'll complete your transformation." He picked up his clothes and started dressing himself.

Creed turned to leave and hissed.

"If you must leave today, I'll wait for you downstairs! I'll summon the demon guardians."

"Yes, Brother, I must!" was all Olin said as he continued to dress himself. With a swift kick, he sent the potions and poultices flying in all directions. "We have more of these at the mansion."

Olin walked down the winding stairs toward the large bar at Jake's Place, Creed was sitting in the corner behind a small table. He walked lively and quick as he continued down the steps.

He didn't want Creed to notice the pain he was feeling every time he took a step. The bullet that Roland had fired had indeed struck him in the ribs, but it had also buried itself deep into his back muscles, passing though one of his lungs on its way. Although the local healers used a lot of magic, the recovery time was taking longer than he had wanted.

With each step, he tried to hide the pain that he was feeling. It was excruciating, but he didn't want Creed to notice. His brother's transformation was all that mattered to Olin, and he knew it was close at hand.

He knew he could recover in the mansion. No one ever came there, and if they did, they would have to face the demon guardians. He could sit in the gardens and feel the sunshine and warmth of a summer breeze, unlike in this dark hole where he'd been since the battle. He had liked Terra Demorte, but now that his own transformation had been completed and he had his body, he favored the world on the surface over this underground world.

Terra Demorte had its benefits to someone like Olin. It was a safe harbor, a place where he was welcome, and no human could ever come. He had friends there who cared about him, or at least pretended to care— gold buys many friends. Most of them were the assassins, and the ones in this part of the Terra Demorte always hung out at Jake's Place. A huge two-story tavern with lots of lights and tables, normally it was packed and loud, but at this hour, most were either in bed, drunk out of their minds and sleeping it off in one of the many rooms Jake's establishment had to offer.

The second floor of Jake's Place had numerous rooms occupied by assassins and warlocks. Some housed trolls and goblins, other rooms had witches. All types of evil stayed at Jake's Place, and most stayed on their best behavior while they were there. Terra Demorte was a dark, evil place, and there was nothing good there at all. Everyone and everything that lived in this world was of pure evil or dealing in it.

The inhabitants there cast their wickedness and evilness on the humans on the surface; few ever created trouble in Terra Demorte.

The dark land housed many monsters, and all were as thick as thieves. Most hated the surface and the humans that lived there, and normally, most managed to get along in their world without killing one another. If they had killing to do, they would go to the surface to get it done.

Olin saw a man sitting across the table from Creed; he was making conversation and using his hands to express himself. Olin stopped on the steps and watched the conversation for a moment. Although the man had his back to him, he knew instantly who it was.

"Morto!" said Olin, continuing causally down the last few steps. "It's good to see you again!"

The man turned, and sure enough, it was Morto, the assassin.

"Master Olin, thank you. It's good to see you again, as well." Morto eased up out of his chair and turned to face Olin. "I'm glad your wounds are better and are allowing you to travel. Master Creed was just telling me that he and you will be returning to the surface today. That's great news, just great!"

"Yes, Morto. Yes, it's great!" Olin said, stepping off the last step. His ribs were throbbing with an agonizing pain, but he continued his stride, trying relentlessly to keep the irritation from showing in his facial expression. He paused again as he looked at the well-dressed man. He remembered the last time he'd seen the assassin, how egotistical and arrogant he had been when accepting his contract to kill Wisteria.

Olin also knew that on that night, Wisteria, instead, had killed the assassin, and that his body had vanished and returned to Terra Demorte. But Wisteria had cut off his head and had stuck it into a sack, so it had not been able to return with his body. If Wisteria hadn't thrown Morto's head over the gates of the mansion, Morto would be lying in a state of death in the Keeping Room and couldn't be reborn until his head was returned.

Even now, the only reason Morto was so polite was that he had lost his medallion. When Wisteria had cut off his head, she had managed to hold on to his medallion, as well, and now it was hers. Once a body is separated from its medallion and the body returns to Terra Demorte, the medallion can't return on its own.

"Well, why don't you join us and return to the surface with us, Morto? You're more than welcome to come with us!" Olin said with a smile.

Morto's eyes narrowed as he stared at Olin, his face turning red. "I can't!" Morto's voice was now very low and sounded more like a growl, a sound one might expect to hear from a mad dog, just before he attacks.

"I'm so sorry, Morto, I didn't quite hear you. Did you say you can't come to the surface with us? Pray tell, Morto. Why not?" Olin leaned against the newel-post at the foot of the stairs; he was teasing the assassin, and what's more, the assassin knew it. "Come on, assassin; tell us why you can't go to the surface with us!" snapped Olin.

Morto was on his feet before the last word escaped Olin's lips. His hands went beneath his cloak; and instinctively wrapped around the handles of his daggers, like snakes squeezing the life from their prey. At this very minute, Morto would have given anything to kill the insolent warlock, but he needed something from Olin, so he slowly removed his hands from under his cloak and wiped his forehead. He ran his fingers through his hair, took in a deep breath, and fished out a pack of cigarettes from one of his pockets. Thumping the pack, the cigarettes jutted forth like magic. The assassin stared at Olin as he gently put his lips on one of the smokes and pulled it from the pack. Lighting the cigarette and inhaling the smoke deep into his lungs, the stare never left his face. He exhaled the smoke and walked slowly toward Olin.

"Master Olin would you like a smoke?" he said.

Olin looked at the assassin and then at the pack of cigarettes. "Sure, why not?"

"Master Olin"—Morto took another draw on the smoke—"the reason I can't go to the surface is because I don't have my medallion, sir. The witch, Wisteria, has it!"

Olin looked at the assassin. It was a disgrace for an assassin to lose his medallion, and Morto had lost his twice. A few years back, he had lost it to Creed, and now to the surface witch, Wisteria. Olin didn't have a conscious, didn't care for anyone or anything; normally he would just as soon kill a person as look at him. The only people he cared about were himself, Creed, and the Great Dark Witch of Terra Demorte. Once, for a few seconds, he had cared about Notor, when the demon guardian Roy had caught him talking to the spirit of the small dead girl Jessica, and now, for some reason, he felt sorry for Morto.

"Well, Morto, we'll just have to see about getting your medallion back, won't we?"

Morto stared at the man in front of him; he assumed Olin was still teasing him about his medallion, so he turned to leave, but Olin spoke once more.

"Well, Morto, are you interested in getting your medallion back or not? If you want it back, have a seat with Master Creed and let's talk." Olin smiled at the assassin and walked over to the table where Creed had been sitting, watching his brother.

"I have summoned the demon guardians, Roy and Ray. They should be here within the next hour," hissed Creed. He kept his cloak pulled tightly around his face and head. His hands were under the black cloak, ensuring no one could see them.

"What about others?" questioned Olin.

"I don't know," Creed hissed.

"Doesn't matter. Two should be sufficient for the moment!" Olin said. "Morto, do you know an assassin by the name of Thor?"

"Thor? Yes, his full name is Thornton. He went to the surface to kill the witch Wisteria and reclaim my medallion. I haven't heard from him since. Why do you ask?"

Olin watched Morto as he sat down at the table. "Well, he's taken up with that witch he went to kill; can you tell me why an assassin would do that?"

"No, I can't." Morto scratched at the top of the table. "You must be mistaken, Master Olin, I find it hard to believe that Thor would ever work for that witch."

"Well, he is!" snapped Olin.

"You lie. He would never!" screamed Morto. On instinct, his hands went under his cloak and grasped the handles of his daggers once more.

"If you value your life, Morto, those hands had better come out from under your cloak"—Olin paused as he stared at Morto—"empty!"

Morto looked at the warlock sitting beside him. His hands were still grasping his daggers, and he would have liked nothing better than to bury them deep into Olin's chest. He hadn't liked Olin when they first met and disliked him even more this very minute. "Thornton is—or was—my best friend, Master Olin. I don't have many friends, and I apologize for getting upset with you for accusing Thor of something like that. I'm sure he would never betray the assassin's code."

"Not only is he working for the witch, Wisteria, but he's working with those two humans that live in Number 12, as well. I can't figure out why he would double-cross Terra Demorte myself. Oh, and apology accepted."

Morto looked uneasy with the way the conversation had gone. Thor had gone to the surface to help him, and he knew that if Thor had betrayed Terra Demorte and the dark side, there had to have been a good reason. "Thor is dedicated to the dark side, Master Olin. That I promise. I still don't be—" Morto paused and rubbed his chin; he took a long draw from his cigarette and blew the smoke up into the air. "Maybe, just maybe..." Morto stopped and scratched at the table once more.

"Maybe what?"

"Master Olin, the night I attacked the witch and moments after you had left, she had me pinned to the floor. She was sitting on me, and man, do you know how much that witch weights? Tons, I suppose!" Morto laughed.

"I suppose," said Olin in a mocking tone. "Maybe what?" Olin looked across the room at the bartender standing behind the bar. Apparently, their conversation was becoming interesting to him, as well, as he had moved down the bar and within earshot of the conversation. "You might as well pull up a chair, Jake, and while you're at it, bring three—no, two ales." Olin looked at Creed. "You want something to drink?"

Creed didn't move. "No!" he hissed softly.

Jake pulled up a chair and slid one of the drinks to Olin and the other to Morto. He looked at Morto and said, "Maybe what, Morto? Continue with your story. What were you going to say?"

"Maybe the witch beat Thor, just like she did me. Maybe she used the gold snake's head dagger on Thor. She used it on me. It's a terrible thing!" Morto picked up the pint of ale and took a long drink.

"For Hades' sake man, spit it out. What were you going to say? Why do you think Thor betrayed the dark side?" Jake said in an ill-tempered tone. He was getting irritated with Morto's scattered conversation. "Thornton is my friend, as well, so if you know something or assume you know something, spit it out, Morto."

"I was going to say that the night she dispatched me, before she cut off my head, she offered me a deal. She wanted me to work with her and to do something to Creed. I can't remember exactly what it was, but I told her no, and that's the last thing I remembered before I woke up here!"

Olin looked at the assassin; he studied his face, body movements, and gestures. He believed the assassin and gained a little more respect for him. "So you told the witch that you wouldn't help her?"

"Yes, I spat in her face just before she, well, you know—just before she dispatched me." Morto lowered his head.

"Don't feel so bad, Morto. I appreciate your loyalty to my brother and me. You've proven yourself, and we will help you recover your medallion. That I promise!" Olin smiled at the assassin. "But it appears that your friend, Thor, didn't have the fortitude to do the same thing. He's betrayed the dark side and the assassin's code. I'm sorry to tell you this, but it's true."

"I can't believe it, and as soon as I recover my medallion, I'm going to find him. He would do the same for me!" Morto said. He drank more of his ale and crushed out the cigarette. "Master Olin, if you and Master Creed help me recover my medallion, I would be very grateful."

"I assumed so!" said Olin.

"Morto," Creed said without moving. His voice hissed softly from underneath his cloak. "We will recover your medallion, but it will cost you something. At this very moment, I can't tell you what it will be, but your payment to me or my brother will be in the form of your services. We will recover your medallion, and you will render your services to us." Creed paused and took a long and raspy breath. The air sounded scratchy and dry as if being blown from a dusty bellows. "Twice we will call upon you, and twice you will do as we request without question." Creed paused and continued with only one word. "Agreed?"

Morto took the cigarette package from his pocket once more and, as before, thumped the bottom of the pack. He withdrew one of the smokes with his lips and slowly pushed the pack toward Olin. "Agreed, sir. If you recover my medallion, I'll be at your service without charge, twice, no questions asked."

"Agreed!" said Creed. He knew the assassins were true to their word, and if Morto said he would render his services, then he would. Creed had another thought: Thor was an assassin, as well, and he had just broken the assassin's code and had betrayed Terra Demorte. Creed looked at Morto from under his cloak.

"Morto, if you break your promise to me or my brother, we will kill you."

Morto looked at the master sitting in front of him, then at Olin.

"Rightfully so, sir. I don't know, just yet, what Thor has done or if he has indeed betrayed our world or the assassin's code, but you don't have to question me or my integrity. I have made several mistakes that cost me dearly the last few years, but I would die before I disgraced the assassin clan. My word on it!"

"Nicely put!" Olin said, lifting his ale. "Nicely put, assassin!"

The door of Jake's Place opened, and a demon guardian peered into the brightly lit bar. He stopped at the threshold and scanned the place, as if looking for someone or something. His eyes landed on the four men sitting in the back corner of the tavern; he picked up his pace and hurried toward them.

"Master Creed, I'm here, sir. I was told that you were returning to the surface today. Is this correct, sir?"

"Back off, keep your distance," shouted Olin rising to meet the demon guardian. The guardian continued his journey across the bar until he was face to face with Olin.

"I don't know you guardian, I haven't seen you before. What are you doing here and what do you want with us?" Olin made ready for a fight.

Demon guardians were common in Jake's Place, they drank there often, but the hour was late and the bar was mostly empty. This guardian was huge, bigger than most and it was obvious that he had some kind of business with Olin and his brother.

"Master, I heard you were going to the surface today, is that correct?" the guardian bowed his head, showing respect for the great warlock.

"Yes," said Olin. Creed sat quietly and didn't offer to move or speak.

"I offer you my services, sir, and that of my partner, if you want it." The demon guardian stood erect in front of Olin and Creed.

"You don't want this one, Master Creed!" shouted Jake. "Get out of my tavern, you miserable thief, you sorry excuse for a guardian."

"I'd be careful with that tongue, Jake," warned the demon guardian. "Careful I'd be."

"Careful is right, Master Olin," Jake continued. "This thing here at one time was a respected demon guardian—and one of the best, there's no doubt about that—but there're questions concerning the last master he was hired to protect. Somehow or another that master has gone missing and hasn't been seen or heard from since this thing and his partner showed up here with their pockets full of gold—his gold, I suspect. I don't think you can trust this one, Master!"

The enormous demon guardian gave Jake a disgusting look, and then focused his eyes on Creed and spoke. "It's true, Master Creed. We did show up with a lot of gold, but the master gave it to us and then disappeared. We don't know what happened to him. He was there one night and gone the next. We waited for a while and then returned back to Terra Demorte after our contract expired, and besides, we didn't have a master to protect anymore."

Olin looked at the beast. "Have a seat." He studied the huge demon guardian from head to feet before taking his seat. He was larger than most and built like a stone house. Olin spoke to barkeeper. "Jake, could you bring our friend some ale?"

"Sure, but this one is under tribunal investigation. I don't think you should trust him." Jake pushed his chair back and away from the demon guardian. "Don't sit next to me, either," he said, walking toward the bar.

The demon guardian pulled up a chair between Morto and Olin. He grunted as he slid down into the chair. The chair looked small in contrast to the huge guardian sitting in it, but nonetheless, the chair accommodated the beast. The guardian's muscles bulged as he rested the massive clubs he called arms on the table. His pig snout nose whistled as he snorted a large blast of air from the small nostrils. Long hairs covered his head, sticking out of what looked like warts. Some were straight, others curly. Some warts housed both straight and curly hairs; there was no rhyme or reason to the way they grew.

The eyes were black and small in comparison to the eyebrows, which resembled some horribly untrimmed bush. His hair was thick, long, and growing is every direction, it was some unnatural color of brown. The ears were large, and the tips flopped over when the guardian wasn't using them to pin point a quarry. As gigantic and ugly as he was, there was no doubt this monster sitting at the table was a perfect specimen of the notorious demon guardian clan.

"And what do they call you?" asked Olin inquisitively.

"My name is Drako."

"We may need a strong guardian like you, but we've got to be honest with each other. I need to know if I can trust you, and you need to know if you can trust me." Olin looked at the monstrous beast. He was wondering if his power and magic were strong enough to take down a guardian this size. "What do you say; can we be honest with each other, Drako? Can we be honest, here today?"

"Sure, yeah," snorted Drako. Jake placed the ale in front of him, and the demon guardian drank it in one continuous motion, gulping several times and then slamming the mug down hard on the table. The mug would have shattered into hundreds of sharp shards if it hadn't been made of thick pewter.

"Want another?" said Olin.

"Sure, yeah!" snorted the guardian. Jake brought more ale, and the huge beast guzzled it down in the same fashion as the first one, finishing with the slamming of the mug on the thick wooden table.

"Really like that stuff, don't you?" Olin said.

Morto had slipped his hands under the table and had wrapped them around the handles of his daggers.

"Yeah!" snorted the guardian. "This stuff makes my head go round and round." The demon guardian snorted and belched loudly.

"Do me a favor, Drako," said Olin. "If you have to do that again, could you please turn your head toward Morto?"

"Yep!" said the guardian. "Yep, sure!"

Morto looked at Olin, then at the huge demon guardian. "Thanks, Master Olin!"

"Jake, bring two more ales for my friend here, please!" Olin said without taking his eyes off the beast. Jake obliged, and slid two more ales onto the table in front of the demon guardian, who quickly picked up one of the brews and gulped it down. He turned his head toward Morto and belched once again. Morto looked at the demon guardian and took a long draw from the cigarette he was smoking.

"I don't think"—Morto paused as he exhaled the light blue smoke— "I would do that again if you value that little pinky finger there. Know what I mean?"

The guardian looked at his hand lying on the table. His pinky was short, fat, and ugly. It had long curly hairs growing on the areas between each knuckle. He didn't take his hand from the table but raised his little pinky finger upward and stared at it.

"What-cha mean, if I value my little pinky finger?" He grabbed the last ale and gulped it down, as well, in the same manner as he had done with the others. He slammed the mug against the wooden table. He turned toward Jake and let out a roar. "Two more. Bring me two more!"

Jake looked at Olin, who gave a small nod; he brought two more ales and slammed them down in front of the guardian. "At your service, sir." The guardian snatched one of the mugs up from the table and started his ritual of gulping the brew without stopping. He finished with the customary slamming of the empty mug on the hard table.

"Now," said Olin, "let's talk. Did you and your former master drink ale, Drako? You seemed to like it so well."

"No, he would never let us drink. He became furious when he caught us drinking, but we found his cellar and it was full of ale. The Master wouldn't drink with us.—too good I suppose—but we drank all the time." Drako stared at Creed.

Olin smiled and interrupted the guardian. "So you and your partner drank a lot when you worked for your master?"

"Yeah, all the time, but he didn't know about it."

"Hey, what's a little drink? Besides, a big fellow like you can handle your tipple, right?" Olin looked at Morto and then at Drako. "Am I right or what?"

"Yeah, I can handle my drink, but Dogger couldn't." Drako picked up the last ale and gulped it down, in the same manner as the others before. He raised his hand and stared again at his little pinky, then turned to look at Morto. His weight shifted slightly, and he tipped toward the assassin. Morto shoved him back upright.

"Easy, big fellow. Don't want you falling out of your chair now, do we?" said Morto. Drako's cloak was damp and sticky, and Morto's hands were now covered with the same substance. Looking at his hands, Morto frowned and slowly wiped them on the shoulder of the demon guardian. He bent forward slowly and took a quick sniff of his hands, made an ugly face, and wiped them again on his own cloak.

"Jake, two more for my friend. He's a drinker," Olin said without taking his eyes off Drako. Jake brought two more large ales and winked at Olin.

"These two will finish him off, I suppose," he said. Drako sized up the two mugs and slowly reached for the first one.

Olin put his hand on the guardian's hand.

"Tell me, Drako. What did you do with your last master?"

"Nothing!" snorted Drako. "Nothing!"

"Come on, if we are going to trust each other and if you want to work for us, you've got to be honest with me. I really don't care what you did with him; I just want to know how a demon guardian like you managed to dispatch a powerful master." Olin looked at Creed. "That must be some kind of feat in itself." Olin shrugged, looking baffled.

"Weren't hard to do!" laughed Drako. "You just have to know how to do it!"

Olin pushed the ale toward Drako and laughed.

"I believe you're right, my friend. Drink up. Jake, drinks all around. Let's drink to my new friend...Drako!" Olin raised his ale and took a small sip. Drako gulped his ale in one long drink, spilling it over his chin and chest.

"This stuff makes my head go round and round!" was all Drako said as he slammed the mug against the table.

"Tell me, Drako, how did you dispatch the master? I really would like to know," Olin said, gently slapping the guardian on the shoulder. "Come on; was it you or your partner that did the dispatching?" Olin smiled at Morto.

"Morto, did you know that it would really take a smart guardian to dispatch a master, and a smart guy is what we are looking for." Olin looked at Drako again. He noticed that the monster was having trouble focusing his eyes, so Olin continued.

"I only need one demon guardian, Drako, and I'll pay two sacks of gold and all of the ale he can drink, but I need a smart one, one that can dispatch a master." Olin let that sink in a moment and then spoke once more. "I guess it was your partner that did the dispatching...right?"

"No, it was me!" snapped Drako. He let out another loud belch and laughed. "I shouldn't do that if I value my little pinker here." He roared in laughter as he pulled on his little finger. He turned to the side and passed a huge blast of gas. "That happens every time I pull on my finger," he said as he turned and looked at Morto. He snorted loudly at him and turned his attention back toward Olin.

"Well, Drako, if you want to work for us and drink all of the ale you can hold, just tell me what I want to know. How did you dispatch the master?" Olin was getting impatient with the guardian and wanted an answer. The obnoxious odor that passed out of the intestines of the guardian was breathtaking. Olin waved his hand in front of his face and continued. "Drako, I need an answer, and if you do that again, I'm afraid—just tell me what I need to know! How did you dispatched a warlock?"

"It was easy; all I did was to..." Drako focused his eyes and looked at Olin. "You're trying to trick me into confessing. Well, it won't work." Drako snorted loudly as he tried to stand, but he was so intoxicated that he couldn't.

The huge guardian slid back into his chair. "I'll kill you just like I killed the other master!" he snorted. "I can do it. I can do it. I killed the other master, and it was easy!"

He raised his chin and laughed loudly. He turned toward, Morto and belched into the assassin's face. The smell was horrific. The monstrous beast turned to Olin again. "I'm going to kill you now, just like I killed the other master who thought he was better than me."

Drako stuck his right hand deep into the soiled pocket of his coat. He moved his hand several times as if searching for something before removing it from his pocket. The enormous fist clutched a small piece of parchment. Placing it on the table, he laid his hand on it. He took his left hand and reached into the pocket on his right side. When he extracted his hand, he was holding a small gold box; he clumsily tried to conceal it with his massive hand, but everyone saw the gold glitter in the bright lights of the tavern.

Morto saw the box first, and his instincts took over. He quickly withdrew one of his daggers and drove it through the beast's hand that was covering the small piece of parchment. Drako let out a loud scream and then snorted loudly. Olin remembered hearing the same painful snort once before—when Max was fighting Thor and Roland in the backyard of the mansion. Max had made the same noise just before he died.

"Quick, grab the box. Don't let him open it. Quickly!" Morto shouted. He was standing now and screaming at Olin. Olin grabbed the monster's hand, but as drunk as Drako was, he had already closed his huge hand around the small gold box and hid it from the ever-searching lights of the tavern. He wasn't about to surrender the contents of his hand.

Morto pulled another dagger and, as before, sank it deep into the wooden table, ensuring it passed through Drako's hand. Drako clutched the small gold box with his free hand and turned to strike Morto. He tried to pull his other hand free, but the two daggers wouldn't release their grip on the hand or the table. Olin grabbed the monstrous hand that was gripping the small gold box, but Drako wouldn't release his clutching grip.

Jake had taken the empty mugs to the bar and returned with a huge club. He lifted it high over his head and struck Drako on the top of the head. It had no effect. Drako didn't flinch. He swung his fist and hit Morto in the face, sending him flying backward out of his chair. He came to a rest under another table, sending flying chairs in every direction. In Drako's mind, Olin would be next.

With one tremendous blow, he hit Olin with the back of his hand, sending him tumbling to the floor; Olin lay there screaming in excruciating pain. The blow alone was painful, but with Olin's recent injuries from the battle with Katie and Roland, hitting the floor was devastating. He screamed louder. Drako attempted to pull the daggers from his hand, but as he did, Jake swung his wooden club once again. The timber split and went flying off in two directions. Drako turned and tried to grab his attacker, but Jake backed off and headed back toward the bar.

Creed hadn't moved but had planted his back firmly against the wall. Drako grabbed Olin's chair and threw it haphazardly toward Creed, striking him on the arm. The dark master extended his arm as if casting a spell, but nothing happened. He looked at Olin, who was moving but not attempting to get up. He could see the pain in his brother's eyes and knew he was hurt. Morto was scrambling to get to his feet, and Jake was behind the bar trying to find another club.

Drako grabbed one of the daggers sticking in his hand, and with one quick pull, removed it. He immediately repeated his actions, removing the second dagger. He turned toward Creed, sat the small gold box on the table, and opened it. A soft yellow glow illuminated from the shiny box. He took the small piece of parchment and slowly, while watching Morto and Olin, starting unfolding it. "Now," he said, "I'm going to dispatch both of you miserable warlocks!"

"Me don't think so!" was all Drako heard as Ray swung his mammoth fist toward the demon guardian. He struck Drako in the back of the head, and the huge demon guardian's face struck the hard tavern table. The gold box fell to the floor, but Drako's massive hand continued to hold on to the small piece of parchment.

Ray grabbed Drako by the arm and, with a fierce thrush, flung the mighty monster across the room into another table. Splinters and chair legs flew in all directions. Ray had already crossed the small area when Drako managed to rise to his feet. Ray kicked him in the groin and slapped his hands fiercely on Drako's ears. The air from the slapping burst Drako's eardrums, and blood oozed into the large cavities and ran down toward his massive earlobes. With one tremendous swing, Ray struck

Drako between his eyes with his monstrous fist. The huge demon guardian fell backward and didn't move.

"Me can rip his head off now?" said Ray.

"Hold on a minute, Ray," said a familiar voice from across the tavern. Roy had entered the tavern and was standing in the doorway. "Master Creed, are you all right? Are you all right, Master Olin?" Before anyone could answer, Roy continued.

"Ray wants to rip this miserable turncoat's head off, but I can't let him do that without your permission. Does he have your permission, masters?"

"No," said Jake. "Take him to the post and let the wood spirits hold him. I'll give him to the tribunal. They'll take care of him. Is everyone all right?"

Morto got to his feet and went over to help Creed. "Master Creed, are you all right, sir?" he said.

Creed hissed. "Yes. Olin, are you hurt?"

"Not seriously, Brother, just my pride a bit." Morto helped Olin to his feet, and both watched Roy and Ray drag Drako to one of the huge posts that supported the second floor of the tavern.

Jake went to the post and rapped on the wood with his knuckles, he called to the spirits within the wood. "Wood spirits hold this demon guardian and don't let him go until I command you to do so."

Two monstrous wood spirits materialized in the huge post. At first, only their heads were visible. They had hair in the sense that it flowed around their heads and vanished into the wooden post. Constructed of a thin layer of wood, each layer was separate from the rest, looking like strands of hair. Their faces were narrow and long, and each had a long beard that disappeared into the wood. They were evil looking, and each gazed upon the demon guardian. Their eyes were round but narrowed as they stared at Drako.

Their ears were hidden beneath their beards and hair, but tips protruded and one could tell they were huge and pointed. The horror of it all was they were evil wood spirits and very disturbing to the eye. Gazing upon them made one nauseated, engulfed by a sick and weakened feeling. Ray backed off a bit. He was huge and muscle-bound, but one could see he disliked the wood spirits. Roy did the same, and Drako stood there, leaning against the post.

They produced arms, and each spirit grabbed one of the demon guardian's arms. As big as Drako's arms were, it was no problem for the wood spirits to grasp and hold him tightly against the enormous post.

Two more arms protruded, one on each side of Drako. They met in the middle and clasped together, binding the huge guardian at the waist. Then, as if magic—and it was—they became solid wood and held the guardian firmly. They pulled on the guardian, and slowly he began to melt into the wood.

"No," shouted Jake. "Bind him. That's all."

The wood spirits moaned softly and then loudly and released the strong grip on Drako. With little effort, they pushed the muscle-bound guardian out of the post. They moaned again, and their faces showed great disappointment.

Roy and Ray each took another step backward. They clearly wanted to keep some distance between them and the two spirit monsters.

Olin and Morto sat down at the table, and Roy and Ray joined them. They all stared at the wood spirits as if in some kind of trance or spell.

Ray finally turned his head and spoke. "Me hates wood spirits. Evil things, me tell you. You can't trust them at all." All agreed, and with the silence broken, the spell released its control of the men.

"Glad me got here just in time!" said Ray. "This guardian is real mean when he's drunk."

"He's real mean when he's not drunk!" said Roy as both of them laughed and then snorted loudly.

"He ain't so mean now!" snorted Ray. The two of them snorted once again as they looked at Drako.

Olin had picked up the small gold box; he studied it for a moment and looked at Morto. "Do you know what this is?"

"Yes, I'm afraid I do—or at least I think I do."

Olin looked at the assassin and then glanced at the door to ensure his privacy. He turned the small box over and inspected every side. "Tell me, then, and tell me what kind of magic and power this box possesses that it can dispatch a dark master."

Morto smiled as he began his story. "There's an ancient tale of a powerful witch—on the dark side, of course—who made a deal with a witch from the good side. A betrayal that was so inconceivable that, to this day, most warlocks and masters only believe it to be a myth."

Olin interrupted. "You're talking about a tavern tale, Morto, a myth. You're referring to a drunkard's tale about a dark witch of death. We've all heard about her—a witch so terrifying and hideous that when she was born her own mother wouldn't give her a name. A witch so evil that even the dark side wouldn't claim her—only the devil."

Morto looked at Olin and continued. "I myself have always thought it to be a myth or tavern tale, but after seeing this box tonight, I don't think so anymore."

Jake spoke softly, "Morto, go on with the story, I don't think I have heard about this witch."

Morto smiled, "the best I can remember, the story goes something like this. There was this witch, so disgusting and evil that no one would speak to her or even look upon her. She lived alone and had no friends or companions. It was on a nightly visit to the surface that she saw him—a strong, handsome young man with skin of bronze and hair the color of her heart. Although she had never had any feelings for anyone on the dark side and although her heart was terribly evil, there was something about this human that captivated her.

"She didn't know what love was and did not understand this strange feeling she had every time she looked upon this man, but it was so undeniable that it drove her insane. She knew she could never be with anyone because of her hideous looks and evil heart, but she couldn't erase the feelings for this human from her thoughts."

Morto stopped and took a long draw on the smoke he had lit. "Some say, she thought he was a god!" Morto released the smoke from his lungs and took another long drag from the smoke.

"The story goes that the dark witch went to a surface witch—on the good side of course—and offered to make a deal. The deal was, if the good witch could produce a potion that would make the evil witch beautiful and give her the knowledge on how to love, then she would give the good witch anything she wanted in exchange. Both witches were very powerful, and both dealt in potions and magic, but the dark witch had no experience in anything that was happy or pure, so she needed the good witch's expertise to make these potions.

"The good witch agreed, but in return for her services, she wanted a way to fight the dark side, especially the dark masters. She requested a magical box that wouldn't only capture the essence or spirit of a warlock or master, but would also allow it to be transferred into a container where it couldn't escape until the container was reopened. The dark witch agreed, and if I'm correct, what you have in front of you is a one-of-a-kind box, a weapon constructed from evil to fight evil, a dark master's worst nightmare."

Olin looked at Morto, who pulled another smoke from the pack of cigarettes and lit it. He slowly rolled the smoke between his fingers. "You don't believe that story do you?" Olin asked.

"Unfortunately I do. Rumor has it that the two witches constructed the box. One represented evil and death; the other represented love and life. Rumor also has it that the good witch carved two figures on the front, one of a woman and the other of a man, holding each other in a romantic embrace. On the backside, the dark witch carved a tombstone with the word *Master* inscribed on it. One of the ends has a large heart, which was placed there by the good witch, and the other end has only one word on it, the word"—Morto paused "*Death*. That word was put there by the dark witch."

Olin examined the small gold box carefully. "Have you seen this box before, Morto?"

"Of course he hasn't seen it before; none of us has ever seen a weapon such as this. Well, until tonight, this thing has only been a rumor," Jake said.

Morto turned and looked at Jake.

"Nicely put, Jake! I wonder where and how this demon guardian came by such a weapon."

Olin looked at the gold box once again. "The box is exactly as you described it, Morto."

Morto laughed and looked at Jake. "Well, if you drank in here as much as I do, you would have heard the tale as many times as I have heard it. It appears that most of the dark side knows about the dark witch that fell in love so long ago. Again, we all thought it was a myth—that is until tonight!"

Jake stood up and looked at Drako, who was still drunk and unconscious. "He'll be out for quite a while. I'll report this to the tribunal." He looked at Olin. "What are we going to do about the box?"

"I'll keep it!" snapped Creed. "We'll keep it safe on the surface!"

"Morto, the top has a picture of a scroll on it; do you think that's the scroll we need to make the box work?" Olin asked, looking at the small piece of parchment lying on the table. He picked it up; there were specks of blood on the outside. He examined it carefully but didn't open it. He stashed it in his cloak along with the gold box.

"I don't know, Master Olin. I would think so, but we might want to ask Drako when he sobers up. After all, he says he knows how to make the box work."

Olin stood up from the table. "We'll take the box and the parchment. We'll see if we can figure it out, and in the meantime, Morto, when Drako wakes up, convince him to tell you how the box works. If you do this for me, I'll pay you handsomely."

"Master Olin, all I want is my medallion back from the witch Wisteria. Get me—"

"We have already made an agreement concerning your medallion, Morto, and that agreement will stand for the time being," Olin said.

"Don't tell the tribunal about the gold box or the parchment. Learn what you can from Drako, and I'll send Ray back with two bags of gold for each of you. Agreed?"

Jake and Morto agreed with smiles on their faces.

Olin looked at the two men and smiled. "When you have learned all you can from Drako, let the wood spirits have him, and no one will ever know what happened here tonight. Pleasure doing business with you gents. Come, Brother. We must return to the surface. Roy, Ray, let's go!"

Creed and Olin headed for the door with Roy and Ray on their heels. As Ray passed Drako, he smacked the guardian in the face and snorted loudly.

Jake fetched two more ales, and he and Morto sat down at the table. "What a night," said Jake. "What a night." Morto smiled and went over to the huge demon guardian, who was still unconscious.

"Drako, Drako, wake up, my friend. Can you hear me?"

"Yes, I can hear you," snorted the guardian. "Get these wood spirits off me; you know you can't trust them." Morto looked at Jake.

"Release the guardian," commanded Jake.

The spirits moaned loudly, and as quickly as they had bound Drako, the wood spirits released their grip on him.

"Come on over here and have another ale," said Morto.

"Sounds good," said Drako. The demon guardian walked over to the table and sat down beside Jake, who had fetched more ale.

"Are you all right?" Jake asked.

"Yeah, sure! It would take more than that to get the best of me." Drako smiled as he lifted the mug of ale and sipped it slowly.

"You didn't tell me you would use wood spirits. You didn't tell me that, Jake. If you had, I would have never agreed to do this."

"Things went a little wacky, Drako. When that happens, you have to think on your feet. Ray wanted to kill you." Jake took a sip of his ale.

"Sorry about the daggers in the hand," said Morto. "I tried to miss the bones." Morto picked up one of Drako's hands. "Looks worse than it is. Does it hurt?"

"Oh no, not at all!" said Drako. "Let me have one of your daggers and I'll show you. Did you have to stick two of them through my hand? Don't you think that one would have been enough?" Drako took another sip of the ale. "They bought it though, didn't they?"

Jake smiled at the huge demon guardian. "You did well tonight, my friend. It was quite a performance."

Morto patted Drako on the shoulder and said. "Did Ray hurt you? He hit you pretty hard?"

"No, I just went along with his punches. My ears still hurt; I'll need to see one of the healers about my ears, not to mention my hand. Oh, by the way, Jake, I thought you were supposed to saw that club in half."

"I did!"

"Well, it didn't work so well, did it? Maybe next time you should saw a little more. I thought you were going to beat me to death with that thing before it broke. At one point, I thought you and Morto were in a contest with each other to see who could hurt me the most. You kept hitting me on the head with that club of yours, and Morto kept sticking his daggers through my hand!" Drako laughed loudly, lifted his head, and snorted toward the ceiling. Jake and Morto laughed as well. Morto mocked Drako and snorted loudly into the air.

"Well, we did it," said Jake. "Good job, guys!"

He looked at the wood spirits "Be gone," he said. They disappeared back into the post, and the post looked normal once more.

# Six

# A Little Capsule

It was noon when Thor rattled the gates in front of Creed's mansion. The warm rays of the bright sun felt good on his exposed skin. The birds were singing their songs and calling to one another, as they too enjoyed the hot summer day. Thor stood in front of the iron gates, and watching the surface world slowly move by, he was amazed. He had forgotten about Creed and the demon guardians and stood wondering why he had always hated the surface so much.

"Still hate it!" he said as he rattled the gates once again. "It's just not home!" He knew he was lying to himself—not so much at the moment, but he knew the more he stayed on the surface the more he liked it. Sometimes he thought it was the sun and the birds, but deep in his heart, he knew it was Wisteria and the Robertses that kept him there.

"Master, there's someone at the gates," said Roy, as he entered Creed's dusty chambers. "I heard them rattling the gates!"

"See who it is," hissed Creed, moving back into the shadows. "Take Ray with you, and don't let anyone onto the premises, Roy!"

"Yes, Master!" Roy said, Popping sounds were heard and Roy disappeared.

Thor put the beauty of the surface world out of his mind as he remembered why he was standing in front of the old iron gates in the first place: the simple task of scanning Creed's mansion for dark spirits. Although he assumed it was empty—same as the days before—he took several precautionary steps toward the end of the great stone wall. Thor had expected nothing, but what he heard were popping sounds on the other side of the wall. He paused for a brief moment, listening carefully. Then he heard what he was waiting for, the familiar sound of a second set of popping noises.

"Hades, they're back!" he said softly. He crossed the street, picking up his pace, and within a few seconds had disappeared down the side street.

"Who's there?" came a husky voice from behind the wall. There was no answer. Roy and Ray stood silently, hiding like thieves, behind the huge great wall. They listened quietly until Roy repeated his question again.

"Who's there?"

"Me don't think anybody's there," said Ray.

"For Pete's sake, Ray, how many times must I tell you not to say *me*? It's *I*. Why can't you remember that. You sound like an idiot when you talk like that."

"Me will remember, Roy. Me—uh, uh, I'll remember it's *I* from now on."

"Well, at least that's a start," Roy said, staring at Ray. "You dumb brute." Roy smiled at Ray and slapped the huge guardian on the shoulder. "No matter how you talk, Ray, I would rather have you beside me and watching my back than any demon guardian I know. He smiled once more at Ray and then said with a mocking laugh, "Me likes you, Ray. Me thinks you are my bestest friend." Both guardians laughed and snorted loudly.

They stared at the huge rock wall, waiting with anticipation to hear something, but no noises came. Finally, Roy shrugged his shoulders.

"I think you're right, Ray. I don't think anyone is out here. If so, I don't think they're trying to enter the grounds. Let's go back and report to the master." Popping sounds were heard and the two demon guardians headed back to the mansion.

Roy knocked before entering Creed's chambers. "Who is it?" hissed a voice from the other side of the door.

"It's me, master, Roy." Roy opened the door and walked up to the large chair sitting in front of Creed's desk. He paused for a moment, distracted by a spider that crawled out of the cushion and came to a rest on the chair's arm.

"Well?" said Creed, impatiently.

Roy looked away from the spider and remembered why he was there. "Master, there was no one at the gates. Just someone walking by, I suppose. I didn't see anyone on the other side of the wall."

From the shadows of his desk, Creed sat looking at the demon guardian. He didn't say anything but delivered a low hiss. Roy continued to stand, expecting an answer, and finally his master did speak. "Where's Olin?"

"He's in the backyard, Master."

"Keep an eye on him, Roy. He's weak, and in the morning he's going for Sarah and the rest of the spirits at Number 12. Tomorrow night I'll have enough power to complete my transformation, and then I'll rule the dark side and this miserable little town they call Johnston." Creed hissed, sliding back into the shadows. "Roy, you stay loyal to me and I'll let you rule all of the demon guardians in Terra Demorte. They will bow to you as they will bow to me. How would you like that?"

"I don't know if I could do that, Master. I wouldn't know how," Roy said, standing in front of his master. Roy knew if Creed's transformation was a success, that Creed would indeed try to rule the dark side and eventually would—or at least would try to—rule all of Terra Demorte.

"Olin and I will teach you, Roy," Creed hissed. "Now leave me and take care of Olin. I have summoned Notor"—he paused for a brief second and in an irritated voice added, "again! When he gets here, show him to my chambers."

Roy backed slowly toward the door. "Yes, Master." Distracted once more by the spider on the chair's arm, he watched the small creature slowly disappear behind the large cushion. The demon snorted softly and left the room.

"If the master thinks I want to rule the Demon Guardian Clan, he's going mad," Roy said to himself. "Mad, I tell you. He wants to rule Terra Demorte, and Ray keeps saying 'me.' Both of them are driving me nuts. I can't take much more of this." He snorted loudly and then walked down the hall, whispering, "I need to kill something."

\*\*\*

Thor hurried down the side street. He wanted to run but knew it would attract attention, so he took long strides instead, stretching his legs as far as he could with each step. He was talking to himself as he headed toward town. "Hades, they're back. I can't believe they're back. All Hades is going to break loose now."

He entered the small restaurant and was greeted by Patty. She started to look for a table for him when Thor spoke.

"Patty, is Wisteria here?"

"No, I'm sorry, Thor, but she's gone home! Is everything all right?" She cast a puzzling look at Thor. He was sweating, and the sweat had soaked through the soft cotton of his shirt. He had retired his cloak during the time Creed had been gone, and since there was no one else to assassinate, he now only carried two daggers beneath his shirt. Wisteria and Katie had fitted him with one of Roland's cotton golf shirts, and he tugged at the soft material, trying unsuccessfully to keep it off his chest as he answered Patty.

"Yes, everything is fine, just fine! I'm going to her house. If you see her, tell her, you know who is back at you know where!'"

"You know what is where?" questioned Patty. "I'm sorry, Thor, but I don't know who you know who is!"

"You don't have to know, Patty. Just tell her, 'You-know-who is back in town.'" Thor smiled at the confused waitress. He was hot, sweaty, and in a hurry, and his patience was wearing thin, but Thor wasn't one to be rude. Even when he was going to kill someone, he was very polite and would inform his victim in advance. "Could you please do that for me?" He smiled again at Patty and stepped toward the door.

Patty grabbed his arm. "Do I tell her, "You know who is back at you know where,' or do I tell her, 'You know who is back in town'?" She laughed aloud and patted Thor on the shoulder. "Just kidding, Thor. I'll tell her."

Thor smiled faintly at Patty and then squinted his eyes. Now poking fun at an assassin would normally provoke a swift draw of a dagger and planting it in one's chest, but Thor liked Patty and had decided not to kill her—well, at least not today.

"Kidding, you say? You're just kidding?" Thor laughed slightly and walked toward the door again. He mumbled softly, "Got to get out of here. Someone's missing a few bats in the belfry."

"I heard that!" laughed Patty.

Thor smiled as he turned to face the inquisitive little waitress. "Just kidding!" he said as he backed toward the door. His smile vanished as his facial expression morphed into one of an evil being casting a wicked spell. Patty suddenly grabbed her backside and let out a blood-curdling scream. Once more, Thor smiled as he left the café.

\*\*\*

Thor stopped on the porch of Wisteria's small cottage and scanned his surroundings. It was a beautiful day, and the sun's golden rays were chasing shadows into hiding and lighting up everything they touched. The birds were singing, and every living creature seemed to be enjoying the gorgeous day. But at this very moment, Thor couldn't take the time to see the wonders of the surface world, but as always, he hesitated before knocking on the old witch's door. If he had learned anything during his stay with Wisteria, it was not to burst into her home. "One never knows what she might be doing," he told himself. He chuckled as he knocked on the wooden door.

"Oh, come on in, Thor. How many times have I told you that you don't have to knock before entering my house?" The voice came from inside, and although it was very welcoming, Thor was leery of entering the old witch's house.

"More than once, my dear lady, more than once!" he answered as he turned the knob and pushed the door open. He expected to feel the cool rush of fresh cold air coming from the dark cottage and maybe a fire in the fireplace sending shadows jumping on the walls and ceiling, but that wasn't what he saw—at all.

What he saw totally shocked and surprised the assassin from Terra Demorte. He wasn't surprised by the fact that a rush of cold air didn't hit him in the face, but more so at what did hit him, which was a blast of hot moist air, like one might expect in a jungle.

The inside of Wisteria's house *was* a jungle, thick and gnarly vines growing everywhere, birds singing and squawking, flying from one branch to another landing clumsily in the thick foliage of the tall trees. He noticed something else was moving. *There, where the corner should be. Yes, there it is. Something's running up that tree.* Thor spoke softly. "A monkey? No...several," he whispered.

Thor watched the monkeys until they disappeared into the vines and foliage high in the umbrella trees. "Funny, I don't remember this house being that high. I don't remember these trees either," he said, again very softly.

"Well, what do you think?" A voice from the deep green undergrowth had spoken. The vines had all but completely taken over the, what now looked to be a large and very high cottage.

"Where are you?" Thor said.

"Here!" Wisteria said as she walked out of the bulky, cumbersome vines. "Well, how do you like it? Isn't it just lovely, dear?" Wisteria finally appeared and walked toward the bewildered assassin. She turned around slowly, and with hands extended, spoke softly once more. "Isn't it just loooovely, dear?"

"Yeah, just lovely, Wisteria. Are we going to sleep here tonight?" Thor asked. "You didn't turn my bedroom into a jungle, did you?" Just then, a very large parrot fluttered from the branches overhead and landed on Thor's shoulder.

"Ho ho ho and a bottle of rum!" said the squawking fowl.

Thor looked at the irritating bird. "Do I look like a pirate to you?" He stared at Wisteria and then, glancing back at the bird, he begged for mercy. "Can you please get this smelly thing off of me?"

Wisteria smiled. "Do you want to look like a pirate, dear?" she asked.

"No!" shouted Thor. "Quit playing around. I've got something important to tell you: Creed's back, or at least his demon guardians are!" Before Thor could say anything else, Wisteria interrupted him.

"What did you say? Creed's back? Quickly, do as I say. Go back outside and stand on the porch. Hurry now. Move." Wisteria pushed Thor gently toward the door.

Thor knew very well not to argue with the old lady, so he pushed the vines open and headed toward the door. He turned the knob and stepped onto the front porch of the witch's house. "Crazy witch," he muttered, knocking the bird poop off his shoulder.

"Thor, dear, would you please be so kind as to come back in here?" Wisteria said. Thor opened the door, and a blast of fresh cold air emitted from the dark room. A large fire danced in the fireplace, throwing shadows on the ceiling and walls. The jungle, birds, and monkeys were all gone. Nothing remained of the lush, thick green undergrowth, and the cottage was back to normal.

"How'd you do that?" Thor asked.

"Do what?" questioned Wisteria.

"You know darn well what I mean. The jungle—how'd you make it disappear so fast?"

Wisterias walked to the center of the room and slowly bent over; she picked something up from the floor and looked at it.

"What cha got there, Wisteria?" questioned Thor.

"Two little capsules, Thor, just two little capsules."

"What do they do?" Thor asked. "What do you use them for?"

"One of these little capsules produces a large jungle, the one you just witnessed, dear," Wisteria said, looking quite proud of her latest concoction. "With one of these and a few magic words, one can produce a thick, luscious, green jungle in seconds…anywhere one wants."

"Can I have one of those?" Thor asked. "You never know when a jungle might come in handy." Thor looked at Wisteria. He knew she was a powerful witch and it would be very unlikely for her to share her magic with anyone, let alone an assassin from Terra Demorte.

"Yes, dear, if you would like. There are only two of these in the world, but here's one for you if you would like." Wisteria handed Thor one of the small capsules. It was dark green and simple, like what one might take for a headache or a cold, certainly not something that would produce a jungle. Thor looked at the small pod with curious eyes. He held it in his hand.

"How do I make it work?"

Wisteria strolled over to him and whispered a spell softly in his ear. She stepped back. "Say those words, and the capsule will do the rest. When you want the jungle to disappear, just repeat the words again, but backward. Now, what did you say about Creed. Did you say he was back, dear?"

Thor looked at the capsule and studied it closely. "Will this really work for me?"

"Of course, dear. Give it a try if you like!" Wisteria said.

"I can wait. Thanks, Wisteria. This is good, and you never know when something like this just might come in handy." He studied the little capsule once again before putting it in his pocket. "Yes, Creed is back—or coming back very soon. I rattled his gates this morning and within seconds heard the popping sounds of two demon guardians."

"Are you sure?" Wisteria said softly. "Are you sure you heard demon guardians?"

"Don't forget I'm from Terra Demorte. I've heard the popping sound of demon guardians all my life. Make no mistake, there are two of them at Creed's this very minute."

"Come, Thor. We must go to Number 12. Katie and Josh could be in danger," Wisteria said as she put the other small capsule in her pocket.

"My thoughts exactly," said Thor, heading for the door. "I don't think Creed would come for Sarah during the day, but one never knows exactly what that warlock is capable of doing."

# Seven

# The Return of the Warlock

Katie and her neighbor Pat were sitting on the steps of Number 12 enjoying the shade that the two giant oaks provided. They chitchatted about the warm summer day, flowers, and things of the past. Pat was very knowledgeable about the Wheeler sisters, who used to live in Number 12, and she was more than willing to share what she knew about the women. One thing Katie had learned from Miss Pat was that all of the Wheeler girls were great women, all were respected in the small town of Johnston, and all loved their wonderful home.

Pat was the first to see the odd pair walking down the city sidewalk; she smiled at Katie and pointed toward the unlikely couple. "Now there's something you don't see every day, an old woman walking a handsome young man."

"Want to bet?" Katie said as she stared at the two strollers. Wisteria was dressed in her usual long lavender dress, and the gentle summer breeze blew softly against it, swirling it around her as if it were alive. Her long black-and-silver hair flowed gently over her shoulders and hung down her back, covering every inch of it. Most was hanging straight, from the crown of her head to down past her waist. It covered her breast and flowed gently downward. Other parts had wrapped itself around her

63

body as if it were holding the old woman together. It resembled a large snake coiled around a massive tree; it surrounded the old woman's body as if trying to protect her from some unseen force.

"I wonder how many of those dresses she has," said Pat, smiling at Katie. "That's all she ever wears. Not saying that it doesn't look good on her, but one might think she would want to expand upon her wardrobe a little."

"Dozens I suppose!" laughed Katie. The women turned their attention toward the tall, slender man walking with Wisteria. He was walking in unison with the old woman, taking small strides, ensuring not to rush her steps. His thick black hair was pulled back into a ponytail that slightly swung from side to side as he walked. He looked quite dashing strolling beside Wisteria. He was wearing a pair of jeans with a slipover golf shirt that he casually wore out. He had a thin waist and broad shoulders, and Roland's shirt fit him tightly, showing off his muscular chest and arms. As he strolled, he looked as if had just stepped out of a *GQ Magazine*, so handsome and elegant, but Thor hadn't just stepped out of a magazine. Normally, his wardrobe, like Wisteria's, consisted of one set of clothing, and for an assassin that was a black cloak with a black suit beneath.

"Who's that man with Wisteria?" questioned Pat. "I've seen him before, walking around town, but never with Wisteria. He's quite handsome, you know."

Katie smiled and only responded softly to her neighbor, "Oh, he's just a friend of hers!"

The unlikely pair of walkers came to the sidewalk leading up to Number 12 and started up the two concrete steps. Wisteria smiled at Katie.

"Well, hello, dear, and how are we doing today?"

Josh, who had been playing in the yard, made a beeline toward the couple and answered Wisteria's question before his mother had a chance.

"I'm fine, Miss Wisteria. Hello, Thor," Josh said, walking beside the assassin. He turned his head upward and flashed a big smile at the tall man.

Thor bent slightly and ran his hand through the little boy's soft curly hair. "Hello, Josh. You doing all right today? I bet you really like playing in this big yard, don't you? It's so lush and green. Reminds me of something else I saw today." He turned slightly and shot Wisteria a quick glance. Wisteria knew that Thor was alluding to her little episode with the jungle, but she made no comment and didn't return Thor's glance.

"Yeah, do you want to play with me, Thor?" asked Josh.

Thor smiled again at Josh. "Maybe later, buddy." He and Wisteria walked down the sidewalk toward the house with Josh tagging alone beside the assassin. As they reached the shade under the two enormous oaks, each—as if being choreographed to do so—looked up into the huge trees. "This shade really feels good!" said Thor. He dropped his head and looked at the two women sitting on the steps. "Hello, Katie. How are you today?" Thor said.

He looked at Miss Pat; he studied her for a moment before he spoke. "Hello, miss. My name is Thor. It's good to see you, and I do hope that you are having a wonderful day." By his manners, one would never guess he was an assassin from the dark side of the world and would cut a person's throat in a second.

Katie spoke first with simple salutations and then gave Wisteria a big hug and a soft kiss on the cheek. She looked at Thor, hugged the assassin, and planted a kiss on his cheek as well. "It's good to see you, Thor. How's your day going?" Before Thor could answer, she continued, "This is my neighbor, Miss Pat Millborn. And, Miss Pat, this is Wisteria, who you already know, and this is her friend and mine, Thor."

"Yes, dear, I already know Miss Pat, and how are you doing today, Miss Pat?" Wisteria said.

"I'm doing fine, Wisteria; it's so good to see you," Pat said with a smile.

"How's your husband Jim, dear? I see he's still running his little antique shop on Main. I do hope he's doing well there. You know, I always thought that little building would make a perfect antique shop."

"He's doing fine, Wisteria, covered up with work. Since his retirement, he's busier than ever, but it keeps him from getting bored. Well, it was nice to see you again, Wisteria, and nice to meet you, Thor!" Pat batted her eyes at the assassin . She gave him a sweet little smile. "I must be getting back to the house. Come and see me when you get a chance, Katie. Wisteria, you and Thor are always welcome to come for a visit too." Pat walked down the steps and smiled once again at Katie, then headed across the yard.

"She's a very nice lady," said Wisteria, "and if you must know, I have over forty of these fine dresses."

"Miss Pat, Miss Pat!" screamed Josh. He ran toward the petite woman, and as he reached her, he held out his arms. Miss Pat knelt down. Josh wrapped his arms around her neck, gave her a big hug, and then gently kissed her on the cheek. She hugged him back and kissed his soft curly hair.

"I'll see you later, Josh. Come on, Poco. Let's go home."

Poco, Miss Pat's crossed-eyed brown poodle, trotted along behind her, stopping every so often to give Josh a quick glance. Since the Robertses had moved in, Poco had become a regular visitor when he saw Josh in the yard. Josh loved playing with the small dog, and they'd become great playmates.

"Bye, Poco!" said Josh. The small dog stopped and turned to give him one last look. He wiggled what would have been his tail but—as with most poodles—was only an inch-long nub. Josh fell into the soft green turf and rolled over repeatedly. Poco couldn't stand it any longer. He turned and headed back toward the small boy. He made a few circles around him and jumped into his lap. Josh rubbed his brown curly hair and, Poco loved every minute of it.

"Send him home when you go inside, Josh!" said Miss Pat. "Apparently he's not ready to come home yet!"

Wisteria and Thor took a seat on the steps of the old house. Katie had offered for them to go inside, but the breeze felt good, and Thor and Wisteria had elected to sit in the shade. Katie sat down and gazed out into the yard; she watched her son playing with the neighbor's dog. "This is how I pictured my days with Josh," she said, "sitting on the porch watching him play in the yard, and just spending time with him. I just love it here, and I love my two new friends, as well." She squeezed Wisteria's hand.

Katie wasn't bashful when it came to telling the people she loved just how much they meant to her. She had always thought it was important to let people know how she felt about them. Especially since she and Roland had moved so often in the past. They had left many friends behind with each move, but all knew just how much she and Roland loved them. She squeezed Wisteria's hand again and smiled at the old woman.

"Now, what on earth brought you two down the street this time of day? You must be hot. Let me get you some lemonade or tea, iced of course."

"Yes, dear, that would be nice. Why don't you get Josh and we all go inside for a spell?"

Katie called for the little boy playing in the yard, and they all went into Number 12. Josh, like Poco, was reluctant to go inside but finally surrendered with a wink from Thor. Katie poured lemonade for her guests and then stuck Josh in the downstairs tub. She returned with a glass of cold lemonade for herself and slid into the oversized chair in the den. She looked at Wisteria and then at Thor. Both looked serious and neither said a word. As she stared at them, she realized something was wrong.

"He's back, isn't he?" she offered.

"Yes, dear, I'm afraid so. Thor went by this morning to rattle the gates, and he heard two demon guardians on the other side. We really don't know if Creed's back, but if he's not, he will be soon. He wouldn't have the demon guardians there unless he was there or on his way."

"I was hoping he wouldn't come back, but I can see how foolish I was in thinking that. What do we do now?" Katie said.

"Well, dear, we'll stay here with you until Roland comes home, and we will all decide at that time. Thor and I didn't want to leave you and Josh alone today, but don't worry, Thor doesn't believe Creed will come for Sarah and the rest in the middle of the day. But we don't want you to be by yourself if he does."

Thor sat quietly and watched Katie's expressions. The longer he stayed on the surface the better he became at reading the facial expressions of humans. "Katie, I know this scares you," he finally said, "but we knew this day would come. Let's not worry about it until Roland comes home and we can decide on what actions we need to take, deal?"

"I'm afraid, Thor, now that Roland's back at work—I'm afraid that Creed or Olin or both of them might show up and hurt Josh or me. It really scares me."

"It scares all of us, Katie, but I promise I won't let anything happen to you or your family. Wisteria has already placed the crystal in your home; it will alert us if any dark spirit enters these premises. If they show up, we'll be right behind them. Would it make you feel better if I came by more often, just to check on you and Josh?"

"Yes, thank you, Thor. I appreciate you and Wisteria, but it still scares me."

Wisteria looked at the young woman sitting in the oversized chair. Although she knew how strong Katie was, at that very moment, what she saw was a frightened little girl sitting alone and not knowing when evil would come for her or her son. Trying to make Katie feel better, Wisteria repeated what Thor had told her earlier. "Well, dear," she said, "Thor and I will be on the alert for Creed and Olin. If they come here, we will be ready."

"Thanks, that makes me feel better," Katie said.

Wisteria and Thor sat in the den of the old house the rest of the afternoon, keeping Katie company. From time to time, the conversation would drift back to Creed and Olin, but Wisteria or Thor would change the topic each time. They wanted to keep Katie's mind off Creed until Roland came home. There was only one thing that could be done concerning the dark side and the two demons Creed and Olin, but convincing Katie and Roland was going to be difficult, and neither wanted to push Katie any harder than was necessary.

Saving Sarah had been a major win in the war against Creed, and actually, the good side had won that war, but now, there was another more brutal war-brewing, one with many battles. And one of those battles would be to save the Robertses from the warlock Creed and his brother. Once the brothers realized that Sarah and the others were gone from their grasp, it would only be a matter of time before they came after Katie and Roland.

Warlocks were powerful, dark, and evil, and most would never want to cross them, a being from Terra Demorte nor a human from the surface. The safest thing to do was to stay as far away from these evil beings as possible.

Once a warlock turned on someone, he wouldn't stop his treachery until he was satisfied with the punishment he'd bestowed upon that soul—or until he had issued it a horrible death.

Things were different with Creed. In the dark history of Terra Demorte and the history of the surface world, never had a warlock ever tried to rule a human town. Warlocks were usually happy with the small surface lots they claimed, and their rule was private and always kept secret from the inhabitants of the surface world.

With the exception of Olin, no other warlock had ever entered into the ancient ritual, trying relentlessly to transform himself back into a human being—being of flesh and bone—and no warlock had ever wanted to rule the dark and evil place known as Terra Demorte. It had always been ruled by the ten clans.

Creed was a vicious warlock, and his brother just as dangerous. And it had been made clear to Thor and Wisteria, after seeing Olin's body, why he wanted to complete the ritual. What spirit wouldn't want the transformation? They assumed the reason he wanted to rule a surface town was to have a place where evil could dwell outside of Terra Demorte.

The history of the dark side wasn't known to many surface dwellers; actually, most humans couldn't imagine the horror that dwelled below them in the belly of the earth. Feeding on the living and trespassing in and out of the human world at will. Of course, these dark and evil monsters know of their own history, the same way those on the surface are aware of much of their own. Nevertheless, on the surface, some things are better left unsaid and certainly not recorded in history books.

Twice since the damnation of man, evil has boiled over its boundaries, and twice the same dark evil has tried to rule great parcels of land on the surface of the earth. Creating places where evil could dwell openly and spread like a disease infecting all living things with darkness and wickedness so that no one would be safe from it, even to the far ends of the human world. These evil beings are brutal and appalling and won't rest until all goodness is banished from the earth and only evil and darkness remain. On earth, they would feed on the living, and the chaos and destruction they cause would be overwhelming.

Both times evil failed, and twice all that is good in this world claimed superiority over the darkness and beat it back, back to its dark and dreary home below the surface of the earth. For centuries, it had been quiet, content living below in the blackness, and the good witches on the surface of the earth, continued to be leery of this evil. They—and they alone—watch and guard the human world from the onslaught of evil.

Thor and Wisteria both knew this history and hoped that Creed's transformation wouldn't be of the same magnitude. Hopefully, this was just one twisted warlock's distorted aspiration and not some well-lain plan to release such horror, once more, on the inhabitants of the surface.

Wisteria and Thor were aware of the dark side's past two attempts to rule on the surface of the earth, and they hoped that the good in humanity would win out over Creed and his followers—but for these two warriors, it was for different reasons.

# Eight

## Evil's First Attempt

It was early in the history of humankind when evil first attempted to rule on the surface of the earth—long ago, when man and things were simple and life was more controlled and dictated rather than left to chance. In those days, mighty pharaohs ruled the lands. Those who were favored by these powerful rulers were indeed favored, and those who were not remained as they were born, in poverty and slavery.

However, there was one pharaoh who loved his lands and its people— all of his people. Unlike his father and his father's father before him, when his time came to rule, he ruled with grace and dignity. He was kind and gentle and changed the way the haves and have-nots lived. His people prospered, and the lowest of humankind that dwelled in his lands never felt the cold pinch of hunger or the fierce bite of winter. All were happy and loved their compassionate ruler.

The mighty pharaoh, loving his land and people as he did, often thought his kindness and generosity would be rewarded in the afterlife. The pharaohs of his time often thought of themselves as living gods, on earth to rule over the common people, nobles, and priests. Upon death, they believed they would join Rah, the Sun god, and the other gods that ruled in the afterlife. Upon death, they would dwell as a god for eternity and, in a dual personality, fight demons in the underworld.

This pharaoh was different from most leaders of his time. Though he did concern himself with the afterlife, he didn't think of himself as a living god, nor did he want to be. He believed that his good deeds on earth would grant him god status in the afterlife and Rah and the other gods would welcome him as a gracious king. So his life was dedicated to loving his people and his lands.

As generous and kind as the good pharaoh was, it's written unto man a number of days he can live and dwell upon the earth. And when this pharaoh's time came, he died and slipped into another world. The people were saddened by the news of their fallen ruler. The wealthy along with the poorest wept, and sadness fell upon the lands. A window of opportunity opened for the nobles and priests, and wickedness began to spread into the land. Dark and evil spirits, united with greed, slowly consumed the lands and the people.

Seeing the sadness and evil that had befallen their kingdom, and unable to see the mistake they were about to make, a group of good witches decided to resurrect their beloved pharaoh. Little did they know that this act of loyalty and love would change the world forever and create unimaginable monsters that, to this day, still lurk in the shadows and prey, at will, on all of humanity.

Thinking only of their kingdom, these witches created a vessel that would indeed resurrect their departed pharaoh. They forged a unique device from the purest gold and then, using great power and magic, gave this vessel the ability to resurrect the dead. It not only gave life, but it also gave the spirit a new body of flesh and bone. As the pharaoh's body had been mummified, a new body was needed.

They were cautious, and in order to protect the vessel and its magic, they also cursed it with a magical spell—a spell that dealt in death and would take the life of anyone that performed the ritual. Anyone, that is, except a good witch.

Once the ritual started, the spirit would be trapped between the essence of a spirit and the mortality of a human. The ritual required much power, more than the good witches had, so they would drain the power or essence from other spirits that hadn't crossed over into the light when they died. They were careful only to capture and collect the power from good spirits, because evil had no place in this ritual.

Once completed, the spirit would be granted a beautiful, strong, and youthful body of flesh and bones, and the memory of its previous life would be fully restored. It would remember death and hopefully be thankful to once again be alive. They called this vessel The Secret of Life.

So on a dark and dreary night, when all was quiet and nothing stirred except the night birds and other creatures of the dark, the witches gathered in a secret place and there, under the cover of darkness, they carried out, for the first time in the history of humankind, their magical ritual.

In the desolate morning hours, their beloved pharaoh came to life, and once again, happiness reigned throughout the lands and the great pharaoh, as in his previous life, ruled with grace and dignity. Evil scurried back into hiding as the mighty pharaoh dealt with the injustices that had consumed his lands, because evil had no place in his domain.

However, once more, the mighty pharaoh met with death, but this time it was most untimely. Some say it was a simple accident, while others say it was an act of murder, carried out by assassins hired by the wealthy noblemen. But, nonetheless, the pharaoh passed into darkness and, once more, fell into an endless sleep. As in the past, the lands fell into dismay and hopelessness as the people mourned their beloved pharaoh.

As with any death, a few didn't mourn the passing of the pharaoh, but rejoiced and wallowed in the reality that the great protector of the lands was, once more, dead. Evil slipped out of hiding, and like an addiction that could never be satisfied, darkness slowly consumed the lands.

Once again, the good witches brought forth life to their much-loved pharaoh. As before, he reigned with grace and dignity, but remembering his past lives and deaths disturbed the pharaoh, and as time passed, the great and mighty pharaoh fell into darkness. He was obsessed with the fear of dying, and that thought alone consumed him. Although he knew the good witches could resurrect him many times over, his fears eroded his confidence and pushed him into great depression.

He began to ignore his lands and people, and his priests, noblemen, and underlings ruled out of greed. The lands fell, once more, into chaos and poverty—this time, during his lifetime. The wealthy took control. Greed and self-indulgence followed.

The healers administered to the pharaoh, but nothing they did could break the powerful ruler's fear of death. Reaching their last efforts, desperation set in, and the healers called upon the good witches, who had restored his life, for help.

"You must help our pharaoh. He's not strong, and his lands are in great despair," pleaded the lead healer.

"What would you have us to do?" questioned the leader of the good witches. "We have resurrected the pharaoh twice, but he must rule on his own accord. We have given you potions and—"

"Your potions are useless," screamed the healer, looking at the old woman standing in front of him. *Death becomes you*, he thought, *you insolent witch*.

"They don't work," he continued. "The pharaoh is still deeply frightened of dying and is slipping deeper into darkness. He won't leave his chambers and can't rule. Others are taking his kingdom from him. This hopelessness is your fault, and you and your group of so-called good witches will have the responsibility of healing our mighty pharaoh. Fix this, or I'll have the whole lot of you beheaded."

The healer's face reddened. He paced in front of the witches, and his voice became louder with each word spoken. He took a long, deep breath and concluded with a simple statement: "Do you understand me?"

The leader of the good witches looked calmly at the healer and paused before she spoke. With a slight flick of her hand, she cast a small affliction spell, a spell that would allow a multitude of bedbugs to join the healer when he slept that night. She spoke softly. "I'll do what I can do, but—"

The good witch didn't finish her sentence; the mighty pharaoh had stirred. He had been sitting silently on his throne as the healers and the witches conversed. He looked down on the witches now and spoke softly.

"There is one thing you can do for me." The pharaoh slightly adjusted his posture, sitting up a little straighter; he looked squarely at the group of witches. His voice became clearer and more dominate. "You need to make me immortal."

"No!" screamed the head witch in panic "We can't do that. We don't have the power or magic to do that. We can't grant immortality."

The ruler looked at the witches, and his demeanor changed as he became irritated and adjusted his posture once more. "Well, if you don't have the power or the magic, then tell me who does." He lifted his hand, and the healers summoned more guards. "Well, I'm waiting. Who has the power to make me immortal?" Two guards stood by the mighty pharaoh's throne and six more by the witches. "Speak, witch," said the pharaoh short-temperedly.

"No one that I know," said the head witch, bowing her head.

"You lie," he shouted. He became furious and stood. "Put her in the dungeon along with the others. I'll keep them there until they tell me who can make me immortal."

The guards grabbed at the witch, but she vanished from their grasp and was gone. The other witches followed suit and vanished as well. They left no other sign that they had been there, but there was a stench, a disgusting odor, that floated effortlessly around the room. The guards gagged and clutched their noses, determined not to breath. As moments passed, their lungs screamed for precious air, but they dared not to open their mouths or release their nostrils.

This infuriated the great pharaoh; he coughed and gagged, and after inhaling the nasty order, he threw his goblet of wine. It scampered across the floor as if some mysterious spell was upon it. They all watched it spin, and no one spoke until the bewitched cup stopped its uncanny dance.

The pharaoh screamed once more while pointing his finger at his guards. "Go to the woods, to the dark witches' encampment, and summon them to come before me. If they refuse, kill them." He paused for a moment, rubbing his chin. "All of them. I'm tired of these insolent magical beings."

Going into the land of the dark witches purely terrified them, but the great pharaoh's men did as commanded. They knew the consequences of disobeying orders. The pharaoh would just as soon separate a man from his head as not. So they marched to the edge of the witches' domain, reluctantly, and entered into the threatening woods where the dark witches lived. No one ever went there. Most, if not all of the people of the pharaoh's lands, were fearful of the witches. By all rights, they were justified to be. The witches were cruel and evil and had no compassion for anything that breathed the breath of life. These witches dealt in the most sinister evil that gathered in the lands, they worked their wickedness to conjure up demons, and they summoned many.

Slowly, but fully alert, the pharaoh's guards continued on their quest. Although they were terrified of the darkness and the shadows that moved with each step they took, they were equally terrified of the pharaoh's wrath, if they failed.

Single file, they inched down the dimly lit trail, the heavy foliage all but blocked out the sun's rays. It looked as if the sun itself was reluctant to penetrate this dark place. There was more to these woods than just darkness and shadows, something more deadly, and it was lurking behind every shadow. Their eyes betrayed them as the shadows and darkness slowly crept toward them, narrowing their advancement, and worse, their escape.

"There's something in there," said a soldier pointing into the darkness. Everyone stared wearily into the thick and musty smelling foliage, fearing some type of monster that would pounce at any moment, but none was seen. They knew something was there, but where?

"And there," said another. "No there, in those shadows."

They all saw something slipping out of the shadows, or was it slipping deeper into the darkness? All saw something, and all saw nothing.

Finally, shadows did appeared out of the darkness and stepped into a dismal glowing light. Two figures stepped forth and stood in front of the pharaoh's men.

"What do you want?" they demanded. Their voices were slightly soothing and came from deep inside their chests, followed by a low whispering sound. "Why do you trespass in these woods?" Their black robes were thin and billowed with the slightest movement. Moving as if alive and not part of the talking heads that protruded from their tops. The witches mesmerized the frightened guards. If only the darkness would give way to more light and let, the guards cast their eyes on the witches' faces. Surely, these creatures were beautiful. They sounded so beautiful.

The figures, stepping deeper into the shadows, repeated their question. "What do you want?"

Awakened from his dreamlike state, the captain spoke in a soft dreamy voice. "We are here to speak to your clan; the mighty pharaoh requires your presence."

"So he does," replied one of the figures. "So he does."

The captain, clearing his head and shaking off the mesmerizing state, came to his senses, stood erect, and spoke, once more. "Why is it so dark in here? What have you done to block the sun from shining in this place?" Then remembering why he was there, he spoke more precisely and clearly. "Will the leader of your clan come with us? The pharaoh—" He stopped for a moment. The word *command* might not be the right one to use. He quickly rephrased. "Forgive me. What I'm saying is that the great pharaoh would like to see the leader of your clan." He stood erect, waiting on the figures to reply.

"Maybe," spoke one of the figures calmly. "Wait here."

Moments later, an old witch and several younger ones appeared from the darkness. The old witch introduced herself. "My name is Zenia." She thrust her staff high into the air, and its gnarly end emitted a bright flame. It chased most of the shadows around the small path into hiding, but the thick woods remained dark and dismal.

The eyes of the distrustful guards danced from one dark shadow to another and then to the witches, who crept onto the long, crooked path, single file.

"Lead on, captain," she said. "We will follow."

When they reached the edge of the woods, the soldiers remembered how the witches looked in the dark dense forest. They remembered how their thin garments had danced around their bodies, evoking beauty, and now that they were out of the dark forest and into the bright sun, they were eager to cast their eyes on such beautiful creatures.

The sun shone brightly as they exited the forest, and as the soldiers looked at the witches, they were mortified. Beauty hadn't befallen these women. Instead, just the opposite. Most, if not all, had long, crooked noses with large nostrils. Warts adorned their faces along with long hairs. Their eyes were as black as coal, only darker, if that were possible. Their clothes were long, black, with multiple layers, not so pleasant to look at in the sunlight. The guards were sure that a comb or brush had never found its way through the thick, long hair that danced about the witches as if it were alive.

The women were hideous, to say the least, and now that they were out of the thick woods and away from the musty, threatening forest, the witches gave off an odor, a strange smell that was repulsive to the nose.

Zenia and the other witches followed along behind the captain toward the pharaoh's palace, and as they neared the majestic palace, no one was surprised by the captain's words.

"We will enter at the back, a secret entrance only known to us soldiers and a few others." He turned toward the witches. "You must use this entrance when you come to see the pharaoh, understood?"

"Yes," was her reply to the captain. "Of course, as you command."

"I'll order my guards to allow you to enter when you come to see the pharaoh."

The old dark witch smiled ever so slightly. She and her dark witches knew of the back entrance. It was no secret to them. They had been in the catacombs many times, unbeknown to the pharaoh and his guards.

Zenia knew she and her witches were outcasts in the pharaoh's lands, and throughout the years of his reign, everyone, including the great pharaoh, had shunned them. Living in the pharaoh's lands for century upon century, they had endured persecution and beatings. When captured, they were killed because of their beliefs in evil magic and the dark arts.

Finally, the good pharaoh had allowed them to settle in a small patch of land near an isolated stone mountain, and there they had survived. The land was unfit for human living, and the water was as black as the witches' hearts. There they made their homes, and there they practiced the most wicked, most menacing magic they could conjure up.

When summoned by the pharaoh, the dark witches had readily agreed. No threats had to be levied against them.

The dark and evil witches welcomed the chance to spread their evil in the pharaoh's lands, and being summoned by the almighty only meant that he needed something—something he couldn't get anywhere else. They had already conspired against the pharaoh with a small number of the more wealthy nobles and priests, using their dark magic to help eradicate their enemies, including many of the poor and defenseless.

They had watched the rich consume more and more riches as greed and unrest crept across the lands. They knew the lands were falling into chaos since the pharaoh's last resurrection and his newly acquired phobia with death, but these witches loved spreading unrest and death.

Upon arrival in the pharaoh's chambers, the dark witches stood before the wanting pharaoh. He explained how the good witches, on his behalf, had conceived a vessel known as The Secret of Life. He explained the power and magic it possessed and how it had resurrected him, not once, but twice. Then he explained how it was lacking, and how it was doing only half the job, and then he looked straight at the dark witches and posed his question.

"Can you make me immortal?"

The witches looked at one another and then back at the pharaoh. Little did he know that the witches had already known about The Secret of Life, of its power and magic. As they stood before the mighty pharaoh, they were certain that he was unaware that they wanted it...for themselves.

Now, Zenia, though dark and decrepit, wasn't stupid. Why should she give the pharaoh anything, especially for free? For that reason, and for her lack of trust in the pharaoh, she decided to keep things simple. Why play out her hand so quickly? So she rubbed her hands softly, and pretending to be hesitant, she spoke. "Maybe, maybe. My witches and I will have to give this some thought," she said.

"How much thought?" questioned the pharaoh.

"Tomorrow, tomorrow your greatness. Tomorrow we will let you know what we can do," said the witch.

"Then you will stay here tonight and tomorrow, and we shall talk again," said the pharaoh.

"And—" The dark witch stopped. She looked at the other witches and then turned back to face the mighty ruler. She smiled ever so slightly at him. "And what of us, your greatness. What's in it for us?"

The ruler studied the witch. What he really wanted to do was have the captain of the guard to strike her down, kill the insolent subject. How dare she ask something from him. She was his subject, and they should be honored that he allowed them live in the woods on his lands. However, the pharaoh needed something from the dark witches, so he simply replied, "What is it you want? What do you require of me?"

He shot a quick glance at the captain of the guard. Julius was standing beside the witches; he stood ready, with his hand grasping his sword's hilt. He was ready to strike at a moment's notice. He only waited for a sign from the pharaoh to do so. As children, they had been friends and had played together, and Julius had never left his side since. The pharaoh had promoted him to captain of the royal guards, the guards appointed to protect the pharaoh's life.

The dark witch smiled. "Your greatness, we will let you know what we require tomorrow. Thank you, your greatness." The dark witch bowed, and then the other witches followed her lead and bowed as well.

"Show them to their rooms," snapped the pharaoh. "We shall meet tomorrow morning."

That night, the witches consorted with one another. They studied their parchments, cards, potions, and spells. They figured, and then re-figured once more. Then as the leader of the dark witch clan studied her curses, she smiled, leaned forward, and spoke softly. "Such a feat has never been done. Our dark magic has never been challenged in such a way, but together, we can do this. Yes, we can."

The next morning, Zenia told the mighty pharaoh that they could and would indeed perform a ritual that would grant him immortality. The ruler was delighted; he thrust his arms into the air and jumped with joy. He smiled at the witches.

"This is what I long for. How long with it take?"

"Two days to prepare, then one night to perform the ritual."

"Then, begin. Come here on the morning of the third day, and we will commence," said the pharaoh. He smiled at the witches. "Thank you," he said with a slight bow of his head.

"Your greatness, what of our wishes?" asked the dark witch Zenia. "You promised us we could have our wishes addressed." The witch bowed slowly but kept her eyes fixed on the pharaoh. She knew of his wrath and his anger, and she wouldn't be caught off guard.

"Anything you want. What do you require?"

"Four things, your greatness." With a slight smile, she studied the mighty pharaoh.

"Go on, what are your demands?" The pharaoh studied the witches, as well. He was thrilled at the possibility of becoming immortal. His power would be limitless, but after this, nothing would make him happier than to kill these smelly, insolent beings.

"First, your greatness, we would like lands of our own, fertile lands where water is plentiful."

"Done," said the pharaoh. "This you shall have."

"Secondly"—the witch bent once more, but again didn't take her eyes from the mighty pharaoh—"we want assurances that your greatness won't harm our clan in the future. Now as it is, we must hide in the lands to ensure we aren't killed by your greatness's men." Sucking up wasn't normally in the witch's bag of tricks, but more demands were coming, so she continued to play her hand slowly. She never took her eyes off the mighty ruler sitting on his throne before her.

"Done," said the pharaoh. "This too you shall have."

"You are most gracious, your greatness. Thirdly, we want you to kill all of the good witches in the land. Pursue them as you have us in the past; wipe this land clean of every last one of them." The witch watched the ruler as he studied her. His eyes scanned the other witches and then focused back on the leader of the clan.

"If you give me what I ask for, this too you shall have. Now the fourth. What do you want?"

"Ah, the fourth, yes," she said, wavering a bit. "Ah, yes, the fourth. We"—she hesitated and then, watching the pharaoh, spoke—"we want The Secret of Life."

"No!" shouted the pharaoh. "That you can't have. Even if I gave it to you, you couldn't use it. Only a good witch can perform its magic. It's useless to you."

"No, your greatness, it will be useless to *you*, as you will never need it again. You won't die and will live forever. You will stay young and handsome, and you won't age, nor will you ever be sick. Your body will heal itself, and disease will have no place in your body. It won't affect you. The vessel we speak of—that is our salvation, and we must have it." The witch spoke clearly and precisely.

The pharaoh studied the witch, and then smiled as if he'd had an epiphany. "You are right. Done. But, I'll keep The Secret of Life until I'm convinced that I'm immortal and that you have kept your word."

"Deal," said the witch Zenia.

The next few days, the pharaoh hid in his chambers, not daring to venture out. Finally, the witches arrived and prepared for the ritual. They produced an object that had seven round cylinders; each looked as if it were made to hold some type of tube. They placed the vessel in the middle of the floor, and autonomously, seven witches slid seven tubes into the cylinders. With the object in the center, they drew a pentagram with a circle around it, carefully letting the circle touch each point of the pentagram. There on each point, they set a candle. They lit the candles.

"There, it's done. We need you to stand here, and we will speak the words."

"What words?" asked the pharaoh.

"The words inscribed on the vessel, magic words. And then you must drink the blood in the seven tubes."

"Agreed," said the pharaoh without hesitation. The only thing on his mind was his pursuit for immortality, and at this point in time, he would do anything they asked.

The witches stood erect and repeated the words inscribed on the vessel. The vessel glowed, and a black ghostly shape rose from and hovered above it. At first, it appeared as a black cloud, but then slowly and precisely, it took on the shape of a most foul, ghostly, and monstrous figure.

"Drink the tubes of blood," shouted the dark witch Zenia.

The pharaoh drank the tubes of blood. One at a time, he lifted them to his lips and poured the red, sticky substance into his mouth. As he drank the last tube, the dark, ghostly shape disappeared into the pharaoh. His chest jutted forward, and he collapsed to the floor.

"Fools, what have you done to our beloved pharaoh?" shouted one of the healers.

"Only what he wanted," spoke the witch. "Your pharaoh is now immortal. He shall live forever."

"Arrest these witches. Put them in chains, and if the pharaoh comes out of this state," said the healer, turning to Zenia, "we shall release you. If not, we shall behead the lot of you." The healers stooped and administered to the collapsed man. He stirred but passed in and out of consciousness. "Take him to his chambers, now," he said to the guards. "Hurry. Do it now."

"He'll be fine," said the dark witch with a smile, but the guards did as instructed and escorted the witches to the dungeon and, there, chained them to the walls. Now, the dark witches could have vanished, disappeared, escaped altogether, but they didn't do so. The ritual had gone well, and the mighty pharaoh would awake from his sleep and find himself immortal. They knew this to be true.

The next day, the guards indeed released the witches and ushered them forth to stand before the great pharaoh. He smiled at them and made gestures with his hands. He held them out, palms up and then waved them like a huge bird getting ready to take flight. His smile was so broad that one might think it painted on. "I feel great this morning," he said, "vibrant."

"Good," said the witch Zenia. "May we go? I don't like sleeping in the dungeon and dislike being chained to the wall." She glanced at the healer, and the healer returned her stare. She noticed hundreds of red whelps on his arms, bites. "Do you need something for those nasty bites? Bedbugs, aren't they?" She grinned, but only slightly.

"No, I have poultices," said the healer, snatching his garments down to cover his arms.

"Well," said the pharaoh, "all is forgiven; my healers were just looking out for my best interest. You will need to stay until I'm certain that I'm immortal. Do you mind?" The pharaoh knew it didn't matter if the witches minded or not. He would make sure that he was immortal before giving up his most valuable possession, The Secret of Life, to the witches.

The leader of the witch clan bowed to the pharaoh. "Oh course not. Your hospitality is accepted. May I approach your greatness?"

"Sure," said the pharaoh, slapping his chest. "I feel really great, invincible."

The leader of the dark witch clan, walked slowly toward the pharaoh. Her hand slid ever so slowly beneath her cloak as she climbed the three steps to the throne. When she stood before the mighty pharaoh, she removed her hand, and before anyone could stop her, she lunged toward the ruler. When her hand came clear of her cloak, she was grasping a huge knife. The knife had a slight curve that came to a very sharp point, which she drove deep into the pharaoh's stomach. The pharaoh screamed and bent over. The guards scrambled to grab the witch, and they held her firmly.

"Give me the word and I'll behead her," said one of the guards. Julius raised his hand.

"No, wait," said the witch. "Look at your pharaoh. He's not dead. He's healing as we speak."

The healers watched their pharaoh slowly stand up. His face was intense with pain, but slowly it changed to a slight smile. He opened his robes, and the healers watched as the deep cut in his stomach closed itself and disappeared altogether.

"That was painful," screamed the pharaoh.

"But your greatness, now you know you will heal. You can't die."

The pharaoh smiled at the witch. "You may go. Take your witches and the vessels with you. I won't need them any longer."

"Thank you, your greatness, and of course you will abide by our agreement to kill all of the good witches of this land, give us our fertile land, and not persecute our kind any longer?" Zenia looked at the mighty pharaoh.

"Of course," said the pharaoh. He motioned to a scribe. "Gives these witches the land they want and decree that no dark or black witch may be harmed from this day forward. Finally, take a legion of men and kill every good witch in my lands. Do this as soon as possible. You know where they live." The pharaoh stared into a mirror. "I look great, and I've never felt better." He gazed upon the old witch, Zenia. "Thank you."

Zenia and her dark witches left the pharaoh's quarters, and with the help of the pharaoh's soldiers, slipped out of the catacombs into the bright sunlight of midday.

"Do you think the pharaoh will keep his word?" asked one of the dark witches.

Zenia, smiled. "Of course not, but we have The Secret of Life in our hands, and in the next few days, we will see how honorable he really is. Greed has its price."

\*\*\*

Minutes later, the guards heard their beloved pharaoh scream. "Guards!" The guards rushed into his chambers.

"Yes, my pharaoh?"

The pharaoh, still staring into the mirror, smiled at himself and then turned to face the captain of his royal guards. "Julius, hunt down those dark witches, and kill them. Bring back to me the vessels they carry, both of them."

The guard bowed his head. "It shall be done." He looked at the mighty pharaoh. "And the order to kill the good witches, my pharaoh?"

"It still stands, Julius. Take the men you need and kill every witch in our lands, both the good and dark. They're filth of the earth, and I want them eradicated from my lands. Report back to me after this has been done."

"Yes, my pharaoh."

The captain and his bloodthirsty guards soon overcame the dark witches. The guards rained down upon them like a summer storm—fast, furious, and hard. Their swords and spears held high into the air, waiting to dispatch all in their way.

However, these dark witches weren't fools, and as they walked toward their homes, they had already prepared for such an attack. As rapidly and abruptly, as the pharaoh's guards rained down on the dark witches, they were much quicker. They disappeared into thin air, taking their possessions with them, including both of the vessels they carried. The Secret of Life and the Vessel of Immortality vanished and were lost to the dark witches.

\*\*\*

In his chambers, the mighty pharaoh became enraged. His plans to recover the two vessels had failed, and the dark witches still lived. His orders to crush and rid the lands of every witch, good or dark, were underway, but failing. He hoped the two vessels he desired would be back in his possession within days, but little did he know, he would never see them again.

Heavy rewards were on the heads of all witches in the pharaoh's lands, both the good and dark. Handsome payments were offered to anyone who could produce the head of a witch or the whereabouts of one. The greed spread like wildfire, and many poor and innocent souls were put to death because of it. Many of these, of course, weren't witches at all, but nonetheless, they fell to the axe or sword.

\*\*\*

The dark witches were mortified and humiliated. They had suspected that the mighty pharaoh might double-cross them, and the few that had survived the endless hunt were now huddled in a small shelter deep in the dark mountain. Zenia wept for her fallen witches, and with the help of the dark witches that still survived, she cast a curse on the mighty pharaoh—the darkest curse ever conceived by a mortal, a curse of living death. A curse that neither man, woman, nor child could ever remove.

In the following days, the mighty, immortal pharaoh became ill. Food and drink turned to ash in his mouth, and yet his appetite continued to grow. With no way to appease his desires to eat and drink, he summoned his healers.

Growing bad-tempered and bitter, he screamed orders at the healers. "Are there any dark witches left?"

"Your greatness, there are a few, and we are hunting for them each day."

"Take the next dark witch alive, and tell her I need to see the dark witch Zenia. That is, if she's still alive."

"And if she refuses to come?"

The irritated pharaoh stared at the healer and slowly pulled out his dagger. "Bring me her head." He thrust the dagger into a nearby guard and pushed the dying body to the floor. Staring at the lifeless man, he spoke softly. "Get this thing out of here."

At that very moment, something strange happened. The mighty pharaoh looked at the warm blood on his dagger. His face was stricken with pain, and his teeth ached. Dropping the dagger to the marble floor, he ran into his bedchambers and, overcome by fear, broke down into tears.

It was the blood. There was something strange about the blood, and he could feel the warmth and the stickiness of the substance without touching it. And the smell seemed to rejuvenate him. The worse part was that he wanted more than anything else at that very moment to taste it.

In the days to follow, the great and mighty pharaoh remained in his quarters. He couldn't eat, as food and drink continued to be of no use. Now instead of enjoying the golden rays of the sun, he hid from it. The sun burned his flesh at the slightest touch, and darkness was becoming the only time he could venture outdoors. His mind would return minute after minute to the blood spilled on his chamber floor, and on his dagger, the smell, the color, the substance—these thoughts haunted him each and every moment.

"Your greatness." Said one of the guards.

"What is it? What do you want?" shouted the pharaoh.

"We have captured the dark witch Zenia."

"Bring her to me."

"Yes, your greatness."

Julius pushed the dark witch Zenia into the pharaoh's chambers. "Your greatness, we have captured the leader of the dark witches. We have her here. A traitor in her clan put these chains on her. They're cursed, your greatness. She can't disappear."

"Where did she get those?" asked the pharaoh.

"From the good witches, your greatness."

"I thought they were all dead."

"Some still live, and we made a deal with one. We told her we wouldn't kill her if she gave us something that would allow us to capture a dark witch, something that would keep her from disappearing. She gave us these.

"We had to make another deal with a dark witch; she is the one who put the chains on this one, while she slept. This allowed us to capture her, your greatness."

"Good work, Julius."

The pharaoh sat in his chambers on his mighty throne; he looked down upon the witch. "Tell me, witch. What have you done to me?"

"Your greatness, I'm sure I don't know what you mean. We gave you immortality. That is all, your gre—"

The mighty pharaoh didn't let the witch finish. "You lie; tell me why food and drink turn to ash in my mouth and nothing satisfies my thirst for both. Again, I'll ask you. What have you done to me?"

The witch looked at the mighty pharaoh. It was exhilarating to see him crawling; or at least she saw it as crawling. He had double-crossed her and hunted her and her witches for days, killing each one they found. Now, he was no more than a beggar in the streets, begging a lowly dark witch for help. How fitting.

"Tell me or I'll have my captain sever your head right here and now. Speak, witch, or die." Julius stared down at the witch, his sword ready.

The dark witch Zenia, knowing she couldn't escape, decided she wouldn't beg. In a low, growling voice, she spoke. "Kill me, you double-crossing aristocrat. You have broken your word to me and my clan; you have killed all of my dark witches, less two. I'll kill the one that put these chains on me when I escape from you." She looked at the pharaoh and then smiled at Julius. "Oh, you can kill me if you want, but heed my word, food and drink will never please your mouth or that insatiable appetite. Nor will you ever feel the sun on your skin, less you burn for it." She lowered her head, waiting for the sword to strike.

"Wait, Julius. Spare her," said the pharaoh. The guard lowered his sword. "Tell me, witch. Can we not come to some kind of agreement?" The pharaoh used a softer tone, now, truly, he was begging. "Can we not help each other?"

"And let you double-cross me again?"

"No, I won't, my word on it. You help me, and I'll free you from those chains."

"And let me live?" she asked.

"As you wish, my word, and anything else you need. Just help me. Tell me what you have done to me...please." The pharaoh was calm, and for once in his life, he was pleading, pleading with the scum of the earth, a dark witch.

"Your word, you will release me and not kill me?"

"Yes, you have my word; I'll release you and I won't kill you. Please, tell me what you have done to me?"

The witch smiled. "I cursed you. And I'm sorry, your greatness, but the curse can't be lifted, not by me or any witch, good or bad, and not by any man, woman, or child on this earth. We, the dark witch clan, gave you immortality, but your treachery caused us to curse you once more, forever. Food and drink will turn to ash in your mouth; and the only thing you can drink now is blood. It will satisfy your desire to eat, but only for a short time."

The dark witch continued. "Blood gave you immortality. The seven tubes of blood you drank held the blood of seven virgins. From this day on, only blood shall you drink. When you first drink, your fangs will show themselves for the monster you are, and be at your beck and call when you drink after that.

"When you drink, your victims will become followers. They won't die but will turn into immortal creatures like you, bloodsuckers. They will fear the daylight and lust for blood. This is your curse for betraying the dark witch clan."

"Why would you do such a thing?" asked the pharaoh softly.

"Because you lied and betrayed me," said the witch. "I'm sorry I can't reverse or remove the curse, but you now wear your treachery for everyone to see, and you will wear it forever, and in the darkness you shall live, like a monster."

"I'll set you free," said the pharaoh. "I'll live with my curse, and you shall live with yours." The pharaoh nodded slightly at the captain of the guards. "Julius will set you free."

"Thank you, your—"

The witch didn't finish her sentence. Julius brought his sword down across her neck, and the witch's head rolled onto the floor. It landed face up and stared into the eyes of the pharaoh. He sat high on his throne and looked at the head.

The head spoke. "One more curse," it said softly. "Wood through the heart will kill you."

"Get that thing out of here," screamed the pharaoh. Julius quickly threw his cape over the witch's head and scooped it up. The pharaoh motioned for him to approach the throne.

"Julius, bring in four more guards, and kill these, as they heard the witch's words and know of the second curse. They will be a danger to me."

Julius nodded and replied, "Yes, your greatness."

\*\*\*

The pharaoh's thirst for blood grew, but before he succumbed to his first kill, he cut his arm and allowed his best and closest friend Julius to drink his blood. The pharaoh and Julius had agreed that he should be the first to be turned.

"Now, you are of my blood," said the pharaoh. "From this day forward, I'll call you Lazarus because I have resurrected you."

This act of loyalty turned Julius, now known as Lazarus, also into a bloodsucker. Lazarus would stay by the pharaoh's side, as his protector, and as his first turned. Not bitten, but turned.

After that, the pharaoh gave into his desires, and on a dark, starless night, the mighty pharaoh made his first kill and drank the blood of a human. From that day forward, the more he drank, the stronger the desire for blood became. He turned countless numbers of people into monsters, and they in turn turned hundreds, and then thousands, into bloodsuckers.

The pharaoh and his monsters bit every person in his lands, and then as the thirst demanded, the pharaoh and his follows extended their search for blood. He and his monsters conquered neighboring lands, and his army of bloodsuckers grew. There was no knowledge of how to defeat the curse of the bloodsuckers. The once-mighty pharaoh was now indeed a monster, and his armies were monsters, but instead of thousands, they were millions, sweeping the lands and conquering them. His desire for blood was now only second to his desire to cast the world into darkness.

He would spread his dark, monstrous curse to every living being in the universe, and eventually rule the world as a living god. However, it has always been said, where there is darkness, there is light, and where there is evil, there is goodness. As with any conqueror or dictator, there is always someone or some force, who will try to take him down.

This force did come—in the form of one good witch, an old witch, who was hunted but never found. Somehow, through all of the chaos that spread across the pharaoh's lands and beyond, she managed to survive the pharaoh and his monsters. Now, she hunted the monster that killed and turned every living thing in the lands into bloodsuckers.

This witch had been the head of the good witch clan, the same who conceived the vessel that gave the mighty pharaoh life after death. She and her clan had resurrected the pharaoh, not once, but twice, and it was she who had refused the pharaoh's request for immortality

\*\*\*

The sun was hot, so she moved deeper into the shadows, and as she did, she thought of that day. *I gave him life twice and refused him once, so he turned to the dark witches, who gave him immortality, and now our beloved pharaoh and our lands are gone.*

After being banished from the pharaoh's palace, she had used her magic on a crow, turning it into a spy. The bird would visit the pharaoh's chambers daily, sitting high on a beam; it would bring back to her the goings and comings of the pharaoh. It was there the day Zenia's head had cursed the mighty pharaoh. So now she knew about the wood-in-the-heart curse, and now she was the only hope to draw the world out of darkness.

It was in the heat of the day when she struck. She had watched the evil pharaoh for months. He was confident, and now that his armies were numerous and strong, he had let his guard down. Taking sleep in an old stronghold in some foreign land, he had left himself venerable. This didn't happen often, as Lazarus was always by his side. However, this day, he had sent his closest friend and bodyguard on an errand, and surrounded by millions of bloodsucking monsters, he felt safe.

On this bright, hot summer day, the old witch crept silently into the stronghold. Once inside, and under the cover of its darkness, she struck. Finding the pharaoh asleep in a pitch-dark chamber, she drove a wooden stake through his heart. He burst into flames, as did the followers he had bitten and the ones bitten by them. The lands were finally free of the bloodsucking monsters...almost.

\*\*\*

There was only one survivor, the captain of the royal guards. Somehow, Lazarus survived, and the race of the vampires continued.

Because he wasn't bitten by the powerful pharaoh, but had gained immortality by drinking the pharaoh's blood, he had received the gift of immortality from his beloved childhood friend, the mighty pharaoh.

The pharaoh had been the first vampire to walk the earth. The vampire clan was conceived through his curse, and after his death, the bloodline survived through Lazarus. Living in Terra Demorte, the mighty vampire would come to the surface to feed, but would not stay after feeding. Lazarus fed on a countless number of innocent people, but he did not turn them into bloodsuckers. Instead, to keep his existence a secret, Lazarus killed his victims, driving a wooden stake through their hearts. No one ever noticed the gray colored ash that remained, and for centuries, he remained unknown.

Later, Count Dracula, a descendent of Lazarus, would come forth. He would be known as the first vampire, but he was not.

This was the first time that darkness tried to rule the surface of the earth, but one old witch wouldn't have it and she alone had beaten it back and sent it into hiding for thousands of years. Nonetheless, the darkness was enduring, and evil waited for another chance to cast the earth into darkness.

# Nine

# Evil's Second Attempt

After the death of the great pharaoh, the darkness was content living in the belly of the earth. After all, Terra Demorte did offer a safe haven for all types of evil, and Lazarus and the few bloodsuckers he had turned were as much at home there as any of the clans who dealt in magic and the dark arts.

For years, all evil in Terra Demorte continued their short visits to the surface. This satisfied their desire to spread darkness and discontent. Their incredible appetite to wreak chaos and havoc on the human population fueled these visits. After years of being quiet, the great, infamous vampire Lazarus began raising an army, a vast army of vampires. He expanded his clan with each visit to the surface, biting innocent victims, turning them into bloodsucking monsters, and now, the vampire clan was many in numbers and their leader was most evil. Some lived on the surface and continued turning men, women, and children, while others followed Lazarus back to the dark world of Terra Demorte.

As time passed, once again darkness raised its ugly head, this time in the form of this fierce and vicious vampire. For the first time in the Land of the Dead, darkness was consumed by greed and anxious to spill over onto the surface once more, and this time forever.

So the great vampire, Lazarus, gathered as much support and backing as he could from the other clans. He then petitioned the council members of Terra Demorte with his desires to cast the surface into darkness. The heads of the ten clans listened to the powerful vampire, and in the end, the vampire, assassins, warlocks, dark witches, demon guardians, lost souls, trolls, goblins, zombies, and lost people clans supported the sadistic vampire. It wasn't that they had any desire or want to rule any part of the surface, but they too were afraid of this vicious and powerful vampire. His wrath was equaled by none.

If the surface world was ever to be ruled and consumed by darkness and evil, then Lazarus was the person who could make it happen. His desire to rule everything was unbearable, as it had been with his former master.

This sparked the deadliest massacre of the surface humans ever recorded in the history of Terra Demorte. With a mighty army, composed of all the clans in Terra Demorte, Lazarus arose. He started in the land now known as America, and in the Southwest part of this great land, his army spilled out of Terra Demorte. They brought death to the native people that had lived on the lands for generations. They raided one tribal village after another, leaving no one behind, but always-allowing one or two to escape. Lazarus and his vampires turned many into bloodsuckers, while assassins, warlocks, and demon guardians killed all others.

As his army grew in number, Lazarus and his army of darkness pushed north, and as they swept through the land, they were like a great plague. The few people that escaped Lazarus's wrath ran to warn the other tribes. The vampires followed their scent and descended on them like hail in a spring storm, and once again allowing a few to escape so they could track them to the next village.

As word of the massacres spread, the people left their villages and fled even farther north. As Lazarus and his army descended on villages, they found them vacated and lifeless. Nations of tribes that had been bitter enemies for years found themselves being herded and funneled toward a great land to the far north, a land of ice and snow. If the dark army didn't kill them, then the cold lands in the North would certainly do so.

If any were to survive, their differences had to be put aside and the great nations of the West had to unite. As they united, food became scarce, and traveling became slower. This was an advantage to Lazarus, as his armies were soon closing the gap between themselves and the last remaining tribes.

At times, many of the warriors decided to stand and fight. This, of course, was a fatal mistake. No amount of warriors armed with bows, arrows, and spears could defeat the fierce army; they were no match for Lazarus and his army.

The monstrous army was equipped with magic, secrets of the dark arts, and dark witches riding broomsticks. The warriors had never seen anything like this and were unable to combat their magic and the spells of the dark arts. They were quickly defeated, but this wasn't good enough. Lazarus wanted them annihilated.

When none of the warriors ever returned to the retreating tribes, the tribal chiefs wouldn't allow other warriors to stay behind and fight. Realizing they couldn't defeat this new enemy, they all fled north.

The tribes moved as swiftly as the men, women, and children could travel, while the warriors hunted for food and searched for water. Feeding the mass numbers grew difficult, and more joined as they pushed northward. The animals sensed the coming evil, and they too pushed north, slightly ahead of the fleeing tribes. This made food scarce.

In the distance, Lazarus and his army could see the tribes. They had finally closed the gap between them, and they watched as the retreating tribes moved slowly into a great valley. By now, Lazarus had conquered the tribal lands behind him. He had pushed the remaining tribes into this one valley. Once he conquered this vast valley, there would be no stopping this mighty warrior. Darkness would have its place on the surface.

Lazarus smiled and rejoiced with his deranged army. They had pushed the people as far North as possible, and now, they were trapped. The great valley was surrounded by massive granite cliffs, nowhere to go. Here they would attack and destroy them all. He knew the tribes were weak and hungry. His previous battles with their warriors only made his army all the more invincible. They were primitive and unorganized. Death would come quickly for them. If any did escape, the land beyond that was ice and snow, and there they would surely die.

Lazarus had managed to spread his evil far and wide. He and his army now controlled the lands from the Great Plains to within a hundred miles of the west coast. Once he had killed these tribes, he and his army would push toward the West Coast. He would turn as many as he could and kill the rest. Then he and his army would push eastward and continue until they reached what is now known as the mighty Mississippi River. He would allow everything east of this great river to live. He and his army wouldn't cross the river. In the future, his clan would need food, and the heavy populated East Coast would be his food supply. He did not fear backlash from the inhabitants of the East Coast, his army and the magic from the ten clans of Terra Demorte, would be greater than they could ever defeat.

The great chief of the valley floor welcomed the other chieftains, and he welcomed the people from all the tribal nations. He and his warriors knew of their plight, and they had prepared for them. The great chief of the valley had many warriors, and there the sought-after tribes would be safe. They would eat and rest and the chiefs of each tribe would be welcomed in the meeting lodge. There, all of them would decide on their future, and the future of all their people's nations.

The chieftains met, and each told their tales of horror. They told how the mighty dark armies descended upon them, killing everything in their wake; taking their food, horses, and cattle; and devouring the animals of the lands. Chiefs told how some of the dark monsters that pursued them descended upon them from above. They told of many warriors who fought these demons, but none survived. They told the great chief of the valley how witches used their magic and how some of the dark monsters, men and women, bit the necks of their people and drank their blood. "Drank the blood of our men, women, and of our children," said one chief.

When the great chief of the valley of the great granite rocks heard this, he was troubled. He had many warriors, but listening to the horrifying tales of death and destruction, he had to rethink his decision to fight. He sat in the sweat lodge and waited for a vision, and a vision did come. He saw an eagle, flying high in the air and disappearing over the northern mountains. As painful as it would be for him, he knew what he must do. The decision was painful because he was a leader and a warrior. He had never run from a battle and had protected his valley many times from many enemies. Now, to protect his people, he and his people must flee north to the land of ice and snow. This land was at best miserable, but there, some of his people and the people of the other tribes might survive.

The great chief stood on a huge stone in the middle of the valley floor. He had addressed his people here many times before, and now he would address them probably for the last time from this stone. He told them of the pursuing darkness, of the monsters that would rain down on them like vultures. He told of the deaths of many warriors and of the monsters that drank their blood. He bowed his head as he spoke.

"My people, we must leave the land we have come to love. We must prepare now to leave in the morning. Pack what you can carry and what is necessary to survive the cold days ahead. We will go into the land of ice and snow."

"No," shouted a young warrior, the chief's son. "We must fight this evil."

"I have spoken," said the great chief. "We will leave tomorrow at noon. Be prepared."

"Father," pleaded the warrior, "this is our land. We can't run. We must fight."

"No, my son. Do as I have told you. Prepare to leave. We can't fight these monsters. Our bows, arrows, and spears have no effect on them. For each one of them we kill, they will kill hundreds of us. We can't win."

The great chief stepped down from the rock. He looked at the young warrior standing tall and proud. He saw himself standing there. He laid his hand on his son's shoulder. "We must leave. Be ready by tomorrow. I'll need your strength for the long journey ahead."

The young warrior leaped upon the rock. He screamed loudly to the people. "I won't leave my home. I'll stay and fight. Who will fight with me?" He looked around; the valley floor where all of the people had met was silent. No one spoke.

The warriors cast their eyes downward. Their chief had spoken, and although they were brave and would willingly stay and fight, their chief had already decided their fate, and they would obey. They loved the young son of their chief, and all knew of his courage, but fighting an army they couldn't defeat was destructive. They departed from the warrior and went to prepare for the move.

The warrior was left alone, standing on the great stone in the valley floor. He watched as the people he loved left to prepare for the long journey.

A soft hand slid into his. He turned to see a beautiful girl standing beside him. "I'll fight with you," she said.

"You?"

"Yes. I won't retreat anymore. You are brave, and I'll stand by your side and protect this valley from those monsters. I was forced to leave my home. I won't run anymore." She held his hand, and although the young warrior knew she couldn't be of any help, he felt something warm when he looked at her. Holding her hand gave him peace, and he softly spoke to her.

"Thank you, but you will go with the others."

"And you?" she said.

"I'll stay. I won't run. This is my home. My forefathers lived and died here. Their spirits live here, as do the spirits of the bears, lions, and cougars. They all died here, and I'll die here too."

"Then, I'll die here with you. I'll fight with you."

"No, go to your people. They will need your courage on the long journey." He squeezed her hand softly and walked away.

\*\*\*

By noon the next day, all of the tribes were leaving. Slowly but methodically they headed northward through the northern pass that would eventually cast them into the land of snow and ice.

The young warrior stood watching the people leave his beloved valley. His thoughts were many as he watched the steady stream of men, women, and children disappearing deeper into the valley canyon. It resembled a giant snake, winding up a rocky trail, and one not actually knowing where it was going. One thing for sure, the snake knew it was moving on to some strange, distant land.

*If the monsters follow them there, then they all will die a miserable death. The ones that are fortunate enough to escape the monsters' wrath will surely die of cold and starvation. Either way,* he thought, *death in the valley floor would be much quicker and more honorable.*

The young warrior sharpened his knife and spear. He gathered many arrows, and by nightfall, he was alone in the great valley floor. He had spied on the dark army that evening and watched as they grew closer to the entrance of the valley. "They will come tomorrow," he said.

He would eat and sleep tonight and tomorrow. *Well,* he thought, *we'll see what tomorrow brings. Regardless, it will be a good day to die.* The warrior loved his home; the great granite rocks were huge and conformed to great cliffs, protecting each side of the valley floor. Huge waterfalls fell thunderously downward hundreds of feet when the snow melted. The rivers and creeks were ice cold, and fish were plentiful. He had hunted the woods for game since he was a boy and had climbed higher on the great cliffs than any other braves in his tribe.

This great land was sacred; it had been sacred to his grandfather and his grandfather's father before him. He didn't know how his father could abandon it. He had talked with his father before the long journey began, hoping to change his mind. His father wept as he explained to his son the reasons why he must go.

"I have loved this land all my life," his father had said, "and as much as I love this land, I love my people more. I must not let those monsters kill them, and we can't fight this evil that approaches us. What do our women and children do when our warriors are all dead? Who will protect them from the monsters that drink their blood? If we all die here protecting these lands, then our race, our people, die here too, and no one will remember us. I must make the right decision, and that decision is to protect our people."

The fierce warrior smiled at his father. "I'm sorry I doubted your courage. I see now that it takes more courage to leave than it does to stay. I'll miss you, my father. I'll miss my mother and my sisters, but I can't leave. I must stay and fight."

"This is your path, my son. I wish I could stand beside you, but I can't. I'm proud of you and wish you well." His father spoke these last words to the young warrior. He and his father had departed as warriors, and yet in his heart, they had departed as father and son. His father led all of the tribes north that day, and as the warrior sat alone by a small fire, he prayed to the spirit fathers.

The next day, the warrior walked to the edge of the mighty valley. He turned and looked at the great granite rock. It was higher than any other cliff in the valley, and somehow, he wished he were up there instead of the valley floor. "I couldn't do much fighting up there," he said softly. "The fight will have to come to me here, on the floor."

He took his spear, and with a mighty thrust, he stuck the butt end into the dirt. Then he stood there and waited for the dark army to approach. Minutes later, he saw them, fierce in number and steady walking toward the entrance of the valley floor. He took his spear and drew a line across the valley floor. "No evil will cross this line," he said.

As Lazarus and his army drew closer, the mighty warrior threw his arms high into the air and sounded his tribe's war cry. He prayed to the spirit fathers.

"Oh spirit fathers, help me in my time of need. This is our land, and a mighty, monstrous army approaches. I can't defeat them by myself, but today I'll die a warrior. Today will be a good day for dying, and I ask for your help. Let my arrows fly straight, and let my spear kill many of my enemies. I pray that my spirit fathers will see how their blood flows through me and when my blood is spilled on this land that it's their blood, as well. I pray that they know that it's for my love for this land that my blood is spilled. I pray that my spirit will be united with you, this day, oh spirit fathers, and that I'll be placed among you and seen as a mighty warrior of the land."

The warrior finished his prayer and prepared to meet Lazarus and his dark army. His thoughts were interrupted as he heard a noise to his left. He turned to fight, but what he saw wasn't some dark and evil force from Lazarus's army, but there, stepping from the trees was a young maiden. The same maiden who, the night before, had pledged to fight beside him and protect his land.

"What are you doing here?" he asked.

"I'll fight beside you. I won't run," she said.

The warrior knew it was too late for her to run now; he would rather for her to die here, beside him, than try to escape. She wouldn't get far, and who knows what they would do to her? He held out his hand, and she took it. Their eyes met and there were things that needed to be said, but their hearts already understood the words. The warrior looked at the beautiful maiden standing beside him. His thoughts escaped him and weren't of the approaching danger, but of one thing, the beautiful maiden holding his hand. If only he could be granted one wish...

"Silly," he said aloud as his thoughts remained unfinished.

"Silly?" questioned the maiden, looking up at the warrior. "What is silly?"

"Nothing."

"Don't you think it's a little late to keep secrets? You said something was silly, so tell me what is so silly. Do you think it silly that I'm standing beside you?" The maiden looked up at the warrior.

As their eyes met, he realized how beautiful she was. He had never seen anything so beautiful. Her thick dark hair flowed about her as if it were alive. It reminded him of the tall grasses that grew in the meadows on the valley floor, massaged by the gentle breezes floating up into the valley. Her hair floated effortlessly into the air as if wanting to follow the wind. As the wind escaped, her hair would be still and gently come to rest about her, once more waiting for another chance to escape. Her eyes were black and dark as the caves carved deep into the cliffs, where he had spent many nights eluding winter storms. They, like the caves, offered solace and comfort in an oncoming storm. Somehow, her captivating eyes evade all light, but he could see deep into them, deep into the heart and soul of this brave maiden.

"I can fight as well as you," she scolded, "so don't think me to be silly." The maiden snatched her hand from his.

"No, not that," said the warrior caringly. He softly took her hand. "I was just thinking that if I had one wish, one wish at this very moment, I wouldn't wish for this dark and vicious army to go away. I wouldn't wish for our people who had to flee this land to return safely. Nor would I wish for only the blood of my enemies to be spilled here today. No, if I had only one wish, I would wish that I had met you months earlier, so I might have spent more time with you. I feel as if I could hold your hand for an eternity." The warrior looked up; he took a deep breath, looked back at the maiden, and smiled.

The maiden smiled. "I love you too."

If there were ever in this world such a thing as love at first sight, this would certainly be it. Maybe, just maybe, this was the beginning of such an oddity. Nevertheless, for these two brave young people, life was ending, and Lazarus and his dark army would make sure of that. They knew death was inevitable, but their hearts flooded with such warm emotions that dying wasn't as important as these few moments they were sharing together in the early morning sun.

The warrior did wish that he had met her months ago, instead of the night before, but somehow he felt complete having her there with him.

Her hand felt soft, not like that of a warrior, but he knew on this day, it didn't matter. With the insurmountable odds, by the time her hands were blistered and calloused, she and he would be dead, anyway.

"Beautiful day," he said nonchalantly.

"Yes," she said. "Are you ready for this?"

"Yes," he said softly. "I won't leave my land."

"Agreed," she whispered.

\*\*\*

Lazarus and his army stood less than 200 yards from the two warriors. He studied them as he stood at the front of his army.

"Two warriors?" he said softly. He really hadn't expected the words to escape his lips, but they did, and the huge demon guardian standing beside him grunted in agreement. Lazarus stood there, pondering what kind of trickery was being planned. He could send any one of his warriors to defeat these two warriors. He wanted to give the charge order but stood in amazement at the two lone warriors guarding the entrance of the great valley floor, which was at least a mile wide. Here, in front of this mighty army, were two warriors, and this was very perplexing to the mighty Lazarus.

Finally, he gave the charge order, and the dark monstrous army charged toward the young warrior and his maiden. It would take a few minutes before the powerful army would be in arrow distance. Lazarus knew that the two warriors would kill as many as possible with arrows, and minutes after that, it would be face-to-face combat. "Little resistance after that," he said.

From a distance, Lazarus noticed one of the warriors raise his hands and shout something. "Too late for that," Lazarus laughed. "Screaming won't help you now."

\*\*\*

The young warrior had indeed raised his hands, and the only one who heard his words was the maiden standing beside him. "Spirit fathers, help us this day!"

There was movement on his left and out of the woods came the spirit of the wolf, followed by a numerous pack. They were larger than the normal wolf clan, and the hair on their necks was standing on end. Their growls were deep and nasty, and they snapped their jaws as if gnawing on brittle bone. Their yellow eyes watched the approaching army. They circled around the maiden and stood facing the forthcoming danger.

To his right the warrior saw the spirit of the bear. They appeared out of nowhere, huge and numerous. Shaking their heads from side to side and pounding the ground with their mighty paws, they circled the warrior and stood by his side.

Then the mountain lion and cougars followed, each crouching and looking at the approaching army. From time to time, they would scream loudly and snap at one another in anticipation of the imminent fight. Eager to charge they held back.

Then a sacred spirit fell before the warrior and the maiden, the spirits of the land. Lighting flashed in the clear, sunny sky, and the wind blew forcefully as if a great hurricane was descending from the sky. Tree spirits bellowed in the wind as they too marched forward into battle. The spirits of the rivers and creeks came forth, and all that breathe the valley air stood beside the warrior and the maiden.

The lightning flashed once more, and the spirit fathers descended and stood beside the wolf, the bear, the lion, and, beside the two brave warriors. On this day, all that was sacred and good in this valley, wouldn't let evil enter without a fight. Seeing the love these two mortal warriors had for each other and the land, they had all called home at one time, they too would fight.

The warrior held out his hand to the maiden once more. She grasped it, and they pushed their hands high into the air and screamed their war cry together. The spirits of the bears pounced up and down, sending their thunderous claws to the surface of the valley floor. The ground shook violently as if struck by an earthquake. Wolves, lifting their heads high into the air, echoed their voices throughout the valley floor, sending out a blood-curdling moan. This prompted the lions and cougars, and they too screamed and dug their sharp claws deep into the trembling earth.

Lightning flashed, and the winds blew. The rivers and creeks rose high into the air and sent a torrential rain, pelting the oncoming army, but the dark army was relentless and continued its deadly charge. Spirits didn't easily deter the dark armies, be they human or animal. Terra Demorte held more than its share of spirits, and most all of them dealt in dark magic. The dark witches uttered a spell and the rains stopped.

The warrior screamed loudly, and all charged toward Lazarus's army, followed by the maiden and the spirit fathers. The spirits of the forest and rivers followed as they too were in the fight. The spirits of the mountain lion and cougar struck first; they were the fastest and plowed their way through the massive army. A beastly demon guardian caught one and slammed it into the ground, but as quickly as he had done this, another cat ripped his head from his shoulders. The wounded cat screamed loudly and limped toward another guardian.

The battle raged on. It was fierce, and as one demon guardian died, another one would step up in his place. The warrior now was down to fighting with his knife. He had speared a huge demon guardian, but the beast had broken the spearhead off in his chest and continued his assault.

The warrior glanced from time to time to see where the maiden was, and as hard as he tried to stand beside her, the distance between them was widening. He saw an assassin attack her, but she quickly dropped him with her spear. A demon guardian hit her from the side, and with a quick thrust of his fist, he saw the spear and the maiden go flying into the air. She fell to the ground but instantly was back on her feet. Not finding her spear, she drew her knife, and leaped toward the huge beast, she planted the weapon deep into his chest. He snorted loudly and then let out a terrifying squeal.

He grabbed for the maiden, but she stepped back out of his reach, and he fell to his knees. She drove a dagger, which an assassin had dropped, deep into the top of the demon guardian's head, and he fell forward.

That's when the warrior noticed that the maiden was bleeding; she had wounds on each side of her head, but those wounds for the most part, appeared superficial. Her hair, matted with dried blood, had soaked it up. He saw a bright-red substance running down each arm and dripping from her hands, he knew those wounds were deep.

He tried to maneuver toward her, but a sharp pain in his back stopped him. He turned to face his attacker. The assassin from Terra Demorte had driven one of his daggers deep into the young warrior's back. He stood and smiled at the warrior, then laughed and pulled two more daggers. In an instant, a huge bear ripped the assassin's head from his shoulders, and he fell to the ground still clutching the two daggers. They quivered slightly in the assassin's hands. Death had come so quickly for the assassin that his muscles hadn't had time to relinquish their grip.

The warrior looked for the maiden. He saw a dark witch on a broom, using magic, snatch up the maiden with one arm. She flung the maiden like a rag doll, who flew high into the air before slamming into a huge rock. The maiden's body relaxed upon impact by the sheer force alone and she was dead.

The lion and cougar let out a loud moaning cry as they saw the maiden's body lying crumpled at the base of the rock. A large lion grabbed the witch from behind, pulling her from her broom; it sank its large teeth deep into her neck, while at the same time wrapping its legs around her body, sinking claws into flesh. The witch, badly hurt, vanished before the lion could complete the kill. She wouldn't fight again this day.

The huge beast, looking confused by its vanishing quarry, locked its eyes on another victim and charged ahead.

The warrior, wanting to go to the maiden, realized it was too late. The wounds she had were draining her of life's essence, and the witch had just quickened her death. To some degree, he was glad. His thoughts of the maiden were sweet, as he remembered her smile, her hair, her presence—but in battle, those thoughts are costly, and as he turned to face another adversary, a powerful warlock struck him down with one blow. His magic killed the warrior instantaneously.

With a mighty swipe of his claw, the warlock was detached from his head. The huge bear snatched the warlock's body, and with a mighty thrust, slung the lifeless body high into the air. Another swipe, and the warlock's head went flying landing somewhere out of sight from the bear.

The bear grabbed the warrior's body and gingerly carried it to the rock where the maiden's body still lay. He softly placed the body beside hers. He lifted his head and growled so loud that the entire battle came to a sudden halt.

Lazarus, thrusting his spear with a mighty force, struck down the bear. The spirit animals lifted their heads and let out a defiant call, and although they were spirits, the magic used against them from the land of the dead struck them down as if they were beastly and alive.

The fight had been honorable, and the spirit fathers, seeing the death of the warrior and the maiden, thrust themselves together and, combining their energy and with the help of the elements, created a mighty cyclone. They hurled demon guardians, witches, assassins, trolls, and goblins out of the valley. All of the dark evil from Terra Demorte, seeing this great force, turned and retreated, but many weren't so lucky.

The great wind circling them drove some into the rocks, lifted others high into the air, and dropped them on the valley floor. The dark witch clan flew quickly from the valley, holding on to their brooms as if caught in a huge backwash. Slower attackers were killed as the wind swept the valley clean.

Lazarus turned to escape, but the spirit fathers captured him, and no matter what he tried to do, he couldn't escape their grasp. They thrust him high into the air and toward the sheer cliff walls. The huge granite wall opened, and Lazarus was flung deep into the dark hole. As soon as the spirit fathers buried him deep in the stone wall, the opening closed and was gone from sight.

The spirit fathers departed, and each came down to the valley floor. The bodies of assassins, demon guardians, and warlocks lay scattered everywhere. Popping sounds echoed, and the spirit fathers watched in astonishment as the dead bodies vanished from sight. Assassins and warlocks returned to the Keeping Room in Terra Demorte, where their clans would resurrect them. These dark warriors could only be kept from returning if they were separated from their heads. The Great Spirit Fathers did not know this.

Within minutes, all of Lazarus's army that had been killed in the fierce battle had disappeared back to Terra Demorte. All that remained were the bodies of the warrior and the maiden. The bodies of the animal spirits had disintegrated when killed by magic. They didn't come back to spirit life, nor had any way of being resurrected. They'd fought for the valley, and their lives had been given in sacrifice to the great valley of the granite rocks. They were no more, just dust, and gone from this world forever.

The spirit animals that had survived the battle stood and watched the spirit fathers as they gathered around the fallen warriors. With an outstretched hand, they beckoned the spirits of the warrior and the maiden to come forth. They both stood in front of the spirit fathers, and as they looked at each other, they felt the same love they had felt minutes before the massive battle.

"Thank you," said the warrior to the maiden. "You fought well. You died well."

"The dying part, I could have done without," laughed the maiden, "but overall, I think we fought a good battle."

"You weren't kidding when you told me you could fight as well as me, were you?" The warrior smiled at the maiden.

"I told you not to worry about me. If you had paid attention to the battle, you might still be alive today. I saw you looking at me. I could hear your thoughts, and I know you were sad, but you shouldn't have—"

"Well, if I had to do it all over again, I would do the same thing," said the warrior, "think of you, that is." He smiled and held out his hand. She placed hers in it and smiled at him.

"Now what?" said the warrior, looking at the spirit fathers. "Do we go with you?"

"No, my son, you must stay here forever, in this valley, to protect it from this kind of evil. I don't think there will ever be anyone as brave as you, great warrior. The spirit of the bear, lion, cougar, and wolf and all of the spirit elements will be your army. Your people will tell of your bravery around their campfires forever, and you will be revered by all of the spirits that have gone before you and the ones yet to go."

The spirit father pointed to a great rock that they called Tissack, which is now the great rock in Yosemite called Half Dome. "There, on that rock, you will watch vigilantly to ensure no evil sets foot inside this valley floor. You also will watch the opening, where the dark one dwells, to ensure no one opens it and lets the evil out."

The spirit father pointed to the great granite rock that they called Too-Tock-Awn-oo-Lah, which is now the great granite rock in Yosemite called El Capitan. The warrior could see the opening and so could the maiden. "You and this maiden are the only one that can see the opening; only in death can you see it. No others will know it's there, and they can't see the place where the dark one dwells. It will be your task throughout eternity to guard this scared place, this great land of the granite rocks."

"This I'll do. I love this land," said the warrior. "What about her?"

"She is now a princess; we all have agreed that if you are to be the prince of this land, then her rightful place is to be the princess of this great land. That is if she accepts and wishes to do so. If not, she'll travel with us to the spirit lands."

The princess stepped forward and eagerly responded. One could still see the little girl in her, so soft and gentle. "Yes, I'll stay here, with the prince. That is, if he wants me to."

"Yes, I do. I really want you to stay with me. I do love this land, but I admit I love you just as much."

The spirit father smiled. "We already knew this, and we knew your fate before the battle. That is why we had to wait until you were killed. Evil will come this way again, and you and your princess will protect all of us from it. You, our prince, will sit on top of Tissack and you, our princess, we will paint your face into the stone wall for all of the nations to see, and you will sit with your prince forevermore."

A spirit warrior pushed forward and shoved an old man into the midst of the spirit fathers. "This one I found over there, watching the battle but not doing any fighting. We think he was a spy for the dark evil one."

"No, I wasn't a spy. They captured me. I'm an old man, blind. I escaped and came toward the sound after the evil ones abandoned the camp. I'm not one of them."

"Kill him," said the spirit father.

"Wait, I know this man," said the maiden. "He isn't part of the evil that was spreading. Many of our warriors were captured. This one is old, and so I guess that's why they didn't kill him."

"Yes, that's why. I offered no threat, blind and old. They just fed me their crumbs and let me be." The old man bowed. At one time, he might have been a fierce warrior, but it was evident that now death would be a gift to him.

"He can live in the valley," said the prince. "Our people will return, and until they do, we will see to his needs. He can tell them of our victory here today."

"Then it's done," said the spirit father. A mighty wind blew, and all of the spirits vanished, except the spirit father. "Before I go I will warn you of a vision that came to me. Many, many moons from now, you will be asked to open the door to where the dark one dwells. You and you alone must make that decision. You must use wisdom, if the evil one escapes, he will not return to the mountain and his wrath would be great." The wind blew once more and the prince and his princess were left standing on the valley floor with the blind old man. The spirit father vanished.

Things would be different now. The prince sent an eagle to bring his people back to their lands. Evil had been defeated and chased back into hiding. Lazarus was entombed forever. Only two people knew the location of that tomb, and those two people were there to guard the valley and the tomb's entrance. However, perhaps, there might be a third person who knew, but he was a blind old warrior, so how could he really know the exact location? And in a few years, he himself would be dead of old age.

Still, evil has a way of presenting itself at every opportunity. This blind old man wasn't dying, as he was already dead. No one had noticed the bite marks on his neck, nor would anyone have known what they meant if they had noticed. Evil will find a way to resurrect itself; it's free roaming and has always found a way to exist. This one old blind man was anything but old or blind, but he was for sure…dead.

This was the second time evil had tried to conquer a piece of the surface. The most unlikely heroes stood and fought this dark force back into hiding both times.

Wisteria and Thor knew of these two attempts. The tales of the dark side's failure had faded in and out of Terra Demorte for centuries. The tales were also well known on the surface, as well. They were always a topic for discussion, and now both Wisteria and Thor were hoping that this great dark witch, Olin, and Creed, wouldn't be the third attempt. Evil had its place, and they knew it was in the bowels of Terra Demorte, not ruling the surface area or its people.

# Ten

## The Decision

"Hello, sweetie, I'm home. You wouldn't believe the day I've had. If you want to open a bottle of wine and slip into something sexy, I'm all for—" Roland stopped in the living room and went silent as Katie quickly sent him a message with her thoughts.

*Wisteria and Thor are here!*

Roland turned the corner and saw the odd couple sitting comfortably in the den. "Oh! I didn't realize we had company. Sorry. As I was saying, sweetie, if you want to go out for dinner, I'm all for it!" Roland's face reddened, and he turned slightly toward the front door wishing he could start the conversation all over again. He knew that was impossible so he turned toward his guests, adjusted his posture, and muttered softly, "I guess we could just stay in and eat."

They all sat calmly and stared at Roland. "Hello, Wisteria. It's good to see you. Thor, how have you been?"

"Fine, Roland, just fine. What was that you were saying about wine?"

Roland looked at Thor. "Not wine, dine—about going out—to eat, tonight!" Thor looked at Roland, his eyes scanning Roland's face. "Why does your face turn so red when you talk about eating?"

Roland didn't answer, and for a second, silence was golden until Wisteria spoke. "Well, it's good to see you, dear. Won't you sit for a few minutes? We really need to talk."

*Katie!* Roland thought. *What's this all about?*

Katie responded with her voice. "There's no need for me to respond with my thoughts, sweetie. Thor's the only one here who can't read them. Wisteria and Thor are here because Creed's back."

"He's back?" Roland's voice had a soft, disbelieving tone. He looked at Wisteria and then glanced at Thor.

"Yes, he is!" said Thor. "Well, at least his demon guardians are back." Roland sat down on the arm of the huge chair beside Katie; she put her arm around his back and rubbed it softly. His mind went back to the night he fought Creed and Olin, right here in his den, the night he pulled the two pistols from underneath the cushion of this very chair and killed a demon guardian. He wondered if it would start all over again, if Creed would come for revenge or if he would just leave them alone. Thor interrupted Roland's thoughts.

"I went by there this morning to scan the place, but as soon as I rattled the gates, two demon guardians popped in on the other side. I vanished down the side street. I don't think they saw me or knew who rattled the gates."

"He's back," said Roland softly to himself. "Well, we knew this day would come. Now what? What do we do now?"

Katie took a deep breath. "Nothing."

Roland turned slightly and stared at her. He could see the little girl that Wisteria had seen earlier, and she looked frightened.

"We don't do anything," Katie continued. "I've been thinking about this ever since they told me Creed was back. I don't think we should do anything. Let them come and see that Sarah is gone, and maybe they will leave us alone."

"Katie, dear"—Wisteria's voice was soft and caring—"it's just not you and Roland. It's Josh and every child in this town, every man, and every woman. If we don't stop Creed, we're all doomed."

Katie broke down and started crying; she covered her face with her hands and sobbed.

"I'm—I'm—I'm afraid—that—that Creed will hurt me and Josh."

Roland rubbed her hair with his hand; she laid her head on his shoulder and sobbed uncontrollably. "Katie, Katie sweetie, it's OK. Let's see what Wisteria has to say, and we will decide what we should do together. Come on, sweetie. We're in this together. I promise I won't let that monster hurt you or Josh. We beat them once. If need be, we can do it again." Roland kissed the soft hair on his wife's head. He took his arm and held her close to him. She could feel the strength in his body, and this was comforting.

Wisteria glanced at Thor and nodded ever so slightly. Neither Roland nor Katie had noticed. Thor spoke very softly but in a clear voice. "I hate to say this, but someone needs to. We have to kill Creed and Olin. We should devise a plan and attack them as soon as we can. We can't let them attack first. If they do, we could suffer serious consequences. These are warlocks we're dealing with, not humans. They're vicious and cruel. They have no consciences, nor do they have any pity on their victims. Once they see that Sarah is gone and they can no longer capture her strength and power, I feel that they will come for you and Roland. I'm sorry, but that's how I see it."

Roland looked at Thor. He knew the assassin was right; he had thought the same things. He paused for a second before speaking. "I suppose you're right, Thor, but what if we attack and fail. Wouldn't this infuriate Creed and Olin and bring them down on us faster and harder?"

"Yes, I suppose so, but one way or another, they're coming for you, anyway. You have cheated them out of something they wanted, something that was very valuable to them, and now it's a matter of honor, a matter of saving face with the dark side. Basically, it's just a pure and simple matter of revenge." Thor watched Roland's expression and then glanced at Katie. She was biting her fingernails, and there were small tears pooled in the corners of her eyes. He knew she was scared, but he also knew many of the warlocks on the dark side. He had worked for many of them and drunk ale with them in Jake's Place. *None would let something like this go without reprisal,* he thought.

"Katie, you know what we should do. What do you say?" Roland said as he gently picked up her hand. He could feel her quivering slightly. He knew it didn't matter what was decided there tonight, what actions they might take, or which direction they might go. By holding Katie's hand, he confirmed what he had always known, that he loved her more than anything else in the world, and that he would die before he'd let anything happen to her or Josh.

"No, please, let's just ignore him. Maybe when he realizes that Sarah is gone, he'll just concentrate on his transformation and be done with it. Once he has completed his transformation, maybe he'll just go somewhere else. Maybe he'll leave Johnston. I don't want to provoke him any more than we already have. Please, let's just wait and see what happens," Katie said. "I think we should just wait."

Roland patted Katie on the hand. He looked at Wisteria and then at Thor. "I don't know what to do!" He ran his fingers through his dark hair. "I'm sorry; I just don't know what we should do."

Wisteria watched Katie and Roland quietly; she didn't want to push these two sweet people into a war that they weren't ready for. She didn't want to persuade them to attack Creed because Roland's comments were right. If they did attack first and if they did fail, which was a good possibility, Creed and Olin would certainly counterattack and bring all the force from the dark side they could muster up.

She smiled at Roland and then spoke very softly. "Katie, dear, I think you're right. If you and Roland want to wait, then that's exactly what we should do." She slowly pushed herself up from the sofa and walked toward the little girl sitting in the big chair. She bent over slightly and kissed Katie on the head. "Don't worry, dear. Things will be just fine. I'm going to make sure the crystal is still working. It will alert us if any dark spirits enters your home." The old woman smiled again at Katie and patted her ever so softly on the shoulder. "Come, Thor. We must be going!"

"No," shouted Thor. "Wisteria, we can't just wait. I know the dark side. I know these demons, and they will come for Roland and Katie, just to save face. Then, they will come for you, Josh, and me. I know these warlocks. I know what they're capable of, and I know how they think."

Wisteria looked at Thor. "Your knowledge is very valuable to all of us, Thor, but we must all be in agreement as to what to do or we will certainly fail. We will wait."

"Roland, please, listen to me. We must attack them first, and do it now." Pleaded Thor.

"I'm sorry, Thor. I just don't know what to do next. Let's just wait a few days and see what happens, and then we can decide. Maybe tomorrow Katie will change her mind and things will be much clearer." Roland said.

"Roland," said Thor.

"Thor, it's decided," said Wisteria. "We will wait."

Thor shook his head and forced a smile at Katie and Roland. "Then wait we shall." He knew Creed and Olin; better yet, he knew exactly what actions any demon or warlock would take if this had happen to them. Creed and Olin would attack the Robertses; he knew this. When, he didn't know, but one thing for sure; he and Wisteria would have to be ready when it happened. He nodded his head and said, "OK."

Wisteria and Thor left Number 12 and headed down the street toward town. Neither spoke a word at first. Each was deep in thought as they slowly walked down the street.

"You know this is the wrong thing to do, don't you?" said Thor.

"Yes, dear."

"We just can't stand by and let Creed and Olin make the first move. If we do, someone will die, and I mean someone in that house back there." Thor rubbed his hands over his hair. He adjusted the band that held his ponytail in a tight little cluster. "So, now what?"

"Now, we attack and kill Creed and Olin," Wisteria said without looking at the strong, handsome assassin walking beside her. "We must act swiftly. Are you with me, dear?"

"You know it!" said Thor. "Is it going to be just you and me, or are we getting any help?"

"I can get help from my order. That will have to do, I suppose. It has been a long time since we have actually had to attack a dark master, but I think the time is at hand. We must stop Creed. I'll send for the help we need. We will plan our actions tonight, and we will attack tomorrow night."

# Eleven

## The Late-Night Visitor

It was precisely three in the morning when Roland heard the noise downstairs. Sitting up in bed, he glanced at the clock. Had he really heard something or was he just dreaming, he wondered. He sat and listened.

"There!" he said softly. "There it is again!" He could feel Katie beside him and could hear her gently breathing. "Josh!" He threw his legs over the side of the bed and slipped onto the floor. He eased ever so quietly toward the bedroom door. He heard the noise again, but this time it was louder than before. Roland glanced into his son's room and saw a little ball curled up in the center of the bed. Josh was sleeping soundly. He walked to the bed and gently scooped up his son. He whispered tenderly as he carried him out of the bedroom. "Hey, buddy. Want to sleep with me and mommy?"

Josh grunted softly and Roland walked into his bedroom.

*Katie!* thought Roland.

*What is it?* thought Katie back. She was startled and sat up in the bed.

*There's something downstairs, in the house. I'm putting Josh in bed with you. Grab your cell and call 911.* Roland slid Josh into bed with Katie.

*Do you think it's Creed?* thought Katie.

Roland slid the nightstand drawer open and pulled out the two pistols. He handed one to Katie and sent her another thought as he pulled on his jeans. He slid three fully loaded clips into his pockets.

*You know how to use this. It's loaded. All you have to do is pull back the hammer, and you're set. Don't get out of the bed. Stay put, stay with Josh, and be careful. Look before pulling that trigger; I don't want you shooting me.* Roland placed the pistol in Katie's hand; he knew she knew how to use it and was glad now that he had shown her how. *Yeah, she might not be the best shot, but when shooting at someone, getting close sometimes is a great deterrent.*

*I heard that.* Katie sent Roland her thoughts. *You be careful, and keep me informed.*

*Will do,* thought Roland.

He turned and glanced into the hall, the small sconce was lighting the stairwell and for once, he was glad it was there. It had bothered him on many occasions when in bed facing the door, but the light was welcoming on this night. He stepped over the creaking threshold and into the dimly lit stairwell. He heard the noise again. It sounded like someone bumping into the furniture, and at times, he thought he heard voices.

He shot Katie a thought as he heard her talking to the police department. *I'm staying upstairs with you and Josh! Whatever it is, it's downstairs, and I can watch the stairs better from here than from anywhere else.*

Roland turned left and stood at the end of the banister, in front of the guest bedroom. He eased into the bedroom and stared over the banister. He could see most of the stairs. *A good vantage point!* he thought. He heard Katie's thoughts as he watched the stairs.

*Police are on their way!*

*Great!*

Roland watched the stairs. He heard more bumping noises and what he thought to be voices. They were faint, and he didn't know for sure. Then out of the darkness at the bottom of the stairs, he saw something. A man dressed in a black cloak starting up the stairs. *Creed!* he thought. The man stepping softly on the steps was moving very precisely, but slowly. He was very quiet and making no noise at all as he climbed the large steps. Then, as expected, something followed behind the man in black. This thing hadn't yet come clearly into Roland's view, but it was obvious that this was what was making the noise. Suddenly he saw a figure, and his thoughts snapped out only two words. *Demon guardian.*

He watched as the monstrous figure walked behind the man in black. He realized he needed to make the first move. He had to catch them off guard, but the timing wasn't right. He wanted to wait until the demon guardian was totally in his line of sight. So he watched the figures little by little walk up the steps. Then he noticed another demon guardian following the first one. The second one tried to whisper something to the first, but his voice wouldn't allow him to do so. Roland heard every word.

"Me wants to kill the little boy!" he said.

"Quiet!" scolded the first demon guardian. Then the man dressed in black stopped and turned to face the two muscle-bound monsters. He held his finger up to his mouth, telling them to be quiet. Roland saw the man in black's face.

*Olin!* he thought. Katie picked up on his thoughts, and Roland heard her reply.

*Oh dear God, no. Please, God, please protect us!* She pushed Josh to the edge of the bed next to the wall, as far away from the door as possible, and then she put her back against the sleeping boy. She turned and faced the open door of her bedroom. If they were going to get to him, they would have to go through her first.

*Roland!* she thought. *Where are you?*

*In the green bedroom, watching the stairs. Olin and two demon guardian are coming up the stairs. If anything comes through that door, empty that gun into it.*

Katie stared out of the bedroom door toward the first landing, she too appreciated the small light the stairwell sconce put forth.

Roland turned his attention back toward the intruders on the stairs. He would wait until Olin reached the first landing. At that point, the demon guardians would be in full sight but bottlenecked on the stairs, and Olin, being on the first landing, would be directly in front of him. This would give Roland the advantage and clear shots at the intruders. Roland watched as Olin took the last step, and stepped onto the first landing.

"Hold it right there, Olin!" shouted Roland. He had already stepped around the bedroom door and had pointed the pistol directly at the war-lock. "Take one more step and I'll shoot. Turn around, get out of my house, and don't ever come back. Do it and do it now!"

Olin stood still; he pulled back the hood of his robe so Roland could see his face. He shot Roland a disgusting look and then a slow grin crept across his face. "I assumed you heard us, Roland. My two accomplices aren't so stealthy in the dark, but that doesn't really matter, does it? I knew you would be waiting, and I suppose you plan on shooting me again?" The demon guardian Ray snorted loudly and looked up at Roland.

"Me going to kill you!" he grunted.

"Well what are you waiting for?" shouted Roland. "Again, Olin, turn around and leave, and it's over! You and Creed go your way and we'll go ours! Go now and leave us alone."

Olin continued to smile at Roland. "Now, you know I can't do that. You've got something I want, and I'm here to collect it." He took a small step across the first landing.

"Stop right there, Olin. Take another step and I'll shoot. The police are on the way. Katie called them the minute you entered the house." Roland raised the pistol as if taking a better aim at Olin. "Get out of here and take those two monsters with you!" Roland did not want to shoot the warlock; he was hoping Olin would be sensible and he and Katie could avoid, yet, another fight in number 12. Then he remembered what Thor had told them earlier, "I know these two warlocks, they will come after you and Katie, just to save face."

"As soon as I collect what I came for!" Olin snapped. "I won't leave until I have what I came for!"

Roland pulled the hammer back on the pistol. "And what is that?" he asked.

"Your son, of course," said Olin in an eerie tone. "I've come for your son!"

"What?" Roland said softly.

"Yes, Roland, I've come for Josh." Olin's tone was still uncanny.

"Why Josh?"

"Because I can," laughed Olin, taking another small step on the landing.

Roland pulled the trigger of the pistol, not once but three times. In his mind, he could see the three lead slugs traveling toward their intended target at a high rate of speed, but as fast as the bullets were, Olin was faster. He had anticipated the move and had already disappeared before Roland pulled the trigger on the nine-millimeter pistol. Roland saw the bullets slam into the plaster wall, each drilling a neat little hole into the plaster, sending small fragments of the hard and cream-colored substance flying into the air and then scattering onto the floor.

The two demon guardians headed for the first landing. They were slow and taking the remaining steps to the top, one at a time. In his haste to reach the top of the stairs, Ray had placed one of his hands on Roy's lower back, pushing him forward. He snorted loudly with each step.

Roland lowered the pistol and fired three more times, but this time it was at the lead demon guardian, Roy. The bullets slammed into his back, drilling neat little holes just as the others had done in the plaster. Roy let out a loud snort and turned to look up at Roland. Blood was running down his back, and he stumbled on the stairs but managed to grab the railing to keep from falling.

Ray tried to get around him, but Roy was too massive and needed all of the space on the stairs to keep his balance. Roland didn't hesitate; he fired three more times, this time into the monster's face. The huge demon guardian fell backward toward Ray and snorted loudly once more, followed by a deep, low moan. It sounded like a foghorn instead of the normal squeal one might expect; it was obvious that blood was filling the mighty beast's lungs, and Roland knew this beast would no longer be a threat. Ray sidestepped his partner and took two large steps toward the first landing. Roland quickly scanned the area for Olin but couldn't locate him anywhere. *Gone,* he thought.

Roy's body fell down the stairs and, with a loud thud, landed on the floor in front of the newel-post. Ray made a fatal mistake and hesitated for a moment to gaze upon his partner. Ray had just reached the first landing when Roland fired again.

The pistol answered his call and sent three more bullets, carrying death toward the huge demon guardian. Three brass casings danced on the wooden floor, spinning and bouncing as if they had no cares, each trying to out dance the other. The three slugs slammed into Ray's chest. He grunted and squealed loudly, looked at Roland, and then took another step across the first landing.

Roland pushed the small button on the gun, and the clip fell to the floor. He reached into the back pocket of his jeans and grabbed another one. As soon as he had shoved it into place, he ejected another cartridge into the chamber of the pistol.

Ray stopped as Roland pointed the weapon at him. He turned, struck a great muscle bound pose, and snorted loudly into the air, sending a spray of moisture everywhere. He grunted at Roland and spat blood in his direction. He realized he couldn't beat the awesome weapon that Roland possessed. Olin had told them about its power and warned them to be on the alert. He had seen Roy fall by this weapon, but he had made up his mind that he wouldn't disappear. He would charge Roland and kill him before the weapon made its deafening sound again.

He felt the pain in his chest, a pain that he had never felt before. He could see the blood oozing through his clothes, running down his chest, and dripping onto the floor. He felt dizzy, and for the first time in his life, the huge demon guardian was scared, truly frightened.

He looked at Roland and managed to say one last sentence that actually made sense. "Me gonna kill you!" It didn't matter at that moment to Ray if he had used the right or wrong words. Roy lay dead at the foot of the stairs, and the intense pain in his own chest confused his brain. His mouth was muttering and sputtering out words on its own, like a runaway locomotive, fully out of control.

Roland fired three more bullets into the monster, who rocked forward and fell to the floor without moving a muscle.

Roland scanned the room for Olin; he quickly sent Katie a message. *Two demon guardians dead. I don't see Olin.* Before he could finish the thought, he realized that something was behind him in the darkness of the green bedroom.

"Surprised, Roland?" It was Olin. Before Roland could turn, Olin struck him with a mighty blow to the head. The force alone knocked Roland, face first, onto the hard oak floor. Softly moaning, Roland managed to turn over onto his back. He lay watching the spinning ceiling. He closed his eyes, trying to shake it off, but when he opened them again, the ceiling hadn't stopped its dizzy dance. His head and body ached with pain, but he managed to raise his gun and point it toward the dark room. Olin had disappeared; he wasn't where Roland had expected him to be. Surprisingly, Olin reappeared on Roland's other side, and now the pistol was pointing in the wrong direction.

"Surprised again, Roland?" Olin extended his hand, and a powerful force hit Roland again, sending him sliding into the spindles of the banister. Roland's gun went skidding into the threshold of the green bedroom. The force had been so great that Roland's body was numb; he stared at Olin and then fell into unconsciousness.

Olin stepped over Roland's feet; he stopped for a moment and looked at the man lying on the floor in front of him. He turned his head and looked into the bedroom where Katie and Josh sat.

Katie saw him standing over Roland; she sent him a message without saying a word.

*Roland, Roland, are you all right?*

There was no answer from Roland. She grabbed the pistol and pointed it toward the door.

Olin didn't know if Katie could shoot the pistol with any kind of accuracy, but he wasn't taking any chances. For a brief moment, his mind went back to their last battle and how deadly accurate she had been with the crossbow. He vanished.

Katie was scared and continued pointing the gun toward the bed-room door, taking short glances at Roland's lifeless body lying in the hall. Her eyes flickered downward then back upward as she wondered about Roland but was equally worried about the whereabouts of Olin. She didn't know if Roland was alive or dead but knew that, for the moment, she was on her own.

"Well, hello, Katie!" It was Olin. He had reappeared behind her, next to the bed. Katie screamed, Josh woke up and screamed, as well. She turned toward her son. Olin had already reached over the small boy and grabbed the pistol from Katie's hand.

"I'll take that!" Olin snapped. With a swipe of his hand, he struck Katie in the face. She fell backward onto the pillow, but her instincts took over and she instantly sat up again. The pain was excruciating, but she ignored it for the time being. She turned toward her attacker, her head ached and her right eye started swelling. She reached for her son, but Olin grabbed her by the nightgown and, with a quick thrust, hit her with the back of his right hand. Katie was dazed; she managed to focus her eyes once more on the warlock standing beside her bed.

Olin returned her gaze, and as he did, his lips quivered slightly before turning into a huge smile.

"I bet that hurts, doesn't it? Well you don't have to worry about another one, because I want you to see what I'm going to do." Katie's eyes closed. Her head was aching so badly. If only the loud gong in her head would stop, maybe she could think. She tried but couldn't focus on Olin any longer.

"Stay with me, Katie. Don't you dare miss this!" he said. Olin tossed the gun onto the floor. He turned, and with a gentle motion, scooped up her son. Katie screamed and grabbed for the boy, but Olin pushed her back. Her head fell once again onto the pillow. Olin walked around the bed and stopped in the doorway. He turned and smiled at Katie. Looking at Olin made her stomach quiver; he had the most evil and menacing smile she had ever seen.

Josh was screaming, he reached for his mother but Olin held him tightly. Stretching out his arms, he shook Josh fiercely, the small boy continued to cry.

"I'll be back, you know, and when I do, I'll kill you and this thing lying on the floor here," he said as he nodded toward Roland. He laughed, walked out of the room, and started down the stairs.

"Roland!" screamed Katie. "Roland!" Roland stirred and moaned softly. Katie slid out of bed. She tried to stand, but the pounding in her head wouldn't allow it. She fell to the floor with a loud thud. The dazed woman tried to stand once more, but she was too disoriented to do so. Dragging herself over to where Roland lay, she touched Roland; he opened his eyes and saw the bruised and bleeding face of his beloved wife. Katie sent him a thought.

*Roland, he has Josh!*

Roland forgot about his pain, and as quickly as he had received Katie's thoughts, he sat up. He prayed for strength as he looked at Katie and heard Josh crying. He turned and saw Olin walking down to the first landing on the staircase. He scanned the area around him and then behind him. He saw the pistol lying in the doorway of the green colored bedroom. With all he could muster up, he grabbed the gun and rose to his feet. As he did, Katie pulled herself up and stood beside her husband.

"Don't let him leave with Josh!" she said.

"I won't!" was all Roland said as he raised the pistol toward Olin. "Stop right there, Olin. Put my son down or I'll shoot." Olin pulled the small boy toward his chest, covering as much of himself as he could.

Josh began kicking relentlessly, trying to dislodge himself from Olin but the mighty warlock wrapped his arms around the boy and held him tight.

"I wouldn't do that, Roland. You might shoot the boy." Olin turn and faced Roland. He started across the first landing, ensuring Roland didn't have a clean shot at him. He glanced down at Ray's body. *He must still be alive or he would have disappeared by now,* he thought. *Maybe I can use him as a distraction.* Olin's thoughts were interrupted by Roland's shouts once again.

"I said stop!" said Roland. He fired the pistol, and the bullet drilled a neat little hole in the plaster, inches from Olin's head. The mighty warlock ducked his head behind the small boy's head. He stopped walking. He could see the determination in Roland's eyes. He studied Roland for a moment; he wondered if the small boy he was holding could cover his entire body, but realized at that very moment that Roland could put a bullet wherever he wanted.

"Why I didn't kill you earlier, I'll never know!" Olin said with a smile peeking out from behind Josh. "Well, now what?"

"Put my son down!" Roland said. "I won't tell you again!"

"I'll make you a deal, Roland. You're a businessman, and I bet you make deals every day in your world. Well here's a nice little deal for you, just a little matter of life or death." Each time he used the word *little*, Olin pushed Josh away from his body a few inches. "You throw the gun away, and I'll promise you that I won't take your son. I'll leave him here. I just need to know that you won't shoot me as soon as I put the boy down." Popping sounds interrupted the conversation between the two men, and Roy and Ray's bodies disappeared.

"Took them a while to die!" said Olin, taking another step across the first landing. "I'm not going that way, and you're not going to shoot me with that pistol," Olin said as he took another small step across the landing, one he had hoped Roland hadn't noticed. But Roland raised the gun, taking aim at Olin's head.

"Throw the gun away, Roland, and I'll give you my word that I'll let the boy go. We'll call it a draw, at least for tonight. What do you say, your son's life for my life?" Olin smiled at Roland. "Come on; throw it away."

Roland looked at the warlock holding his son. "How do I know that I can trust you?"

"I give you my word. I'll let him go," said Olin. "I promise. Even a warlock like me has some honor!"

Roland didn't want to put the gun down, but the longer he held Olin at gunpoint, the longer Olin had a chance to change his mind. Roland took a moment to ask himself one simple question, could Olin disappear with a live human in his arms? He had seen him disappear into walls before, but never with a live human in his arms.

"OK, give me your word that you will let my son go!" He was hoping that warlocks did have some kind of honor, even in the darkness of their world. He didn't know, but he was hoping that he was making the right decision. "Your word, Olin!"

Josh was still screaming and kicking. "Hold still you little brat," Olin scolded.

"I promise that I'll let the boy go! I'll leave here alone, my word!"

Roland dropped the gun to the floor. Olin watched him and smiled as if he had won the battle. "Kick it away with your foot," he said.

"Roland, do you think that wise?" asked Katie softly.

"No choice, sweetie. We've got to trust him."

Roland placed his foot on the pistol and gave it a gentle push; the gun slid several feet away and came to a rest in front of the bathroom door. Slightly pushing Josh away from his body, Olin held the small boy out in front of him. His arms dangling the small boy as if taunting the couple standing at the rail. He smiled a victorious smile. "I'll keep my word, as promised." As he spoke, he walked across the first landing to the head of the stairs. He stood there facing Katie and Roland. "It was here that my brother Creed killed Sarah Wheeler, and it will be here that I do the same to your son!"

With a quick thrust and his arms fully extended, he held the small boy out over the staircase. Then with a gentle motion, he brought Josh back to his chest as if giving him a hug. He shot a smile toward the couple at the rail. "Children are precious, you know, but as promised, I'll let your son go." The words had barely escaped his lips when he extended his arms and pitched the small boy high into the air. Katie screamed, seeing her son rise high in the air. Roland looked at his son; Josh was crying loudly and gasping for breath. Roland saw the terror in his son's eyes as he paused for a brief second midair before starting his fall toward the oak steps.

Olin smiled and then, as if taunting the couple once again, he laughed. "As promised, I'll leave Number 12 alone, without the boy!" He turned slightly and vanished into the wall.

Josh started his decent; he had stopped crying and Katie and Roland watched in silence as he fell helplessly toward the bottom of the stairs that would surely bring sudden death, as it had with Sarah so many years ago.

Within seconds, there was a loud, terrifying thud on the wooden steps. Josh bounced slightly and rolled head over heels to the bottom of the stairs. He, like the demon guardians had, finally came to a rest at the foot of the stairs. His small body lay still.

Olin reappeared at the head of the stairs, on the first landing. Once again, he looked at Katie and Roland and spoke in a taunting voice. "Never trust a warlock, Roland, never. We have no honor!" Olin turned once more and disappeared into the stillness of the night air.

*\*\**

Roland sat up in bed; he was hot and dripping with sweat. He could feel Katie softly sleeping at his side. She was taking long, deep breaths as she slept. He wished he could do the same, but most nights, the night-mares would come and they were becoming longer and more realistic.

The night air was still, hot, and muggy. The huge windows were open but offered little assistance in cooling the humid night. There was no moon to speak of, the night was dark, and the only light Roland could see was jutting forth from the small sconce on the wall in the stairwell. He slid out of bed and walked into the dimly lit room.

"Another nightmare, Roland?" questioned Katie.

"Yeah, I'm just going to check on Josh. Do you mind if I bring him in here with us?"

Roland had made the turn, and was already stepping into his son's bedroom when Katie answered him.

"No, not at all, sweetie," said Katie. "Are you all right?"

"Yeah," said Roland. "I can't explain these horrible dreams. I don't know what they mean, or if they mean anything at all. I just hate having them!" He returned with Josh and slid him into the bed beside Katie.

Josh turned toward Katie and threw his arm around his mother. His breath smelled like honey, but this was normal, and Katie could smell the scent of strawberries from the shampoo she had used to wash his hair. He cuddled up beside her and softly said, "I love you, Mommy!"

Roland slid back into bed, and as the early morning air slightly stirred, he fell back into a light sleep. He felt better having Josh in the bed with him and Katie. His dreams were getting longer and steadily becoming more horrifying. They always involved Josh, and rarely a night went by without the dreams involving some horrible creature from the dark side.

# Twelve

## The Council

"Silence!" screamed the hooded figure standing at the head of the large, rectangular table. The table was huge and carved out of granite. There were two tall candelabras sitting on the massive stone table, arms extending in every direction, lighting the cold surface. Wax dripped from the large candles, splattered like raindrops, and then froze as if some kind of spell kept them from spreading any farther.

The hooded figure at the head of the table spoke. "You know why we have called the council together once more. Before we start, I'll call out each clan by name, and we will ensure all clans are present before continuing."

"The warlock clan."

"I'm here," said a well-dressed warlock.

"The demon guardian clan."

"Here," snorted a beast.

"The human soul clan."

"Here," said the head of that clan.

"The goblin clan."

"Here," said the goblin clan leader. He looked at the other clan members but did not acknowledge any of them.

135

"The assassin clan."

"Here," said the assassin.

"The vampire clan."

"Here," said the head vampire. He hissed loudly and cursed under his breath.

"The zombie clan."

"Huuuuu, here," said the clan leader, but the words were slow coming.

"The dark witch clan."

"Here," said a witch. She took her finger and pointed it at one of the candles, it went dark and then with another flick of her finger, it produced a small bright light.

"The troll clan."

"Here," shouted a huge troll as he slammed his fist on the stone table. "I'm here!"

"Last, the creature clan."

"Here," said a creature with a snake like head. "I'm here." He then transformed his head into a human head. He smiled and a long forked tongue flickered from his lips.

"That's everyone, all accounted for," said the hooded creature.

There was a brief pause as the leaders of the clans looked at each other. They had been there before, at this same table discussing matters of importance, solving disputable issues, and creating, as it were, laws for the inhabitants of Terra Demorte.

The witch rose from her chair and picked up a tray of small cups. The tray was large, and the cups didn't have handles but were stacked one on top of the other in two stacks. There was a pitcher, as well, on the tray. A strange-colored mist rose out of the pitcher. At first it was red. Then it turned green. And now, floating effortlessly upward into the huge hall, it was blue, and it formed a small cloud. She sat a cup in front of each clan member and slowly poured the brew. No one touched the drink until she had finished and performed the same ritual, for herself, at her seat.

"Drink up!" the hooded figured said. All picked up their cups and drank the mixture.

"As you know, by drinking this potion, if any of you speaks a word of what is discussed in these chambers, without permission of this council, you will die." The creature paused for a moment as if wanting that part to sink in. "You will die the most excruciating death possible." All of the clan leaders laughed and drank the potion.

The hooded figure drank the potion, too. He was one of a kind being, evil in all aspects. He had much magic but most of the inhabitants of Terra Demorte hadn't seen the power of his magic, but all knew his magic was strong. He was gentle in nature; rumors were he wasn't from this world. He had no clan, and no family. He mixed well with the assassins, warlocks, but had no use for the witches, goblins, trolls, or demon guardians. The rest, he tolerated. The ten clans of Terra Demorte had elected him as head of the council. He was evil and strong, but had never eluded to any kind of agenda. He just needed a place to call home. He never went to the surface; he was transparent to the surface world.

The figure at the head of the table spoke once again. "You know why we are here; we are here to discuss the warlock Creed. I have it on good terms that he is trying to complete his transformation, giving up his spirit body and cloaking himself with a body of flesh and bones."

"Good terms? What good terms? You have no knowledge of what Creed is trying to do. This is all hearsay," said the leader of the warlock clan.

"Here, here!" said the head of the assassin clan. "There's no proof of what Master Creed is trying to do, and I don't see why the council was called together to discuss this matter."

The rest of the clan leaders nodded in agreement. The hooded figure spoke once more. "My spies tell me things about Master Creed that are—"

Before the figure could finish his statement, the warlock clan leader spoke again. "What Master Creed does on the surface of the earth is none of this council's business. Our laws tell us that my clan can do whatever we like on the surface of the earth, so whatever Master Creed is doing is no concern of this council."

The rest of the clans joined in, and all agreed with the warlock, all except the head of the demon guardian clan.

"The demon guardian clan, you aren't agreeing with the rest of the clan leaders. May I ask why?" said the hooded figure.

"We all have heard the rumors about Master Creed and his transformation, and that is none of our business, because he is doing it on the surface of the earth." The demon guardian sat back in his chair and belched loudly. "My clan is protecting him now, making sure he is safe, but there are strange goings on in that house, things I'm not allowed to talk about."

"What types of things?" snapped the head of the warlock clan.

"Strange things," said the demon guardian. "Strange things."

The warlock leader jumped to his feet. He walked the floor impatiently and spoke loudly. "There is no proof that Master Creed is breaking any of our laws. Again, I tell you, what my kind does on the surface of the earth is our business and no one else's. It doesn't concern the other clans and is no concern of this council."

The hooded creature spoke softly. "You are right, of course. What the warlocks—or any of the clans—do on the surface is no concern of anyone else, unless…"

"Unless what?" snapped the warlock.

"Unless whatever is done on the surface spills over into Terra Demorte and violates our laws and agreements here. I believe that Master Creed is doing just that."

"You have no proof of that. Yes, I agree that Master Creed is trying to complete his transformation, and we all know that his brother, Olin, has already completed the same transformation, but again, he's doing it on the surface of the earth, and that's no concern of this council or any business of the other clans. He has shown no transgression here."

"I have proof," said the hooded creature.

"You what?" said the warlock. He faced the hooded creature, for a moment in an aggressive manner. "You say you have proof. Then show us this proof you speak of."

"I can't," said the hooded figure. "I have proof, and all of you have heard the rumor that if Master Creed completes his transformation, he'll rule Terra Demorte and your clans."

The room went into an uproar; everyone was speaking at the same time. The hooded creature waved his arms. "Silence. My proof is undeniable; this you must believe."

The warlock sat back down. Watching the hooded figured he spoke. "Show us your proof or we are done here."

The creature stared at the warlock, then at the rest of the clan leaders. He didn't want to play his hand, but the leader of the warlock clan was right; he must produce proof or the meeting would be over.

"I have a spy in Master Creed's house," he admitted.

"You have a spy in Creed's house?" said the assassin.

"My spy tells me that Master Creed has spoken of ruling all of the dark masters and Terra Demorte. He has made his brags that he'll rule all clans. He has told his demon guardians that they will rule all demon guardians as soon as his transformation is completed."

"You lie," shouted the warlock as he rose from his chair. "You lie, you filthy creature."

The hooded figured rose abruptly and pointed his finger at the warlock. "How dare you?" he said.

"He doesn't lie," said the head of the demon guardian clan. "He speaks the truth. Roy told me that Creed offered to let him rule all of my clan and that he would teach him how to do so."

The warlock and the hooded creature sat down. The warlock looked at the demon guardian, then at the hooded creature. "Who is your spy," said the warlock. "You say he is in the master's house?"

"No, I didn't say he was in the master's house."

"Yes, you did," answered the warlock. He rose once more, aggressively to his feet.

"No, *he* is not in Master Creed's house, but *she* is. My spy is a she." The hooded figured looked victoriously at the warlock. He had won a small battle with this mighty warlock, and it was won with words.

"Yes, she's been there since he started his transformation, ever since the rumor started."

"You have no right to spy on a warlock. No right. What are you doing with spies? You have no clan, why do you need a spy and who else do you spy on?" the warlock shouted. His voice quivered. "I demand to know who this spy is. You say it's a she; bring her forward. We all need to speak to her; we all need to see her."

The hooded figure had risen to his feet, "we all have spies here, I'm no different. I don't answer to the warlock clan, so your questions to me are irrelevant."

The warlock was furious, he shouted once more at the hooded figure. "I demand to see your spy."

"For her safety, I can't."

The warlock stood up. "Again, I tell you, you have no right to place a spy in a master's house. You have violated—"

Before the warlock could finish, the hooded figure spoke. "Sit down. Most of you know of my spy rings. They've helped this council many, many times before with no complaints. The warlock clan knows this. As the leader of the mighty warlock clan has stated this day, what the clans do on the surface is no concern of this council. Well, what I do on the surface is equally no business of this council. Equally, no concern unless it spills into Terra Demorte, and this does."

"Then tell us of your spy," said the leader of the dark witch clan.

"I fear for her safety," said the hooded creature.

"We all drank the potion," said the warlock. "No one in this room can talk to anyone about this. We need your proof, and we need it now."

"Here, here," sounded the entire room. Every clan agreed with the warlock, so the hooded figured stood up slowly. He produced a small box from under his cloak and sat it on the table. He raised the lid slowly, and out crawled a small spider. It came to a rest on the huge stone table.

"Deidre, show yourself." The small spider crawled over to the edge of the table and, as it leaped off the table, transformed into a young woman.

"I'm here, Master," she said.

The table was silent. No one spoke, and all watched the slender woman as she spoke.

"I'm Deidre; I have spied on Master Creed and his brother, Olin, since he started his transformation. I live in his house in the chair that sits in front of his desk. I have heard him on many occasions speak of ruling all of the dark masters that dwell here and ruling Terra Demorte. I heard him tell the demon guardian Roy that he could rule all of the demon guardians and that he and his brother would teach him how to do so. What my master is telling you is the truth."

The monstrous demon guardian snorted loudly and raised his voice. "She's telling the truth, no one knows that except me, we have kept this a secret. The guardian Roy told me this in private and the only others that know this is the two masters he works for, master Olin and master Creed."

"Deidre, go back to Master Creed's house until I beckon you again. If you learn anything new, let me know." The hooded creature bowed slightly at the young woman, and she did the same. She left the council.

"Now," said the hooded figure, "are we ready to talk?" All of the clans agreed. The warlock sat down in his chair and smiled at the hooded creature.

"Let's begin," said the warlock.

# Thirteen

## Olin's Visit

The night air hung over the small town of Johnston like a huge web. There was no breeze, and if the wind stirred, it only lasted for a few seconds. On this dreary night, the only things moving were the crickets and night birds. They were singing their nightly songs, as if tomorrow would never come, each trying to out sing the other. Days earlier, the moon had changed from a beautiful full moon lighting everything in its path to a small slither, giving no light to the earth below. The dew had fallen, and the heat picked it up and mixed with the stale air, making the humidity worse.

There was one other thing moving within the shadows that night, something foul and evil, something that hadn't yet been unleashed upon the small town of Johnston. Master Creed hadn't wanted to draw attention to the dark side and his locale until his transformation was completed, so he'd kept this monster on a short leash, a very short leash.

That foul creature was Olin Thomlin. Olin was one of the deadliest warlocks in the history of the dark side, being fully human and spirit. He walked slowly, taking small steady strides. His long, dark cloak had long sleeves and a hood that covered his head; no parts of his body were visible. Leaving a small shuffling sound in his wake, his cloak dragged the ground. The crickets and night birds stopped their singing as he walked by, for they too feared this evil being. Olin kept up his steady pace until he reached Calhoun Street.

Walking slowly past the houses, he came to a stop in front of an old two-story house. He had been there many times before, staring into the huge windows of the house. He had often wondered how life would have been if he had been Horace Wheeler's son instead of his father's. How life would have been living with a caring family instead of one where the children were terrified of—

"Enough of that!" snapped Olin. "This night, this very night will be the greatest night that my brother and I will ever have together. Tonight, we will have the necessary power to complete his transformation. Tonight, within minutes, I'll have the spirits he needs." Olin vanished and then, within moments, reappeared out of the living room wall in the old house everyone knew as Number 12.

Olin went right to work; he assumed that Wisteria had cast a spell to protect the house, so he wasted no time calling for the spirits that he had come to collect. "By the powers of the dark side, I summon all spirits that belong to us to appear. I summon you, Sarah, Horace, and Melissa. You now belong to the dark side, and I command you to appear." Olin held out his hands and waited for the spirits to appear, but to his surprise and dismay, none did. Not understanding what had happened he repeated his incantation, but again nothing happen.

"How could this be?" he said softly. For the third time, he repeated his command. "I order the spirits living in this house to appear. I command you to show yourselves to me. I command you to come to me!" To Olin's disappointment, nothing happened, and no spirits appeared. He turned slowly and saw the glowing crystal. It glowed softly at first and continued becoming stronger until its light shone forth, putting out an enormous ray of red light, a blinding light that irritated Olin's eyes. He turned and vanished into the living room wall, and as he did, he spoke only three words. "That witch, Wisteria!"

It was still dark when Olin walked back toward the mansion. He didn't hear the crickets or the night birds, nor did he hear all of the other creatures that talk to the cool night air. They would stop as Olin walked by, only to begin again as soon as the evil passed. Although they were chirping and singing with all their glory, he was deep in thought, trying to figure out why Sarah, Horace, and the nanny hadn't come forth when he had commanded them to do so. The noise escaped his ears.

He knew the triangular séance had failed the night Wisteria had performed it—he was sure of that. After all, he had witnessed the botched performance and remembered quite well staying until the clock struck its final note sharply at midnight.

He also knew that once a triangular séance had failed, there was no reversing it, and there was no way that anyone could change the outcome. Even the most powerful magic couldn't change the ritual that had been put into motion. It was a dangerous practice for the witch that conducted it as well as any spirits she might call upon.

All of the spirits that had been summoned should now belong to the dark side, he also knew this.

"I don't how to explain this to Creed!" he said softly. "I have no explanation. He's going to be furious. He was counting on Sarah and the rest being there, counting on me to bring them to him *tonight*." Olin cursed as he walked onto the grounds of the mansion, still confused by the events that occurred in the early morning hours at Number 12.

Roy met him in the courtyard and looked around, trying to see the obedient spirits. Finally, when his curiosity got the better of him, the demon guardian spoke.

"Master Olin, where are the others?"

"They weren't there Roy. They're gone."

"Gone, Master? Where?"

"I wish I knew, Roy. I wish I knew." Olin cursed once more before entering the old house. "I guess I might as well tell Creed. He's going to be livid."

"Do you want me to go in with you, Master?" asked Roy.

145

"Not if you value your head, no thanks, Roy. There's no need." Olin shook his head and gave Roy a final order. "Keep a sharp eye, Roy. Stay on the alert. After he gets the news, he'll probably want to kill something."

"Yes, Master!" Roy said, leaving the kitchen and going back out into the courtyard. "I'll be upstairs in a minute," he said. Olin nodded in agreement without actually having heard what Roy said.

Hesitantly, Olin tapped on the door that opened into the dark chambers of his brother's room. He and Notor had done this many times before; he noticed the spider webs running from the door to the door's facing. He watched the webs stretch as he gently pushed the door open; they clung to the door as long as they could and then as always, gave way and snapped as the door opened wider.

"Olin, you're back," hissed Creed, easing out of the shadows. He put his elbows on the dusty old desk. "Did you bring them? Did you bring them back with you, Olin?" His voice was raspy and scratchy, but his manner was like that of a child waiting for a parent to relinquish some type of sweets or goodies from inside a coat pocket.

"No." Olin didn't pause or sidestep the question. He was straightforward but made no explanation why he hadn't brought back the spirits that dwelled in Number 12.

"What, why?" asked Creed in his usual raspy voice. "Why?"

"I'm sorry, Brother. Sarah and the others weren't there!" Olin said, sliding down into the chair in front of Creed's desk. "Somehow, they're gone." Olin expected Creed to come unwound or to lose it. He had expected Creed to become irritated, and at the very least start cursing and swearing, but that wasn't what followed.

"What? You say they didn't appear?" Creed's voice was soft but still raspy and scratchy. "Did you call them to come forth? Did you command them to show themselves?"

"Yes, Brother, several times. I tell you, something has happened. They're gone."

Creed slumped back into the shadows. He didn't say another word, but Olin could hear his rough breaths as he sucked down the early morning air and then released it.

"Are you all right?" Olin asked. It was then that Creed's demeanor and his patience seemed to shatter—snapped into fragments.

Creed screamed, standing up behind the old wooden desk, "No, I'm not all right!" He stepped forward and struck the lamp on the desk with his hand, sending it scampering to the floor. The small bulb flickered and went out. The room was dark.

"Light!" shouted Olin. The small lamp floated back to the desk and put forth its small light, once more lighting the surface of the desk.

Roy, who was now back upstairs, guarding the hallway, entered the room and stood looking at the two warlocks.

"Master, is everything all right?" he said.

"Fine. Get out," snapped Creed in an arrogant voice. He was still standing behind the desk, and Roy, looking confused, turned and left the room, pulling the door shut.

Creed slowly raised his hands and pulled the hood off his head. "Look at this. Do you see how I look? Do you think for one single moment that I want to look like this for another day? Especially after seeing you, the way you look, the way your hair and skin look? The way you sit in the sunshine day after day?" Creed dropped his head.

He was, at best, hideous. The skin on his face and head was thin, stretched tightly over his skeleton. His white hair was thin but long, and the blood vessels running throughout his head resembled nothing less than a huge roadmap. His black and shallow eyes were sunken back into his head. His nose was defined but not complete. His mouth looked like a dark hole spreading from one side of his face to the other. He had no lips, and his teeth were long and sharp like needles. He stared at Olin.

"I asked you a question. Do you think I want to look like this forever?" He didn't give Olin time to answer. "I needed those spirits. I needed their power. They can't be gone. It's some kind of trick by that witch,

Wisteria. It's got to be!" He grabbed the edge of the desk and, with a quick thrust, flipped it high into the air. Creed's power was astonishing. The desk floated in the air, then turned a full three-hundred-sixty degrees, and as if powered by magic, landed back in the same spot on the floor.

The lamp floated in the air and, as if possessed, which it was, floated back down to the surface of the desk.

"Nice trick," said Olin. "Nice!"

"This isn't funny!" hissed Creed. "Look at me. Do you think this is funny, Brother?"

Olin pulled a piece of lint from his trousers and watched the small spider that lived in the chair run from the arm of the chair back into the cushion.

"No, Brother, I don't think it's funny; forgive me if you think I'm taking this lightly. I know how much you needed them, but they were gone. They didn't appear when I commanded them to do so. I agree with you that this must be some kind of trick, but what? There isn't any way that witch could have pulled this off after botching the séance. We know that. We heard her call for Sarah and the others; we stayed until midnight, until we knew without a doubt that the séance was doomed. Sarah and the others should be there. They should be there waiting for us…but they aren't."

He sat looking at the monster standing behind the desk. He wondered if that was how he had looked during his own transformation. He had seen himself but couldn't remember looking that hideous. His had been quick, not long and drawn out like his brother's. He knew that his brother was disappointed, and he wanted nothing else at that very minute but to rise from his chair, go back to Number 12, and kill Katie and Roland and then Thor and Wisteria.

"No, there's something else going on there. The witch has moved them, hiding them or something. She's got them somewhere, and I aim to find out where." Said Olin.

Creed had settled back down into his chair. He slowly pushed his chair backward into the shadows. "Maybe, maybe," he hissed. "I need them, Olin, and I need them now. I can't wait any longer to complete this blasted transformation. If I don't get them soon, I'll lose the power that I already have, and then—well, you know what happens then." Creed sat in the shadows and didn't move.

Olin sat in the chair and didn't say a word. He knew what Creed was alluding to and that his brother had waited far too long to complete his transformation. What he didn't understand was what the witch, Wisteria, had done with Sarah and the others.

"Olin, get the dark witch, Odium. Find her, and bring her to me," Creed hissed.

"Yes, Brother, and if she doesn't want to come?" asked Olin.

"You see that she does. Do whatever it takes, but have her here as soon as you can. I'm going out!" Creed said as he rose from the shadows.

"Where are you going?" questioned Olin. "Do you think it wise to go out?"

Creed walked around the desk and over to where his brother sat. Olin stood up to meet the warlock standing in front of him. Creed rubbed Olin's hand with his long, bony fingers. "Don't worry about me, Olin. I'll be all right. Just get the witch."

\*\*\*

The alarm clock exploded its not-so-good morning alarm sharply at six. The noise was more of an irritating echo than anything else, but it went off as preset. Roland quickly fumbled with the clock until he found the snooze button. "nine more minutes," said Roland, "just nine more minutes!"

The clock made its *beep, beep, beep* sound twice more before Roland slid out of bed. The room was bright, and the morning sun had found the three large windows in front of the house and flooded the room with a brilliant pallet of colors. The hand-blown glass in the huge windows cast the golden rays in every direction, changing the light into small specs of greens and blues mixed with yellows and golds. The sight was magnificent.

Roland remembered why he and Katie loved the old house so much. He stood there wondering if what they were going through was worth the trouble. Yes, there was something about the house that was building a bond with Katie and him, and although Sarah had passed over, the old house was still very magical. It was calling to them, baptizing them in its array of colors and beauty, and now it was stronger than ever. Roland didn't know exactly what the mesmerizing influence was—or if it was really anything at all. It was just a feeling that he had.

He turned back toward his small son and wife, who were sleeping in his and Katie's bed. The light from the windows cast a blanket of transparent colors over them, as if trying to cover them with a protective blanket.

Roland smiled and walked out of the bedroom. He turned at the threshold of his bedroom and glanced at his family once more. He loved them with all of his heart, and he wanted nothing more in this world than to believe that the old house would protect them.

"Watch over them, please!" he said. "Take care of them while I'm away!"

***

It was just after eight when Wisteria and Thor rang the doorbell at Number 12. Katie had just gotten out of bed and had left Josh lying under the sun's magical blanket. She hurried downstairs to answer the door. She smiled at the sight of the old woman standing on her front porch.

"Well, it's nice to see you this morning, Wisteria. Won't you come in?"

"Yes, dear. Would you do me a favor and get your things together? I want to take you and Josh to breakfast." She and Thor stepped into the house.

"All clear," said Thor, scanning the house with his scanners. "Something dark has been here, but what, I can't tell you!" he said, glancing at the small crystal. The crystal was still glowing but casting forth a soft reddish light.

"Olin," said Wisteria. She turned back toward Katie and smiled. "Quickly, dear, get your things, and let's go. Thor can't pick up Olin on his scanners, as far as we know, he might be here now. You won't be coming back to the house. Thor and I don't want you to be alone today, so get everything you need."

"Olin was here?" questioned Katie. "Josh!" She rushed up the stairs. She found her small son right where she had left him, curled up in the center of her bed, sleeping soundly. She gently stroked his hair, woke him up, and asked him if he wanted to go to Wisteria's Café for breakfast.

Josh sat up in the huge bed and rubbed his eyes. Katie couldn't help but notice how small and precious he looked in the middle of the overly large four-poster rice bed. Such a small little package in the enormous bedroom.

"Yes, Mommy. Let's go eat at Miss Wisteria's café. I'm hungry!"

Minutes later, all four of them walked out of Number 12 and headed down the sidewalk toward town.

"Are you sure that Olin had been in our house?" Katie asked.

"Yes," said Thor, "I can't tell exactly what, my scanners indicates nothing, but the crystals say something different, and it was something dark.

"When?" asked Katie.

"Last night. Actually, early this morning before Roland left for work. I assume he came for Sarah and the rest of the spirits," Thor said, watching Katie's expressions.

Katie looked worried, she had always assumed the dark side would come for Sarah, Horace, and the nanny eventually, but as time passed, denial consumed her thoughts and her hopes chased reality away. She started believing they wouldn't.

"So, dear," Wisteria said, "he knows by now that they're gone." Wisteria paused before continuing, then in a calm and reassuring voice she said, "We don't want you to be alone in the house today. Just precautions, that's all, dear!"

Katie pulled her hair back behind her ears. "I guess we can do some shopping until Roland comes home."

"Well, if you get bored, let Thor know, and he can bring you by my house. Who knows? We just might get into something," Wisteria said with a huge grin. "Have you ever seen a monkey swinging from a tree, Josh?"

"No. Do you have a monkey, Miss Wisteria?" Josh said, looking up at the old woman.

"You just never know, Josh. I just might," Wisteria said, looking at Thor. "I just might!"

\*\*\*

Breakfast was good and the conversation was the same. They all sat and prolonged ending the meal as long as they could before Wisteria finally excused herself and said something about some errands that she needed to run. She instructed Thor to stay with Katie throughout the day, but Katie quickly objected.

"Please, Wisteria, Thor doesn't want to babysit us all day.

"Sure, I do," said Thor.

"We can take care of ourselves; I think we will be perfectly safe in town. We'll just shop until lunch and then hang out here in the café until Roland comes home, if that's all right with you?" Katie said, looking at Thor. "Nothing personal, Thor, but I'm sure you have more to do than hang out with us all day."

"Actually, I don't," said Thor with a big smile. "It would be my pleasure to hang out with you two."

"Well, thank you, Thor, but Josh and I will be fine. We've got some shopping to do and some errands to run. I'll call for you if we need you, and I know where to find you,"

Katie said standing up. "Thanks again, Thor, but we'll be fine."

"I'll be here if you need me, Katie. Just let me know," Thor said. He knew Katie really didn't want his company at the moment, and he certainly didn't want to intrude. He decided he'd just hang out in the café. "I don't think Olin or Creed would try to harm you while you are in town, so just do what you want and check in with me every once in a while. That way, I'll know that you are all right."

Katie thanked Thor and hugged Wisteria before she left. "Thanks, Wisteria. Don't worry about us. We'll be fine."

Katie left the café and walked around town looking in every store she passed. Every minute that passed seemed to be at least ten minutes, and Katie realized that it was going to be a long, long day. She hadn't gone very far when she turned the stroller around and headed back down the street toward Number 12. She was determined not to let Olin keep her out of the home she loved so much. Katie pushed the stroller up to the front porch of the old house. She picked up her son, put her key into the lock and slowly gave it a turn; she heard the lock slide back and paused for a moment before opening the door.

# Fourteen

## The Dark Witch, Odium

Olin watched his brother leave his chambers and stroll slowly down the long stairs to the first floor of the mansion. He knew where his brother was going; he had witnessed the same sight many times before. He wanted to stop him, but he also knew if Creed wanted to go out, nothing he could say or do would prevent him from doing so. It was early morning, still dark, but not for long. If the sun rose and struck his skin, even for a brief moment, he would burst into flames.

"Be careful," said Olin. He shot Roy a quick glance. Roy followed behind the two masters; he wanted to help but stood dumbfounded at the head of the stairs. His master was disturbed, but he was only a protector and had no words of wisdom for this situation. He knew that his partner Ray would offer up a remedy, his remarks would simply be, *if you want to feel better, master, kill something, that all ways works for me.* He nodded slightly as Olin spoke. "Watch over him, Roy, and don't"—Olin looked at the demon guardian—"leave his side!"

"Yes, Master," Roy said.

Ray, who had been at the other end of the hall listening, walked quietly—well, as quietly as the huge demon guardian could walk—to where Roy stood. He knew something was wrong with his master and moved closer to see if he could help.

Roy turned slightly to watch his muscle-bound partner. Ray glanced down the stairwell, and Olin and Creed had stopped moving and stood staring at him. The racket he was making might have easily registered a three on a Richter scale every time he took a step.

"What?" said Ray, shrugging his shoulders. Again, Ray wasn't endowed with stealth, nor was whispering one of Ray's traits. "The master needs to kill something," Ray said, "always makes me feel better."

Olin, glancing at the monstrous figures standing at the head of the stairs, shook his head slightly. He and Creed continued down the stairs, they felt more content knowing the demon guardians were there. As loud and clumsy as they were, the brothers knew Ray and Roy could be trusted and would be there for them in a crisis.

"Who's Odium?" Ray said.

"Don't know, but I think we'll find out shortly. Go with the master and guard him. Let me know if you need anything. I'll be there shortly; Master Olin wants to talk to me," said Roy.

Roy watched as Ray followed Creed into the back of the house. He heard the kitchen door open and then shut and assumed they had left the house. Roy walked down the stairs to where Olin was standing. Olin turned and whispered to the demon guardian; he placed two bags of gold nuggets into his hands. He turned and began to walk away but turned back to face Roy.

"Here, this one is for you and Ray." Olin tossed another bag of gold nuggets toward Roy, who watched the bag as it sped toward him. When the bag was close, he took one quick swipe with his huge arm and snatched the bag out of midair.

"Thanks, Master!" he said, turning to leave.

\*\*\*

It was daybreak when Olin walked down the crooked gravel road toward the small cottage sitting in the woods. The sun was just rising and shadows ran for cover, as if alive, hiding in cracks and crevices, until the sun extinguished them altogether. The trees, vines, and flowers drank from the night's gift of life. The dew, at this time of day, was thick, and each plant drank its fill. The morning was bright, but the small cottage under the trees was dark, and it seemed to creep deeper into the shadows as the sun rose.

The old house itself was crooked in every way, built that way. The windows were set within the walls crooked. Although he assumed they would open and close with ease. He could see from a distance that the door, as well, wasn't set straight. The chimney rose high into the air, and flowing from side to side like a giant weed growing out of control, it too was crooked. The banisters that fronted the porch were lower on one side than the other, and all of the spindles were crooked.

"Yes!" he said emphatically, "the signs of a witch's house." He walked upon the porch, knocked gently on the door, and within seconds, heard a voice from within.

"Yesssss, yessssss, who's there?" The voice belonged to an old woman, and as Olin waited for the door to open, he thought he heard a second voice, a man's voice. It was low and raspy like Creed's.

"My name is Olin; I have a message for you from Master Creed, the warlock who rules this lot. Open the door; I must speak with you. That is if you are the dark witch, Odium." Olin waited for a reply.

The door opened, and standing in front of him was a small, frail-looking old woman. She stared up at Olin and smiled. "Yesssss, yessssss, Master Olin, please, yessssss, please come in!" The old woman smiled again, and Olin returned the smile. It seemed she liked to drag the word yes out and at times repeat it often, sometimes she would drag it out longer than other times. There was no rhyme or reason to it. "Yesssss, yesssssssss, what can I do for you Master, yessss, yessssss?"

"I have a message from Master Creed. He wishes to see you," Olin said, glancing into the house. He eyes quickly scanned the large room, searching every corner for the source of the other voice he had heard.

There were no internal walls, just the outer walls of the large room. They were adorned with various types of pots, jars, and strange dried plants, all tied neatly together at one end. There were dead birds hanging by their necks with some sort of old string, held to the wall by rusty nails or tacks. Dried blood had run down the wall, staining the old faded wallpaper.

There was a small sitting area in front of a rather large fireplace. There were several old ragged chairs, which had clearly been used quite a bit. The mantel had various items on it; Olin couldn't make out exactly what they were, but the odd things scattered throughout the old house intrigued the warlock.

There was a large kitchen in the back with cabinets hanging on the wall and a huge butcher-block counter that divided the kitchen from the rest of the house. Numerous, large dried puddles of something dark covered it. *Blood,* thought Olin.

"May I come in?" He asked.

"Yessssss, yessssss, please, yes, please come in, yessssss, yessssss!" The old woman stepped aside, allowing Olin to pass. "Yessssss, yessssss, Master Creed. Yes, I'll go see the Master. Tell him, yessssss, yessssss, tell him that I'll come see him tomorrow, yes, tomorrow."

"I apologize, madam, but the master wants to see you now. You're to come back with me"—Olin paused; he disliked using the word please, especially to a witch, but he decided at the last moment to ask politely—"please."

He knew of the old woman's reputation; she was one of the most powerful dark witches ever known to walk on the surface. She was cruel and most evil. She would dispatch anyone or anything that got in her way, if she desired to do so. She herself was very powerful and highly respected by the dark witch clan; however, she was a witch, not to be trusted—at all.

Odium looked at Olin, turned, and walked slowly toward the kitchen. "I'll see the Master tomorrow, yessssss, tomorrow!" she said. "Around seven o'clock." She spoke softly and didn't turn to face Olin.

Olin hardly knew the old woman, just stories about her and her magic. He knew she had been around for an extremely long time, but already he had a dislike for the witch.

"Look, witch, we can make this easy, or if you like, we can make it hard, but one way or another, you're coming with me. Which is it, the easy way or the hard? This is your master who summons you. You will show him respect, and you don't want to keep him waiting. He does allow you to live in his lot."

Olin positioned himself to fight the witch if indeed he needed to. Actually, he wanted to fight this witch. He had awesome powers, magic, and abilities, but up to this point hadn't been allowed to use them. His brother was keeping him on a short leash, but here in this small house, away from everyone, he would welcome a fight, and a fight against such a powerful dark witch would be even more welcomed.

In Terra Demorte, it was forbidden to fight another dark spirit, but this wasn't Terra Demorte, and Olin was eager to see how his powers would hold up against this insubordinate witch. Of all the dark, evil, and miserable people in Terra Demorte, he hated the Dark Witch Clan the most. They were foul, stinky, and slimy, a poor excuse for women.

Odium turned to face the visitor that was standing in her home; she immediately saw the determination on Olin's face and the position he had taken. "Yessssss, yessssss, no one allows me to live anywhere, I live where I want and do what I want. I was here in this lot many, yessssss, yessssss, many years before your Master, yessssss, yessssss. So, Master Olin, yessssss, so you want to fight the most powerful witch, Odium, yessssss, yessssss, you do." Odium smiled at her handsome visitor. "Yes, yessssss, yessssss, you don't want to do battle with me, Master Olin, yessssss, yessssss. No—you—don't—want—to—do—that!"

"One way or another, witch, you're coming with me. Again, your choice," repeated Olin.

"Yessssss!" said Odium slowly. "Yessssss, keep your shirt on. Give me a few moments and we can go, yessssss, yessssss!"

Olin smiled at the witch, turned, and walked out on the porch. He felt that he had won a battle, just maybe the old witch had heard of him and his powers, as well. "I'll wait out here if you don't mind. Take your time!" He lit up a cigarette and inhaled the smoke deep into his lungs, as he exhaled the smoke he mocked the old witch. "Yessssss, yessssss, you don't want to do battle with me, yessssss, no, you don't."

"You mock me!" said a voice from behind Olin. He turned and the witch, Odium, struck him in the face with her hand.

Olin looked at her and smiled. "Better be careful, witch. I'm not in the best of moods this morning!" He turned his back to the witch and took another draw from the cigarette, but before he could exhale the smoke, a great force struck him in the back. Olin fell from the porch—or, rather, was flung from the porch to the ground with a violent force.

Lying on his face, he turned to see what had hit him, but before he could turn over, something big and heavy landed on his back. He felt it straddle him as he tried to turn over. He felt another great blow to the back of his head and heard the thing on his back let out a loud growl. He quickly vanished, and as quickly as he had vanished, he reappeared again, only this time he stood to face the thing that had attacked him.

Olin was angry. "So she's turned a monster loose on me!" he said. "If a fight's what this witch wants, then a fight she'll have, I should never have turned my back to her." He narrowed his eyes and searched for the monster, but the only thing standing in the yard was Odium. She had her purse in her hand and a large hat perched on top of her head. It looked like a cinnamon bun, icing and all.

"I'm ready, yessssss, yessssss. I'm ready to go now!" She smiled at Olin. "We can take my car. It's over, yessssss, it's over there." Olin looked to where the witch had pointed, and sitting half in and half out of a very crooked garage was, indeed, an old car.

"What was that thing that attacked me. Where'd it go?" Olin snapped. He glanced around, but there was no monster to be found. He looked at Odium. "You think that was funny? I'll ask you once more who attacked me and where the beast went. You will tell me or I'll kill you!"

"Yessssss, yessssss, I didn't see any beast, Master Olin. You ask me a question that doesn't have an answer. I have no beast that attacked you, nor did I see anything attacking you." Odium turned to face Olin. "But, yessssss, yessssss, if it's a fight you want, then I'm, yessssssss, yessssssss, I'm ready." The old witch stood looking at Olin. Her purse clutched in one hand, keys in the other.

"Fine. Make your move, witch!" Olin shouted.

Odium smiled at Olin. "Get ready, Master!" She turned, farted, and wobbled off toward her car. Olin watched and expected at any time for her to turn on him, but Odium didn't turn until she was on the driver's side of her car. "Coming?"

Olin relaxed and started walking slowly toward the car; he took his eyes off Odium and scanned the area for the monster that had attacked him. "Stupid witch," he said softly under his breath. He hadn't wanted Odium to hear his remark, but as old as she might have been, she responded quickly to it.

"Stupid, yessssss, yessssss, and stupid you say! We will fight, Master Olin, yessssss, yessssssss, we will, but not today. I don't like you, yessssss, yessssss. No, I don't like you at all."

Olin walked toward the car. He stared at the old witch. He didn't make any hand gestures, but a violent force struck Odium in the back. The force bounced her off the dusty garage and she fell to the ground. For an old woman, she responded quickly and was back on her feet in an instant. She looked at Olin.

"Good, witch. Then you must know that I don't like you much either, but I came for you and I'm sure my brother needs you or he wouldn't have sent me. Yessssss, yessssss, yesssssssss, we will fight one of these days, but I agree with you, it won't be today!" Olin laughed as he mocked the old witch. He threw his hands up in the air and waved them wildly as he mocked her again. "Yessssss, yessssss, we will fight, yesssssss, yessssss."

Odium ignored Olin. She brushed off her clothes, and clouds of dust came forth. She opened the door, got into the car, and cranked it up. The car's exhaust quickly filled the old garage with a thick blue and gray cloud. As if conquering the world, it eased out of the crooked garage and surrounded the car. It resembled an early-morning fog, thick and mysterious, deviously encroaching upon the car, ready to devour it and its contents.

"Are you sure this thing you call a car will run?" Olin said, sliding into the passenger's seat. He waved the stench of smoke away from his face. Odium, once again, ignored Olin's arrogant comments.

She put her hands on the steering wheel and focused her eyes forward; she sat there looking out of the windshield but didn't put the car in gear.

Olin looked at the cranky old witch with uncertainty. "Now what?" he said. "You gonna make me sit here until I suffocate?"

"I'm waiting," Odium said calmly.

"Waiting for what?" snapped Olin.

"I'm waiting for you to fasten your seatbelt!" said Odium. She didn't turn toward Olin but sat still, focusing her eyes on the darkness within the garage.

"I'm not wearing this thing!"

"You are if you're riding with me. We wouldn't want anything to happen to you, now would we? Besides, it's against the law."

Both knew that the dark side had no use for surface laws, and none obeyed them. They were from the dark side of the world, surface laws were for others, not them.

Olin looked at Odium and then at the contraption she had strapped across her breast and lap. He searched for the belt and secured it tightly around his chest and waist.

"Are you happy now, witch?" he snapped.

Odium didn't answer. She slowly backed the car out of the garage and away from the thick smoke.

Olin turned, once again, to look at the old crooked house. *One day!* he thought. *One day-I'll burn this place down and kill this stupid witch.* He sat for a second, staring at the old house. *And I'll burn this stupid car too.*

Odium and Olin didn't speak as they headed down the street toward Creed's mansion, not until Olin smelled the most obnoxious odor. "Did you do that?"

"Yes, pleasant aroma, don't you think?" Odium said. "Collards!"

Olin reached for the window; he was holding his breath as he spoke. "How do you get this blasted thing down?" he said.

"You have to turn that handle there, yessssss, yessss, you do," said Odium. She smiled, took in a deep breath, and pointed toward the door. Olin grabbed the small handle and started violently turning the knob. Nothing happened.

"Nothing is happening," screamed Olin, still holding his breath. The urge to breathe was excruciating, and although he resisted, somehow, he could still smell the terrible stench. Somehow, he could taste it in his mouth.

"Yessssss, yesssssssss, it doesn't work, yessssss, yessss, it quit years ago," said the old woman.

Olin couldn't hold his breath any longer so he let out what air he had in his lungs and inhaled the nasty odor. "By Hades, I can taste it," he said. He quickly fumbled in his pockets for a cigarette.

"You can't smoke in my car, yessssssss, yesssss, yessssss, you can't, and smoking isn't good for you!" said the annoying chauffeur.

Olin looked at her and stuck the cigarette into his mouth. He lit the smoke and inhaled another blast of air into his lungs.

"You could kill someone with that stuff, you know!" he said.

"Yes." Odium smiled. "I know!"

As they approached the front gates of the mansion, Olin spoke once again to the old witch. "Pull down to the end of the wall there. We can enter at the back of the mansion." Odium did as instructed and stopped just past the great stone wall.

"Ah, yessssss, yessss, demon guardians," she said, looking at Olin. "Are you still using those old dinosaurs for protection? You should be using witches." She laughed as she walked with Olin down the small path leading to the back gate. "I knew your father and mother, you know!" she said. "Yessssss, yessss, I did."

"Shut up, witch. I really don't care who you knew or what you know or think you know. Just shut up!"

"As you wish, Master Olin," Odium said. "That's a nasty bump on the back of your head," she said as she opened her purse and produced a small bottle. "Rub some of this on it, and it'll be better in no time. We wouldn't want that to get infected, now would we?"

Olin ignored the offer. The crooked little path finally disappeared at the end of the stone wall, next to the old iron gate. Olin quickly climbed to the top of the wall and jumped to the other side. As he stood, he saw that Odium was standing next to him, holding her purse in one hand and smiling. He gave her a dirty glance and headed for the kitchen door. He knew of the gate, and it would have been simple to pass through it, but he'd wanted to see if the old woman could tackle the wall. It backfired.

"Halt," came a voice from behind the overgrown shrubs. "Sorry, Master. I didn't know it was you," said Ray.

Olin glanced at Ray. "Watch her, Ray! Stay behind her and keep your eyes on her, both of them!" Olin snapped the order as soon as Ray came into view.

"Me will, Master. Me will!"

Odium glanced at the demon guardian. She muttered a few words and pointed her finger at the monstrous figure. He snorted loudly and fell to the ground, rubbing his eyes. He finally managed to stand, but Odium pointed at him once again. She muttered a few words, and Ray snorted loudly and looked at the witch. "You blinded me, you stupid witch. Me gonna kill you!"

"Not so fast, fellow. You take one-step toward me and I'll blind you forever. Do you understand me? I was just showing Master Olin that if I wanted to do any harm here, you couldn't stop me." Odium laughed, turning away from Ray. But taking one's eyes off a demon guardian that is standing so close isn't always the smart thing to do, and a dark witch should have known that.

Odium had just started to take another step when Ray hit her from behind with one of his gigantic fists. Stumbling, she pitched forward and hit the ground face first. The cinnamon-bun hat rolled off her head and came to a rest on the path. Ray stomped it with his mighty foot, then with a twist of his mighty leg, ground it into the dirt. Odium didn't move, and at first, Olin thought she was dead.

"Good move, Ray! Good show!" he said with a laugh. "I think you killed her!"

"Me will!" Ray said as he took another step toward the witch. Odium stirred and slowly stood up; she muttered a few words, and Ray fell to the ground. He lay still.

"By Hades, witch, what did you do to Ray?" said Olin with a smile. "Did you kill my demon guardian? Roy'll probably take that personally."

"For the moment, yes. Yes, I did."

*Funny,* thought Olin, *she didn't stutter.*

"Well, bring him back to life as I need him." Said Olin.

She muttered a few words and looked for Olin, but he had vanished. He appeared on the other side of her. He pointed at her and smiled.

"Are you finished? If not, do what you want, but follow me." He watched the old witch.

"No, I'm not!" shouted Odium. She muttered a few more words and pointed at Olin. Olin smiled at the witch.

"Your magic won't work here anymore today, Odium." Olin pointed his finger once again toward her. "If you provoke me once more, I'll dispatch you on the spot. You understand me?" Odium pointed her finger again at the warlock standing in front of her, and again she muttered more of her magic words, but as before, nothing happened to Olin.

"Yessssss, yessssss, Master Olin, your magic is truly, yesssss, yesssssssss, truly powerful. You win this time, Master Olin, yesssssss, yessssss, this time. I'll never underestimate you again. Yesssssss, yesssssssss, yessssss, no, never again." Odium paused and bent down to pick up her hat. "Master Creed wanted to see me?"

Olin looked at the dark witch. At this very moment, he could easy dispatch her—and how tempting it was—but she was right. Creed did want to see her, and although Olin didn't know why, he knew it must be important if his brother was wasting his time with her. Olin pointed a finger toward Ray and spoke. "Spell be gone. Life restored." Ray opened his eyes and snorted loudly; he stood up and looked at Olin.

Once a demon guardian has died, no one can restore his life. When they die on the surface, they will disappear back to Terra Demorte, and there, their clan buries the body. Their life is gone.

165

Olin knew that Ray wasn't dead, but under a spell the wicked witch Odium had cast. A spell that resembles death, and left in this state, would eventually die. Olin also knew that Odium would not be so bold to walk onto her master's grounds and kill one of his protector. The consequences would be too, great.

"Thanks, Master!" said Ray.

"I've disabled her powers, Ray, she's harmless now." Olin said smiling at the big brute.

"Me gonna kill her now. Now she has no power over me!" Ray said, taking a step toward Odium.

"Easy, big fellow," said Odium. "Your Master wouldn't like it if you killed me before he has a chance to talk to me, yessssss, yesssss, He wouldn't like that at all!" She stepped back as Ray approached her.

"It's OK, Ray. Maybe later!" said Olin, smiling at Odium. "She's right. The master wants to speak to her, and I promised Odium that she could leave here alive. I must remember to be a gentleman and treat you as our guest." He turned to Odium. "Please, madam, forgive me for my hostility toward you, and please allow me to help you to the mansion."

Olin smiled at Odium, turning on his charm, a charm that could have talked a squirrel out of his last nut on a cold winter's day. He had beaten the witch and now had nothing else to prove. He was the victor in this battle, the battle he had wanted so badly earlier that day. She had bested the demon guardian, but not him, and now she was standing there with no magic power. He had won.

"Come with me, please!" Olin walked through the overgrown garden followed by Odium and Ray. They resembled three ducks all in a roll as they headed toward the kitchen door, the old witch following Olin and Ray following her.

Odium turned quickly and stared at the guardian. Olin didn't notice and continued making his way down the narrow garden path. With a slight wave of her hand, she pointed a crooked finger at Ray. Instantly, a huge swarm of bees dove from above and attacked the demon guardian, stinging and biting him. He snorted loudly and swung his heavy fists toward the flying insects in a feeble attempt to scare them away, which failed.

Olin heard the commotion and turned to see what was happening. Ray was standing under the tree, snorting loudly and swinging his arms. He looked like a huge turkey trying to take flight.

"What the—?" Olin shouted. "Ray, get in the house!" Olin turned and ran toward the kitchen. The old witch Odium did the same, and both reached the house one behind the other, swatting the bees. It was pretty obvious that if it moved, the bees were attacking it.

Olin entered the kitchen with Odium right behind him. They heard Ray swearing and cursing in some type of foreign language that neither understood. Olin laughed as he headed out of the kitchen and into the large foyer. "This way, witch!"

Odium smiled and followed Olin. She turned once again, and with a flick of her finger, locked the screen door that allowed access to the kitchen. Ray had just landed on the wooden porch and made a dash for the screen door. When he attempted to open it, he was surprised to find it locked. He pulled once again, but the door wouldn't budge. He stopped for a moment to swat, once again, at the swarming insects. Then with a thrust of his huge body, he ran through the door, breaking the wood and smashing the screen.

He quickly flung the kitchen door shut and managed to swat down the bees that had made it into the house. Odium smiled at the demon guardian and turned once again to follow her host.

Olin tapped on Creed's door, which, as usual, was standing partially open. The spiders had rebuilt their webs, and as before, they snapped as Olin pushed the door open.

"Master Creed, Odium is here," he said.

"Come in," came the raspy voice from the shadows behind the desk. Olin showed Odium to the overstuffed chair sitting in front of the desk; he pulled up another chair and sat down beside the witch.

Creed came out of the shadows and placed his elbows on the desk. "I need your help, witch."

"Yesssss, yesssssss," said Odium. "Yessssss, yessssss, how can I help you, Master Creed, yessssss?"

"Do you know about my transformation?" questioned Creed.

"Yesssss, yes, Master Creed, yessssss, I do!"

"What do you know?" hissed Creed. "About my transformation, that is?"

"I know you wanted me to capture you a newbie, yessssss, yessssss. I did that for you, Master Creed, yessssss, yessssss, I did, I did that for you. I showed you where she was, do you need, yessssss, yessssss another one, Master?!" Odium said. "Do you need another newbie like, Jessica?"

"No, not a newbie, not now. Do you know about the little girl who lived in Number 12?"

"Yes, yessssss, yessssss, I did, Sarah Wheeler, yes, yessssss, I did. You've been trying for years to catch her, yessssss, yessssss, you have." Odium sat staring at Creed. "Yes, yes, did you finally succeed in capturing her?" She didn't stutter this time.

"Odium, the witch, Wisteria—"

Before Creed could finish, Odium let out a loud scream.

"What did that meddlesome old witch do? She's always poking her nose where it's, yessssss, yessssss, not wanted. What did she do?"

"She held a triangular séance," Creed said. Odium sat and this time didn't interrupt her master. "Olin and I interrupted it, and we fought with her until the stroke of midnight."

"So, she failed?" asked Odium. "Yessssss, she would have failed."

"Yes," said Olin. "We made sure of it, but somehow, when I went to collect the spirits this morning, they wouldn't come to me."

"Yessssss, yessssss, that's impossible. They must come, Master, yessssss, yessssss, yes, they must. They have no choice in the matter," said Odium.

"They didn't respond to Olin's commands this morning, Odium," hissed Creed. "We were wondering if you could help us determine why they aren't in Number 12."

"Yessssss, yessssss, they, yessssss, yessssss, they must be there, they have to be!"

Odium stopped. "Yesssss, yesssss, unless she tricked you someway, yesssss, that's the only way the spirits wouldn't have obeyed your commands to appear this morning. Yesssss, yesssss, she's tricked you."

"But how?" questioned Creed. "How? We were there when the clock struck the final note of midnight. How could she have pulled this off?"

"I can't tell you, Master Creed. I don't know, but yesssss, yessssssss, she has tricked the, Master. Yesssss, she has. There is no other explanation," Odium said. "Yesssss, no other explanation." She paused as she sat thinking. "But how?"

Olin looked at the witch and lit up a smoke. "We don't know, Odium, but this morning when I went to collect Sarah and the others, none of them were there. They're gone!"

"Yesssss, yesssss, you're speaking of Horace and the nanny. Yesssss, yesssss, they were in Number 12, as well. Yesssss, yesssss, they were. I knew that, I knew they were there." Odium said.

"How did you know that?" hissed Creed.

"Master, yesssss, yesssss, Master, Odium knows all spirits that dwell on the surface in this area, and other areas, as well. Yesssss, I do! They hide, but Odium seeks them out." Odium looked at Olin as if she thought he should be impressed. Olin stared back at the witch and then, taunting her, stuck out his tongue at her.

"Odium, so you know all of the spirits stuck on the surface, the ones who haven't passed over and the ones who haven't succumbed to the dark side?" Creed asked.

"All, yesssss, yesssss, most all of them, Master. I know the ones that haven't crossed over and the ones that have. Both the good and the bad, I also know the ones that have not succumbed to the dark side," Odium replied.

"Odium, I need three spirits with great power, three that have been here on the surface and haven't succumbed to the dark side or been robbed of their power. Can you help me with that?" Creed asked.

"Yesssss, yesssss, no, Master Creed, there are none that have that kind of power left in your lot, yesssss, yesssss, none at all," Odium said.

Then she flashed Creed a huge smile. "Yes, yes, Master Creed. I do know of four such spirits. Yesssssss, yessssss, they have been dead for years and haven't passed over or drained of their power. Yesssssss, yessssss, I do know of them," Odium said.

Creed sat up straight in his chair and then spoke once again to Odium. "Tell me where they are, Odium. I need them."

"Yesssssss, yes, Master Creed. I assume you do. They have great power and strength. Yesssssss, yessssss, they do." She spoke softly; she had his attention.

"Tell me where they are, Odium," Creed hissed. "I need them and I need them quickly. Can you get them for me?"

Odium looked at the great Master Creed. At this very minute he was doing nothing less than begging her to produce the whereabouts of the four powerful spirits he needed. She looked at Olin and then back at Creed. This, at last, was the chance she had been waiting for since she had heard about Creed and Olin's transformations.

"Yesssssss, yessssss, Master Creed. I can get them for you, to be sure, but there's something I need from you, Master, yessssss, yessssss. Yes, there is something I need from you." She bowed her head, showing an act of respect for the master, but the old witch wasn't sincere. She was only setting the stage, play acting as it were, to get what she really wanted, and what she wanted wasn't to help the warlock Creed.

"What is it, Odium? If it's within my power, it's yours—if you can produce the spirits that have enough power for me to complete my transformation. Quickly, tell me what it is that you want," hissed Creed.

"I want, yessssss, I want The Secret of Life."

Olin stood up in a flash. His brother did the same, and before the witch had a chance to react, Creed bellowed an answer to her request.

"Never! How dare you to come into my house and demand such a thing? Do you think for one minute you can barter with your Master? I have let you live here—here, in my lot—and haven't requested anything for payment until now, and you want to barter with me? You want the most precious gift the dark side has ever seen? No, I won't give you The

Secret of Life." Creed sat back down in his chair. He gave it a gentle push and disappeared back into the shadows behind his desk.

Odium looked at Creed; she could feel Olin's rage as he stood beside her. "Yessssss, yessssss, Master Creed. I didn't mean to offend you, but that's the bargain, four powerful spirits for The Secret of Life, after you have completed your transformation, of course. I want The Secret of Life all for myself; it will make me beautiful and young again. I must have it. Yessssss, yessssss, I want to be young again."

"You heard the master, Odium. No deal. Tell us where these spirits are. I have no knowledge of any powerful spirits dwelling in our lot. We have captured and converted all the ones that have any power. Sarah, Horace, and the nanny were the only spirits left that had any kind of power worth salvaging. Where are these spirits that you say have such great power?" Olin said.

"Yessssss, yessssss, I know where they are. Yessssss, yessssss, I do. And I can capture them for you if you promise to give me The Secret of Life." Odium didn't turn to look at Olin; she stared into the shadows where Creed was still lurking.

"No!" hissed Creed. "I won't give you The Secret of Life. Never."

Olin started to strike out at the witch; he wanted to call her an insolent, ungrateful scavenger, living in his brother's lot, who, now that Creed needed something from her, wanted him to pay for it. He decided that he would just dispatch her and look for the spirits himself. He raised his hand and then paused.

He looked at the old woman, a witch who wanted to be young and beautiful again; he changed his mind and didn't attack. The witch was old, frail, and decrepit—or at least that's what she portrayed. He suddenly understood her wants and needs.

"Odium, what if we promised to transform you next? What if my brother and I promised to transform you, as soon as, his transformation was completed? We won't rest until we complete your transformation. What would you say to that?" Olin said. Creed sat in the shadows and made no comment as he waited for Odium's answer.

"Yessssss, yessssss, no, no I don't believe I could trust you. I don't believe you would transform Odium. Yessssss, I don't believe you would," she said.

"I give you my word, Odium," said Olin.

"And mine," snapped Creed.

"Yessssss, yes I know the word of a warlock isn't to be trusted, as you know that the word of a witch is the same—especially mine." Odium laughed and continued to speak.

"But I guess I'll just have to trust you, yessssss, yessssss, I will. If both of you promise to transform me to a beautiful young woman, I'll bring to you the four spirits. Yessssss, yessssss, I will."

"Where are they, Odium? Where do they hide that we can't find them here in our lot?" Olin said.

"Yessssss, yessssss, there is still another thing I'll need from you, Master Creed. The four spirits aren't in your lot. They're in your neighbor's lot, and I'll need your help in"—Odium looked around, ensuring no one was listening to their conversation—"yessssss, yessssss, I'll need your help to kill Master Umberto. Yessssss, yessssss, you know Master Umberto?" she asked.

"Yes, we do," said Olin. "So the spirits are in his lot?"

"Yessssss, yes they are, Master Olin, and he knows they're there. We will have to kill him. Yessssss, yessssss, we will if we are to capture these spirits. Will you agree to these two things, Master Creed?" She turned to look at Olin. "Will you agree as well, Master Olin?"

"Yes, we will," said Olin. Olin had answered before Creed had a chance, but Creed knew if he was to complete his transformation that he would have to work with the witch, Odium.

"Yes, we agree," said Creed. Odium sat quietly in the large chair. She knew she couldn't trust the two warlocks sitting there in the room with her, but her desire to become young again and to be beautiful once more consumed her fears of trust, so she decided to join forces with the two warlocks.

"Yessssss, yessssss, Master Creed. I'll be loyal to you and Master Olin, and I'll go for the spirits as soon as—" Odium stopped. "Yessssss, yessssss, as soon as Master Olin kills, Master Umberto. He is a very powerful warlock, and I don't believe I could kill such a master all by myself."

Now, Odium knew quite well that she was conniving and shrewd enough to kill any warlock if she could get the drop on him. She had many years of experience in killing, everything from adults to children, and she knew very well how to do it. She also knew that in a full-frontal fight she had better than a fifty-fifty chance of defeating a warlock, but why take the chance?

Creed needed the spirits, and Olin wanted to fight someone, so why not let Olin do the fighting? If Olin succeeded in killing Master Umberto, then she was on her way to being transformed. She would be next. If Master Umberto killed Olin, then she could and would kill Creed and take The Secret of Life from him. Creed was very vulnerable in his current stage, and killing him would be easy.

She sat and stared into the darkness where Creed was sitting. The two demon guardians were no threat to her; they would be easy to dispatch. In Odium's opinion, she had nothing to lose by letting Olin kill the dark master. There was also, in her opinion, an added bonus.

Warlocks weren't supposed to trespass on another's lot, and if a warlock found another warlock trespassing on his lot, they would go to war with each other until one was dead and his spirit sent back to Terra Demorte, hopefully into the Keeping Room. Either way, Odium figured she would come out ahead of the game. Only on the surface could a warlock kill another warlock and get away with it. If Master Umberto caught Olin or Creed trespassing, he might kill both himself, leaving her a clear path to The Secret of Life. She sat quiet for a moment and then pushed the idea a little harder.

"Yessssss, yessssss, Master Olin. You will need a plan if you are to kill Master Umberto. Yessssss, yessssss, you will!" Odium looked at Olin, waiting for a response.

Olin suspected Odium was playing him for the fool and hoping one way or another that he himself might be the one killed. He knew he couldn't count on Odium's help, so if he was to do the killing, he would indeed have to come up with a plan. When killing a warlock, one usually had to kill a couple of demon guardians, as well.

"I'll have a plan when the time comes, Odium. Just let me know when you have convinced the spirits to convert to the dark side. Once they're ready to come to the mansion, I'll dispatch Master Umberto. We will finish Master Creed's transformation that very night. Killing another master can bring great consequences from his friends. But we can't delay the transformation any longer, agreed?"

"Yesssss, yessssss, I agree. Don't worry about me, Master Olin. I'll do my part! Yesssss, yessssss, I will. Yesssss, I will! There will be enough power to transform both of us. Yesssss, yessssss, it will."

Olin pulled the gold box from his cloak. He stared at it patiently and then held it between his two thumbs and index fingers. "Do you know what this is?" he asked.

"Yesssss, yessssss. Where did you get that? Yesssss, yessssss, that's the dark witches' gold box you have there. Yesssss, I'm sure of it. May I see it, please, yessssss, please?"

"In a moment," said Olin. "Do you know how this works?"

"Yesssss, yessssss, I do. Yes, I do"

"Will you show me?"

Odium sat for a moment before answering. She stared at Olin and wondered where he had gotten such a rare item. As she stared, she knew that such a weapon in the hands of Olin and Creed could easily make them so powerful that they, indeed, could rule the dark side and all of the other masters.

At that very moment, doubt flooded her evil dark mind. She wondered if she should help these two warlocks at all. She wondered if she should show them how to unleash the magic of the gold box. Odium turned her face back toward Creed, who was still sitting in the shadows.

"Yes, I can show you how the gold box works; do you know what power it possesses?" she asked. This time, the old witch didn't drag out the word yes and spoke very clearly and precisely. "Do you know what that gold box can do?"

"Dispatch a master warlock," said Olin.

"Yes," said Odium. "You need the box and the parchment that comes with it. Do you have the parchment?"

"Yes," said Olin. He opened the box and took out the parchment; the box put forth a golden glow. "Yes, I have the parchment here. Do you want me to read it?"

Odium looked at Olin. Here was the warlock that mocked her and thought he had beaten her in the garden just minutes earlier. And here was a warlock that had no idea how close he was to death. She looked at Olin, and then with the small light that the lamp was putting forth, she noticed Olin's body. Although she had been with him most of the morning, she hadn't paid that much attention to his appearance. His skin was beautiful and smooth as bronze. It glowed like that of a statue, and she noticed his dark hair, his green eyes, and his smooth face. "Not one wrinkle," she said softly.

She hadn't meant for Olin to hear her remark, but he had and so had Creed. Olin smiled at the old witch and said softly, "It's remarkable, isn't it?"

Odium was caught up in the fantasy of being beautiful again herself, and she replied softly, "Yessssss, yessssss, very remarkable." Odium was powerful and a shape-shifter—at a moment's notice could change into a young beautiful woman or a huge, dirty, mangy beast—but with age, it was very painful and the spell didn't last very long. It was almost unbearable.

As she looked at the handsome man sitting beside her, the thoughts of being young again and living forever in that state flooded her mind. The thoughts of being a beautiful woman all but consumed her. She decided she would stay true to her bargain with Olin and Creed.

Odium realized that after ones transformation, they would not age but be young and beautiful forever. However, they were not immortal. This was the issue the mighty pharaoh faced, and that was the reason he wanted to be immortal. If killed on the surface, their body would disappear back to the Keeping Room in Terra Demorte, where their clan would resurrect them, if they elected to do so.

"Yessssss, yessssss, don't speak the words on the parchment, Master Olin. Where did you get the box?" she asked.

"If you must know, I got it in Terra Demorte," Olin said. "I took it from a demon guardian who was drunk and had been accused of dispatching his former master."

"Yessssss, yessssss, in Terra Demorte. Did it, yessssss, yessssss, did it ever occur to you how a priceless possession like that ended up there? You know, yessssss, yessssss, it wasn't made for the dark side. Yessssss, yessssss, no, it shouldn't ever be in Terra Demorte. Yessssss, yessssss, it shouldn't."

"Doesn't matter how it got there. What matters, Odium, is that I have it now! I just need to know how to use it. I assume you just open the box and read the words." Olin took the parchment and unfolded it; he held it up and began to read the words.

"Stop, Master Olin. Don't read the parchment. Yessssss, yessssss, you must stop now."

Olin stopped and looked at Odium. "What? What's wrong? Why do you stop me?"

Odium sat silently for a moment and then spoke. "Master Olin, let me see the parchment. Yessssss, yessssss, let me see the parchment." Olin looked at the witch. He wondered if he could trust her with the parchment and the gold box. He quickly decided he couldn't, so he handed Odium the parchment and kept the box.

Odium studied the parchment and then smiled at Olin. "Yes, yes, someone wants you dead, Master Olin. Yes, they do. You see, yes, if you had read this parchment with the box open, *you* are the one that would be trapped within its walls. This isn't the parchment you need, Master. No, it's not." Odium folded the parchment and placed it on the arm of the chair.

"What do you mean, Odium? What do you mean if I'd read the parchment I would have been trapped within the box?" Olin questioned. "The demon guardian said he read this parchment with the gold box open and it trapped his master. You must be mistaken."

"No, Olin. I'm not mistaken. The spell on the parchment will trap within the box the one who reads the parchment. Yes, someone wants you dead, Master Olin." Odium looked at Olin. "Would you please, yes, let me see the box?"

Olin looked at Odium and then at Creed, who had slipped out of the shadows and was now at the desk. "Let her have the box, Olin," Creed said. "Roy! Roy, come in here." Roy entered the room and stood by the chair on the other side of the witch. "Watch her, Roy. Keep an eye on her."

Odium looked at Creed. "Yessssss, yessssss, I'll show you that you can trust me, Master Creed. I stopped Master Olin from reading the parchment and saved his life. Now you must show me you can trust me. Send this demon guardian out of the room."

Creed studied the witch for a moment and then spoke softly to Roy. "You may go, Roy."

"Yessssss, yessssss, now, Master Olin, would you, yessssss, yessssss, would you give me the box?" Olin rose from his chair and handed Odium the gold box. Odium studied the box; she turned it and looked at the drawings and figures on all sides. Then, as if she knew what she was doing, she closed the box and pushed on the heart that was on one end. The top divided into two pieces and slid open. It was magic, because there was no line dividing the top. By all appearances, the top was one solid piece of gold. Odium handed the gold box back to Olin.

"Yessssss, yessssss, Master Olin. Yessssss, yes here's your parchment," she said. Olin looked at the box. He slid the top open farther, which revealed a small cavity. And there, lying in the cavity was a small piece of ancient parchment. Olin took the parchment out and sat the box down on the chair's arm. The top of the box slid back shut and concealed the small cavity once again. Olin studied the parchment and looked at Odium.

"How did you know about this?" he asked.

"I was told about this box and how to use it many years ago when I was a—" Odium stopped. "It doesn't matter. What matters, yessssss, yessssss, what matters is that you know where the real parchment is kept."

"Why did the demon guardian have this box, and why did he not have the right parchment?" Olin asked. No one spoke. All looked at the gold box and then at the small piece of parchment that Olin was holding.

"It was a trap, yesssssss, yessssss, a trap. Someone wanted you to open the gold box and read the wrong parchment, yessssss, yessssss, that piece of parchment there." Odium pointed to the parchment on the chair's arm. "If you had done that, you would be trapped in the box, and neither you nor Master Creed would know how to get you back out. Yesssssss, that's it. Yesssssss, someone is trying to trick you!" Odium smiled at Olin and then turned to Creed. "Does this prove my loyalty, Master Creed? I just saved your brother's life. In fact, once Olin was trapped in the gold box, you Master Creed would have been easy to kill."

Creed looked at the witch sitting in front of him. He had no choice but to confirm his trust in her. "Yes, Odium, I do trust you now, and I'll keep my word and transform you once I have completed my transformation. Thank you for saving my brother." He made a low hissing sound. Odium smiled at Creed and bowed her head slightly.

Creed knew the old witch had no loyalties to him or Olin. She wanted The Secret of Life and would stop at nothing to get it, but for the time being, he knew she would be satisfied with the thought of being transformed into a young and beautiful woman. He also knew that in order to be transformed, she had to be...dead.

Olin looked at the gold box; he took a seat and sat quietly thinking. He raised his head again and looked at his brother. "They tried to trick us, Creed. Terra Demorte, everyone in Jake's Place, they've tried to trick us.

They wanted me to read this parchment and become trapped in the gold box. They knew you wouldn't be able to get me out and would seek help in Terra Demorte. Once I was out of the way, they would surely have killed you."

"Why?" hissed Creed.

"Don't you see, Brother? They want your transformation to fail. They're on to us, somehow. They know if you succeed in being transformed, that our next move is to rule the dark side and all of the surface masters. They have to know, or at least suspect it; why else would they try to trick us with this gold box?"

Creed stood up. "Those devilish dogs, those spineless dark devils. They will pay for this, and we will make sure of it." Creed slid back into his chair. He took several deep, raspy breaths. "We can't trust anyone, Olin; we need to complete my transformation. This gold box will buy us a few days, but sooner or later they will send someone to see why you haven't tried to use the box and why you aren't trapped in it."

"Yessssss, yessssss, they won't have to send anyone. The spell on the parchment that they gave you will let them know when Olin is trapped within the box. Yessssss, yessssss, someone is trying to stop your transformation. Yessssss, yessssss, they are."

Odium smiled as she looked down into her lap.

"We can use this for our advantage, Creed. Odium, can you teach me how to use the gold box correctly?" Olin said, turning to Odium. "Do you think they knew the real parchment was under the lid?"

"No, no one knows that except the dark witch and the good witch that conceived the box." She smiled at Olin.

"Then how on earth did you know?" questioned Olin.

The old witch smiled at the handsome warlock. "As I said, no one knows that except the dark witch and the good witch that conceived the box."

"So, you devised this contraption?"

"Yes."

Olin paused and stared in amazement at the old woman sitting in front of Creed's desk. At that moment, he realized that Odium was much more than just a dark witch. Somehow—and he certainly didn't understand why—he admired her.

"Will you show me how to use it, Odium?" he said, respectfully.

"Yes, yessssss, it's quite easy. Once you are in the presence of the master you want to trap, open the box and read the words on the parchment, and when you have finished reading it out loud, just speak the name of that master that you want to trap in the box. Yesssss, yessssss, then close the lid. Yesssss, yessssss, just close the lid.

"You can set a trap by setting the box in the opening and reading the parchment, and when the dark master gets close, just speak his name. Once you have captured the master, read the parchment backward and touch the gold box to any container, and the spirit will be transferred into that container. Yesssss, yessssss, very easy to do, yessssss.

"You can use a jar or a bottle, anything that has a top that you can seal. Once you have sealed the container, yessssss, the spirit can't escape until someone, anyone opens up the container. Yessssss, very easy, once you know how. Once the container is opened, the master will be transformed back into his old self, and looking for revenge, I would suspect."

"If I capture a master, will Terra Demorte know? Will the gold box or parchment alert the tribunal?" Olin asked.

"No, no, no one will know. Yessssss, yessssss, no one will know," Odium said.

"This will work to our advantage. Yes, it will," said Olin. He looked at the box once more and stuck it, along with the parchment, under his cloak. He looked at the fake parchment lying on the arm of the chair. "This might come in handy, as well." He stuck it in his pocket and flashed a big smile at Odium. "Thanks, witch, I, as well, will keep my word to you and will see that you are transformed back into the young and beautiful woman that you desire."

Odium smiled at Olin. "Thank you. Yessssss, yessssss, thank you!"

"So they want to keep me from my transformation, do they?" Creed said. He had regained his breath. He now was ready to condemn Terra Demorte for their deception. "Olin, we need to know who was behind this trickery." Creed struggled again for breath.

"Don't worry, Brother. I'll find out, and we will take revenge on each and every one of them. We have to assume that the demon guardian Drako was in on it, maybe he is the only one. I can't believe Jake would turn on us. Maybe, Morto. Maybe," Olin said. "I vow to you, I'll find out who did this, and when I do, I'll kill every one of them, in or out of Terra Demorte. It doesn't matter to me."

Creed rose up in his chair and put his elbows on the desk. "Now, about my transformation. Odium, can you get me the spirits I need?"

"Yessssss, yessssss, I can, but tonight we must capture Master Umberto in the gold box. Then I can collect the spirits and bring them to you tomorrow night. His spies will alert him the minute I cross into his lot," Odium said. "He has warned me not to—"Odium stopped and looked sheepishly at Olin.

"He warned you not to what?" asked Olin.

Odium smiled. "Not to ever trespass on his lot. Yessssss, yessssss, 'Never,' he said, but that's good. Yessssss, yessssss, that's good."

"How is that good for us, and how do we get into Master Umberto's house without his demon guardians catching us? If his spies alert him that you are coming, or we are coming, he'll be waiting for us. It's hard to attack a master where he lives, almost impossible. If he thinks we've come to harm him, he'll be fully protected or just disappear to Terra Demorte. Then the dark side will certainly know that we plan to harm the other surface masters."

"Yessssss, yessssss, you're right, but we won't capture him in his house. You will capture him in my house." Odium laughed slightly and then started choking on something, which she coughed up and then spat out of her mouth, onto the floor of Creed's chambers. Olin watched as it slowly crawled away. Disgusted, he scrunched his face and shook his head. Creed and Olin sat looking at her in repulsion.

"Oh, if you think that's something, you should smell the vicious, wicked, odor when she farts." Said Olin.

Odium moved slightly, and a loud noise erupted within the chair. She then sat still, and a malicious-smelling odor filled the room.

Olin moved his chair away from the witch. As he stood up, he stared at her. "Must you do that?" he said.

"Yessssss, yessssss, do what?" Odium said abruptly.

"Part with that nauseating odor," Olin said.

"Yessssss, yessssss" was all that Odium said. "Collards and turnips."

The stench was unsettling, and although the obnoxious odor still hung heavy in the air, Olin decided to open his mouth and ask another question to the witch. "How are you going to get Master Umberto to your house?"

"You leave that to me, Master Olin. You just be at my house tonight at seven o'clock. Be there and don't be late! Bring the gold box, and we'll take care of Master Umberto."

Creed spoke softly. "Why can't you bring me the spirits tonight, after you have captured Master Umberto?"

"It will take some time to capture Master Umberto, and more time for me to convince the spirits to convert over to the dark side; I'll also need your help with that, Master Olin." Odium turned and looked at Olin. "Will you help me?"

"Of course. Yes, yes."

"Good. See you at seven o'clock. Yessssss, yessssss, at seven." Odium stood up and wobbled toward the door. She left without speaking another word.

"Roy," hissed Creed. Roy entered the room. "See that Odium leaves the yard."

"Yes, Master!"

Creed and Olin sat for a moment in silence. Then Creed spoke in a soft, raspy voice. "What about the good witch, Olin. How are we going to handle that?"

Olin smiled at Creed. "The same way we did during my transformation. I have already selected the witch, and she has two young, beautiful daughters!"

"Tricked and robbed by that witch, Wisteria, and now Terra Demorte has turned against us. What next?" Creed muttered. "It appears that we have a lot of work to do when my transformation is complete."

"Yes, and don't forget about the two humans who live in Number 12." Olin rubbed his shoulder. "We've got a score to settle with them, as well." He stood up and walked toward the door; he turned and looked at

Creed. "Once Odium gets you the spirits you need, I'll kill her. She must be demented thinking we would transform her." Olin laughed.

Creed stood up and walked over to where his brother was standing. Roy entered the room and informed them that the witch, Odium, had indeed left the house and the yard.

"Yes!" hissed Creed after Roy had left. "I too wanted to kill Odium— that insolent witch, wanting to bargain with me—but she might come in handy after she has been transformed. We might need a witch, especially one as evil as Odium."

"I don't think we could trust her!" Olin said.

"Nor do I," hissed Creed, "but we could use her until we didn't need her any longer, I think we could keep her on a short leash, if you know what I mean." Creed hissed again, turned, and walked back behind his desk. "I'm tired, Olin. I'm going to rest!"

"Rest, Brother. I've got an errand to run, and I'll be back to check on you!" Olin said, taking off his cloak. "I won't need this. My street clothes should do for this little errand."

"Where are you going?"

"To make a visit to one of our friends!"

"Olin, don't go stirring up trouble. Let it lie until my transformation is completed, then you can kill those two meddlesome humans. Let it lie for now!" Creed said. "We've got a lot of killing to do, after I'm whole." That was the first time Olin had heard Creed refer to his transformation as "being whole."

"I'm just going to pop into Number 12 to see if Sarah is really gone. I'll wait until the house is empty and just poke around a bit." Olin walked toward the door. He lit a cigarette and walked out of Creed's chambers and down the steps, vanishing into the foyer wall.

# Fifteen

# The Attack

Katie took a deep breath, pushed the door open, and stared curiously into the living room. She breathed a sigh of relief; the house looked exactly as she had left it earlier. She quickly entered the house and went straight into the den. She put Josh on the sofa and headed into the kitchen to get her bills.

"We've got to hurry, baby!" she said, walking down the hall. "Wisteria doesn't want us to be in the house today. She wants us to wait until Daddy comes home." She grabbed the bills lying on the table and retraced her steps back down the hall heading toward the den. "Do you have to pee pee before we leave, baby?" she said. The small boy she had left on the sofa didn't answer. Katie returned to the den and stopped dead in her tracks.

"What are you doing here?" she said. "Put my son down!"

"Why, Katie, you're not glad to see me?" asked Olin. He was sitting on the couch, holding Josh in his lap. "Nice boy!" he said. "Odium would like him. Although she prefers the blood of small girls for some reason, I'm sure his blood would taste just as sweet?" He looked at Katie and flashed a smile. "Yes, I'm sure she would enjoy him."

"I won't tell you again. Put him down," shouted Katie. She glanced at the crystal and noticed immediately that it was dark.

"I wouldn't worry about that there," said Olin, also glancing at the crystal. "You certainly don't think that I couldn't counter that little old security spell, do you?"

"They'll be here any second. Put my son down and leave!" Katie said, standing her ground. "I won't ask you again." Olin could tell that Katie was a very strong woman—not so much physically but mentally—but he immediately saw Katie's weakness…her son!

"No one is coming, Katie, and all I want from you today is a little information. I'll put your son down, but first, tell me what Wisteria did with Sarah Wheeler." He put his hands around Josh's neck. "So soft," he said. "Quickly, tell me where they are and I'll leave."

"Put my son down and get out of my house," shouted Katie. She took a small step toward the warlock.

Olin gently slid the small boy from his lap onto the couch cushion. "You sit right there," he said. "As you wish, Katie. I'm leaving." Olin rose from the sofa and walked over to her. "You are a strong woman!" he said. "I like that." He turned slightly, and with a quick thrust of his hand, he slapped Katie in the face. The unbelievable force propelled her backward; she managed to grab the arm of the huge chair to keep from falling to the floor. Olin reached down with one hand and pulled the dazed woman up by her hair. He stood in front of her and watched her left eye start to swell. He released her hair and squared her up with his hands.

Josh, seeing his mother beaten by Olin, began to cry.

"Did that hurt?" Olin said with a smirk. "I think I'm going to kill you." He grabbed Katie's throat and pulled the unsuspecting woman a little closer. With his free hand, he struck her again, hitting her in the same eye. Katie started to fall, but Olin pulled her back up. "Don't get wobbly on me, Katie; you still haven't answered my question. Now I'm going to ask you one more time. Where is Sarah Wheeler?"

Blood was running down Katie's face and dripping steadily onto the floor. She focused on Olin and spat at him. "I'm not telling you anything;

now get out of my house." Olin pulled her close; he turned and looked at Josh, who was crying hysterically.

"Mommy, mommy!" cried Josh.

"Shut up, you stupid little creature," shouted Olin. "Shut up. Stop that crying!" But the more Olin shouted at Josh, the harder he cried. Olin pulled Katie closer. "I'll not ask again. If you value that boy on the couch, you will tell me what I want to know. I will kill him if you don't. Where is Sarah?" Katie closed her eyes. She felt her head spinning, and she knew she would have to tell Olin where Sarah had gone. She would tell him everything and anything to keep him from hurting Josh.

Before Katie could speak, Olin hit her again, this time with his fist, and struck her on the other eye. It, like the left eye, started swelling immediately. A large gash spewed blood down her cheek and into the corners of her mouth. "Nice," said Olin. "It matches the other one!"

Olin laughed and pushed Katie down into the large chair. He walked toward the little boy, who was crying on the sofa. "I thought I told you to shut up," he said. He stood, staring down at Josh, and with a hard swing, he backhanded the small boy, sending him off the sofa and onto the floor. "I think I'll just kill you both," he said.

Katie tried to get to Josh. Her legs wobbled and with her head spinning, all she managed to do was take one-step before she fell in the floor. Olin grabbed the large coffee table with one hand and flung it toward the living room. It crashed onto the hard wood floor, and the glass broke, sending small shards everywhere.

Katie crawled to her son. His mouth, nose, and eyes were bleeding. He wasn't crying now, but lay still on the floor. He was unconscious. Katie pulled the small boy up into her arms; he was breathing and moaned as she rubbed the blood from his face. "Baby!" was all she could said.

Olin, snatching the small boy from her arms, flung him back onto the sofa. He grabbed Katie by the hair, and with a mighty blow, kicked her in the face. She rolled backward and let out a loud cry. Olin kicked her again, but this time in the chest and then again in the stomach. He pulled her up by the hair and pushed her back into the chair.

"I'm going to ask you one more time, and if you don't tell me what the witch did with Sarah Wheeler, I'm going to kill that little boy. Right here in front of you." Olin laughed and stood erect. "Well," he said, "I'm waiting."

"She's gone. They're all gone, and I'm glad you can't have her!" Katie folded her arms around her chest. The pain was excruciating, and her face was bleeding profusely. She wiped the blood on her shirt and tried to clear her eyes so she could see the monster standing in front of her. As she wiped her eyes, she realized it wasn't the blood keeping her from seeing; both of her eyes were swollen shut. It was at this very moment that she realized she and her son were at the mercy of Olin, a dark warlock, a demon from the dark side.

"Where did they go?" asked Olin. "Quickly. I'm getting bored with this!" Olin reached down and stroked Katie's hair. "Quickly, Katie, and I'll make it quick for you and your brat!"

Katie jerked her head back and then replied to Olin's question. "They crossed over. They crossed over into the light, and now they're gone, gone from you and that miserable brother of yours." She was crying now. There was no hope. She was alone with this deadly warlock, and she and Josh would surely die.

Her thoughts ran wild, skipping from one to another, but there was one thought that calmed her, one thought that made her fears subside. Katie smiled and felt a warm feeling flood her body; she curled up in the chair and was engulfed in this one thought: the thought of Roland and how much she loved him and how much he loved her and Josh. She wanted to hold her son one more time before she died, but her swollen eyes wouldn't allow her to get to him. She listened for him but heard nothing but Olin's voice.

"How?" asked Olin.

"My husband is going to kill you."

"I doubt that. Quickly, tell me how."

"How what?" snapped Katie.

"How did they cross over? How could they cross over when Wisteria botched the séance?" Olin screamed.

188

"She ran the clock back twenty minutes. She tricked you and that hideous creature you call your brother!" Katie snapped again at the warlock, she spat more blood toward him. "Go ahead, if you're going to kill me, get it over with."

"Oh I'm going to kill you, Katie, but first, I'm going to kill this little boy here. I'm really sorry that you can't see this, but maybe he'll scream for you."

"Please, don't hurt him. He's just a small child. Please, Olin, I beg you. Kill me, but please leave him alone. Please!" Katie was choking on her own blood, but the pleading words continued to escape her lips. She cleared her throat and spat the pooling blood out. "Please!"

"Do you think for one minute that it matters diddly to me that he's a child, a small boy, a baby?" Olin took a step toward the sofa. "Well, it doesn't. I'd just as soon kill him as you, Katie, and after I kill him, I will kill you!"

"I don't think so," shouted a loud voice. Katie strained to hear who it was; her head was ringing so loudly that she couldn't make out to whom the voice belonged.

The voice belonged to Thor. With a quick leap, he dove to the floor, and with a quick shoulder roll, he stuck one of his daggers into Olin's stomach.

The warlock screamed, and as Thor stood up, he swung his fist and struck the warlock squarely between the eyes. Katie strained to open her eyes as she heard Olin scream. She couldn't see a thing, but at that very moment a faint ray of hope filled her heart. She didn't know what was going on, but she knew she wasn't alone, that someone was trying to help her.

Olin fell backward and hit the wall. He didn't vanish into the wall but flexed his hand and shot a fireball toward Thor. Thor held up his hand, and with a small movement, the fiery ball bounced off an unseen force and burned out.

Thor flung one of his daggers and smiled as the sharp instrument of death hit Olin in the chest. He followed the dagger and with a huge leap, he kicked Olin in the chest, just missing the dagger. Olin let out another painful scream and vanished into the wall. Thor waited, searching every corner of the room for Olin to reappear, but the warlock was gone.

"You coward," shouted Thor. He let out some strange words, undistinguishable to Katie. "Come back and fight, you miserable warlock!" Thor scanned the room but remembered that his scanners wouldn't pick up the transformed monster. He glanced down and saw Josh lying on the couch. He saw the dried and clotted blood that had run from the small child's face.

"You sorry dog," shouted Thor. "You sorry demon! Come back and fight, you sorry coward!" Again, he spat forth-strange words, words that a warlock would understand, but not a mere mortal like Katie. He dropped to his knees, stroked Josh's hair, and rubbed the boy's head with his hand. He remembered the small boy asking him to play just days earlier, and how he'd sat in Wisteria's Café coloring while they all talked that very morning. How could anyone hurt such a small child? Josh let out a small moan. Thor could hear him breathing and knew that he was alive. These strange feelings of love were new to Thor, in his past he hated surface people. Although he didn't want or like these feelings, they flooded his heart.

"Katie!" he said. "Are you all right?" Katie was crying softly. She knew someone was there, and now, as Thor rubbed her hand, she recognized the voice.

"Thor," she said softly, "is Josh all right?"

"Yes, Katie. He's alive. How are you?" The huge man looked at the battered woman. Tears filled his eyes as he stroked her cheek. "I'm sorry, Katie. I'm sorry this had to happen to a wonderful person like you. You're going to be all right. I'm here, and I won't leave you." He glanced at the crystal and shook his head.

Wisteria suddenly pushed open the door to Number 12. "Thor, are you here?"

"Yes, Wisteria, in here. Hurry. Katie's hurt, and so is Josh!" Thor stood up to meet the old woman. He wanted to help Katie and Josh but had no idea what he should do. His skills were in fighting and assassinating, not healing.

190

"Can you help her, Wisteria?" Thor asked.

"Yes, I have all I need here in this bag. How's Josh?" she said.

"Alive," Thor said. "That's all I can tell."

Wisteria looked at Thor. "Go get me some warm water, dear, and then sit in the dining room. I'll call you if I need anything else. Both will be fine, dear, just beaten and battered a bit! I'm glad you got here when you did. A few minutes later and..." Wisteria stopped. "Get the water, dear! Thor, be alert. Be on the alert for Olin. He might return."

"I wish he would, that piece of..." Thor left the den and headed down the hall to get the water Wisteria wanted. "I'll kill Olin Thomlin," he called from the kitchen. "I'll kill that brother of his, too, if it's the last thing I do."

Thor returned with the water and watched as Wisteria rubbed something on Josh's face. He glanced at Katie and saw that the same poultice had already been applied to her face. He watched, as the brown substance moved about Katie's face. It seemed to be alive. This was nothing new to Thor; he had seen poultices like this before.

Wisteria reached in her bag and pulled out something that resembled a large, loosely rolled cigarette. She lit it, and a light-blue smoke emitted from the end. She pushed the smoke toward the moving poultice. She closed her eyes and started speaking strange words. She stopped and looked up a Thor. "Go into the dining room, Thor. Please, dear."

"Yes, of course." He went into the other room and sat in one of the dining room chairs, gazing into the living room. His mind went back to the many times in the past when had visited the surface. The times he had come to the surface to kill humans. He had had many contracts and had always fulfilled them. He wondered what would have happened if he had ever gotten a contract on a child. Would he have killed such a precious being? He looked at the empty cold fireplace across the living room. *Was my heart that cold? Is it now?* he thought.

Thor shook his head in disbelief. *Yes, before I would have, with no questions ask, but not now. I could never kill such a precious being now!*

191

Thor sat thinking about his life as an assassin. He had always known only evil and had only lived in Terra Demorte. He had always hated the surface and most of all the humans that inhabited it. He had his own set of skills and magic, and now after seeing what Olin was doing to an innocent girl and her son, he wondered if he could ever go back home, back to the land he had loved. He had wanted to—it was home. But although he didn't like the surface, the more he stayed there, the less he liked home. "Quite a quandary," he said softly.

Wisteria worked in the den. Thor could hear the incantations, and every once in a while, he thought he heard strange sounds like bells ringing. Wisteria had managed to make Katie a bed on the couch and a small place for Josh at her feet. Their faces were covered with multiple shades of concoctions that Wisteria had rubbed on the bruises and cuts. Both were sleeping quietly, and as they slept, Wisteria was chanting words and burning incenses.

*** 

It was something after six when Thor heard Roland's car pull into the drive. He stood and went into the living room. "It's Roland, Wisteria. I'll meet him."

"That's fine, dear," Wisteria said. "Bring him in here; he'll want to see Katie."

"Sure," Thor said, walking out onto the front porch. He waited on Roland, attempting to keep his facial expression from giving anything away. Although he felt many emotions, showing them was something else; after all, he was an assassin from Terra Demorte.

"Thor, what a surprise. How are you doing?" Roland saw Thor standing on the front porch. He looked at his friend's face and knew instantly that something was wrong. No matter how hard Thor tried, his changing heart reflected itself on his face.

"What's wrong, Thor? Is Katie all right?" Roland picked up his pace and was on the porch within seconds. "What's wrong, Thor?"

"Katie's hurt, Roland, and so is your son." Tears came to Thor's eyes; he couldn't believe the feelings he was having. Tears were no strangers to Thor, but having them in his own eyes was strange. He had seen them many, many times in the eyes of his victims, but not until this trip to the surface had, he ever felt them in his own eyes. He wiped them away and followed Roland into the old house. "They're alive, Roland, just beaten up a bit."

"Katie, Katie," shouted Roland, entering the living room, "Katie, where are you?"

"We're in here, Roland, in the den," said Wisteria. She met Roland at the two large French doors that divided the living room from the den. "They are all right, Roland. I've given them something to make them rest, dear."

Roland walked over to the sofa. Tears filled his eyes when he saw the two people he loved the most lying on the makeshift beds. Katie's eyes were swollen shut, and the deep cuts about them were packed shut with the greenish-brown concoction that Wisteria had placed there. Her lips were cut and swollen. Most of her face, although covered with the potion, had turned black, blue, and greenish brown. His eyes followed her bruises down to her neck and then, as he lifted her blouse, he saw that in the middle of her chest was one great, big bruise. Both sides of her breasts were covered with the same multiple colors as her face. "Who did this?" he said.

His gaze shifted to the small boy lying at the feet of his wife. "Josh!" Roland walked to his son and knelt down beside him. He saw the crusted blood inside his son's nostrils, the soft tender skin on the face of his two-year-old son was bluish green, and Josh's right eye was swollen. Roland placed his hand on his son's forehead and softly kissed his bruised cheek. Tears rolled down Roland's face, and like a small child, he broke down and sobbed uncontrollably. He placed his head on Josh's chest and hugged his son. "Who did this, Wisteria?" he said again.

"Olin," said Wisteria. "It was Olin!"

"Shouldn't they be taken to the hospital, Wisteria?" he said softly.

"No, dear. There are no bones broken; they're just bruised up. The cuts will heal, and there will be no scarring. I have them sedated so the potions will work, and tomorrow they will be much better. Don't worry, dear. I promise they'll be just fine!"

Roland wiped the tears once more from his face. "I'm going to kill him, Wisteria. What kind of monster would do this to Katie, and especially to a small child like Josh?"

"A monster like Olin," said Thor. "You don't have to worry about killing him Roland; I'll do that for you!"

Roland looked at Thor. "You mean that?"

"Totally," said Thor.

Roland tried to reach Katie with his thoughts, but nothing was returned. He bent down, kissed Katie on the forehead, and turned toward Thor.

"Get your stuff. We're finishing this, and I mean now!" Roland said standing up.

"I'm going with you. You'll need me," said Wisteria. "These are masters you're dealing with, and you're going to need my help."

"No," said Roland. "I need you to stay with Katie and Josh. In their condition, they only have you to protect them. Please, Wisteria, please stay with my family. We're taking care of Creed and Olin!"

Wisteria looked at Roland and could see the worry in his eyes. She knew at this moment he wasn't worried about the battle with Creed or Olin, but she could see the worry concerning his wife and son. "OK, Roland," said Wisteria. "I took the liberty of moving my belongings into the green bedroom. I'm not going to leave any of you until this thing is finished."

"I didn't see you bring any belongings, Wisteria!" Thor said.

"Of course not. If you are to kill Olin and Creed," she said, changing the subject, "you'll have to get past his demon guardians. If Olin and Creed realize you are coming, they'll disappear, and you won't be able to find them. You have got to surprise them, dear!"

"I can handle the demon guardians," said Roland. "How do I kill that miserable dog, Olin?"

"In their state, the same as any mortal, but once you have killed them; you must cut off their heads. Otherwise their bodies will disappear back to Terra Demorte, and they will be restored and back here within two days. You have to sever the heads and put them in a sealed container," Thor said.

"Let's go!" Roland said. "Let me get some things. I have something for you, Thor."

Roland went upstairs and returned with his green duffel bag. Wisteria walked into the dining room where the two men were standing.

"Remember, dear, you have to surprise Olin and Creed, or they'll be gone before you get in the house. Do you want my electrical gadget?"

"No need tonight, Wisteria; I purchased some additional things that will help us kill this dog!" Roland unzipped the bag and stuck one of his hands deep into it. He fished out something from the bottom and showed it to Thor and Wisteria. It looked like two small pipes.

"What are those?" Wisteria said. "What do they do, dear?"

Roland looked at her and smiled. "This, my dear, is how we get past the demon guardians. These are silencers." Roland pulled out a nine-millimeter pistol. He screwed a silencer onto the barrel of the pistol. "When you pull the trigger, no one hears anything," Roland said. "And I mean no one!"

"Roland, do you think you could give me one of your pistols?" asked Thor. "They're far superior to my daggers. I hate to ask, but I would really like to have one of those and one of those things on the end. Would you mind if I took one of yours?"

"Yes, and I won't give you one of mine, Thor, but you can have these. I purchased them for you." Roland opened the duffel bag, and there were more of the same, pistols and silencers. "Mine are right here!" These are quiet and better than the Tasers or crossbows. I have plenty of ammunition, as well." Roland handed two of the death machines to Thor. "Do you know how to use these?"

Thor quickly slid a clip into the bottom of the handle of the pistol. He slid the chamber back, and a brass cartridge slid neatly into the chamber of the pistol. Thor repeated this nine times. All of the cartridges performed the same action, and he caught them one at a time as the pistol belched them up. He pushed the small button on the side of the pistol and the clip slid from the handle into his waiting hand. He reloaded the clip without ever looking at the bullets or clip and neatly slid it back into the handle. "I'm a quick learner," he said. "Let's wait until dark, and we'll go!"

Roland loaded all of the clips, and both men checked and rechecked their gear. "I have some clothes for us upstairs, Thor. Let's get dressed." Minutes later, the men came back downstairs dressed in tight black attire. They had two shoulder holsters tucked neatly under their arms and multiple pockets on the black pants. Thor had his daggers draped neatly around his waist, and the men stuck numerous clips into their pockets and stuck their pistols in the holsters under their arms. "I'm ready," said Roland. "I'm going to make them pay for what they did to Katie and Josh. Tonight those dogs die!"

"Wisteria, do you need anything for protection? I have a shotgun here that will tear a hole in anything that comes near you!" Roland said.

"No, dear. Don't worry about us. I've got magic that you've never seen, and tonight I'm going to use it. No one will find us until you return. Don't worry about us. We'll be just fine."

Wisteria could see that the man standing in front of her wasn't the Roland Roberts that she had met weeks ago; he had changed and somehow seemed much braver than before. He was armed and determined to take on and attempt to kill two of the most evil entities that roamed the surface of the earth.

It was finally growing dark, and Roland and Thor decided it was time to leave. "We'll take my car and park down the street from the mansion; we'll enter from the back. When the demon guardians come, we will take them out as quickly as we can and then go for Olin and Creed. We must act swiftly. We can't hesitate or slow down, and we must get into the mansion as quickly as possible. The first one that reaches Creed's chambers must take them out as quickly as he can. If one of us should get hurt or fall, then the other one will leave him and go for our goal, which is to take out Creed and Olin. We have only one chance to do this. We must not fail."

"Let's go," said Thor. "We've got scores to settle!"

The two men slipped out of Number 12 by the back door and left in Roland's car. Neither spoke as they drove toward the old mansion, which housed Creed and his demons. Roland pulled up alongside the stone wall and drove past it until he reached the end. He turned the engine off. He sat in silence for a moment, wondering just what he was doing.

Here he was, sitting in his car with two pistols strapped to him—his pockets filled with bullets—working with a creature from the belly of the earth, who also had pistols strapped to his chest. He couldn't imagine how many laws he was breaking by just being in possession of the guns and silencers. Both men were trying to sneak into what police would think was a deserted house to kill a warlock, a demon with magical powers, something no one on earth would believe if he were caught in the house. He laid his head back onto driver's seat. "This is insane," he said softly.

His mind went back to the sight he had just witnessed, the bruises on his wife and son's faces. Like the dawning of a new day, realization sat in. The warlock in this mansion had attacked his wife and son. If Thor hadn't shown up, Katie and Josh would be dead by now. He had to finish this, and he had to finish it tonight.

"Ready?" he finally asked.

"Yes, I'm an assassin; I was born ready. But there's something I need to tell you, Roland—something I need for you to know before we go in," Thor said.

"Don't worry about it now, Thor. You can tell me later. We've got things to take care of in this house." Roland opened his door. "If you're ready, let's go!"

"Been ready," Thor said, opening his door. The men slipped along the rock wall, down to the back of the old mansion. Roland looked at his watch. "Seven thirty. Let's see who's home."

# Sixteen

## Master Umberto

Olin had left the mansion in plenty of time to get to Odium's house before seven o'clock. He walked slowly down the street smoking a cigarette. He wondered how the old witch, Odium, was going to get a master warlock out of his house and, more importantly, over to her house. He knew that masters usually only left their quarters to take care of business at Terra Demorte or just to visit there.

At times, they would leave to take care of some serious business or matters they alone had to handle within their lots, but this was rare and only done if their servants or assassins couldn't handle the problems for them. In these rare cases, they always traveled at night and with their demon guardians.

Olin walked down the crooked road to the crooked house Odium called home. He could see a small light glowing from within the witch's house. The soft glow illuminated the large room inside of the cottage, but when Olin entered, he had no problems finding a spot in the corner where he could crouch and not be noticed.

He reached inside of his cloak and fished out the small gold box. He pressed on the heart at the end of the box and the top slid open. He pulled the parchment out and placed it on the floor in front of him. He placed the small box, with the lid open, on a small table next to him. The lamp's glow camouflaged the light that emitted from the enchanted box.

\*\*\*

Odium stood in the shadows, watching four small girls playing in a vacant lot. She had stood there before, watching these girls. She knew they played there often, and what luck, they were just were she wanted them to be tonight. "Yessssss, yesssssss, just what I need," she said.

\*\*\*

"Master Umberto, the witch Odium is back in you lot, sir," said a huge demon guardian. "Your servant John is here, sir. He wishes to see you. May I show him in?"

"Yes, Drako. Show him in. I've asked him to keep an eye on her and to keep me informed of her antics and especially if she ever came back to my lot. Get Dogger. If she is trespassing on my lot tonight, we will kill her. I've warned her not to kill in my lot." Umberto stood up to meet, John, one of his lowly spikes that he used as a spy.

"Master, the witch Odium is in your lot. I believe she's here to kill again," said John.

"Where's she at now?" Umberto asked.

"Near the playground, Master."

"Drako, get Dogger, and let's go. We've got a witch to kill."

Drako left his master's room, and within minutes, was back with another huge demon guardian. "We're ready, Master."

"How is your hand? Is it better? I'll need for you and Dogger to be in top shape tonight, if we're going to kill this witch. She's old but powerful."

"My hand is healed up pretty good, Master. The healers did a good job on it." Drako made a fist. It looked like a huge sledgehammer when he neatly rolled it into a ball. "I'm fine, Master."

"Good. Let's get going. We will end this tonight. We will kill this witch."

\*\*\*

Odium watched the girls playing in the empty lot. The streetlight offered plenty of light for them, and as Odium approached them, the small girls didn't see her until it was too late. She didn't move like an old woman, but like a much younger and stronger person. Her hair wasn't thin and gray, but long and black, and it flowed down past her shoulders. She stood upright and moved quickly.

One of girls noticed the dark shadow approaching. She let out a loud scream as Odium struck her with her walking stick. The small girl fell to the ground. Odium turned quickly, watching the other small girls scatter, screaming.

Odium managed to strike another girl, knocking her to the ground. The small girl made no attempts to get up. She didn't move. The witch ran, quickly overtaking still another girl within a few strides. The witch's walking stick came down hard on the back the girl's head, sending her to the ground as well. The fourth girl ran across the street screaming loudly.

Odium turned and strolled back to the first girl she had attacked; she was moaning and had managed to pull herself up on her knees. Odium raised the stick high and struck the small girl again on the head, then again, and then one last blow to ensure she was dead.

"Yesssss, yesssss, that should do it. Yesssss that should do it just fine!" She stooped and pulled out a small bottle from beneath her cloak. Opening the lid, she watched breathlessly as the young child's blood filled the bottle. "Yesssss, yesssss, this is good, yesssss, good!"

She capped the bottle while hearing voices from across the street. She stood and licked her fingers. The warm blood tasted sweet and sticky. She knelt down and rubbed them in the girl's warm blood once more. She brought her fingers back to her mouth to taste the red substance.

"Halt," said a voice. "Stop. Don't you move or I'll shoot!" It was the voice of a man. He was running down the street with two more following in close pursuit. Odium watched the three men cross the street. She gave the dead girl another look and, with two leaps, vanished into the woods. She heard gunshots and saw flashlights scanning the edge of the trees.

\*\*\*

Master Umberto and the demon guardians were two blocks away when they saw the dark witch, Odium, running into a nearby patch of woods. "She's moving fast. She's shape-shifted into a younger woman!" said Umberto.

"We can catch her, Master," said Drako. "Come on, Dogger."

"No need, Drako; we know exactly where she's going. She can only stay that way for a few more minutes, and then she'll have to shape-shift back to her old self. We can catch up to her at her home. That's where she's heading."

"But, Master, she lives in another lot. She lives in Master Creed's lot, and we know what he's up to. Do we want to go there, Master?" Drako asked.

"Tonight, yes, Drako. We won't be there for long. Odium will be very weak after shape-shifting, and this will be the perfect time for us to kill this miserable witch—her magic will be weak. She'll not be expecting us, and we can kill her and be back in my lot in no time. Master Creed will never know the difference—and who cares if he does?" Umberto smiled at Drako and repeated the last sentence. "Who cares if he does?"

"Hopefully by this time, his brother, Olin, is already dead," said Drako.

"Dead? What do you mean, dead?"

Drako looked at his master. "Not dead, Master. I was just thinking out loud, sir."

The warlock looked at Drako. "Is there something you aren't telling me, Drako?"

"No, Master, no, just thinking out loud."

"You're thinking about the gold box, aren't you?"

"Yes, Master. I was hoping that Olin would have tried the parchment by now and would be trapped inside of the box. Then his brother, Creed, wouldn't be a problem to kill, sir."

"Yes, Drako, I agree, but you must never speak of the gold box again. If Terra Demorte finds out what we are doing, it will be—"

"Will be over for all of us, right, Master?"

"Yes, Drako. Yes, it would be, but I won't let another warlock take over my lot, nor will I be a servant to another warlock. I'm my own master, and this is my lot. When we are finished with this witch, we will kill Creed."

"Good," said Drako.

***

Odium walked slowly into her house. She glanced around for Olin and then, knowing her house as she did, spotted the gold box on the table. "Yessssss, yessssss, get ready. They'll be here in no time. Yessssss, yessssss, they will."

"I'm ready," said Olin in a soft voice. Odium walked to the back of the large room and turned to face the door. It wasn't very long before the door burst open, and in walked Master Umberto and his two demon guardians.

"Well, witch. What did my servant John tell you?" Master Umberto snapped.

"Yessssss, yessssss, Master Umberto, your spy, told me not to come back into your lot. Yessssss, yessssss, he did. Yessssss, he did!" Odium said. She stood there weak in body and stared at the warlock standing in her house. "Yessssss, now would be a good time for us to speak. Yessssss, yessssss, it would." The old witch stared at the warlock, Umberto. He stared back at Odium and wondered what she was talking about.

"Well, I don't know what you're talking about—we have nothing to speak about—but you know why we are here, right witch? We'll going to kill you for coming back into my lot. You've killed another little girl, haven't you?" Umberto said, looking at the blood stains on the witch's cloak.

Olin picked up the small parchment and read the words inaudibly to everyone else in the room. At the end, as he added the two words "Master Umberto," he raised his voice.

Umberto, hearing his name, turned to see what was happening. He saw a man dressed in black crouching in the dimly lit corner. He started toward him, but as he moved, his body started to disintegrate into small particles. They floated upward, and then like a mighty whirlwind spiraled toward the small gold box. The two demon guardians watched in amazement as their master disintegrated into small specks. They were dumbfounded, watching the specks fall into the gold box. When the last particle vanished, the box slammed closed. It was done.

Olin stood up. He was ready to do battle with the two demon guardians, Drako and Dogger. The guardians hadn't moved since their master disintegrated. Drako looked at the man dressed in black, his cloak covering his face. His glanced at the gold box, which he recognized immediately. It was the same gold box that he had given Olin in Jake's Place. He spoke one word before he vanished amid a flurry of popping sounds: "Dogger!"

Dogger vanished seconds after Drako. Olin and Odium were alone in the room. Olin stood erect and pushed back the hood of his cloak. "They're gone," he said. "I wonder why they decided not to fight, but no matter. We got what we came for. We've got Umberto?"

"Yessssss, yessssss, you've got him, Master Olin. Yessssss, you have!" Odium said.

***

Roland and Thor peered across the stone wall. They had decided that Thor would go directly for Creed and Olin and Roland would take care of the patrolling demon guardians. Thor had magic, and he would need every trick in his bag when it came to fighting two warlocks. He knew Creed was harmless until his transformation was complete, but Olin— actually no one knew how much power and magic he had. Thor was doing what he had been sent to the surface to do; tonight he was going to fulfill his contract and kill Creed and Olin.

Roland and Thor crossed the stone wall, and headed toward the back of the mansion. Roy and Ray noticed them immediately. "Master, there are two intruders at the back," said Roy. "I need for you to go to the laboratory; we can protect you better there." He turned and looked at Ray. "You go with the master, Ray. I'll be there shortly."

Ray stomped around. "Me wants to fight, Roy. Me wants to kill the intruders." He snorted loudly.

"No. Master Olin left us our orders. Take Master Creed to the lab-oratory, and I'll be right there. Now get going, Ray." Ray looked at his master and headed to the laboratory. He mumbled words about fighting but, obeyed Roy.

"Roy, is Olin back?" Creed said, walking toward the door.

"No, Master, but he gave me instructions this morning to get two more demon guardians, and they're here. He wanted them for your transformation tomorrow night. They weren't supposed to arrive until tomorrow morning, but they showed up early. I'll send them to stop the intruders; Ray and I will protect you in the laboratory."

"Are you sure there are intruders?" Creed asked.

"Yes, master, I don't know who, but we will find out." Said Roy, he turned to leave.

"Ray, get the master to the laboratory, now," snapped Roy.

Creed saw the demeanor in Roy change. Once again, he saw Roy taking charge in a serious situation.

"Roy, there are two intruders at the back of the house," said a demon guardian, coming into Creed's chambers.

"Take what's his name and go kill them, now!" shouted Roy. "Don't let anyone in the mansion. Get going," Roy said, pointing toward the door. "I'm going to the laboratory to protect the Master."

"Don't worry. We won't let anyone in," said the huge demon guardian. "Come on, Sid," he said, turning to his partner. "We've got some killing to do!" The two demon guardians left and headed down the stairs. They weren't quiet. Both were huge, and like Roy and Ray, they had muscles bulging everywhere. They reached the bottom of the stairs and headed toward the kitchen.

\*\*\*

Thor read his scanners. "Two demon guardians heading this way. As soon as they come out of the kitchen door, I'll slip by them and you can take care of them. Creed must know we are here. He and two more demon guardians are on the move, going down to the basement."

"Here they come," said Roland.

The screen door opened, and out came two huge demon guardians. Roland backed up and headed back toward the stone wall.

"Get him, Sid," said Thad, the larger of the two. "Get him." Sid jumped from the porch and gave chase to Roland. Thor watched as Thad jumped from the back porch, but he didn't give chase. "There are two," said Thad, "but I can't locate the other one!" Thad looked around but didn't leave the side of the porch. If Thor were to get into the mansion, he would have to take the demon guardian out.

Roland looked over his shoulder and saw the slow-running demon guardian chasing after him. He stopped and turned to face the muscle-bound monster. He slid his hands onto the grips of the two pistols, and with a quick pull of his arms, the pistols were in his hands and cocked.

Roland waited for Sid to get closer; he could see the hate in the monster's eyes and knew that the only thing on the creature's mind was to kill him.

He remembered the battle he'd had in that exact spot with the first demon guardian that he had ever seen. He remembered killing him with a bolt through the head. He also remembered the fierce battle in his home and killing a demon guardian there. He had shot Shep, Creed's former demon guardian, in the chest and then in the head, not once but several times.

Focusing on the fight in front of him, he took a firm stand and spoke softly to himself.

"Don't waste your time, Roland. Shoot to kill. Shoot him in the head." Roland raised the two pistols; he looked down the barrels and lined up the two sights. He focused them on the face of the fast-approaching demon guardian.

As Roland pulled the triggers, the guns worked in unison. Both jerked as the hammers came down, hitting the firing pins and sending the bullets on their way. He fired each pistol three times, the noise barely noticeable. The pistols worked their magic and sent forth small pieces of lead carrying excruciating pain and death. The pistols then belched out the empty casings, and in one continuous motion, slammed two more cartridges deep into the guns' chambers.

Roland pulled the triggers again, and the guns performed the same ritual, sending death from its barrels. He watched in slow motion as the casings were belched out of the guns and floated in air before heading down toward the turf. He had seen this many times, but never in such a slow motion. It was if his mind had taken control and had slowed things down so it could calculate every move of the demon guardian. He was in full control as the bullets struck their target.

It was apparent that Sid had never seen a gun or had the slightest idea of what one did. The six bullets struck the huge monster in the face simultaneously. He let out a loud squeal and fell to the ground.

Thor had repeated the same actions as Roland; he'd pointed the two pistols at Thad and pulled the trigger on each pistol twice. The demon guardian turned just in time to see Thor point the pistols at him. Thad had just seen Sid fall and saw the blood spewing from his face and neck. He let out a loud squeal in desperation just before Thor started firing.

Thor's bullets hit their mark, and the huge demon guardian wobbled slightly before crashing to the ground. Thad managed to grab his face with his huge hands before falling. He, unlike his partner Sid, didn't let out a dying squeal.

Roland and Thor ran into the kitchen. "Careful, Roland. My scanners can't pick up Olin. He could be anywhere," Thor said, scanning the old house. "Two demon guardians and a master, has to be Creed, are in the basement in some kind of room. I don't see anyone else. Follow me." Thor went into the foyer and down a set of stairs leading to the basement.

The men stood outside a large wooden door, the kind one might see in a castle, a thick door that opened inward. The hinges couldn't be seen from the outside and there was no way to open up the barricaded door from where they stood.

"That's why he didn't disappear," said Thor.

\*\*\*

The door had indeed been barricaded from the inside, and both Roy and Ray were standing on the other side waiting for someone to enter. "There's no way anyone can come through that door, Roy. It's over a foot thick. We're safe in here," Creed said.

"Who do you think it is?" questioned Creed.

Roy turned toward his master. "Not sure, Master, but if they made it in the mansion, that means they had to kill Sid and Thad."

"Me wants out," shouted Ray. "Me will kill them for you, Master. Let me out!" Ray started for the beam that secured the large door. Roy stepped in front of him.

"No, Ray. Master Olin gave us our orders. We're to stay with Master Creed and not let anyone into the laboratory."

"Olin must have suspected something like this. Do what he says, Ray. Sit down!"

Creed was hissing now. His voice was raspy, and he worked hard to gasp what little air was flowing into his lungs.

\*\*\*

Roland looked at Thor. "We could burn them out," he said.

"Wouldn't do any good, Roland? They would just disappear and reappear somewhere else away from the fire. We've missed them. I had no idea that they would have hired additional demon guardians. No one told me, and they should have!"

Roland looked at Thor. "Who should have?"

"Later, Roland. Let's search the house and see what this miserable dog has been doing."

Roland and Thor went back upstairs to the first floor of the mansion. "Don't worry about Creed. I'll keep an eye on him. We'll have to assume that Olin is in there with him and his two demon guardians. I wonder why he didn't come out and fight. That's not at all like a master. Normally, you don't have to push them too hard to get a fight out of them."

"Nothing here," said Roland, after checking out the first floor. "Let's see what's up stairs."

"I've been here before; Creed's room is the first one on the left at the top of the stairs. I don't pick up anything upstairs on my scanners—everything looks clear. Just keep on the alert for Olin. I can't see him," said Thor.

"I hope he sticks his head out." Roland said, pointing one of his pistols upward. "I'll put a couple of holes in it for him."

"That would be nice, but if he was going to show himself, he would already been here!" Thor took the stairs two at a time. When he reached the top, he glanced at his scanners once again and pushed open the door to Creed's chambers.

The men stood at the door, looking at the large room. There were several drawings on the floor and a circle drawn around them. Large candles sat on the circle; they weren't lit but were placed in strategic locations. There were two boxes drawn inside the circle as well, one across from the other one, and in the center was another small circle.

"He's ready to complete his transformation, Roland," Thor said. "Somehow or another, he's found the power he needs, and by the looks of it, he's getting ready to perform the ritual. Let's get out of here; we need to let Wisteria know about this."

"What makes you think he's ready?" Roland asked.

"He wouldn't be doing this unless he was certain he could pull it off. He's ready!"

"Where do you think he got the power to complete his transformation?"

"I don't know, Roland, but let's get out of here. There's nothing more we can do here tonight. One thing is for sure: we need to stop *this*." Thor pointed at the floor. Roland turned and started out of the door when Thor stopped him.

"Roland, stop." Thor walked behind the desk and pulled open the drawer. He stared into the drawer and then looked back at Roland. "Empty," he said. He glanced at the coat rack and saw the bloody cloak; he noticed the small pools of blood that had dripped from the cloak's hem. "There, there in the corner, Roland. That's twice I've seen a bloody cloak hanging on that rack. Something's not right about that."

\*\*\*

Olin had taken his time returning to the mansion. He thought about Number 12 and the beating he had given Katie. He was disappointed that he hadn't been able to kill her and that brat of hers, but nonetheless, he had gotten the information he wanted from her.

"So they used a simple little trick to fool us? Well, that won't happen again," he said as he spat. "But at least now I know how they pulled it off!"

His thoughts continued, and he smiled, rubbing his stomach and then his arm. He had escaped serious injuries when Thor had attacked him; it was nothing but sheer luck that prevented him from being hurt worse or even killed. The dagger Thor had thrown had cut his arm, but only superficially. The one Thor had plunged into his stomach had hit the small gold box, which acted as a shield, leaving him untouched by the weapon's sharp point. "Soon," he said, "I'm going to kill that assassin."

\*\*\*

Roland and Thor had just stepped off the kitchen porch when the small gate squeaked as someone pushed it open and entered the backyard. "Get down. Someone's coming," Roland whispered.

They ducked behind the bushes and the long, prickly briars; they crouched down and headed down the winding stone path toward the small pond. They stopped every once in a while to peer over the tall flowers and grasses, trying to see the man in black.

"It's Olin," whispered Thor. "Stay down!" The men dropped down to the ground and huddled around the small stone pond. Thor slipped his arm silently into the water as he crouched beside the pond.

"He sees the dead demon guardians," whispered Roland.

Olin stooped down to examine the first huge beast. He rose slowly and scanned the backyard. He took several steps and stared down at the second demon guardian lying at his feet.

Roland stood up. He was boiling with anger. There, standing in the yard, was the man who had beaten Katie and his son. Now it was payback time, and he wanted Olin to know who he was and why he was there.

"You miserable dog. I'm going to kill you, Olin!" Roland shouted. The warlock turned to face the intruder.

Thor grabbed Roland by the arm. He too had risen rapidly to his feet. "If we are going to beat this warlock, we've got to split up, Roland." Thor took several steps into the garden; he wanted distance between himself and Roland. "Be careful, Roland. He can vanish and the reappear right next to you. Stay alert."

As Thor spoke, Roland did what he did best when in a fight—he pulled the triggers on his two pistols. The pistols did exactly as they were designed to do. They spat lead slugs straight toward the unsuspecting warlock. It was apparent that Olin hadn't had any experience with silencers, as he had proudly taken a full-frontal stance to fight Roland and didn't move even after Roland fired his shots. The lead bullets struck all around him before he realized what was happening, and the steaming bullets hit him several times. He wobbled slightly and vanished instantly.

Thor wasted no time. He emptied his pistols in the same direction and sprayed the back entrance of the house. He quickly pressed the button on the sides of the pistols and reloaded the deadly machines.

"Make ready, Roland. He may appear anywhere."

Olin did appear. And he was madder than a wet hen on Sunday morning. He managed to fling a fireball at Thor before Roland emptied his pistols in his direction once more, and then he vanished once again. Thor ducked and muttered a few words, and the fireball vanished.

Roland reloaded and stood ready. He moved toward the mansion. Thor started in the same direction but kept a sharp lookout in the gardens.

"You never know where he might show up, Roland. Be ready."

Olin reappeared, and with a wave of his hand over a shrub, a huge wolf like creature came to life. Thor emptied his pistols toward the demon, and two more hot lead slugs struck the warlock in the chest. He fell to the ground and vanished. Roland took aim at the charging monster. He fired all of his rounds into the beast, but it didn't stop, nor did it stagger. It was charging straight at Roland.

The mighty beast was closing ground on Roland, and when it was closer it leaped toward the warrior. Roland ducked, but to his surprise, the beast was on top of him. Both fell to the ground and in an instant, the huge beast turned back into a shrub.

Roland pushed the green shrubbery off him and stood up. "What happened?"

"It was only a distracting spell, Roland. I noticed it at once. We use it often when we need to distract someone. The first time I had one of those things coming at me, I messed my pants. Scared the living daylights out of me."

"Do you think you could have told me this? I thought I was dead. I couldn't kill this thing. It just kept charging me."

Thor laughed. "I knew you weren't in any danger. I had to keep my wits and keep an eye out for Olin. Surprisingly enough, he hasn't reappeared to fight. I think he's gone into the house, probably down to the basement with the others. We both shot him. He's in pain and may be dead by now. One way or another, he's hurt.

"Well, I guess we can go home, since they don't want to fight." Roland looked down at the shrub. "This thing scared the life out of me."

Thor laughed. "If you want to kill one of those things, Roland, just don't water it. That will usually do the trick." Thor kicked the shrub. "You were never in any danger. Just remember this. Olin will probably use it again. If you had been by yourself, he would have reappeared behind you while you were watching this beast, and it would have been easy to have killed you. Just be aware of this type of thing. It's magic mixed with trickery. Warlocks love this type of thing."

Roland kicked the shrub once more, and the men headed for the gate.

"The ones you have to watch out for is the dogwoods, but don't worry. Their growl is much worse than their bites." Thor laughed and patted Roland on the back.

"Is that you I smell?" asked Thor.

"Could be," said Roland. "I'll have to check when I get home."

"No, seriously, Roland, don't you smell that terrible stench? It's the water." Thor lifted his arm slightly and watched the water run down his arm. It fell in little droplets onto the stone walk; Thor rubbed the liquid with his hand.

"It's not water, Roland. It's blood, and the pond's full of it. And there's something else in there too. I touched it when my hand slid in the water. It felt like flesh!"

"Let's get out of here while we can," said Roland. The two men left the pond and slipped around to the stone wall. They gave the kitchen porch one last look before starting over. "Wait," said Roland. "We've been scaling the wall and Olin walks through that gate. Come on. Let's go this way."

Roland and Thor left through the gate; the rusty chain and lock had been removed and was wrapped around the gate's bars. The gate made a small creaking sound as they pulled it open. Roland glanced back toward the porch. "Nothing. Come on!" He stopped. "Oh, Thor. I smell you now. Jeez, what did you stuck your arm into?"

Thor raised his arm and smelled it. "That nasty pond, Roland. That was what I was telling you. It's full of blood and meat."

*** 

Olin hobbled up the stairs and saw Creed's door standing open. "Creed," he said. There was no reply, and Olin stepped into the room. "Creed, are you in here?" Again, there was no reply. Olin vanished and reappeared down in the basement. He saw that the huge laboratory door was shut, so he vanished once more and reappeared in the laboratory.

"Olin, you're back," said Creed with a raspy voice. "We had visitors while you were gone, intruders on our property."

"Me can go now?" Ray interrupted the conversation with his dreadful use of English vocabulary. "Me wants to get out of here and kill somebody. Can me go now, Roy?"

"Yeah, go check on the two new demon guardians, Sid and what's his name. You know, the other one," said Roy. "Check the property too. Take them with you and check every inch of the estate."

Roy looked at Olin. "We didn't fight them, Master Olin. We did as you commanded us to do, and we brought Master Creed to the laboratory and locked him up with us. They couldn't get in, so I guess they left, but it doesn't matter. If they're still here, Ray will find them."

"No one's here, Roy," said Olin angrily. "The intruders are gone." He glanced at Ray. "Don't worry about checking on your two new friends. They're dead. They're in the backyard."

"Me will go check," Ray said as he headed out of the laboratory.

"Master Olin, do you know who it was?" questioned Roy.

"Yes, I think I do. It was probably Roland, Thor, and maybe that busybody witch, Wisteria. Who knows?" Olin said with a smile. He looked at his brother and flashed a huge grin. "Creed, I have Master Umberto here in this box." He shook the box from side to side.

"Odium was successful in helping me capture him," he continued. "She's going tonight to see the spirits we need. Tomorrow, I'll go with her and bring them back here. Then your transformation will be over!"

Creed looked from under his hood. "Good," he whispered. "What about the witch, Olin? We need a good witch to perform the ritual."

"I've got that covered, Brother. It shouldn't be a problem," Olin said. "It never is!"

"Good," hissed Creed. "Then tomorrow it is!"

"Yes, Brother, tomorrow night we celebrate your resurrection, your transformation, your rebirth into a new world." Olin smiled at Creed and then at Roy. He snapped an order at the demon guardian as he sat down at the table. "Keep a sharp eye out tonight, Roy, and tomorrow, as well."

"Will do, Master Olin. Do you want me to get more help?"

Olin sat quiet for a moment before answering. "Yes, as soon as possible."

The door to the laboratory was open and had remained that way since Ray's departure. He had left to go kill someone, anyone. It didn't matter to Ray. Roy heard popping sounds in the hall and heard Ray grunt as he came in the opening. "Roy, they're dead, both of them. They vanished back to Terra Demorte. Me can't find anyone else on the property."

"Dead?" said Olin, taunting Ray. "Who's dead?"

"The two new demon guardians. Their faces were bloody and all messed up. Me started to help them, but they disappeared back to Terra Demorte. Do you want me to get more, Master Olin?"

"Yes, Ray, and yes, they were dead. Didn't I tell you that before you left?" Ray looked dumfounded at Olin and then at Roy.

"They're dead. Me knows it now. Me knows it for me self." He puffed up his chest and turned to walk out of the laboratory.

"Yes, two more, Ray, and get them tonight if you can. We must have plenty of protection tomorrow. I'm sure the intruders were Roland and that renegade assassin; they probably came for a little revenge. We'll stay here tonight, Roy, but I'll need to leave sometime after midnight. I have an appointment with a good little witch who's going to help us tomorrow night," said Olin.

Creed pulled his cloak around his bony body; his hood, as usual, covered his face. He sat still and took in small, shallow breaths that sounded like someone blowing through a pipe. He hissed softly as Roy shut the huge door.

Olin looked at his brother. He knew that time was running out for him and that the transformation had to be completed soon. He smiled and said, "I had a little talk with Katie this morning. She told me that Sarah, her father, the nanny, and the small newbie had all crossed over. She told me how that witch Wisteria had tricked us. Creed, they set the clock back twenty minutes and that stupid fool, Notor, fell for it." Olin smiled. "And so did we.

"Well, I'm not falling for any more of their tricks, and after your transformation, we need to kill all of them. If we don't, they'll be a thorn in our side until we do." Olin leaned back in the chair; he lifted his legs and placed his feet on the table.

"I was going to kill her and her son this morning, but that two-faced assassin showed up. He tried to stick me with one of his—actually, two of his daggers but missed. If he hadn't shown up, there would be two fewer Johnstonians tonight. You should see them, Brother. I beat the tar out of them. They looked pretty bad if I must say so myself."

Although no one could see it, Creed smiled underneath his hood. "Good!" He snorted like a demon guardian, and both he and Olin laughed.

"Do you think we can trust Odium to bring the spirits we need?" he asked.

"Sure. She wants something from us. I'm not sure what. I mean something more than the transformation she wants. She'll bring the spirits, but we can't trust her beyond that." Olin smiled. "It will be my pleasure to kill her. Yessssss, yessssss, it will!" He laughed again as he mocked the old witch.

Olin sat silently for a few minutes. He looked as if he were sleeping, but every once in a while, he would take a deep drag off the cigarette he was holding. Roy jumped as Olin suddenly scrambled to get to his feet. Within seconds he was standing. "Hades, Creed, they might have seen the ritual site. If they went upstairs, they had to have seen the candles and drawings. They must know that we are going to try to complete your transformation." Olin walked toward his brother. Then, like a lion in a small cage, he starting pacing the floor. "We need a plan, something that will keep those meddling fools away from the mansion and away from us." He paced several more times, and then an evil grin crept across his face.

He sat back down and stared at Creed. "Don't worry about that, Brother. I'll come up with something before tomorrow night. I'm not letting anything mess this up!"

Olin sat for a while and then decided to tell his brother and Roy about the fight he'd had in the garden. "When I returned tonight, I was ambushed in the garden. They've changed their pistols, Creed. They don't make any noise. I didn't know they'd fired any shots until they hit me…"

"You've been shot again?" Creed said.

"Yes, Brother, but not to worry. The first ones they shot at me missed, well, mostly. Two hit me, but nothing serious, superficial wounds mostly, one in my arm and one in my side; I have already taken care of those. The second time they shot at me, this little gold box saved me. Two bullets hit this thing. That's twice today this box has saved my life.

"I did a little distracting spell and vanished into the house. I'll kill those fools before too long. Right now, though, we need to complete your transformation." Olin rubbed his side and arm. A little sore but, nonetheless, nothing serious. He sat and looked at the gold box. "Glad I have you."

# Seventeen

# The Evil That Men Do

It was after midnight when Olin left the mansion. The rusty, old gate squeaked softly when he pulled it opened and then repeated the same irritating sound as he gently pulled it shut. He strolled silently through the darkness, staying in the shadows as much as he could until he came to a small white house facing Calhoun Street. Although it was on the same street that Number 12 faced, it was many, many blocks farther down the street, one of the last houses before leaving the city.

He stood outside and watched the dark house attentively, scanning every nook and cranny. He took a drag on a smoke and exhaled the smoke high into the cool night air. He listened as the crickets, frogs, and night birds sang their never-ending songs. He waved one of his hands, and everything became quiet, deadly quiet. He gave another small wave of his hand, and the noise started again. He chuckled softly to himself.

The walk had reminded him of the wounds he had suffered that evening. They were still aggravating and sore, but the poultices were working their magic and the pain, for the most part, had vanished

He walked inaudibly to the front porch and stepped ever so softly upon the wood that decked it. He knew the witch that lived there. He had spied on her weeks before the battle at Number 12. She was a good witch, one that belonged to Wisteria's Order of Witches. He had checked out several other witches before the battle, as well, but had chosen this witch because of the bargaining chips she possessed.

Only a witch could perform the transformation ritual, but she couldn't contain any evil or darkness. She had to be a good witch, and Olin knew this one was. The Secret of Life wasn't to be used by anyone that was dark or evil. The vessel was conceived into being as a way to bring life back into a good king, one that had died too early. Only the most pure and noblest kings would be offered this ritual and the right to live again.

Olin spoke a few words, and everything became quiet once more. It was if time was standing still. The birds became quiet; their night songs ceased. No crickets sang or chirped. Everything was silent, deadly silent.

With a wave of his hand, the door opened. It made no noise, as it swung open; it was as silent as the moon's beams slipping into the darkness of the night. He walked into the house and down the hall to a small bedroom. The night-light gave just enough light for him to see a small girl lying in the center of a bed. He slowly backed out of the room, crossed the hall, and peered into the next bedroom. Another nightlight was shining, casting its dim light over the room. He noticed another small girl lying in her bed. She looked slightly larger than the first, maybe a year or two old, maybe a little older. He walked closer to her bed.

*\*\*\**

A few minutes later, Olin walked into the last bedroom. In this bedroom, he saw the witch that he would need for his brother's ritual. She too was curled up in the center of her bed. Her chest would heave up and then collapse with each breath she took. He waved his hand, casting a small spell to ensure she continued to sleep. He stuck a large note on the mirror and went back to the first bedroom, where the smaller of the two children slept. He scooped up the little girl and headed out of the house.

\*\*\*

The morning sun was shining brightly, and the heat from its golden rays was busy chasing the mist and fog from the corners of the yards and drying up the dew. Gloria sat up in bed and stretched. It was such a lovely day, and she and her two beautiful daughters had made plans to take a long summer stroll to town this morning. They were expected for breakfast at Wisteria's Café. She smiled. "It will be good to see Wisteria," she said.

She slid her legs over the side of her bed. Instantly the stench of evil smothered her, taking her breath. It hit her like a ton of bricks. "Something evil has been here, here in my home," she whispered. "Eve, Dawn, come here, quickly," she called. "Come here."

Her feet had just touched the floor when she noticed the paper stuck to the mirror. She called for her two daughters once more as she read the note aloud. "Eve, Dawn, come here, quickly. Please come here now!" There was no answer.

She screamed, running down the hall to the bedrooms where her daughters slept. She turned the corner and saw instantly that the bed where her smallest daughter slept was empty. She crossed the hall and saw the most terrifying sight.

The bed in which her eldest daughter lay was covered in blood. Her daughter was lying in the center of the bed. She, like the linens, was covered with the red substance. She started toward the bed and heard her daughter moan.

"Dawn, don't move. Let me look at you." The small girl lay still. Her face, arms, and legs had already turned black, blue, and bluish green. Bruises covered most of her body. There were cuts on her arms and legs, and her eyes were swollen shut from some type of horrific blows to the head. The cuts were oozing blood, slower now than when first delivered.

Gloria brushed away the blood from her daughter's face and watched more of it, gushing now, from two large gashes over her eyes.

She stood up and held out her arms. She spoke words that only a witch would understand. She left the bedroom and returned with her bag and some wet towels. She cleaned the blood from her daughter's wounds and rubbed poultices on them. The strange goo moved slowly, covering the cuts, hiding them under their healing powers.

She opened the small bag, took out several herbs, and put them in a small, round bowl. With her hand, she crushed the leaves. Her hand was shaking so badly that she had a hard time getting the match out of the small box, but after several attempts, she managed the task. She lit the substance and spoke more incantations.

Tears rolled down her cheek while she worked on her daughter. No time to worry about Eve. Dawn needed her, and for the next two hours, the good witch worked her remedial powers on the small girl and prayed that God would spare her life.

She changed the linens and spoke softly. "It's done, darling. Lay and rest. Mother is here with you. You'll be fine, my darling." Gloria sat quietly beside her daughter. She held her hand and rubbed the cool cloth over her face. She jerked slightly when she saw, lying on the floor, the note that Olin had left. During all of the praying and healing rituals, it had tumbled from the bed. She unfolded it carefully and read it once more. Tears filled her eyes as she read the words.

*I left the oldest one alive, just barely, but alive. I'm sure your GOOD magic and potions will heal her in no time. However, your youngest daughter is now in my care, and if you don't do exactly as I instruct you to do, your GOOD magic won't be able to help her. Keep my little visit to yourself, and don't tell anyone. If you do, your daughter will die. Be at my brother's mansion tonight sharply at eight o'clock. If you aren't, your daughter will die. We will need you to perform a small ritual. If you refuse, well, let's put it this way, I know a dark witch that will drink every drop of this little girl's blood. Not to mention that, before she does, I'll torture your daughter until she can no longer stand the pain. Be there at eight o'clock, not a minute late. Remember, tell no one, and don't try any tricks, or your daughter will die the most terrible death you can imagine.*

*Yours truly,*
*Olin Thomlin*

*PS. I'm assuming you and your order know all about my brother and me. If you don't, you had better find out where I live and do it very discreetly. No one must know you're coming here tonight, and you had better show up alone. We will be watching!*

Gloria folded the note and held it in her hand. She bowed her head and said a prayer. "God, Lord of all creation and master of all that is good and holy, please, Lord, watch over my Eve. Let her, dear God, return to my loving arms, alive and unhurt. We love you dearly. Amen." She wiped the tears from her eyes and kissed her daughter on the forehead. She rubbed her cheeks, curled up beside her on the bed, and cried softly as she hugged her daughter.

*** 

Olin walked into the mansion sometime around three o'clock in the morning. He carried the small girl to the laboratory and laid her on the table. She was under one of his dark spells that would keep her sleeping for hours, and if she awoke, he would just cast it again. "I don't want to hear any crying!" he said. "I hate children, kids, or whatever they're called now."

"So," said Creed, "I see you were successful with the good witch. Good job, Olin. Things are coming together rather nicely. Have you thought of a way to keep that meddling witch, Wisteria, and her friends away tonight?"

"Yes, actually I have!" Olin smiled at Creed. "Roy, put this thing in another room and keep an eye on her. Whatever you do, don't let her out of your sight. If she wakes up, let me know and I'll put her back into a deep sleep. I don't want to hear a peep out of her. Do you understand?"

Roy bowed slightly, picked up the small girl, and carried her into another room. Olin sat down and threw his feet on the table. "Lights out!" The room went dark and quiet.

\*\*\*

Roland and Thor had just made it back to Number 12 when the clock struck ten. Gong, gong, gong! The clock chimed its last three harmonious notes and then went silent except for the methodical sound of the pendulum swinging back and forth, relentlessly and systematically gnawing away at time.

Wisteria was sitting in the overstuffed chair in the den watching, so it appeared, over Katie and Josh. Her head lay back against the cushion, her eyes shut and her mouth slightly open. Her huge breasts gently rose with each breath and then gently deflated as she exhaled the life-giving air.

"Are you asleep?" whispered Roland.

"She never sleeps," said Thor. "She's probably meditating. You never know what this old witch might be doing. She's probably setting a trap; if you ask me, you know, that 'Oh, I'm asleep' routine. 'Let's get her while she's asleep' trap."

"I'm protecting the house, dear." Wisteria whispered in a soft voice, but the voice didn't come from the old lady sleeping in the chair. It came from behind them. Both Roland and Thor turned quickly but saw nothing. They turned back toward the chair and Wisteria was gone. Confused, they turned back around to where the voice was heard, and standing behind them was the old witch, smiling at them.

"What's wrong, dear, trying to sneak up on a poor old sleeping witch?" She said.

"No, just trying to figure out where in blue blazes you are," said Thor, "where you really are. And why do you have to do that? I mean, why do you always have to be…you?" Thor stopped talking, rolled his eyes, and shook his head from side to side. "You're just showing off, aren't you?"

"No, dear, just keeping you on your toes, and it worked, didn't it?" She paused. "A lesson for both of you: what you see isn't always what's happening. Think before you act on what you see. You should know that, Thor. You are an assassin, aren't you, dear?"

She flipped her head, and her hair came alive and floated around her. She sat down in the huge chair. Her weight forced a small upward gust of wind, and her hair came to life once more and floated in all directions. "You couldn't sneak up on deaf mule," she muttered.

"What are you talking about? I wasn't trying to sneak up on you. I knew you were here, and we came back to tell you about something we saw at Creed's. What's all this stuff about sneaking up on someone?" Thor ran his fingers through his hair. "I could've snuck up on you if I had wanted to, but I didn't want to. Why should I?"

"I'm just messing with you, dear. I was just testing a little of my magic," Wisteria said, smiling at Thor. "I'm sure if you had wanted to, you could have snuck up on me. Of course you could, couldn't you, dear?"

"You're driving me nuts is what you are doing, and yes, I could have snuck up on you if I had wanted!" Thor murmured. "I'm an assassin. Of course I could!"

"If you two are finished with your little 'I can do this and I can do that' routine, we really need to talk about what we just saw at Creed's." Roland chuckled and then glanced at Katie and then at his son. "They're looking much better, Wisteria. Thank you."

"They're doing a lot better. Let's talk, and then we'll put them to bed. I think it would be better if they slept in their beds tonight, dear, I think they would be more comfortable." Wisteria crossed her hands and looked at Roland. "What did you see at Creed's, dear. Did you kill that miserable demon?"

Thor bend over, picked up several colorful feathers, and then a small piece of green vine. Inquisitively, he looked at the items. He looked at Wisteria and smiled. "Trying out a little magic, are we?"

Wisteria returned the smile and repeated her question. "What did you see at Creed's, dear, did you kill that miserable demon?"

"No," said Roland. "We did kill two demon guardians and by the time we made it to Creed's room, he had locked himself, along with two demon guardians in the basement. He locked himself in a room with a door that had no handles."

"Olin wasn't at home, as we were leaving, we saw him come into the courtyard." Thor added. "But that's not all we saw, Wisteria. In Creed's room, we saw a huge circle drawn on the floor. Candles surrounded it, and inside of the circle, there were different symbols, Egyptian I think. What do you suppose all of that means?"

"Wait, Thor," Roland said, standing up and looking at the two un-likely detectives. "There was something else drawn in the circle, remember, Thor? There were two squares directly across from each other, and a small circle in the center of the big circle." Roland looked back at Thor. "Remember?"

"Yeah, you're right. There were two squares and a small circle. What do think this means, Wisteria?" Thor posed his questioned for the second time.

Wisteria sat for a moment, digesting and processing the information she had just gotten. Then, with a slight move of her huge body, she spoke. "He's found a way to start his transformation. He must have found other spirits, spirits with a lot of power. He's getting ready to start the ritual. He must be.

"I'm not familiar with the actual ritual, but if he's drawing penta-grams on the floor, I would think he's getting ready. He's getting the power he needs elsewhere. I wonder where…" Wisteria looked puzzled. "Where would a demon get such powerful spirits? It was only yesterday that he found Sarah and the rest of the spirits gone from Number 12."

Once again, she sat pondering the uncertainty. "If he knew there were other spirits with that kind of power, why would he have been so set on getting Sarah?" Wisteria rubbed her knuckles softly and looked at Roland and Thor. The men could see that the old witch was deep in thought, and neither wanted to interrupt her complex thinking process, so they waited for an answer.

"He's getting help from someone; he has to be, but whom?" she said softly. "You said you saw Olin coming into the back courtyard?"

"Yes, we were leaving, and he just barely missed seeing us. Lucky for us, we heard the gate squeak before he saw us. We hid in the shrubs and tall flowers. He didn't see us until Roland shouted at him and then emptied his guns on him. I think he hit him several times, but we aren't sure. Then I emptied mine. I have no idea if I hit him or not. All we know is that we sure let a lot of bullets fly his way. One thing for sure, we did kill two demon guardians, but we did that before Olin arrived," Thor said.

"There was something very strange," said Roland. "There's a pond back there, but it isn't full of water, Wisteria. It's full of blood. It stinks like there's something's rotting in it. Thor accidentally stuck his hand in it, and there were pieces of something in the water, some kind of flesh. Well, that's what Thor though it was, chunks of something." Roland looked at Thor. "Tell her, Thor. Tell her what you saw."

"That's pretty much it, Roland. The pond's full of something sticky, and Roland's right; it isn't water. I think there might be bodies or parts of bodies in there." Thor looked for Wisteria's reaction, and when he didn't get an answer, he pushed the old woman for one. "Well, what do you think this means?"

"I don't know, dear. There have been a lot of little girls killed these last few weeks, but all of their bodies were found. They were brutally attacked—some say by a monster, others say by a dark figure—but none of their bodies or body parts were missing. If so, the newspapers didn't report it. There are no reports in the newspaper of missing children or adults." Wisteria sat quite perplexed as she pondered over their bizarre story.

"One other thing, Wisteria. There's a bloody cloak in Creed's room. The time I was there to steal his gold, I saw one, as well. Whatever's in that pond, Creed's killing it. I'm sure of it." Thor looked at Roland and then back at Wisteria. "Maybe he's killing people that no one would miss. You know, homeless people or migrant workers."

"But why, dear?" asked Wisteria. "Why would he need to kill people...unless that's where he's getting the power he needs for his transformation? Newbies don't have much power, but they do possess some, and maybe he's trying to kill as many people as he can to get enough power. It's ridiculous, but he's desperate, and desperate people do insane things. I wonder if he is insane enough to try that."

"Would that work?" asked Roland. "Could he get enough power that way?"

"I wouldn't think so, but who knows? Who knows what a warlock like Creed would do, dear?" Wisteria said. "Who knows?"

The room was quiet for a while, and the seconds that passed felt like hours. Thor and Roland sat thinking as they watched Wisteria. She as well sat for a spell without speaking. The sound of the grandfather clock ticked softly as time drifted away. Finally, after many tick tocks of the old clock, Wisteria spoke.

"One thing for certain, Olin and Creed have to assume that whoever was there tonight has seen the diagrams and circles. I assume they will think it was us."

Roland interrupted. "Do you think they will come back here? Do you think they will try to stop us from interfering?"

"Certainly!" said Thor. "I think so, anyway."

"Well, let's think about that, dear," said Wisteria. "Olin attacked Katie and Josh this morning, and you and Roland paid them a visit and killed two demon guardians. I thought that would have been the two they called Roy and Ray. Then you Thor said you saw Creed in the basement with two demon guardians, is that right?"

"Yes," said Thor, "my scanners picked them up."

"Then that tells me that Creed and Olin must have gotten two more of these guardians to protect him. I think they might have learned from tonight's little episode that if they mess with us that we will seek retribution. If I'm right, I don't suspect they would want us back there until Creed's transformation is complete. I might be wrong, but I believe they'll acquire more protection, dear. I believe they'll probably go into some kind of lock-down mode until the transformation is completed."

"Then what?" asked Roland. "What if we wait until the transformation is completed, or what if we can't get back into the place. Then what?"

"If Creed completes his transformation, then he'll come after all of us and won't stop until we are all dead," Thor said. "He and Olin will unleash their magic on all of us; we've got to stop them before they complete this thing, and certainly while Olin is on a short leash."

"I agree, but I don't see how. If we attack, they'll just go to that room in the basement, and we'll just end up killing more demon guardians or getting killed ourselves," Roland said. "But after what he did to Katie and Josh, I say let's go for it."

Wisteria sat quietly and looked at the two men, and then a faint smile crept across her face. "We could use this as an advantage to avoid a fight and get back into Creed's house for a good look around. We could get in without a fight; just walk right into the place."

"And how do you expect us to do that?" Thor asked.

"Easy, dear. We'll just walk in, right behind officer Jim," Wisteria said.

"Behind Jim? How's he getting into—" Roland stopped for a second, and then mirroring Wisteria's expressions, he smiled. "You're a genius, Wisteria, pure genius. Such a good idea!" He stood up and paced the floor a few times. "Do you think Jim will let us go in with him?"

Wisteria smiled and then chucked. "With a little of my magic, he'll let us lead the charge," she said.

"What charge? What are you two talking about? What charge?" asked Thor.

"Well, for an assassin, you're pretty slow, dear," Wisteria said.

"Don't start with me again, witch. Just tell me what in the Hades you're talking about. What charge?" Thor stood up. He was flustered. Wisteria and Roland were making plans, and he hadn't a clue as to what either of them was talking about. He repeated his question. "What charge?"

Roland looked at Thor. He couldn't help but to gouge his partner in crime—or his partner in fighting evil. "You really are slow, aren't you, Thor?"

"Hades, Roland, don't you start with me. What in the bloody Hades are you two talking about? Don't you have to go and change your pants?" Thor gouged back at Roland. "You still smell funny."

Roland laughed and then explained their thoughts to Thor. "My pants are fine, Thor, but do you remember the pond, the blood, and the pieces of bodies in the pond? Remember the bloody cloak in Creed's room and the circle, candles, diagrams, and all of the symbols?"

"Yeah!" said Thor.

"Well, if one of us were to place an anonymous telephone call to the local police department and inform them that we think the person or persons killing the little girls was holding up in the old empty mansion, then they would raid the house and cover every inch for clues. If we could get in there with them, then we could get a better idea of what is going on and maybe stop Creed."

"Exactly, Roland!" said Wisteria. "Good for you. I couldn't have said it better myself. With a little help from me and my magic powder, Officer Jim will escort us right in, and once we are in the house, we can do a little investigating ourselves."

"Hades, why didn't I think of that?" Thor said. "Do you think it will work?"

Roland laughed and slapped his friend on the back. "Of course it will, Thor, like clockwork. Twenty minutes after we make the call, that whole place will be crawling with police, hundreds of them, and once they find the bloody pond, they'll tie that place up for days."

"When do we make the call?" Thor asked. "Can I make it? I've never called the police before." He laughed slightly, rubbing his chin. "It might be fun." He rubbed his chin again and said, "Actually, I've never used a telephone before."

"You've got to be kidding me. You have never used a telephone?" said Roland.

"No. Why should I? What do you think I would do; call my victims or the police before I showed up to kill them?"

"Hadn't thought of that," laughed Roland.

"But," said Thor, "I have ran from the police on several occasions, and once or twice, just for the fun of it, hung around so one of them could shoot at me a time or two." He laughed, and then seeing that Roland and Wisteria weren't laughing, moved on. "Well enough of that. Can I make the call?"

"Yes, dear, if you insist, I guess you could do that." Wisteria said. She winked at Roland. "Make it tomorrow at four. Thor will stay with Katie and Josh, and I'll be at the gate when the officers arrive. You, Roland, will be at work and won't be associated with the call or raid at all. You need to stay out of this."

"But why? Why do I need an alibi? I thought I was going in with you," said Roland disappointed.

"And me too!" said Thor. "You'll need us!"

"I appreciate the offer, dears, but someone will need to be here with Katie and Josh. Roland, you'll need to be at work. That way you'll have a good alibi and won't be associated with any of this." Wisteria smiled. "This is the only way I can get all of the information I need while Olin and Creed are scampering away. They won't be able to lock themselves in the basement. If they do, the police will knock down the door."

"Where will they go?" asked Roland.

"Well, with the demon guardians, they'll probably disappear back to Terra Demorte. They will stay there until it's safe to return to the house.

Olin and Creed could hide in the walls, but the demon guardians won't let themselves be seen by humans, the normal ones anyway, and they can't hide in the walls. Therefore, they'll go back to Terra Demorte and wait until it's clear to come back, and in the condition Creed's in, he won't let the demon guardians go far without him. Olin may be badly wounded, as well," Wisteria said. "It's foolproof."

"What if they come here?" asked Roland. "What if they disappear and come here to hide?"

"I doubt if they will do that, Roland. They have to know that we are here, and they wouldn't risk a fight with the demon guardians, especially in the daylight hours. I'm sure they know that Wisteria has moved in and probably know that I'm here, as well. I agree with Wisteria; once they see all of those surface people pouring into their house, they'll head toward Terra Demorte as quick as they can. All of them leaving the place for Wisteria to poke around in—wonderful idea. I'm glad I thought of it!" Thor said, grinning. "Aren't you, Roland?"

"I'm really glad, Thor. Good idea!"

"Hogwash!" said Wisteria. "You two are hopeless!" They all laughed, and Thor and Roland sat back down. "Then it's all settled. Thor, we will give you the number, and tomorrow at four o'clock you will place the call to the police and tell them that—"

Thor interrupted Wisteria. "I know what to tell them, Mommy. Just give me the number." Roland burst into laughter and looked at Katie to see if he had disturbed her.

"Don't worry about her and Josh, Roland. They're sleeping soundly, and we won't disturb them. Thor and I talked before you left to go to Creed's, and we decided that once you returned, we would try to cheer you up by picking on Thor a little. It seemed to have worked, dear."

"Is there anything you don't know how to do?" asked Roland.

"Yes," said Wisteria. "Yes, there is."

"And what would that be…?" asked Roland.

"It's how to get close enough to Creed so I can kill him." Wisteria stood up. "We need to carry Katie and Josh to their rooms. Oh, by the way, why was Thor inquiring about your pants, Roland. Did you have an accident, dear?" questioned Wisteria.

"No, of course not. When we were fighting Olin, he transformed a bush into a terrible beast—a wolf of some kind—and it attacked me. I shot it several times, but it didn't do any good. It jumped on me, and when I hit the ground, it was only a bush on top of me. It scared the living—uh, daylights out of me. I thought I was a goner."

"Oh that. Yes, dear. That's a scary thing, but it's only a distraction spell. Quite harmless, dear." Wisteria chuckled. "If anything could, that just might be the thing that would make you mess your pants. They're terrible looking, especially when attacking you."

"Could you or Thor not have warned me? One of you might have told me something about a distraction spell, but no, you let me find it out the hard way. Scared the—"Roland stopped talking and adjusted his posture. "Well, it scared me."

Wisteria and Thor laughed, and then Wisteria spoke softly. "Well, Roland, we can't remember to tell you all that's out there. There is a lot of magic out there, and believe me, dear, the dark side knows most—if not all—of the spells. Besides, dear, at least it wasn't a dogwood tree—"

Roland interrupted. "Oh, Thor has already told me that one. Their bark is worse than—"

Thor and Wisteria joined in with Roland's last few words, "their bite." All laughed and pointed at one another.

"Oh, Thor, you said you had something you wanted to tell me when we were in the car. What was it?" Roland asked. Wisteria and Roland looked at Thor.

"Uh, uh it was nothing, Roland. I can tell you later." Thor stood up. He did have something to tell Roland, and it was very important, but he didn't want to talk about it in front of Wisteria. He looked at the old woman. He knew he would have to tell her too, but Thor knew that there was a time for everything. And now certainly wasn't the time for what he had to say. "Just garbage about you surface people. I'll tell you later. Don't worry about it. Let's get Katie and Josh to bed."

\*\*\*

It was early morning when Roland heard the door of his neighbor's pickup slam. As the cool morning air flowed across his bed, he heard the engine crank. "Seven," he said, "always at seven!"

Roland smiled. Now he appreciated the punctuality of his neighbor's morning ritual. After all, this was how he had figured out how Wisteria had carried out the botched triangular séance.

After yesterday's excursions, it was good to see Katie sleeping soundly beside him. They had put her to bed on her back, and she hadn't moved. He was surprised to see her bruises—although they were still very colorful—weren't as intense as the day before. The cuts above her eyes were closed tightly, and the swelling was completely gone. Wisteria had concocted a sleeping potion before she had gone to bed, and Katie was still under its dreamy spell, sleeping soundly.

Roland slipped out of bed and smelled the sweet aroma of coffee brewing in the kitchen. *Who's making coffee?*

"Good morning, dear," Wisteria said. "I let you sleep in a bit this morning. I have your breakfast ready, and here's your coffee, dear." She poured the steamy brew into a mug and then repeated the same action for herself. "Just can't start the day without a cup of good coffee." She smiled at Roland and pointed at a chair. "Go ahead, dear. Sit down. Thor's upstairs practicing dialing the telephone."

"I can't believe he has never used a telephone," he said.

"Well, Terra Demorte hasn't much use for our modern-day gadgets, but don't let that fool you. They have lots of magic, and it's very deadly."

"I believe that," said Roland. He laughed and pulled out one of the chairs. He sat down and took a sip of the delicious brew. "You really like picking on him, don't you?" Wisteria smiled and didn't answer.

"I've decided to stay home with Katie today, Wisteria. I have an important meeting today, but I can cancel it. I really need to be there, but I need to be here too."

"Now, don't worry about Katie, dear. The sleeping potions I've made for her will keep her in bed most of the day. She won't know you're here if you do stay, dear. Thor and I will watch over her while she's recuperating," Wisteria said. "How's your coffee, dear?"

"It's great, thanks. And thanks for helping Katie through this, but I worry about her, and I feel like I need to be here watching over her. I don't want to leave her alone."

"You do what you need to do, dear, but I would prefer that you had a good alibi this afternoon. I'm sure Olin and Creed have spies watching every move we make. They know you are supposed to be at work today. I think you should go. Katie and Josh will be perfectly fine. We can protect her. That I promise." She sipped her coffee and looked at Roland. "You do what you want, dear. It's your decision."

Roland ate his breakfast—or at least pretended to. He moved his eggs to the other side of the plate, cut his bacon into little pieces, and moved it around. Pinching his toast into tiny pieces, he stacked the small pieces neatly on top of his eggs. His plate was a mess, and Wisteria was sure that he hadn't taken a bite.

"You need to eat something, dear!" she said.

Roland picked up the telephone and dialed his office. He was thinking about the meeting, and although it wasn't intentional, he ignored Wisteria.

"Linda? Roland. I'm sorry, but I can't make the meeting today. Something came up here at the house, and I need to take the day off. Can Dave or someone else sit in my place?" Roland paused, while listening, and pushed his eggs to the other side of his plate. He piled the small pieces of toast into the corner and then stirred all of it up into one pile.

"I'm really sorry, but I don't see how—" He paused. "You're kidding. He's coming too? Why didn't you tell me yesterday? Oh! Well, that certainly does make a difference." He paused again and drew circles on the tablecloth with his finger. "Hold on a minute." He looked at Wisteria. "You think Katie and Josh will be all right if I go to work?"

"Yes, dear. They'll be fine!" Wisteria said. She smiled at Roland and patted his hand. "Go to work, dear. Thor and I won't leave Katie's side until you return home. I promise."

"Linda, I'll be there. I'm on my way." Roland hung up the phone. "Thanks, Wisteria. I really worry about them, you know. I still feel that I need to be here with them."

"Thor and I will be with Katie and Josh until we solve this issue with Olin and Creed, dear. We will protect all of you, as best we can, until this thing is over, or we will die trying. Go to work. If you stay home today, what about tomorrow? Eventually, you'll have to go to work. You can't stay home all the time. Katie and Josh will sleep most of the day, so off you go, dear. Go ahead. Scoot!"

Roland thanked the old woman and stood up. He walked past her and then turned and gave her a huge hug. "I hate we got into this mess, Wisteria. I wish we had moved into another house, but since we didn't, I'm really glad you're here with us!" he said.

The old witch didn't move or acknowledge Roland's affection toward her. She only replied. "You were chosen for this, Roland. You had no choice in the matter, and if you had a choice, you would be doing exactly what you're doing now, fighting the dark side and Creed."

Roland sighed and walked out of the kitchen. He knew she was right, but why was *he* chosen to fight Creed and his demons? He had no magical powers or special talents for doing this kind of thing. All he had was Katie and Josh. He smiled and said softly, "Yeah, well, maybe that's enough!"

He turned once again toward Wisteria. "What if Creed and Olin show up today? With just you and Thor here, are you sure your magic can fight them off and keep Katie and Josh safe?"

Wisteria smiled at Roland. She placed her hand in the large pocket in her dress. "Roland, close your eyes for a few seconds." Roland did as instructed.

Wisteria spoke softly. "Now open your eyes, Roland." Roland opened his eyes, but he didn't see his house, nor did he see Wisteria. What he saw was a massive jungle with birds and monkeys flying and leaping in the trees above. There was a rather large river flowing recklessly down a sloping valley floor.

As he looked up, he saw massive trees and vines blocking all of the sun's rays. He could smell the moisture of the jungle as if it had just rained. He could feel the small droplets of water dripping onto his head and clothes. He saw birds flying from one tree to another, but the monkeys were just sitting now, watching him as if eyeing their next meal.

"Wisteria," Roland said softly.

"Yes?"

"What is this? Where am I?"

"You are in your house, dear."

"This stuff is so thick I can barely move. Wisteria, where are you?"

"I'm right behind you, dear."

Roland turned around, and as he did, he found himself staring into the eyes of a huge snake, not just any ordinary snake, but a snake with a gold head and glowing red eyes. The snake hissed loudly as it started to coil, getting ready to strike.

"Wisteria!" shouted Roland, "help. Help me." Roland heard a soft voice, one he had heard many times before, Wisteria's voice.

"Close your eyes, Roland." He immediately did as instructed. "Now open them, dear."

Roland opened his eyes, and there standing in front of him, in his house, was Wisteria. She smiled at Roland. "I can protect Katie and Josh, Roland. I promise I can."

"How did you do that?" asked Roland.

Wisteria simply replied, "Magic, dear."

# Eighteen

## The Hanging Tree

It was noon when Katie walked into the kitchen. Her cuts were mostly healed. The gashes were tight, and the swelling had all but subsided. Small scabs outlined the once blood-oozing cuts. The bruises were of a lighter shade but stilled roamed the surface of her face, some lighter than the others, appearing to cast the woman's face into a state of camouflage. She walked slowly and with a noticeable limp.

"Hello, dear. We've been expecting you!" said Wisteria. Katie gave the old woman a hug and sat down at the table. "Feeling better, dear?"

"Much better," said Katie. She sat for a moment and stared at the hot coffee steaming in her cup. She looked over at Thor and smiled. "Thanks for coming by yesterday, Thor. You saved our lives. Thank you!"

Thor smiled and looked at the battered woman sitting in front of him. "You look much better today. I apologize for not getting here sooner. The crystal only gave a slight alarm before Olin immobilized it. You were lucky Olin didn't kill you!"

"Really, Thor, do you have to be so truthful? You could have stopped after telling her how good she looked," scolded Wisteria. She looked irritated and shook her head.

"What?" said Thor, looking puzzled.

Katie patted the assassin on the hand and smiled at him. "It doesn't matter. You saved my life, and I'll be forever grateful."

Wisteria revealed to Katie their plans to slow Creed's ritual by having the police scour the area. She talked about the pond filled with blood and body parts. "Once the police see this, they will be on the site for weeks trying to find evidence and figuring out just what's going on over there. I think it's a good plan!" she said.

"Couldn't Olin and Creed hold the ritual somewhere else?" questioned Katie. "Couldn't they just move to some other spot?"

"I don't think so. When I go in with the police today, I want to take a good look at the markings on the floor. Normally when you start something like that, you have to finish it where it was started. The markings are drawn with magic and blood. Once drawn, that's where the ritual has to be held." Wisteria leaned back in her seat. "Let's hope this is the case here."

"Why do you have to go in that place, Wisteria?" Katie asked. "Do you think the police will just let you walk in?"

"We need all of the information we can get, and once I get in there, I can gather a tremendous amount of it. My magic will let me see things most can't see," Wisteria said. "Don't worry about the police, I—"

"You can just blow a little powder in their faces?" said Thor.

"No, Mr. Smarty-Pants. I've worked with the police before on certain things. They'll let me in," Wisteria said, looking at Thor. "Not everyone has to sneak around all the time like assassins do." Thor laughed and shook his head. He knew crossing wits with this old witch would be a losing battle.

Katie couldn't believe Roland and Thor had gone to Creed's mansion for revenge. She listened intently as Thor explained every detailed of the fight and the killing of two demon guardians, how they barely escaped Olin, and how they had stumbled upon the blood-filled pond.

"It's with regret that we didn't get to Creed. He hid in the basement with his two demon guardians. If I could have gotten to him, this would be over." He had decided not to tell Katie about Roland and the distraction spell, he laughed slightly. "You would have had to be there to really appreciate what I say." The women looked at Thor, but neither said a word.

What came next totally surprised the assassin and the witch. Katie took a sip of her coffee and looked Thor directly in the eyes. "Well, you're going to get another chance, and if that fails, another one and then another one, until we kill both of those warlocks. I knew that nothing short of a miracle would save me yesterday. Olin was going to kill Josh right there in front of me." Tears filled Katie's eyes; she wiped them with her hand and took another sip of her coffee.

"Katie, it's OK. Don't think about it!" Thor said. "It's not the past we have to worry about; it's the future."

"No, Thor, we need to think about it. If Olin could hurt such a sweet child like Josh, it's hard to tell what he and his brother, Creed, could or would do after Creed's transformation. We've got to stop them. I realize this now; I made the mistake of thinking they wouldn't come back to Johnston. I was so foolish thinking we would get off that easy. It's them or us, and I'm not letting it be us anymore!" Katie wiped her eyes again and choked down the saliva that had collected in her throat.

"Yesterday I realized this is a war, and after seeing Olin wanting to kill a child, I'm convinced that we've got to stop him. Your plan to send the police in there is great, and I agree with you, when they find the blood and body parts they'll turn that place inside out." Katie smiled and continued. "We need a plan, Wisteria, a plan to kill Olin and Creed."

"Yes, dear, we do. Thor and I have been thinking about that. With Creed's demon guardians and his ability to vanish in an instant, there's no way we can get close enough to him to kill him. He's not going to leave the safety of his mansion. However, Olin seems to be quite comfortable doing whatever he wants around this town. If we can catch him out of the mansion, we might be able to kill him.

"With Olin dead and out of the way, Creed would be easier to kill, and if he needs Olin to complete his transformation, we might just squelch those plans as well." Wisteria sipped her coffee and looked at Thor. "I know what you're thinking, Thor. Once we kill Olin, we have to sever his head from his body and put it in a container of some kind, or his body will disappear back to Terra Demorte. There, he'll be restored as powerful as ever," Wisteria said. "Then when he returns, he'll be as mad as ever and set on revenge. If we are going to kill him, we need a good plan, one where we can get his head."

"Once he falls, you have about fifteen seconds before his body disappears. Once it's gone, you're right, he'll be back, with a vengeance. It only takes a few days in Terra Demorte and he'll be as right as rain and madder than Hades. It's a matter of pride, not resurrection," Thor said. "Things being resurrected in the Keeping Room is big gossip. It seeps in and out of Jake's Place quickly. It usually means something or someone lost a battle somewhere. It's more embarrassing than anything else."

Katie looked at the witch and the assassin. "Then we need his head!" she said.

Wisteria agreed, and then looking at the assassin sitting at the table, asked, "Have you ever been resurrected, Thor?"

"No." The assassin didn't elaborate.

***

Odium walked slowly to the place where the four spirits dwelt. She knew this place well and had often visited it as a young girl. In the last few years, though, she had come weekly if not daily. At least that had been her normal routine until Master Umberto had forbid her to trespass in his lot. She had cursed him and refused his requests to stay away, but his spies reported her comings and goings daily. Twice, she barely escaped Umberto's efforts to catch her. "Yessssss, yessssss, Master Umberto didn't want me to talk to these spirits. Yessssss, yessssss, he didn't want Odium to know about these spirits. Master Umberto's gone now, yessssss, yessssss. Odium can come back now. Yessssss, yessssss, she can!"

She knew the four spirits that dwelt there; she had known them when they were alive, but no one had knowledge of that. Once she realized they hadn't crossed over, she did visit them often. "Yesssssss, yesssssss, you never know when you might need a spirit as powerful as these, yesssssss, yesssssss!" she said.

She remembered the earlier days when many spirits lived here. Master Umberto had slowly captured them, casting them into slavery or using them as spies. The dark masters in Terra Demorte—trolls, goblins, and warlocks—would purchase such spirits for servants, working them relentlessly. The Master had stripped them of their strength and power before selling them, all of them—except these four.

"Yesssssss, yesssssss, I wonder!" she said. "I wonder why." Odium walked toward the huge old tree. She wondered why he had let them stay here for so many years. They were so powerful, so strong in energy, but Umberto had never attempted to capture them, and she knew that he knew they were there.

In the old days, Odium had watched the decent townsfolk of Edgefield many times hang criminals from the tree. The hanging tree was huge and had always been used to serve up a good dose of justice to the people found guilty of crimes. Mostly, the hanging tree was used for the migrant worker or strangers passing through the small town. They were the ones whose days in court usually consisted of a pot-bellied sheriff issuing a guilty sentence and a mob ensuring the death sentence was carried out quickly. There were never any questions about who was hanged or the antiquated way justice was served. It was appropriate to see the good folks taking care of business and ensuring the safety of the small community.

After each hanging, late into the night, the old witch would come by to see if the spirit or spirits had crossed over or passed on. She had watched many times as Master Umberto coaxed the spirit into following him and not crossing over. There was no bright light for most. Most were criminals, and when death came, only blackness followed. Warlocks like Umberto were waiting, and if the spirit didn't follow him, he would forcefully capture them in a void and send them straight to the Keeping Room in Terra Demorte—most decided to follow their new Master.

Odium stood gazing up into the huge tree; she looked at its branches and massive trunk. It looked so evil, stretching its twisted arms in every direction, and she loved it. She could feel the energy and power of the tree. It seemed the old tree had grown a new branch for every person hung there. "So many, yessssss, yessssss, so many!" she said with a grin.

She walked under the tree and sat down on the barren ground. No flowers or grasses grew under the tree; the ground was dead, dead—as some would say—as dirt. She noticed small pieces of rope ingrown into the bark of some of the branches. "Yessssss, yessssss, such a lovely tree."

She sat for a moment, feeling the wickedness the tree emitted. She absorbed the obscurity, feeling it uniting with her foul spirit. She welcomed it, and it made her feel bitter deep within her old bones.

"I command the spirits of the tree to come forth. Come forth and sit with me. I'm the dark witch, Odium, and I have come to talk with you. Yessssss, yessssss, come forth for I'm of darkness as you are of darkness!" she said. "Yessssss, yessssss, come forth!"

Odium sat quietly and waited. She could feel the spirits, and like so many times before when she had visited with them, knew they would come, but only in their time.

"Odium, why do you visit us? Why do you call on us? Our master has told us not to speak with you. He has warned us, told us not to communicate with the dark witch, Odium, and if we did, he would send us to the Keeping Room. Why do you bother us? Leave this place and don't ever return," said one of the spirits.

"Yessssss, yessssss, I know what Master Umberto has told you, but your Master is gone. He's been captured by the warlock Master Olin, who is your new master. Master Olin and Master Creed have taken this lot, and I'm in their service. Yessssss, yessssss, I am, and I must take you to them, so come forth and follow me!" said the witch, Odium.

"We have been instructed by our master not to leave this place until he comes for us. He warned us that you might try to trick us into leaving, but we won't leave. Our master is the only one that can command us to leave; he is helping us, helping us find the answer."

Odium sat quietly for a second. "Yessssss, yessssss, you say your master is helping you find an answer. Yessssss, yessssss, what answer?"

One of the spirits spoke. "The answer we seek only he can provide. Leave this place and don't come back, witch!"

"Yessssss, yessssss, I won't leave until you come with me. Your new master commands it. Yessssss, yessssss, you don't want to face him with your insolent behavior. He'll send you to the Keeping Room, yessssss, yessssss, I'm sure of it. Now stop this foolish talk about Master Umberto and come with me." Odium sat and waited, but the spirits didn't show themselves, and although Odium made numerous attempts, the spirits fell silent.

Slowly, the old witch walked backed toward her house. She mumbled, and when she wasn't talking to herself, she cursed aloud. She had to tell Olin and Creed that still another obstacle stood in their way of completing Master Creed's transformation. She would need Olin's magic to capture the spirits and physically force them to follow her to the mansion. "Yessssss, yessssss, always something, always something, never easy!" she said softly.

Odium had as much power and magic as any warlock, but she was a witch and not a warlock. Only warlocks could force spirits into servitude.

# Nineteen

## Everyone Has a Plan Or Do They?

Olin walked slowly down the sidewalk. His spirits were high as he went over his plans again in his mind. Since early that morning, he had pondered and pondered over his brother's transformation, and the never-ending problems that continued to plague it. In his infinite wisdom, he had conceived a devious plan of his own to stop Katie, Roland, and that meddling old witch, Wisteria, from interfering with their plans. At this very moment, he was on his way to put his plan into action. It was four o'clock, and Olin had just turned the corner onto Calhoun Street, strolling toward town.

\*\*\*

Thor looked at the huge grandfather clock in the living room. "Four o'clock!" he said. "It's time to use the telephone." He dialed the infamous three numbers that had been weighing heavy on his mind since the day before. He just couldn't understand how he could dial three numbers and someone far away could talk to him. "Marvelous!" he said, "simply marvelous!" He waited patiently until someone answered.

"911. What's your emergency?"

"I'm calling about the old Thomlin mansion. I've noticed some strange things going on over there. I believe the person that's killing the little girls is staying there—I mean hiding there." Thor hung up the telephone and smiled. "That's cool. I liked that!"

\*\*\*

"Hello, sir? Sir? Who is this?" The dispatcher hung up the telephone; she keyed her mic and began talking. "Dispatch to 318."

Jim heard the call and responded. "318."

"318, I just got a call concerning the killings in Edgefield, standby."

"Ten-four" said Jim. The dispatcher called the local Edgefield police, and within minutes had instructions on what to do next.

"318, proceed to the old Thomlin mansion. Edgefield police will meet you there along with an agent from the FBI. Don't enter the mansion until backup arrives. If there are suspects at that twenty, they're considered armed and dangerous." The dispatcher released the key on the mic and waited for a response from Jim.

"Ten-four, my ETA at that twenty is ten minutes. 318, out!" The emergency lights flicked and danced as they put forth their beams of light. The siren blared and yelped as the cruiser headed for the old Thomlin mansion.

"318 to dispatch."

"Go ahead 318."

"Who reported this?"

"They hung up before telling me their name, and for some reason, the ANI and ALLY, did not show up on my console. I have no idea, 318."

\*\*\*

Wisteria had left Number 12 minutes after Thor had made his call. "Simpleton!" she said. "Don't even know how to use the telephone, such a nincompoop!" Thor had been left to watch over Katie and Josh. Wisteria had warned him not to let them out of his sight. She had cast a spell to block the number of the phone Thor used, and it worked well.

"Thor, take care of them, whatever you do, don't let them out of your sight." Thor said mocking Wisteria. He sat and muttered something about treating him like a child, always giving him instructions and telling him what to do. "After all, I'm an assassin from the dark side; I can protect life as easy as I can take it." He said still mocking Wisteria. His preference was taking it of course, but with the Robertses, he would protect them with his life, no matter what.

\*\*\*

Wisteria walked slowly down the street toward Creed's mansion. She smiled as a police cruiser passed her, lights flashing and siren screaming. "Looks like everything is going to plan and working quite well," she said with a slight smile. However, the smile left her face just as the cruiser sped past. She stared across the street at a figure walking toward town. It was Olin. He noticed Wisteria, too, and stopped to face her motionlessly.

"Well, well, look who's out for a stroll," he said softly. "I should just cross the street and kill that witch now, right here in broad daylight. There's nothing stopping me, and that might put a stop to her meddling in our business." He laughed as he stared at the old witch.

Wisteria also looked intently at Olin. *Wonder where he's going?* she thought. She stared at the warlock, and then as if to insult him, she raised one of her hands and waved at him. But as she dropped her hand, she muttered a few words.

Olin turned to continue walking but then grabbed his throat as if some invisible vice was closing its jaws around it. He quickly glanced at Wisteria, but the old witch had turned and continued her walk down the street. He muttered a spell and took a deep breath. The warm air filled his lungs, and he was able to breathe once again.

"One day I'm going to kill that witch," he said, muttering a few words and waving in Wisteria's direction. Wisteria continued down the street. She had contemplated Olin's move and cast a simple protection spell. Whatever Olin had tried had no effect on the old woman.

"That'll give him something to think about!" Wisteria said softly as she strolled.

"Witch!" snapped Olin. "One day, one day very soon!"

"One day, I'm going to kill that warlock," she said. "One day, one day very soon!"

\*\*\*

Odium had returned to the crooked house she called home. She wondered about the spirits at the tree. She knew she had to tell Olin and Creed about the insolent beings and laughed as she gathered her keys and headed out toward her car. "Yessssss, yessssss," she said. "This will certainly infuriate the masters. Yessssss, yessssss, they won't like this at all."

Odium paused for a moment before turning off the crooked gravel road onto the paved street. "I wonder what Master Umberto has promised them, what answer are they looking for."

Odium drove slowly onto the paved street. Three police cruisers passed her with lights flashing and sirens screaming. "Such a pleasant sound, yessssss, yessssss, it is. Maybe someone has died. Yessssss, yessssss that would be nice."

\*\*\*

Creed sat in the darkness of his chambers; tonight he would be transformed back into something beautiful, back into a human, back into a being that could walk among the surface people, as he had done so many years ago—these were the people he hated most and the people who would soon, hate him. He also knew that after his transformation, they would have a choice but to serve him and his brother. As soon as his transformation was completed, he had scores to settle and, just for amusement, people to kill.

He made a soft noise that resembled a laugh. "After tonight, my brother and I will show these people what the dark side is really about."

\*\*\*

Jim was the first to reach the gates; he had stopped the wailing of the siren minutes before he turned toward the old mansion. He pulled his car in front of the old stone wall and picked up his mic. "318, to dispatch. I'm at the Thomlin mansion, waiting on Edgefield police. I'll be standing by!"

"Ten-four, 318. Edgefield is in route." The radio went silent.

Wisteria saw the Edgefield police turn up the street toward Creed's mansion. She stopped at the corner and watched the police officers line up their cars in front of the old stone wall and step out of their cars. Another car pulled up. It was gray, and a man wearing a dark suit got out and walked toward the officers. He gave some instructions, and the officers scattered.

Four went down the street and around to the back of the mansion. Four others went around the other side. At least ten other officers, including Jim, stood at the gates, watching the man in the gray suit cut the lock that bound the two huge gates together.

\*\*\*

Roy burst into Creed's chambers. "Master, there are humans at the front gate, at least ten, and eight more in the back. I believe they're coming in. We need to go, Master Creed, and we need to go now!"

"Has Olin gone?" Creed whispered.

"Yes, Master. He left earlier."

Ray came scurrying into the room, looking perplexed and worried. "Roy, they're coming in. We gotta go."

"Get the girl; hide her in the vault. No one knows the combination, and no one can get in there. Let's go. I'll need to put a sleeping spell on her to keep her quiet," Creed said. Creed and the two demon guardians walked hurriedly down the stairs. They continued their descent until they were in the basement.

Roy grabbed the young girl from the small bedroom just before a loud bang came echoing down the stairs into the basement—the noise was the sound of the front doors of the old mansion being forced open by huge battering rams.

At the same time, the other officers forced entrance into the house from the kitchen. Creed and the two demon guardians darted into the laboratory. The master hastily opened the vault. Roy and Ray kept watch in the hall. "Master, we must hurry. They're all upstairs. We must go, Master."

Creed pulled open the huge door to the vault and pushed the small girl inside. He cast a simple spell to keep her quiet, but it didn't work. Eve screamed as loud as she could. He tried again, and once more the spell was unsuccessful. The girl continued to scream. Creed raised his hand and struck the small girl in the face several times until Eve fell unconscious. "That should keep her quiet." He shut the vault door and vanished into the walls of the laboratory. Roy and Ray slammed the laboratory door, popping sounds came forth and they vanished to Terra Demorte.

\*\*\*

"OK, boys, check every nook and cranny. If there's anything here, I want to see it. Check the grounds and turn over every rock. Get dispatch back on the horn and see who called this in!" The man in the gray suit shouted his orders, and police officers scattered in every direction once more. "Jim, you stay with me. We'll check this floor first."

"Yes, sir!" Jim said, following the FBI agent into the living room. Officers scurried everywhere. Four went upstairs, and four went downstairs to check the basement.

"Check everything well, boys. Let me know if you see anything," said the man in the gray suit.

***

Wisteria walked up to the gates of the mansion. They were flung open, inviting all to enter. She strolled up the drive toward the old house.

Two officers noticed the old woman and swiftly intercepted her advancement. "Sorry, madam, but you're not allowed here. This is a police investigation and you'll have to leave." One of the policemen said.

"I'm with Jim Coffee; it's all right for me to be here," Wisteria replied.

"I'll have to check, madam," said the police officer. "What's your name?"

"Wisteria," replied Wisteria.

He spoke into his radio. "212 Edgefield to 318 Johnston!"

"318, what's up?"

"There's a huge—"the officer looked at Wisteria. "Sorry, madam. I mean there's a woman here, by the name of Wisteria, she says she's with you. Is it all right for her to come onto the premises?"

Jim answered, "Yes, let her in."

"Sorry to have bothered you, madam. Please go ahead!"

"Thank you so much, dear!" Wisteria said. "Please tell you wife, Mary, that Wisteria sends her greetings."

"I will!" said the police officer. "Hey, how did you know my wife's name? Do you know us?" Wisteria had already turned and continued to walk toward the front door, ignoring the officer's question.

A police officer came running from the backyard waving his arms. "Over here. Over here. There's something in this pool—blood and lots of it. And there's body parts or something in it. Come on, guys, over here."

Police officers scurried toward the officer, all but the two guarding the front gates. Wisteria continued toward the front door, walking slowly up the steps, and for the first time in many, many, years, stepped into the foyer of the old Thomlin mansion.

***

Olin continued down the street toward town. He went over his plan once again in his mind. He whistled while walking the last block toward his destination.

\*\*\*

Odium drove slowly toward the mansion. As she turned the corner, she saw the police cruisers lined up in front of the old stone wall. She slowed her car, passing the old iron gates of the mansion. Seeing the gates flung open, she scoured the premises. She could see police officers searching the yards and gardens. She smiled and drove on.

"Yessssss, yessssss, looks like Master Creed and Olin have their hands full at the moment. Yessssss, yessssss, it might be a good time for me to steal The Secret of Life from them, yessssss, yessssss, it might." She stopped her car a stone's throw from the end of the stone wall and got out. Slowly, she walked through the gates, an old woman meandering. She, like Wisteria had done, headed toward the mansion.

"Excuse me, madam. Are you a friend of Officer Jim's, too?" said the police officer sarcastically. "If you are, I'll still have to get permission from the chief to let you continue."

"Yessssss, yessssss, of course you will," said Odium. The officer laughed.

"It looks like Officer Jim's entourage of high society friends are here today. One would never know that this was a police investigation. I just let another elderly woman in a few minutes ago. I believe her name was Wisteria, or something like that. Are you a friend of hers as well?" he asked.

"Yessssss, yessssss, you say Wisteria is here?"

"Yes, madam. I just let her in. She's going in the house now. Oh, there she is on the front porch. Just a minute and let me get you cleared, and you can go on up!"

"Yessssss, yessssss, no need. I was just leaving. Thank you." Odium turned and strolled back out of the gates. "Yessssss, yessssss, I wonder what that old witch is up to. Yessssss, yessssss, I wonder!"

***

Wisteria walked into the large foyer. She paused. Closing her eyes, she could feel the evil that dwelt there, and she sensed it, cold and dark. She shuddered and walked slowly into the living room.

A two-way radio made a beep, and an officer's voice echoed throughout the house: "Captain, you need to come up here. Second floor, first room on the left. You've got to see this!"

"Roger that. We're on our way," said a rough voice. The FBI agent and the chief of the Edgefield police department walked into the foyer, heading toward the stairs. Jim followed the two men. He didn't speak but continued scanning the area. They turned to go up the stairs when the FBI agent noticed the strange old woman standing in the living room.

"What in the blazes is she doing here?" he said.

"Oh, sorry about that. She's with me. She's all right; I told your officers that she could come in," Jim said. He smiled at Wisteria and nodded. "Good afternoon, Wisteria!"

"Good afternoon, dear. Thanks for letting me in. I'll just wait here for a spell so I can catch my breath. An old woman like me can't climb all of those stairs, you know."

The FBI agent repeated his question to Jim. "What is she doing here? Is she one of your investigators?"

"Actually, no. I mean yes, unofficial that is. I mean she helps sometimes; you know, she's a psychic."

"You mean she's clairvoyant?" said the FBI agent.

"Yeah, something like that," Jim said, closing the gap between the FBI agent and Wisteria. He whispered softly, "You know, she's a witch!"

"What?" shouted the FBI agent. "You called on a witch to help? Are you nuts?"

"No, not at all. She's helped our department before, and she's quite good at what she does." Jim paused.

"And just what does she do?" said the FBI agent.

"I don't know, exactly, but whatever it is, she'll do it pretty well!" said Jim, looking at Wisteria. Wisteria had her back to the men and stood motionless. Her hair floated around her waist as if trying to protect it.

"Well, tell her not to touch anything, and keep her out of the way. If she sees anything or feels anything—" The FBI agent stopped and looked at the chief. "Oh, for Pete's sake, if she can help you, tell her to give you a shout. After all, this is your jurisdiction. Let's get upstairs and see what's going on up there."

The three men made their way upstairs, and Jim turned and looked at Wisteria as he vanished up the stairs. She was still standing in the living room, looking around as if she had heard nothing. "Morons. I already know more than they will ever find out," she said, heading for the stairs.

"Chief, check this out!" said an officer. "Strange markings of some kind on the floor and these candles sitting around. Looks like some kind occult has been meeting here, probably those devil worshipers. You know they meet in places like this."

"Yes, this is strange," said the chief. "Looks like they were planning some kind of ritual or something. The candles haven't been lit, so it looks like they haven't started. It appears we might have scared them off, or even better, they might be coming back later on tonight."

"It looks to me, dear, that someone plans to make some kind of sacrifice here, maybe a young girl," said Wisteria.

The FBI agent, the chief, and Jim turned quickly to see Wisteria standing in the room, looking at the markings and candles. She looked at the desk and the bloody cloak hanging on the rack. She remembered Thor telling her about it. "There." She pointed at is. "What's that?"

An officer walked over to the dark corner. "It's a cloak of some kind, and it's covered with something. Oh, my gosh. It's covered with blood!"

"Get it bagged and send it to the lab," shouted the FBI agent. He looked at Wisteria and smiled. "Do you know anything about these markings?"

"Yes, these particular markings are used for a sacrificial offering, usually that of a young child." She paused. "Or maybe a small animal. Let me study this for a while, and I'll see what I can make of it, dear," Wisteria said. "It may take a few minutes."

The two-way beeped once again, and a voice said, "Chief, you need to come out to the backyard. There's a small pool with blood everywhere and body parts scattered in the water, chunks of it. You really need to take a look at this."

The chief keyed the mic on the two-way and spoke. "Yeah, sure, we're on our way out."

"Take all the time you need, madam. I'm going outside for a spell. If you come up with anything, just let me know," said the FBI agent. He turned to Jim. "Jim, I'm glad you brought her. She just might be able to help with this. Let's go, boys. We need to check the pool." The agent smiled at Wisteria, and like two little ducks following their mother, the FBI agent and the chief of police followed Officer Jim from Creed's chambers and headed for the pool.

Wisteria studied the markings on the floor and at the candles sitting precisely on the pentagram. *They're ready!* she thought. *They're still waiting on something, but they're preparing to complete the transformation. Somehow or another, Creed's found the power he needed to complete his wretched transformation.* She walked slowly around the markings, making sure she didn't touch or move anything. She stared at the drawings on the wooden floor; she held her hand over them and looked surprised. "No magic, nothing, just markings."

She glanced at Creed's desk and slowly walked over to it. She wanted to know more about the monster who sat there. She wanted to know more about his plans. She moved quietly around the desk and sat down in the chair. She closed her eyes for a moment, and then with a violent jerk, she opened them. They rolled back into her head and then came forward and stared out into the room.

Wisteria looked at the room. She saw a demon guardian standing in front of the desk. He spoke. "Master, there are humans at the front gate, at least ten, and eight more in the back. I believe they're coming in, We need to go, Master Creed, and we need to go now." She couldn't see Creed but heard his voice. It was coming from her.

"Has Olin gone?" it whispered.

"Yes, Master. He left earlier," said the demon guardian.

She saw another demon guardian enter the room. He scurried toward her in a panic. He looked perplexed and worried. "Roy, they coming in. We must go."

Again, she heard Creed's voice come from where she sat. "Get the girl. Hide her in the vault. No one knows the combination, and no one can get in there. Let's go. I'll need to put a sleeping spell on her to keep her quiet." The voice was harsh and scratchy, but she knew it instantly. She watched as Creed and the two demon guardians walked bristly toward the door.

Wisteria's head jerked backward. She closed her eyes and then opened them once more. A small trickle of blood oozed from her nose. She took her handkerchief from her dress and wiped it gently. She rose from the chair and walked slowly to the bloody cloak. She placed her hand on the cloak, and once again her head jerked violently backward and her eyes rolled back into her head. Like before, they opened and quickly focused on the room. Once more she saw into the past.

She was wearing the cloak and peering out from the hood. She saw an empty room and a desk with a small light. She saw a bony hand with long fingers and yellow nails claw at her throat in an attempt to untie the cloak. She looked down and saw the blood running from the creases of the garment. The long, bony fingers were covered with blood. She watched as they raked the blood from the cloak and the blood-soaked hand rose toward her lips. She could taste the warm substance but continued peering into the past.

Wisteria wanted to see more, but the bloody fingers were smearing the blood over her face and in her mouth. She finally had to break her concentration, or she would certainly have to puke. More blood oozed from Wisteria's nose, and she wobbled slightly, walking toward the door.

She walked by the large chair sitting in front of Creed's desk and noticed something shiny lying on the cushion. It looked silvery, like the thread of a spider's web.

She paused and very gently picked up the strange object. She noticed very quickly that it wasn't part of a spider's web. Instead, it was a hair, a very long hair. "A woman's hair," she said softly.

Wisteria wiped her nose again; the blood was oozing now in a gentle flow. She squeezed her nostrils tightly to prevent the sticky substance from continuing its journey down to her lip.

She held the hair. As before, her head jerked violently, and once again her eyes rolled back into her head then focused on the center of the room. She saw Creed sitting in the darkness behind the old desk. She heard him speak, addressing her.

"I need your help, witch," he said. Wisteria listened, hearing the warlock in the darkness talk about his transformation, how he had been searching for Sarah Wheeler for years and how he needed her strength and power, that same strength and power that her father and nanny possessed. She listened as Creed told her how Olin had gone to Number 12 that very morning only to find that the spirits were gone. She listened, and finally the witch spoke.

"Yessssss, yessssss, I know about your transformation, and I know about Sarah Wheeler, her father, and the nanny. I knew they were there, there, yessssss, yes in Number 12, and I knew, Master Creed, how badly you needed them. Yessssss, yessssss, I know they were there." Wisteria's eyes focused on the empty room where she stood. She knew immediately that the voice belonged to none other than Odium, one of the most evil witches that roamed the surface.

Wisteria listened to Creed and the old witch's conversation, and the more she listened, the more intense the pain in her head became. The blood flowed freely now from her nose and dripped steadily onto her purple dress. She stood motionlessly and listened to the conversation between Odium and Creed. She listened intently until she couldn't stand the pain. She collapsed onto the floor.

\*\*\*

"318," came a voice over the two-way. "318, come in!" The two-way squawked again.

"318, go ahead!" said Jim. He was standing beside the small pool, watching the FBI agent poke at something in the bloody water. "Hold on, dispatch!" he said. "What on earth is that?"

The FBI agent and the Edgefield chief stood staring into the murky, bloody water. They turned and looked at Jim, and finally the FBI agent spoke. "Well, I don't know. But we will bag it and have the crime lab look at it. There's plenty of blood mixed with this water. Maybe it's all blood. Who knows? As far as the parts, maybe human, maybe not. I don't know. It's too decayed to tell."

The chief shook his head. "Boys, when the FBI crime lab gets here, help them out as much as possible." The other officers shook their heads and stared, bewildered, into the small pond.

"318," said the voice again from the two-way. "318, I need you!"

"318. Go ahead, dispatch. Sorry about that," Jim replied. He excused himself and walked back up the winding rock path toward the old mansion.

"318, I have a situation. There's been a terrible accident on Highway 69, in the curve at the old Brooks farm. I need for you to investigate it." The dispatched stopped and waited on a reply from Jim.

"Ten-four, I'm on my way," said Jim.

"318, there's one other thing. I believe you know the person involved in the accident. It's our newest resident, Roland Roberts." The dispatch paused.

Jim responded. "What? Mr. Roberts? Are you sure, Lola?" Jim forgot about proper police and radio protocol. He paused for a second and repeated his question. "Lola, are you sure it's Mr. Roberts?"

"Yes, Jim, and there's more. He's in bad shape, pinned in his car against that huge old oak tree. He's asking for his wife, Katie. Rescue is telling me that if they move him, he'll die within minutes."

Jim walked toward his cruiser. "What next?" he said to himself. "This is turning into the worst day I've had in years. Mr. Roberts is such nice guy and has such a nice family."

"Jim!" called dispatch.

"Yes, Lola. Sorry. I'm here. I'm on my way," Jim responded.

"There's more. I need for you to stop by his house and pick up his wife. This will probably be her only chance to see her husband before"— the dispatch paused—"you know, before he dies."

"Ten-four," said Jim. "Jim, don't take his son. He's too small. Get one of the neighbors to look after him. Do you copy?" The dispatcher released the key on her mic.

"Ten-four," said Jim. He cranked his car and headed for Number 12. The lights on his cruiser flashed as he turned onto the side street that led down to Calhoun. The siren screamed loudly, and for the first time in years, he purely hated the sound.

"Jim." The radio squawked once more. "Jim, do you understand that you aren't to take the boy?"

Jim eased off the gas pedal and turned onto Calhoun Street. He cut off the lights, silenced the screaming siren, and responded to dispatch. "Ten-four, copy that, Lola. I'll get a neighbor to watch Josh." The big engine in his cruiser roared as he punched the gas pedal once more.

He shook his head and squinted. *Funny,* he thought. *How did I remember the kid's name?* He had only met Josh a time or two at Wisteria's Café, but the small lad had made an impression on him. It wasn't just that, but for some reason, he really liked the small boy.

Jim had no kids of his own, nor was he married. He never had the time; it was as if police work was all he was interested in, and for some reason he hadn't really thought about a family of his own. Though it wasn't really professional, Jim and Lola had been seeing each other for years, and although they were considered a couple, neither ever mentioned marriage or kids.

\*\*\*

Wisteria stirred. She had hit the floor hard when she passed out but hadn't hurt herself. She pushed herself up from the floor, and upon standing, wobbled a few seconds before walking toward the door. "Odium!" she said.

She walked down the hall and peered into the other bedrooms. Nothing. Then, remembering the conversation Creed had with his two demon guardians, said, "They've locked a small girl in the vault; I've got to get down there."

She walked down the stairs and met the FBI agent and chief coming back into the house.

"Well," said the FBI agent, "did you find out anything about those markings and candles?" He looked at the old woman. "You're bleeding. Are you all right?"

"Don't worry about me, dear. I'm fine," she said, trying to make her way past him.

The FBI agent, blocking her passage, handed Wisteria his handkerchief and prompted her once more. "Did you determine what the drawings and candles were all about?"

"Yes, dear, I did. I'll meet you up there in a few minutes and we can discuss it. I'm going out on the porch to get a breath of fresh air. I'll be back shortly."

"Are you sure you're all right?" asked the chief. "You don't look so good. You're pale. May I help you?"

"Now don't worry about me, dear. You two go on upstairs, and I'll be up in a few minutes. Go on, now, and scoot." Wisteria made a scooping gesture with her hands. "Go on. Don't worry about an old woman like me. You've got police work to do."

The two men climbed the stairs and headed back to Creed's chambers. Wisteria walked slowly toward the front door. She turned and watched the two men disappear into the upstairs hall. The moment they were out of sight, she headed for the basement.

The basement consisted of a very wide hall and two small rooms—one on each side. At the end of the hall was the laboratory, which consumed most of the basement.

She peered into and searched the contents of the two rooms. The first room was dusty and dirty, full of cobwebs and small spiders. It was apparent no one had been there or used it for years.

The second room had a small bed, and although it wasn't much cleaner, there was something unusual about the bed—there was a small impression on the blanket, and the blanket itself was free of dust and dirt.

"Something or someone has being lying on the bed, something small," she said. She entered the room and walked to the bed. She stared closely at the blanket and then softly laid her hand on the bed. Her head jerked violently backward, and her eyes rolled back into her head. Then as before, they rolled forward and she stared straight ahead.

She saw a demon guardian and recognized him immediately—Roy, the same one she had fought at the front gates. He walked toward her and picked up a small bundle. Wisteria moved slightly, and as the demon guardian walked out the door, she saw that the bundle was a small child. She stood and watched the demon guardian disappear into the hall. Wisteria followed.

In the hall, Wisteria saw Creed, dressed in his black cloak. She stared at his face, and although the hood covered most of it, she could make out its bony features. It was covered with a soft, whitewashed skin. The nose was still not complete, and the eyes were sunken deep into the eye sockets. "Horrible!" she muttered.

She watched as Creed and the demon guardians walked into the laboratory. Creed turned the vault's lock and pulled on the huge door. It opened with ease, and Wisteria watched the demon guardian drop the small child onto the floor of the iron vault. The child screamed and started ed whimpering.

Wisteria watched in disbelief and wondered what a small child was doing in Creed's mansion. Then to her horror, Creed snatched up the frail child, stared for what seemed to be a very long time at her, and then with a forceful blow, slapped the child across the face using the back of his hand, which he repeated several times. The small hood on the child's head fell off. Wisteria saw the face of the helpless child for the first time. It was a small girl, a girl she knew.

"It's Eve. Dear God, no, not Eve!"

Eve lay still on the vault's floor after Creed had released her. Wisteria heard Creed hiss something about how that should keep her quiet. "That monster!" shouted Wisteria. Blood oozed again from her nose, but Wisteria continued to watch as Creed shut the door to the vault. He disappeared, and she heard popping sounds as his two demon guardians disappeared, as well.

Wisteria's head jerked slightly as she came out of her trance. She walked over to the vault and softly laid one of her hands on the tarnished iron. She knew the small girl lay within the thick, dark walls of the cold tomb. She also knew she was still unconscious, but alive. She wanted to help, but there were questions that needed to be answered before she could rescue the small girl. She cast a protection spell, one that would keep Eve in a deep sleep until the spell was lifted.

Wisteria walked slowly back up the steps to the first floor. She worried about the small girl in the vault and wondered about her mother. She knew Gloria quite well; actually, she was one of her closest friends.

"She's a powerful witch," she whispered.

She walked out onto the front porch of the old mansion. She wobbled back and forth slightly and grabbed for one of the columns.

"Easy there," said a voice. It was the FBI agent. "Are you all right?"

"Yes, dear, just a little tired after climbing those stairs."

"Can I get you something?" he asked.

"No, I'm fine, dear. Thank you." Wisteria stood erect and shook slightly; her large lavender dress floated softly around her body. She walked toward the steps when the chief spoke.

"Madam, would you be so kind as to take a look at something for us, please?"

"Yes, dear, but only if you call me Wisteria. That's my name, you know."

"It's down here, by the stone pond. Let me help you." The chief took Wisteria's arm and helped her off the porch.

"I warn you there's something strange here. There's blood in the water and pieces of"—he paused—"something else in the water. We don't know what. We were hoping you could tell us."

Wisteria walked over to the stone wall that surrounded the small pond; she stared for a moment into the dark water and then sat down on the wall. Then ever so gently, she placed her hand on the stones. Her head jerked violently backward and as before, her eyes rolled back into her head and then focused straight ahead. This time she saw something sitting on the wall; something dressed in a black cloak. She watched the figure and realized it was Creed. He had his back turned toward her, but it was evident that he was struggling with something.

He raised his arm, and the sleeve of the cloak slid down toward his elbow. Wisteria could see that his transformation was truly in the advanced stage. His arm was complete but very pale. She could see the blood vessels running under a thin layer of skin. He held a knife in his hand, and with great force, he plunged it several times into whatever he was struggling with. It made a terrible scream and everything became quiet.

She watched as the warlock brought something to his mouth. It was bleeding profusely, and Wisteria watched as Creed drank its blood. The blood ran down his arms and onto his cloak, then in little rivers down toward the ground. Creed drank more and more of the blood. His arms, face, and cloak were covered with the red substance.

He picked up the knife once more and cut a huge chunk of flesh from his victim. He brought the meat to his mouth and gripped it with his long, bony fingers. He gnawed on it and she could hear him sucking out the blood.

He tossed the large chunk of flesh into the pond, and using his knife, cut another chunk of the bloody meat. Wisteria sat on the stone wall that surrounded the pond and watched Creed feed. He tossed another chunk of flesh into the pond and stood up. He picked up what was left of his victim and tossed it, as well, into the pond.

She softly pulled her hand off the wall and laid it on her lap. Her eyes rolled back into her head, and then focused back again on the pond.

She stared into the pond, wondering what she should say, wondering if she should tell the FBI agent and the chief what was in the pond. She knew that their investigation would eventually tell them, but her mind went back to Eve and the question of why she was here, and what was Creed doing with her. There were other questions, as well, but the one question that disturbed her the most was why Gloria hadn't confided in her.

Wisteria looked at the two officers and she shook her head. "I'm sorry. I can't help you, dear. I'm not feeling very well, dear. Would you mind if I went home?"

"No, madam. You can go. Have a nice day." The FBI agent turned and headed up the path. "Let's leave this to the lab, boys. She can't help us."

"Where is, Jim, dear?" Wisteria said.

"He's not here. He had a call," said the chief. "Do you need a ride?"

"No, I was just wondering where he was. I'll be leaving now!"

The FBI agent spoke softly to Wisteria. "Madam, you said you would tell us about the markings in the house."

"Yes, dear. Let me go home and do some studying, and I'll let Jim know as soon as I interpret them." She smiled a weak smile and turned to leave.

She left the pond and walked down the drive to the gates; she crossed the street and headed away from the old mansion. When she reached Calhoun Street, she didn't turn toward town; instead she headed the opposite direction.

\*\*\*

Odium sat in her car and watched Wisteria walk out of the gates. Once Wisteria was out of sight, Odium walked back through the gates and headed for the mansion.

"Excuse me, madam. You can't go up there until I get you cleared," said a uniformed officer. "You did say you were a friend of Jim's didn't you?"

"Yes, of course," said Odium, nearing the officer. She held out her hand and blew a fine powder into the eyes of the officer. She muttered a few words and headed up the drive.

"You can proceed, madam. You've been cleared," he said.

"Thank you. Have a nice day," said Odium. She walked in the door of the mansion and headed straight for Creed's chambers. She walked into the room and saw the drawings and candles on the floor. "Yessssss, yesssssss, he's ready. Yessssss, he is. He's waiting on the spirits I promised. Yessssss, yessssss, he is." She scanned the room but couldn't find what she was looking for. "Where, yessssss, yessssss, where would he hide something like that?"

The evil witch closed her eyes and muttered something. Her head jerked back the same way Wisteria's had done earlier. Her eyes rolled back into her head and her nose started to bleed. When her eyes refocused, she looked back into the past.

Odium watched Olin draw the diagrams on the floor, and after he had finished, he sat the candles in the small circles. She heard him speak. "We'll let the good witch bless the drawings with her magic, Brother."

Creed left his chambers and slowly walked into one of the other bedrooms. His two demon guardians stood in the hall watching him. He disappeared into the room. He closed the door, but Odium followed him.

He walked over to a large bed and stared down as if someone was lying there. He stood there for a while and then turned and shot a quick glance at the door. He stared at Odium for a second; it was if he sensed her and knew she was there, but she knew, there was no way he could actually see her.

He looked at a large panel wall beside the bed. There were round porcelain knobs in one of the panels over the nightstand. The knobs created the shape of a large tree—small knobs making up the trunk and limbs and eight large knobs making up what seemed to be some kind of fruit.

There was another, matching panel on the other side of the bed and from the door; Odium noticed how lovely they were.

Creed pushed on one of the knobs and then another. He moved his hand down the trunk of the tree and pushed softly on one of the smaller knobs. The panel clanked and snapped opened.

He reached inside and pulled out a small package wrapped in an ancient cloth. He took it back to his chambers, and Odium followed him. He placed the package in the center of the diagram. The drawing on the floor illuminated. "It's ready, Olin. As soon as Odium brings the spirits I need, we can finish my transformation."

Odium's head jerked slightly as she came out of the trance she was in, she smiled and walked toward the panels. "Yessssss, yessssss, so that's where he keeps it."

"Hey, you, you there, old woman, what are you doing here?" It was the FBI agent. He and the chief had decided to recheck things in the house since Wisteria was of no help to them. "What are we running here, Chief, an old folks home? Is this one of Jim's friends?

"I know you," said the chief. "This is an evil woman, an evil witch, so I've heard. Get her out of here, and I mean now. She's no friend of Jim's. Jim and I have had more conversations about her than I can count. Get her out of here."

Two officers grabbed Odium by the arms. "Get her off of these premises, and make sure you escort her out of the gates before turning her loose. Put the cuffs on her and don't let her move her hands. Matter of fact, keep her hands behind her back. She's not to be trusted." The chief shouted his orders. "Go ahead, get her out of here! Get two more officers in here to help!"

The two officers handcuffed Odium and walked the old woman out of the house. They met two more officers outside, and they all escorted the old witch down the drive to the gates.

"Don't come back," said one of the police officers.

"Yessssss, yessssss, I won't," snapped Odium. "I should turn you into toads or something. Yessssss, yessssss, that's what I should do."

The two men turned and scampered up the drive. They passed the two other officers, who were supposed to be guarding the entrance. "Don't ever let her in here again. The chief is pretty ticked off; he found her in the mansion."

"You got it, Sergeant," said one of the officers.

The sergeant looked at the two officers. He bent toward them and said, "The chief said she's a witch."

"You don't mean it?"

"Yes, an evil witch at that. Don't let her back in, and whatever you do, don't look at her. She threatened to turn us into toads or something," said the office with a laugh.

"You don't mean it?"

"Yeah, keep sharp, men, and whatever you do, don't look into her eyes. The chief said if you look into her eyes she could turn you into anything."

"No way!"

"Yes," said the sergeant. "If you want to keep your head, you two had better not let her back on the grounds." The sergeant laughed, and he and the other officers headed back to the mansion.

"Do you think she's a real witch?" asked one of the officers.

"I've heard she is, and you know what they say about witches and crooked houses. I've been to her house before on a complaint, there was a terrible stench that stunk up half of the county, and it came for something she was cooking outside in a huge kettle. Well let me tell you, everything on her house was crooked, including her windows and doors," said the other officer.

"You know where she lives?"

The officer squinted and turned up the corners of his mouth. "Of course, and it's really spooky down there!"

Odium walked slowly toward her car. "Yesssssss, yessssss, now I know. Yesssssss, yessssss, I do!"

* * *

On the other side of town, an hour earlier, Olin looked at the woman sitting behind the desk. "Very good." He laughed. He stood motionless and stared at the helpless woman. His mind was asking two questions: "Should I kill her or let her live?"

Lola returned Olin's stare. She sat there patiently waiting for Olin's next move or command. She was totally in his control. Anything he wanted, at the moment, Lola would do.

Olin thought about the repercussions if he did indeed kill the dispatcher and what would happen if he let her live. He knew he could erase her memory of his being in the police station, but the desire to kill her was overwhelming. He cast another spell and left the police station.

# Twenty

## The Kid napping

Wisteria rapped loudly on the wooden door. She stood and waited for an answer.

Gloria opened the door. "Wisteria?"

"Yes, dear. May I come in?"

"Wisteria, my daughter is sick. I wouldn't want you to catch anything. Would you mind if I ask you to come back tomorrow?"

"Hogwash, I certainly would, Gloria. You know quite well, dear, that I don't catch anything unless I want to catch it. Besides, Dawn may be sick, but Eve is in trouble, and we need to talk." Wisteria looked at her host. "Now move over and let me in." Wisteria walked through the door and down the hall toward the kitchen. "Make some coffee, dear. This might take a while."

Gloria followed the old woman to the kitchen and instantly started scurrying around the kitchen, preparing the coffee. "I'm sorry, Wisteria. I should have called you!"

"You certainly should have, dear. You know we stick together. What is Creed doing with your daughter?" Wisteria looked at Gloria and asked a question that she hoped had good news. "And where is Dawn?"

Gloria started crying. "A warlock named Olin came last night and took Eve. He beat Dawn. She was barely alive this morning. Have you seen Eve? Is she all right?"

"She's alive; Creed has her locked in his vault. I wanted to rescue her, but I need to know what she is doing there. No one knows she's there, and you need to tell me everything, dear."

Gloria showed Wisteria the note that Olin had left. "They want me to perform some kind of ritual. If I don't, they will kill Eve. I know all about Creed and his transformation. Apparently they need a witch to perform the ritual, a witch like me."

"Why didn't you let me know, dear?" asked Wisteria. "You should have summoned me."

"I know, but as you can see by his note, he said he would kill Eve."

"Well, dear, I have her in a sleeping spell; she won't feel anything and won't be any trouble for Creed. So he wants you to perform the ritual, does he?"

"Yes, Wisteria. What do you want me to do?" asked Gloria.

"You, my dear, will do as instructed. You will perform the ritual," said Wisteria.

The two women talked about the ritual, and Wisteria shared exactly what she wanted Gloria to do. "You do know, dear, they will kill you and Eve as soon as the ritual is over, don't you?"

Gloria looked at her hands. She folded them and placed them in her lap. "I won't let them kill Eve. I've got to save her, Wisteria. Even if it costs me my life, I can't let them kill my little girl."

"No, dear, we won't let them kill either of you. Let me know when they contact you. They won't have their ritual tonight; I've made sure of that!" Wisteria stood up. "Thanks for the coffee. Let me see if I can help Dawn."

"She's—" Before Gloria could finish her statement, Wisteria finished it for her.

"In her bedroom. I know, dear."

* * *

It was a beautiful afternoon, and things had shaped up nicely for Wisteria. Her plan to have the police raid Creed's mansion had turned out perfectly. "That should keep that monster away for a few days," she said with a laugh. She walked down the street and headed back to the abandoned mansion of the infamous Thomlin boys.

Even with all of the police officers standing around and searching every inch of the grounds and house, the old witch managed to find herself back in the basement of Creed's mansion, undetected. She walked slowly to the locked laboratory door, and with a wave of her hand, the huge, heavy door eased open. She walked in and went to the vault.

Replaying, in her mind, what the trance had shown her earlier, she saw Creed slapping Eve when he locked her in that tomb. She muttered words under her breath and then, with a slightly happy voice, said, "I'm going to kill that warlock, one day, as well."

Wisteria placed her hand on the vault. Numbers weren't her strong suit, but nonetheless, she turned the old dial to four numbers, and then with all of her might, she opened the vault door. There, lying on the floor was Eve, sleeping soundly. Her cheeks were bruised, and her mouth covered with dried blood. Other than that, Eve was in good condition.

With a small wave of her hand, Wisteria pointed at the child and said, "Eve, my dear, wake up. It's time for you to go home. Come on, dear. Let's get out of this place."

Eve opened her eyes and looked up at the old woman. "Wisteria, can I go home? I miss my mother."

"Yes, dear, get up and I'll take you home."

Wisteria and Eve walked out of Creed's mansion without anyone paying them any attention. They turned and started down Calhoun Street; minutes later, they walked onto Gloria's porch.

"Eve," said Gloria. "Oh, honey, it's so good to see you." Gloria grabbed her daughter and hugged her tightly; she kissed her on the head as tears dropped into Eve's hair.

273

Wisteria patted Gloria on the sleeve. "You let me know if you hear from Olin or Creed again. They will be looking for another good witch to complete the transformation. You call me if they come here again. I'll alert the others in our order."

"I will, Wisteria; don't worry. I have put several spells around this house. They may be able to counter them, but not before I'm warned."

"Good, dear. I have cast a few myself."

\*\*\*

Jim pulled into the drive of Number 12. Of all of the calls he had been dispatched on in years past, this one was running close to being the worst. He hadn't known Katie and Roland very long, but the few times he had met Johnston's newest couple, he had fallen in love with them. "I really hate to do this," he said, walking upon the front porch.

"Jim, how are you? Please come in. Is everything all right?" Katie had seen the cruiser pull into the drive and met Jim at the door.

"I'm afraid it's not, Katie. We don't have much time, you need to come with me," said Jim. He paused, "I'm sorry but it's your..."

"It's Roland, isn't it?

"I'm sorry, but I'm afraid so. He's been in an accident, and I need to take you there. I'm sorry, Katie, but he's been injured, and he's asking for you," Jim said, watching Katie's expression change from that of a mature woman to that of a small child. Her eyes welled up with tears, and she started to shake. "Get your things, Katie. I'll take you to him." Jim noticed the bruises and cuts, and Katie saw him staring at them. Neither spoke a word about them.

Katie turned and headed into the den. "Thor, Roland is hurt. Would you please get Josh? We need to go to him." Katie's emotions were un-containable. She finally broke down and started sobbing hysterically.

Thor rushed to her side. "Are you all right?"

"No, not really. Get Josh and let's go. Roland's hurt," she said.

"Katie, I don't believe we should take Josh. The dispatcher requested that we leave him with a neighbor, that is if you don't mind," said Jim. "Do you know if any of your neighbors are at home? Is there anyone we can leave Josh with?"

"No, only Thor," said Katie. "No, wait. Miss Pat is home. I saw her this afternoon in her yard. Thor, would you take Josh over to Miss Pat's house. I'm sure she wouldn't mind keeping him for me, tell her it's an emergency." Katie turned to Josh. "Baby, I need for you to stay with Miss Pat while Mommy runs an errand. Do you mind, sweetie?"

"No, Mommy. I don't mind. I wike Miss Pat. She gives me ice cream," Josh said.

"I'll stay with Josh, Katie," said Thor. "You go on with Jim, and I'll stay and keep an eye on Josh. Hurry now. Get going. Me and Josh will hang out here, won't we, Josh?"

"Yeah, we'll hang out here," said Josh, smiling at Thor. He started playing with his toys again but then stopped. "No, I want to go to Miss Pat's house. She has ice cream."

Katie started crying again. "Please, Thor. I don't think I can do this alone. Would you please go with me? Josh will be fine at Miss Pat's."

Thor gave Katie a hug and a small kiss on the forward. "Sure, whatever you need."

Thor grabbed Josh's bag and headed for the door. They all left the house and walked briskly toward the patrol car. "I'll be back in a second." Said Thor.

"No problem," said Jim. "I'll call in and let dispatch know we are leaving."

Thor picked up Josh and hurried toward the neighbor's house. He walked onto the porch and rang the bell. Pat answered the door with a big smile and a warm hello. Thor told her about the emergency, and of course, Miss Pat agreed in an instant to watch the small boy.

"Come on in, baby. Would you like for Miss Pat to get you some ice cream?" she asked Josh. The boy readily agreed as he walked into the house. Thor left the porch, and as soon as his feet hit the grass, he broke into a run. Jim had the engine running, and Katie had already taken a seat in the front of the cruiser.

Thor jumped into the back, and Jim backed out of the drive and headed toward town. He flipped on the lights and siren.

"318 to dispatch. We are leaving Number 12. I have Mrs. Roberts and her friend. Our ETA is fifteen minutes or less. Do you have any additional word on her husband?"

"No, 318. Just that he is requesting his wife to be brought to the site," said Lola.

"318, out!" Jim looked at Katie and offered a faint smile. "We'll be there in a few minutes, Katie. I'm really sorry about this. I hope it turns out all right."

"Me too," said Katie. She sat quietly and listened at the siren making its urgent cries. She had always wanted to ride in a police car but not like this, not heading to a crash site where the only man she had ever loved lay injured and possibly dying. She wiped her tears once more as the car sped down Highway 69.

"It should be right up here, Katie, around the next bend. It's the old Brooks farm. It sits right beside the road, and there's a huge oak tree in the yard. It's always been a bad curve, and that oak tree is right in the way if you don't make the..." Jim realized what he was saying and quickly stopped. "Sorry, Katie, just rattling a bit. Here we are."

He had been to this site many times before and had seen countless accidents. Most were fatal; it was as if the old tree didn't like giving its victims second chances. The owner, John, had promised many times to cut the tree down, but he had not.

\*\*\*

Olin walked upon the porch of the Millborn house. He peered through the glass storm door and could see a small boy sitting in the den on a huge rug. A woman with shoulder-length gray hair sat on the floor playing with the child. She was on her knees with her back to the door. He realized that the couple in the den of the house had no idea of what evil was watching them. He knew that, even on a good day, neither had a chance of escaping, and he—and he alone—would decide who lived and who died today. He slowly turned the door's knob, but the door wouldn't open. It was locked.

"Well, we'll just have to do this the easy way," he said. He reached out and rang the doorbell. He watched through the glass as Miss Pat came to the door.

She looked through the glass and saw the handsome man standing there with a magical smile on his face. "May I help you?" she said through the glass.

"Yes, my name is Olin. Katie sent me for her son, that small boy there." Olin pointed over Miss Pat's shoulder. "The one in your den," he said.

Miss Pat looked into Olin's eyes. Olin smiled at her and then glanced away. "Come on, let me in."

"I don't think so. I think I'll keep Josh until Katie returns. You need to leave," she said.

"I think not," screamed Olin. He grabbed the knob once again and gave it a quick but very hard pull. The door snapped open, but Miss Pat had anticipated Olin's move and was already pushing the solid wooden door closed. The warlock gave the door a swift kick. The force of his kick was so brutal it sent the door violently back against the wall. Miss Pat ran toward the den. The intruder was now in the house.

Pat grabbed the small boy and pulled him up on her hip. Before she could take a step, Olin grabbed her by the hair. She screamed and dropped Josh onto the floor. She tried to turn to face her assailant, but with a quick push, Olin pushed Miss Pat's head straight down into the coffee table. He pulled her head up and spun her around. Her eye was bleeding profusely. He looked into her eyes, and he could see that she was on the verge of passing out. He shoved her head once again into the coffee table. The wood didn't budge, but the soft skin did. Blood was running down her face and spewed from her nose and mouth. Olin released his grip on the woman's head and watched as she fell to the floor.

Josh started crying, remembering Olin. He screamed as Olin picked him up. Olin sneered. He hated kids, and even worse, he hated them the most when they cried. He held Josh with one hand, and with the other cast a small spell on the screaming boy. Josh immediately fell asleep and became quiet. "That's more like it, no noise," said Olin.

\*\*\*

"318, to dispatch."

"Dispatch. Go ahead, Jim."

"I'm here at the old Brooks farm, but I don't see anything. Repeat the twenty on Mr. Robert's accident."

"You are at the right place, 318, the old Brooks farm, the big oak tree."

Jim passed the old tree and looked over at Katie. "Something's wrong here. Let me turn around, and we'll go back. I didn't see anything that resembled an accident."

"Thank God," said Katie.

Thor listened from the back seat. He watched as Jim turned the cruiser around and retraced the drive back to the old farmhouse.

"Dispatch, there's no accident here. Are you sure about the location?"

"Yes. No. I don't know, Jim."

"Dispatch, who called this in?"

A soft, confused voice came back across the radio. "Jim, I'm not sure. I didn't make a note. I don't remember."

"Jim look, there goes Roland now. He just passed us. That's his car!" shouted Katie." He's all right, he's not hurt."

"Dispatch, this must be some kind of a joke. Mr. Roberts just passed us in his car. I'm taking Mrs. Roberts back to her house." Jim paused. "Lola, are you OK? You don't sound as if you are."

"Yes, Jim. No. I don't know," came a frightened reply over the speaker.

"Lola, as soon as I drop Katie off, I'm coming to your twenty, 318 out." Jim shook his head and hung the mic on the radio. "This has been some day."

Katie was relieved to have seen Roland's car, with the beating yesterday, and now this, it was just about all the poor woman could take. She let out a heavy sigh as tears ran down her face. "This was such a wicked thing to do."

"Sick joke, Katie. This must be some kind of sick joke. I'm so sorry." Jim spoke softly as he headed back to Number 12. His lights were flashing and his siren screamed once again.

"Sick joke or a distraction," shouted Thor. It became quiet inside the car for a few moments, very quiet, until Thor broke the silence with one word. "Josh!"

Roland pulled into his drive and peered into his rearview mirror. "That's Jim," he said. He sat thinking for a second as the cruiser pulled into the drive behind him. "I'm sure I wasn't speeding." He watched in the rearview mirror and saw Katie and Thor getting out of the patrol car. "Josh," he said, getting out of his car.

Katie ran to Roland. She threw her arms around him and hugged her husband. "Someone said you had an accident and that you were hurt."

"Katie, this can wait. We need to check on Josh!" said Thor. "Roland's all right. Let's check on your son!" Thor headed across the soft green turf toward Miss Pat's house; he had taken only two steps when the door sprung open.

Miss Pat staggered out of her house and onto the porch; blood covered her face and was dripping down onto the front of her dress. One of her eyes was swollen shut, and she could just barely make out shadows with the other. She let out a moan and fell forward. She made a feeble attempt to grab one of the small columns on the porch but missed and tumbled head first off of the porch into the soft, green grass with a thud. Katie, Roland, and Thor rushed to the injured woman.

"Dispatch, 318. I need the EMT boys at the Millborn residence immediately." Jim was shouting orders into the radio's mic. He popped the trunk of his car, grabbed a first aid kit, and headed across the yard.

"Miss Pat, what happened?" said Katie. The injured woman lay still in her semi-unconscious state. With every raspy breath, she let out a small moan.

"Pat, Pat, what happened? What happened to you?" Katie gazed at the bloody woman and then a terrifying thought passed through her mind. "Pat, where's Josh?"

Katie rushed into the house. She saw the trail of blood left by Miss Pat. She screamed for her son, but there was no answer. She searched the house and couldn't find the small love of her life.

By the time Katie returned to the moaning woman, the paramedics had arrived. Jim directed them toward the bloody woman lying in the yard. Katie bent over the crumpled woman. "Miss Pat, where is Josh? Can you hear me?"

"A man came for him." Miss Pat moaned and passed out. The paramedics loaded her onto a cot, and minutes later, the ambulance pulled out of the drive and headed toward Edgefield.

"Olin," snapped Thor.

Katie screamed loudly, "Where's my son?" She looked at Roland and collapsed, but Roland was there for her. With one scooping motion, he lifted his wife up in his arms.

"Thor, search Miss Pat's house. See if you can find Josh. When you're finished, meet me in Number 12. We need to talk." Roland knew his son wasn't in the house. He knew what Miss Pat meant; he knew exactly who the man was. "Olin," he said softly.

"Olin? Who is Olin?" said Jim.

"No one, Jim. Sorry about that. I was just thinking out loud," said Roland.

"Roland, where's your son?"

"I don't know, Jim. As you know, I just got here. I'm not quite sure what's going on here. Let's get Katie in the house and maybe we can see what's happening." Roland watched Thor come out of the Millborn's home. He skipped two of the steps as he jumped into the yard and headed toward Roland. When his eyes met Roland's, he shook his head slightly.

Roland's eyes dropped toward Katie. He knew what Thor was telling him. He carried Katie into the house. He choked back the tears, realizing his son was missing, and knew without a doubt that his small son was now in the hands of a vicious warlock, a demon from the dark side of the world.

"Roland, take care of Katie, and see if you can make any sense of this. I'm going to check on Lola, and I'll be back in a few minutes. I'll have to drive to Edgefield and see if Pat can tell us anything about your son. Check everywhere, Roland. If you don't find him in the next fifteen minutes, we'll get the FBI involved and start a full-scale search of the neighborhood." Jim smiled a faint smile at Roland. "I don't know who's behind all of this, but I'm glad you're safe, Mr. Roberts. That was a mean trick for someone to play on Katie, calling in and telling all of us you were hurt, dying. Don't worry, Roland. We'll find out who's behind this, and we'll find your son!"

Roland thanked Jim and carried Katie into the house. Thor followed and shut the door to Number 12. No one spoke a word until Roland laid Katie on the couch.

"Roland, you know who's behind this, don't you?" said Thor.

"Where were you, Thor? You and Wisteria weren't supposed to leave Josh's side. Where's Wisteria?" Roland shouted. "Where is she?"

"I'm here, Roland. I met Jim in the drive. He told me what happened. Have you found Josh?" the old woman said, walking slowly into the den.

"My son was at the Millborns', someone attacked Miss Pat, and now Josh is missing," snapped Roland. "I thought you were going to stay with my family, Wisteria. Where were you?"

"I left Thor here, Roland. I thought—"

Roland interrupted the old woman. "Well you thought wrong!" His voice suddenly changed. He spoke softly, bewildered. "My son is missing, and I don't know where he is. He's gone." Roland slid into the overstuffed chair. He put his head into his hands and attempted to force the tears back, but the tears came anyway.

"Well, look who's balling like a baby!" mocked Olin. "What's the matter, Roland, missing something—or should I say some*one?*"

They all looked toward the living room just in time to see Olin walk out of the wall. Roland jumped to his feet and started toward the dark demon. Thor had already made the same move; he had plunged his hands beneath his shirt and was holding two daggers.

"Stop right there," shouted Olin, "or the child will die." Thor stopped and blocked Roland's advancement with his arm. He put the daggers away and grabbed Roland's arm as he was passing him. Both had made it to the double French doors between the den and the living room. They had stopped just short of where Olin was standing. "Now, back off and plant yourselves in the den. I've got something to say to you."

Roland started toward Olin again, and Thor restrained him. "Let's see what he has to say, Roland." The men backed up slowly, and neither took their eyes off the warlock. Thor slowly pushed Roland back toward the chair.

"Take a seat, Roland," he said.

Katie sat up and stared at Olin. "Where's my baby?" she said. "What have you done with him?"

"Your baby is fine, Katie, and if you want him to stay that way, all of you will do exactly as I say or—" Olin paused. A faint smile came over his face as he stood looking at the people in front of him. He savored the moment.

Sitting in front of him were his archenemies—well, at least the only surface people who had ever given him any trouble to speak of and survived—and now they were like puppets on strings, ready to obey his every command.

He stared at Wisteria. "You are undoubtedly the most powerful witch the dark side has ever known, and here you are, sitting powerless and helpless, obeying my every command. Doesn't that bother you, witch?" Wisteria sat quietly and didn't answer.

"Of course, let's not forget about you two, the two do-gooders. You are the only two surface people that I can remember that have ever given my brother or me a hard time and lived to tell about it. Both of you have been nothing but a thorn in our sides since your arrival in this forsaken town they call Johnston."

"You've shot me with those bows and shot both of us with your guns." Olin paused for a second, and his faint smile disappeared. "Wow, that must make you two feel really good. Does it? Come on. Does it make you feel really good?" Olin bent forward, waiting for an answer. No answer came as Katie and Roland sat quietly.

The smile came back to Olin's face. "Well, it's time for some payback."

He looked at Thor. "You are a traitor to the dark side, assassin, and you will be appropriately dealt with when the time is right."

Thor looked at Olin. "What's the matter with now, Olin?" Thor took a step toward the warlock. "Let's finish this between you and me. Come on. Let's do it now."

Olin paused. "Your time will come, assassin, but not now. I'll kill you, but that's not what I'm here to talk about, is it?" He looked at Katie, "Your son, that precious little boy of yours, is in my care and if you don't do exactly—and I mean exactly—what I tell you to do, I'll kill him." Olin flashed a quick but vicious smile toward Katie. He paused a little longer to savor the look on everyone's face. "Well, no. No, I won't kill him!"

He paused once again, and the smile vanished. "I'll give him to an evil witch I know; she really loves the taste of children's blood, especially the young ones. Yesssssss, yessssss, that's what I'll do." Olin raised his hands and shook them violently. He was mocking Odium, and his audience, and enjoying every moment of it. "Yesssssss, yessssss, that's what I'll do." The smile returned, and he dropped his hands.

"My brother was going to complete his transformation tonight, but someone has the cops combing our house and grounds. Now, I wonder who might have thought that up?" he said. "But, regardless, they'll be gone in a few days, and we will complete the ritual as planned, and if any one of you does anything to interfere with it again, your son will die—and I mean in a most agonizing way."

"And if we do as you say?" asked Katie. "Will you give my baby back to me?"

"Yes," said Olin calmly. "You have my word on it!"

"And can we trust your word?" asked Katie.

"No," said Olin, "but that's all you're getting!" The smile came back to the warlock's face; he bent forward slightly and spoke softly. "Of course I'll bring him back. What do I want with a little noisemaker like him? I have no need for him. Yes, I promise I'll return him to you!"

"If you hurt my son, Olin, I'll kill you, if I have to follow you to Hades," Roland said. He hadn't taken his eyes off the demon.

"And I'll help him, warlock," said Thor. He too hadn't taking his eyes off Olin. "And I've already been to Hades!"

Wisteria sat and she, as well, hadn't taken her eyes off the warlock. It was if she was studying him, contemplating some type of attack or movement. She was muttering as if talking to herself.

"Whatever," said Olin. "But let me tell you one thing right now; if any one of you as much as comes near our house, you'll never see that kid alive again. Do you understand me?"

Roland glanced at Katie; she was sobbing quietly and trying to wipe the tears away with her hands. He spoke softly. "You win, Olin. Just give me back my son, and I won't interfere with you or your brother again."

The smile on Olin's face had returned. "Now, that's what I wanted to hear, but it's still a little late for that." He stood erect and smiled at everyone. "Oh, one other thing. I don't care how you do it, but get those police officers out of our house and off of our grounds now, or I'll kill that brat of yours just for the fun of it." He laughed loudly. "Well, this certainly was a nice visit, maybe I—"

Before Olin could finish his sentence, Wisteria leaped to her feet so fast that no one actually saw her move. With a wave of her hand, a mighty force hit Olin. She muttered a few words, and another force knocked the warlock to the ground. He tried to disappear but could not.

"What's the matter, dear, lose your powers?" Wisteria asked. She stretched out her arms, and Olin was snatched to his feet in a violent manner. His head snapped backward and then violently forward. His hands tightened into huge fists. He dropped his eyes to see what was happening to them, and faster than a lightning bolt, his right fist struck him squarely in the mouth. A small trickle of blood rolled down Olin's lip to his chin and then dripped onto his cloak.

"Now, that won't do, dear," Wisteria said. With another wave of her hand, the left fist struck Olin in the same place as the right had, enlarging the cut. Olin staggered but couldn't fall, some mysterious force held him up. Now a large stream of blood flowed steadily down onto his cloak, and there was a large gash in his lip. Then, before Olin could blink, another right, then left, then right, then left. Olin's eyes started swelling; his lips were swollen and bleeding profusely. His nose poured a sticky red substance.

"Look at me, warlock," shouted Wisteria. Olin opened his eyes. He was weak, but Wisteria's magic wouldn't allow him to fall to the floor. Wisteria raised her hands and muttered more words. She shuddered all over and sent a flash of purple lightning toward the dazed and confused warlock. The force flung the demon back against the wall; he tried to speak but could not. He stared at the witch but knew nothing but a miracle could save him. He was paralyzed by the old witch's magic.

"Do you feel helpless and powerless, warlock? Well, do you?" Wisteria smiled at Olin. "Well, let's try this one." She placed her hands together and rolled them over until a gray mist emitted from them. She muttered more magic and flung her hands toward the demon. He stumbled back against the wall once more. The mist surrounded him, and he gasped for air, but none was to be had. His eyes rolled back into his head, and he tried to breathe, but the mist sucked out all breathable air.

"What's the matter, Olin?" Wisteria said. "Having a hard time catching your breath?" She waved her hands, and the mist vanished. Olin gasped for air. He looked at Wisteria and tried to speak, but once again, the words wouldn't come. He remained silent.

Katie, Roland, and Thor watched in amazement and shock as Wisteria worked her magic. Olin's dark, black hair had turned gray; so had his eyebrows and all other body hair that could be seen. He stood in the middle of the living room floor trembling. Wisteria smiled at her handiwork.

"Now, warlock, I'm going to remove your head with this." Wisteria's hand disappeared beneath her dress and when it reappeared, she stood there holding the gold snake's head dagger.

"Do you know what this is, Olin?" Wisteria said with a smile. "Yes, yes you do. I know you do, and I can see the fear in your eyes. I can taste it, just like the assassin, Morto. The air tasted the same way just before I killed him."

Wisteria walked slowly toward the trembling warlock. "Do you know what will happen if I let my little friend here bite you? She took the point of the dagger and slowly traced the outline of Olin's face. "One little bite and it's all over for you. Know what I mean, dear?"

Olin's eyes widened. He wanted to scream, but his voice continued to fail him. His lips were swollen twice their normal size, and the blood oozed from the wounds. He stared into the eyes of the old witch. He knew what had happened to Morto. He remembered that Wisteria had thrown his head over the gates of the mansion.

"Wisteria, please, stop," said Katie. "He knows where Josh is, and if you kill him, we may never find him."

Wisteria looked at the warlock. She knew he would never drop his guard like this again. He had come to Number 12 tonight full of pride and arrogance. He'd had the upper hand, holding all of the cards, and that was the biggest mistake he had ever made. He had dropped his guard, underestimated his opponents, and Wisteria had taken full advantage of the moment. She had cast her spells that temporarily blocked his powers. She knew that after tonight Olin would never let anyone strip him of his powers again. Just as she had the power to strip him of all his powers, he had the magic to prevent it.

Wisteria turned slowly and looked at Katie. She muttered a few words and spoke. "Don't worry, dear. He can't hear us now. Katie, tonight we caught Olin off guard. If I release him, he'll never let his guard down again, not like he did tonight. Let me kill this warlock. Please, dear!"

"He's the only one who knows where our son is," was all Katie managed to say. "He's the one who took him."

Wisteria knew better. She figured Josh was at Odium's house, but she couldn't be sure, and if she killed Olin tonight—and if she was wrong and Katie was right—they may never find him.

"She's right, Wisteria," Thor said. "I certainly would like to see you kill this miserable dog, but she's right." Thor looked at Katie and then at Roland.

"I don't like telling you this, and I know it's not the time, but you've got to realize that Olin will never give your son back to you. You need to realize that." Thor said, pausing for a moment. "We will have to take him, one way or the other. We will have to find Josh and take him. That much I know."

Katie broke down once more. "He said he would give Josh back to us. He promised."

"Katie, dear, this is a warlock, a demon of the worse magnitude. Thor is right; he'll never let you have your son back. He would keep him just to get even with us. We'll have to find him ourselves. So I'm going to kill him." Wisteria turned toward Olin and raised the gold dagger high into the air. The snake's eyes glowed bright red, and its body moved slowly around Wisteria's hand.

"No, Wisteria, please don't," shouted Katie. Roland rose from the chair and walked toward his wife. Katie rose to meet him. "Roland, please. Not now. Not until we find Josh. You heard him. They'll kill our son."

"Wisteria, let him go," said Roland. "I'm not asking."

Wisteria looked at both of them. She knew of their feelings—the pain, the hurt, and the hope. "Oh, the hope!" she said softly. Her mind recalled a similar situation many years ago. She had made the mistake of letting a demon live, a demon named Creed, and now Katie and Roland were making the same mistake with his brother.

*Ironic how things come full circle,* she thought. The same mistake, so many years ago, had cost her dearly, more than anyone would ever know, and she didn't want Katie and Roland to ever feel that kind of pain. Her mistake to let a demon live had cost her the life of her sister, Magnolia, and it had cost her Magnolia's spirit, as well. One thing that a good witch feared more than anything else was that the dark side would collect or capture her spirit when she died, and keep it for evil.

Wisteria, holding the dagger, dropped her hand to her side. She looked at the demon standing in front of her and muttered a few words. All assumed she was going to let him live. Katie signed slightly. Then with a mighty effort and quick as a flash, Wisteria grunted loudly and raised the dagger high into the air. She brought the dagger down with all of her might, and the dagger, finding its mark, struck Olin. It struck him squarely between the eyes, and he collapsed to the floor.

Wisteria, looking down at the demon, shook her head slightly. "If only I hadn't turned the knife around," she said. She muttered a few words, and Olin vanished.

Wisteria had indeed turned the knife around, and instead of the sharp point hitting Olin between the eyes, it was the other end, the blunt end of the handle. The snake's eyes glowed brightly and then slowly diminished and went dark.

"Probably a big mistake, but it's done. He'll wake up shortly and remember everything vividly, and I wouldn't have it any other way." Wisteria laughed slightly. "At least he'll be alive."

*** 

Odium sat staring at the small boy lying on her couch. Her mind wandered back to the small girls she had killed; she had tasted their blood and now craved the taste even more. She wondered if a young boy's blood would taste the same. "Yessssss, yessssss, so sweet. It tastes so sweet."

She walked toward the couch, making sure, she made no noise, but the spell Olin had cast on the small boy was strong, and Josh slept soundly. She paused for a moment and stared at his soft, white skin. She knelt down and picked up Josh's arm. "Just a little taste," she said. "Yessssss, yessssss, just a little taste!"

The door of Odium's house burst open, and the gray-haired warlock staggered into the witch's house. He stared at the witch, seating himself in an old chair. "Get away from him, and put that knife down. Get me some hot water," he said, "and a cloth, preferably a clean one."

"Yes, Master, yes!" Odium dropped the small arm of her prey and looked at Olin. She wanted to ask what had happened to him but knew better. Whatever Olin had tangled with—she laughed slightly—certainly won the battle. She went into the kitchen, fetched a hot towel for Olin, and walked slowly over to where he was sitting. She looked at what used to be dark-black hair. She handed Olin the towel and slowly backed away. "Yessssss, yessssss, are you all right, Master?"

"Fine, just fine," shouted Olin. "Did you get the bloody spirits?"

"No, Master. Yessssss, yessssss, it seems we have a problem, Master!" said the witch.

Olin had placed the hot cloth over his face. "Why should I not be surprised?" He moaned softly, sat quietly for a moment, and then spoke tenderly. "I thought you said you had that covered?"

"Yessssss, yessssss, Master, I did, or at least I thought I did. It appears that Master Umberto has made some kind of pact with the spirits, and they say they will only obey him." Odium paused for a second and then told Olin all about her afternoon and how the spirits wouldn't leave the tree unless Master Umberto commanded them to do so. Olin sat without making a sound and listened to the old witch's story.

"Fine, that's fine for now. We can deal with that. I still have their master. I guess he'll be useful after all." Olin pushed his head back deeper in the chair and sat quietly.

"Do you need anything else, Master Olin?" asked Odium.

"No, not at the moment. Just let me know if company comes, and stay away from the kid!" Olin said. He pressed the cloth against his face. "Get me another one of these!"

# Twenty-One

## A Different Story

There was an intense conversation taking place at Number 12. Katie and Roland were distraught, to say the least. The kidnapping, of course, had taken its toll on them. Wisteria had mixed a potion to help them cope with the disappearance, and after they'd consumed it, Katie and Roland were less tense.

"What now, Wisteria?" said Roland.

"We get Josh back, Roland, and quickly."

"What do we need to do?" Roland asked.

"Well," said Wisteria, "Josh can only be one of two places, Terra Demorte or at a dark witch's house, a witch by the name of Odium. She lives close by."

"Wisteria, there is no way Creed and Olin would take a human to Terra Demorte, no way," said Thor. "Absolutely no way. Our laws won't allow that, even for a warlock. That's serious business."

"It's only serious business if they get caught. Creed and Olin don't care, Thor. Josh is one of two places. I'm going to Odium's house to see if he's there. I'll be back soon. Thor, keep an eye on this place. Stay sharp. Roland, get your guns and be ready for anything."

Wisteria stood up, and as she did, there was a knock on the front door; she walked slowly toward the door. "I'll get it," said the witch.

"Hi, Wisteria. May I come in?" It was Officer Jim. He was shaking, and his eyes were red as if he had been crying. "I need to talk to the Robertses."

"Jim, is everything all right. Are you all right?"

"No, Wisteria. No, I'm not all right. Where is Mr. Roberts?"

"Here, Jim. I'm right here," said Roland. He stood up to meet the officer. "How can I help you, Jim? It's not a good time for me right now, but what can I do for you?"

"Well, Roland, it's not a good time for me either, but I need to know what's going on here. Where is your son? Did you find him?" Jim was still shaking; he looked around the room and wobbled over to the sofa. "Where's your son? Tell me what is going on."

"Jim, you're shaking. Please sit down," said Wisteria.

"Wisteria!" snapped Jim. "For the love of all that's holy, what is happening with you folks? Who is so mad at you all that they would kidnap the Robertses' son?"

Wisteria slid her hand into her pocket. When she pulled it from her dress, she had a small white ball neatly tucked away in her palm. She rubbed her hands together, and the small ball turned to powder.

"Wisteria, don't even try to blow that powder into my face and think it will work. I need to know what's going on with Mr. Roberts, and I need to know now!"

"How do you know about this powder?" Wisteria questioned. "When it's used it erases the memory of it from your mind."

"Not on me, Wisteria, not on me. This is the last time I'm going to ask you. What's going on?"

The radio made a loud beep, and Lola's voice came in loud and clear. "Base to 318. Jim, come in."

Jim shot to his feet. "Stop it, Wisteria. Quit this foolishness and tell me what's going on. Stop trying to use your magic to get rid of me. That's not Lola. Lola's dead! Someone killed her over an hour ago, and whoever did it sounded just like her when I called for help for Miss Pat." Jim sat back down on the sofa.

"What did you say, Jim?"

"I said Lola is dead. She was beaten and then torn to pieces. Blood was everywhere. Whoever did it must have realized that she was a—"Jim stopped.

"A what, Jim?" Wisteria rose slowly. "A what, Jim?"

"Different is all, Wisteria—just like me, just different. Now, she is dead, and I need to know if her death is linked to Mr. Roberts's son being kidnapped."

Wisteria straightened her dress. She looked at Jim and softly replied. "Yes, Jim, we know who took Roland's son, and I suspect he is the one who killed Lola. He's a warlock from the dark side of the world, an evil and dangerous demon."

"The same one that lives in the mansion we raided today?"

"Yes, dear, the one and the same," said Wisteria. Thor, Roland, and Katie sat staring at Officer Jim.

"I felt the same presence at the station as I did in that old house; I knew it was the same evil."

"Is that what you meant when you said Lola was different?" Wisteria asked.

"Yeah, both of us—we feel things, know things. I can't explain all of it, but I know that most of your little potions and spells don't work on me, but I went along with the powder in the face thing just to not give myself and Lola away. Now she's dead, and I mean to kill the person that did that to her. It doesn't matter what it takes. I'll find that demon and kill him, but first, let me help you get your son back, Mr. Roberts. Let me help you save your son. What are your plans?"

"Jim, are you offering to help us? You do know we can't report Roland's son as being kidnapped? We have to do this ourselves, no police, just us. Do you understand that?" Wisteria looked inquisitively at Jim.

"What I'm going to do to that demon is outside of the law, so yes, I understand. Let me help you. You are in charge. I'll do it your way, but let me help. What is your plan?"

Wisteria looked around the room. Thor was on the edge of the sofa staring at Jim. Roland and Katie looked at Jim and then at Wisteria.

"Why not? We can use the help," said Roland. "I'll tell you, Jim, I've always liked you, but this is my son we are talking about here. I'm sorry about Lola, but there's nothing we can do for her now, but we can save my son. I don't mean to sound uncaring, but I want my son back—alive. So if you want to help, you have to follow instructions and do exactly as we say. Understand?"

"Understand, Roland. I understand. Let's save your son, and afterward, I'll kill that warlock for you." Jim sat back on the sofa, and a faint smile came across his face. "I'll kill that demon and his brother, as well."

"How did you know about his brother?" shouted Wisteria, rising to her feet. She raised her hand and was ready to strike.

"Whoa, Wisteria. Yes, I know of his brother. I felt his presence, as well, in that old mansion. There are two of them, both evil and both up to no good. So where do you think Mr. Roberts's son is?"

"In one of two places," said Roland. "Wisteria thinks he is either in Terra Demorte or at an old witch's house, a witch by the name of Odium."

"Roland, quiet," scolded Wisteria. She rose from her chair again, and as she lifted her hands, Jim disappeared into the sofa.

"What the—" shouted Roland. "Wisteria, what happened? What happened to Jim?"

Wisteria muttered a few words and sat back down. That wasn't Officer Jim. I don't know who or what he was or even if he was a he, but…how could I have been so blind?"

"A spy for Creed, my guess," said Thor.

"Yes, of course, exactly. I've got to move fast if Josh is at Odium's, but I'm guessing that if he was, he's gone now. I'll be back shortly; in the meantime…don't let anyone in, even if you know them."

Wisteria turned to leave when a blast of warm air struck her with a mighty force. As suddenly as it struck her, it turned into a glowing green ball and vanished into the stairwell. Everything and everybody went quiet; no one moved. Wisteria was the only one who had felt the hot blast of air, but all saw the glowing green ball.

"Wisteria, what's wrong? What is it?" asked Thor. He had risen and had daggers in hand, waiting for something.

"Can't be. This can't be happening—" Before Wisteria had a chance to finish the sentence, a voice spoke.

"Sure it can, and it's happening."

Everyone looked around the room; there was no other person in the room. They all gawked in wonder as to whose voice they heard. The glowing green ball floated through the stairwell door. It hovered across from where Wisteria was standing, and then slowly materialized into a shape.

They all watched as the shape took form, standing there in his ghostly form, was Notor.

"Hi, Wisteria. It's good to see you." He slowly walked over to Katie. "It's good to see you, Mrs. Roberts. I'm sorry to hear about your son."

Wisteria, still in shock, finally spoke. "Notor, what on earth are you doing here?" Roland, Katie, and Thor just stood there with their mouths open and their eyes as wide as if they had seen a ghost. In actuality, they were looking at one.

"I'm here to help Mr. and Mrs. Roberts get their son back."

"You help?" Wisteria was gasping for air. "How on earth did you return here? Who sent you?"

"It doesn't matter who sent us, Wisteria." This time the voice wasn't that of Notor, but another familiar voice. It was that of Horace Wheeler. His form then appeared next to Notor's.

"Horace, what on earth are you doing back here? What's going on?"

"Wisteria, please, have a seat. Let me explain. Notor wanted to soar through the old house one more time before we showed ourselves,"

Horace said. He chuckled slightly. Everyone sat staring at the two ghosts standing in the den. Wisteria, acting like a kid in school, did as Horace had instructed her to do and took a seat. Thor followed suit. Katie and Roland had already taken their seats, and all stared intently at the two new visitors.

"What are you two doing here?" asked Wisteria. "How on earth did you return?"

"We heard about Katie and Roland's son, and know who kidnapped him, but we have no idea where he is. Notor and I volunteered to come back to help. We were told that this was impossible, but we begged and pleaded. They warned us that once we came back, we might not be able to return...ever. Both of us agreed that no matter what the cost, we wanted to help, so by the grace of all that is holy, here we are."

Roland looked at Notor and Horace; a small smile crept across his face. "You two came back to help us?"

"Yes, Roland. You have given and done so much for us, we couldn't let this happen to you without offering our help and assistance." Notor paused. "We are here to do whatever it takes to get your son back."

"Well," said Wisteria, "quite a pair you two make, but nonetheless, you just might come in handy, but I still would like to know how in blue blazes you managed to cross back over."

"I was told you might ask that very question, Wisteria. Here is your answer: where there is love, there is hope; where there is hope, there is faith; and where there is faith, there will I be also."

Katie looked at Notor and at Horace. "Thank you for offering your help and returning to help us. Thank you so much."

Wisteria stood up. "All of you can talk. I'll be back in a little while. I need to go see an old dark witch."

"Odium," said Notor.

"Exactly, Notor."

"Do you think she is the one that kidnapped Roland's son?"

"No, Olin kidnapped Josh, but I hope she is hiding him."

# Twenty-Two

## The Hiding Place

Roy flung the doors of the pub open; they bounced off the walls with a crash and then shivered as if they were cold. Roy stepped aside and allowed Creed and Ray to enter. Jake was behind the counter wiping down the bar...again. Roy carried two large bags, and Ray had two, as well. Creed walked tall and upright. His cloak covered his body. He walked defiantly to the table in the back corner. He was furious.

"Take my bags to my room, Roy," Creed commanded. "Olin's as well. Get us three rooms, and make it quick."

Roy stopped in front of the bar. "Give me three rooms for my master, Jake, and make it quick."

"Sure."

"Jake." It was Creed speaking. "I want all three rooms adjoining— our usual rooms, plus one more."

"Sure, Master Creed. Glad to have you back."

"Roy, you and Ray square our luggage away and come back down here as soon as possible," Creed said. He motioned for Roy, and as Roy moved closer, Creed whispered into his ear, "I need for you to stay by my side until Olin gets here, so make it quick and get back down here."

"Yes, Master," said Roy.

"Good to see you, Master Creed. Where's your brother, Olin?" Jake said, making small talk.

"If you have to know, Jake, he's on his way. He'll be here shortly," Creed said with great effort. He remembered that Jake was there the night they took the gold box from Drako and didn't know if he was trustworthy.

Jake could hear his wheezing from where he stood. He realized that Creed wasn't as healthy as he had been the last time he was there.

"He'll probably be glad to see you, Jake," Creed managed to get the words out, but they were harsh and scratchy.

Jake broke out in a sweat; the memories of the gold box flooded his thoughts. He wiped at the bar and replied, "Yeah, it'll be good to see him too."

*** 

Creed and his two demon guardians sat at the table. They had been there for hours when Olin came through the door. He looked tired. His long hair hung loose around his neck, and small drops of blood dripped from his nose. He attempted to wipe the blood away, but with every wipe, more oozed from his nose and dripped onto his cloak. His eyes were swollen from the fight, and his face was battered and bruised. He carried a large bag and quickly headed to the table where his brother was sitting.

"What happened to you, Master Olin?" Roy asked.

"Not now, Roy. Take this bag to my room. Do it and be quick about it."

Roy stood up and grabbed the bag; he headed up the stairs. Within minutes, he returned to the table. He raised his hand and ordered ale for the table.

"Olin, what happened to you? Was this Wisteria's doing?" Creed asked. As Olin answered, Jake started setting the ale on the table.

"Here you are gents." Jake smiled and slowly started his trek back to the bar. He strained to hear the conversation, but all he heard was that Wisteria had indeed beaten the warlock. He smiled a little but only for a brief moment, then grabbed a rag and started cleaning the bar.

\*\*\*

Wisteria stood outside of Odium's house wondering how she was going to do this. She knew Odium quite well, knew she was most evil and—above all—dangerous, very dangerous. Wisteria was most powerful in her own home, and she knew Odium would be more powerful in hers.

"How am I going to do this?" she said again.

"Let me," said a voice from behind her. "Let me do the snooping, Wisteria." It was Notor.

"What are you doing here?" Wisteria scolded. "I told you to stay put."

"I know, but I thought you might need a little help getting inside without a fight." Notor smiled. "I can help...watch." Notor walked to the front door and, as hard as he could, knocked on the door.

"Who's there?" said a voice from inside the house.

"Me, Notor. I've come to speak to Master Olin."

"Notor? Creed's little Notor? His little spike?"

"Yes, that would be me, witch."

The door sprang open, and there stood the old witch staring at him. "Well, at least you had the good sense to come before me in your ghostly form. If you had not, I would have—well, never mind. Come in Notor." The witch stared into the darkness and quickly closed the door behind Notor.

She knew of this little spike. She also knew she had nothing to fear from Notor, so she wobbled over to a chair and sat back down.

"Well, what is it that you want?" she asked.

"I have come to speak with Master Olin, but I don't see him any-where. I thought he was supposed to be here."

"Who told you that?" said Odium calmly. She sat staring at Notor. She didn't blink, nor did she move. She just sat there looking at the ghost with her cold, dark eyes.

"Roy, the demon guardian, sent me to deliver a message to Master Olin." Roy was the first name Notor could think of, and as usual, he blurted out the first thought that crossed his mind.

"Well, go back and tell your demon guardian that Master Olin has left for Terra Demorte, along with that small boy." Odium grabbed her own mouth, as if she shouldn't have said that. "Well, doesn't matter. Since Creed owns you, I guess you know about the boy?"

"Sure," said Notor. "The Robertses' little boy. Sure, I know about him."

Odium stared at Notor. "Well, is there anything else?"

"No, witch. I guess not."

Then, as if something strange had come over her, Odium smiled at the spike. "Notor, do you like your master?"

Notor looked at Odium, and for the first time in his life, he didn't speak the first thought that came across his mind. His reply was that of a question. "Why do you ask, witch?"

"Well, I'm a dark witch, and I have a lot of power and magic. I realize that a spike like you has no magical powers and is normally used as a spy or messenger. I was just wondering if you and I could make a deal of some...kind." Odium took a few seconds to finish the sentence with *kind*.

"What *kind* of deal?" asked Notor. He stared at the old witch. He knew, that at any moment she could totally annihilate him, so he just sat there and went along with her. "What kind of deal?"

"Well, yessssss, yessssss, a good deal for you, Notor, yessssss, yessssss."

Notor stared at the old witch. All of a sudden, she was stuttering. Until now in the conversation, she had not, and he wondered why now. However, only Odium knew why, when she stuttered, it was only because she wanted to; it was a way for her to annoy one.

"Yessssss, yesssssss, you and I can make a good little deal together, and I'll give you anything you want, even killing powers." Odium smiled at the frail little man. "Yessssss, yessssss, what do you say, Notor?"

"What do I have to do in return, witch?"

Odium stared at the ghost and then spoke very precisely. "This has got to be between you and me, Notor. Do you understand? If you tell anyone else, I'll dispatch you. I may even sell you to the troll clan." It was rumored in Terra Demorte that all spikes that walked the surface of the earth were afraid of many things but that their worst fear was being sold to the troll clan for the purpose of servitude.

"Yes, I understand. What is it you want from me?"

"I want you to spy on Creed and Olin for me. Just let me know what they're doing and what they're up to. If you do this for me, I'll do a lot for you...agreed?"

Notor had gotten the information he had come for. He knew that Olin had left for Terra Demorte and had taken Josh with him; all he wanted to do now was to get away from the foul, evil being that sat in front of him.

"Agreed," said Notor. "I agree, but I want my killing powers." He knew if he didn't barter for something, she would know there was a difference in him. "I want my killing powers."

Odium sat up in her chair. She looked at the ghost sitting in front of her. "I knew that was what you wanted. You bring me some good news and keep me informed; I'll give you the power and magic to kill. I promise you, Notor."

"Agreed," said Notor. He stood up to leave, and Odium spoke once more.

"Remember, Notor, this is our little secret." The old woman shook violently, and in a second, she shape-shifted into a monster, something that resembled a wolf but was much bigger. Then she shook violently once more, and as suddenly as she had transformed, there sitting in front of Notor, once again, was the old witch.

"If you disappoint me, Notor, the monster inside of me will tear you to pieces."

"Yes, of course," said Notor. "I'll keep my ears and eyes open, and as soon as I hear anything, I'll come straight to you." Notor knew that the monster he had just seen couldn't tear him to pieces. He knew that Odium's shape-shifting performance was for show and nothing more. However, he also knew that she could trap him, take him to Terra Demorte, and trade him to the troll clan, and that, at one time, had been his worst fear.

Odium was happy; she now had a spy of her own. She knew Notor wouldn't let her down. She also knew he would be too afraid to lie to her. Notor smiled and headed for the door. He turned the knob and didn't look back. The old witch smiled. "Lights off," she said. The old house went dark.

Wisteria was waiting for Notor and as they walked back to Number 12, Notor told Wisteria all about the conversation between him and Odium.

"Well, dear, you did all right tonight," Wisteria told him. The conversation continued as Notor questioned Wisteria about the kidnapping and about Creed, Olin, the old mansion, and Josh. It was as if he couldn't get enough information. She felt a difference in Notor; he seemed sharper and smarter than before. Although one wouldn't have to be very sharp to be smarter than the old Notor. She chuckled as she walked beside him.

\*\*\*

Olin walked up the stairs toward his room. His gray hair was combed back, and he had slipped a leather band on it. His ponytail danced with each step he took. He had tried to turn his hair back to the jet-black color it had been, but with each attempt, his hair turned a whiter, lighter shade of gray. It was now streaked with long strands of white hair. He cursed it as he passed a mirror on the wall.

He entered his room and opened the bag sitting on his bed. He stared at the contents, quickly grabbing the bag, he flipped it over, and Josh rolled out on the bed. The small boy was in a trance, a spell that Olin had cast upon him before bringing him to Terra Demorte. He knew if anyone found the boy, it would be certain death to him and his brother.

"The trance will keep you quiet, and after my brother's transformation, I'll kill you and dump you in the pit. No one will be the wiser." He threw the bag under the bed and headed down to join his brother.

He and Creed had decided not to mention the gold box, as only Jake, Morto, and the demon guardian, Drako, knew about its existence. Olin and Creed figured that if Jake and Morto were in on trying to capture Olin in the box, they would think that he hadn't yet tried to use its magic.

Olin sat staring at his brother. He, Roy, and Ray all drank numerous pints of ale, talking softly and making plans to finish Creed's transformation.

Creed sat silently and listened. He knew for once that he and Olin had the upper hand. Creed felt something now that he hadn't felt since he'd started his transformation; for the first time, Creed felt happiness. He also knew if anyone found out that, they had brought a human to Terra Demorte, even a child…"Well, no one must know or find out," he said softly. "The consequences would be devastating."

# Twenty-Three

## Plans

Roland, Katie, Horace, and Thor sat listening to Wisteria and Notor. When Wisteria told them that Olin had taken Josh to Terra Demorte, Thor instantly jumped to his feet.

"What in the Hades are they thinking?"

"What do you mean, Thor?" said Roland.

"I've told you, Roland. No human is allowed in Terra Demorte. If any of the ten clans finds him there, it's over for all of you. They will totally wipe out your bloodline—every man, woman, and child. It's our law. As it's written, so shall it be, and every clan has sworn to this in blood."

"What will happen to Creed and Olin if Josh is found in Terra Demorte, Thor?"

Wisteria pointed to the sofa. "Please sit down, you're making me nervous. Let's think about this and come up with a plan. Every minute that passes is very valuable and is one more minute that Josh is stuck in that horrible place. No offense, Thor."

"None taken. It would be the Keeping Room for both Olin and Creed, and you are right—we need to get Josh out of there, and I mean quick. Olin's probably got him in a trance; this is good as it will keep him quiet and, for the moment, safe." Thor was pacing again, thinking… thinking like an assassin from Terra Demorte.

"Do you know where they're hiding him, Thor?" Wisteria pointed to the sofa again. "Please sit, Thor."

"Of course I do. They'll hide him at Jake's Place, a local pub with lots and lots of rooms, and I mean lots. A very private and secure place. They can hide him in one of the rooms upstairs, sit downstairs, and watch everyone that comes and goes. This might be good for us, as they don't know that we know where they've taken him.

"Thanks to Notor, we do. This gives us valuable time. Now all we have to do is figure out a way to get him." Thor sat down. He looked worried. "But that…may be our biggest problem."

"What do you mean, Thor?" said Roland.

"I'm the only one here that can go to Terra Demorte, and since I've taken up with Wisteria, I'm not welcome there and would be thrown in the Keeping Room if I showed up. That's the reason they took him to Terra Demorte. They know none of us can touch him there. Even if we found out where he was, none of us can go there. Good planning on their behalf."

"What would you have to do to get back into the good graces at Terra Demorte?" asked Wisteria.

"I don't know, Wisteria. I'm not exactly totally exiled from Terra Demorte. I must tell you something. I tried to tell Roland when we went to kill Creed and Olin, but the timing wasn't right. I'm not sure it's right now, but I need to say this."

"Say what, Thor?" asked Katie. Roland watched the assassin. He knew that, no matter what Thor was about to say, he was a friend and would stand by him and Katie until they got Josh back. This, he knew, and would bet his life on.

Thor looked at Katie and then, like a viper watching its prey, slowly slid his eyes toward Roland. Thor had never known friendship outside of the assassin clan, and Terra Demorte, and he knew now—at this very minute—he had to make a decision and choose between friendship and loyalty to his clan. Little did Roland know that friendship and loyalty were two different things to an assassin. Thor was an assassin and loyal to the assassin clan; it was bred into him, engrained into his being.

"I was sent to the surface by the council—not by all ten clans, but only a few. Sent here to see what Creed and Olin were doing and, if possible, to kill both of them. You see, the council has a spy in Creed's mansion, and our spy tells us that once he completes his transformation, Creed plans to rule Terra Demorte and all of the ten clans. He also plans to bring everything that is evil to this small town, and then like a cancer, he plans to conquer and take over the lots of the other masters, spreading evil as far as he can. Normally, we don't care what a master does on the surface, but Creed plans to rule the ten clans of Terra Demorte, and that just won't do."

"So you didn't come for Morto's medallion when you came to my house?" said Wisteria. She stared at the assassin.

"Well, yes and no. I came for the medallion and thought if I could kill you, I could take your head to Creed, and he would welcome me into his house. There I could kill him and Olin, but as luck would have it, you bested me and I had no choice but to throw in with you. If you had killed me, I wasn't so sure you would have thrown my head over Creed's gates, as you did Morto's. If you'd kept my head, I couldn't have returned to Terra Demorte, and my body would be in the Keeping Room.

"Once I made a pact with you, I met Katie and Roland, and then all of you slowly changed my life. At first, I was just using you, thinking that I would find a way to dispatch you, and then gain Creed and Olin's confidence. Then I would carry out my orders to dispatch both of them. However, the more I became involved with all of you, the more I realized that I was wrong in my thinking and the more I knew I had to kill Creed and Olin in some other fashion."

"So now what?" asked Wisteria.

"Now it will be hard for me to go back to Terra Demorte. The only ones who will welcome me are the council members, and only some of them. I'm an outlaw, an outcast. I don't know how I can go back and have any respect. The minute I'm seen, I'll be thrown into the Keeping Room, and for how long, I have no idea. Hundreds of years, I suppose."

"How could they throw you in the Keeping Room, Thor?" asked Notor. He knew about the keeping room, a dark place where they kept spirits until they were sold, bartered, or traded for something. It was a bank of sorts, where masters locked away spirits for punishment or for later use.

It was a place assassins would go if separated from their heads, a place where their bodies would lie dormant until their heads were returned—sometimes forever, if a good witch killed one of them and put his head in a container on the surface. His body would return to Terra Demorte, but his head never would.

"How? Easy. Once they saw me, they would separate my head from my body and keep it that way until a decision was made as to what they were to do with me." Thor looked worried. "I have to go back. If anyone here is to save Josh, it has to be me. I'll just have to take the chance that no one will see me until I find your son, and then I'll have to get him out of there without being seen or caught." At this very moment, Thor realized he was an assassin, and an assassin he would always be. Loyalty over friendship.

"I'm going too," said Roland.

"Me too," said Katie.

"You can't go; it would mean sudden death for both of you and for Josh. No, I'm the only one here that can go, and I don't see how I'm going to do it. Besides, you need a medallion to enter the portal, and none of you have one."

"I have Morto's medallion," said Wisteria. She knew something was up with Thor. She had seen the worry on his face for days, and now something worried her about the assassin from Terra Demorte.

"I know," said Thor. "I'll need that as a bargaining chip if I get caught in Terra Demorte."

"Will that help you, Thor? Will taking Morto's medallion get you off the hook if you get caught?" Katie said.

"No, not even close, but I have no choice. That's all we got."

"Maybe we all would have been better off if you had killed me, Thor." Wisteria said. "This is my fault, my entire fault. Bringing all of you into this, it's my fault," Wisteria said. She knew this wasn't true. She knew that fate brought Katie and Roland to Johnston, but she wanted to see how Thor reacted to that statement. She sat watching Thor's expression; she wanted some kind of assurance that the assassin sitting across from her was still an ally. To her relief, the assurance came.

Thor laughed slightly. "You did what you had to do, Wisteria. No one's blaming you. If we had to do it all over again, I'm sure Katie and Roland would have done the same thing."

"We did the right thing, Wisteria, but right now, we need to come up with a plan to get my son back." Roland smiled at the old witch, but the smile faded quickly. "It's OK. We all did the right thing, but now it has backfired on us, and we need to change our course of action."

Notor sat up in his chair. His mind was spinning, sending thought after thought into his cluttered mind. He shook his head and spoke. "I have an idea."

Thor, Wisteria, Katie, Roland, and Horace turned toward Notor. "Well, dear, let's hear it. We need some kind of plan, and we need it now. Time is very valuable," Wisteria said, looking at Notor. "What is it, dear?"

For once, since his life after death, Notor felt very important. Everyone wanted to hear what he had to say, and for once, he felt he was part of something big, but as usual, he opened his mouth and out rolled his thoughts.

Thor listened to Notor's plan. Foolish little spike, he thought. "Does he ever listen to what rolls out of his mouth?" he whispered. Wisteria glanced at Thor; again, she studied the assassin and then slowly turned her attention back to Notor's plan.

Listening to Notor's plan, the assassin had an epiphany. Notor's plan would work well and right into his plan, a plan he wouldn't share. "Very well," he said softly.

Time was running out for Thor. He wanted to help Katie and Roland; he wanted to get Josh out of Jake's place. He had taken a liking to the little boy, but he had a contract on the surface that needed filling, and as an assassin, he would fulfill it. He sat and wondered how things had gotten so messed up.

Why had he allowed himself to be consumed by friendship with Wisteria and the Robertses? He knew better than to let something like that happen. Maybe it was because he hated Creed and Olin so much. He knew Olin was vicious, and the more he was around him and his brother; the more he hated them. Beating a young woman and her baby boy was something that even an assassin couldn't stomach. Killing them was one thing—that he could do quickly and painlessly—but beating them? That was different altogether.

Thor snapped back to reality. He had his own plans now, and with all that was going on, sacrifices would have to be made, and tonight, he needed to think like an assassin and figure out a way to fulfill his contract and do what he did best…and that was to kill.

# Twenty-Four

## The Double Cross

The night birds chirped and the crickets sang as Thor, Roland, Wisteria, and Notor walked down the street. The night air was cool, and the dew had started to fall, giving the flowers their nightly drink. The sky was dark and resembled a huge lake with tiny lights dancing everywhere. The clouds were thin and looked like small, white ripples in a lake when something was disturbing the water.

Horace had stayed at Number 12 with Katie, and both wondered if the unlikely foursome could carry out Notor's plan. Little did they know that there were multiple plans waiting to be unfolded this night.

The witch's house was dark. There were no lights to break the darkness. Nothing sang around her house—no night birds, no crickets. All was quiet, deathly quiet. For once in his life, Roland could feel unadulterated evil, and although nothing was stirring, he could feel the evil surrounding him. It encroached on his space, trying to engulf everything in its path.

"What now?" asked Roland.

"Notor, you know what to do. Go ahead. Do it. Do it now." Thor spoke softly. "It's up to you…be brave. We will go back up the street and wait. We don't want to be too close to this witch's house."

Wisteria shot a quick glance at Thor. This wasn't part of the initial plan. Thor was changing it, but, nonetheless, they all moved back up the road and disappeared into the darkness.

Notor was frightened, but even so, he made his move on the evil witch's house. He wondered if could fool the old witch. Even if he did, he wondered if he could pull this off. "Well," he said softly, "I've got to try."

He stood on the porch and stared at the crooked door. A soft voice broke the silence. "Come on in, Notor. Come inside."

Notor opened the door; a small light flickered in the fireplace as he walked toward the witch. The light cast shadows in the room, and everything seemed to be alive, dancing and moving as if watching him. He shuffled toward the figure sitting on the couch.

"What do you want, Notor?" Odium whispered in a low voice. She knew that the only thing that would bring this spirit to her door at this time of night was news—something Notor had heard that he deemed was so important that he would risk coming back before her.

She also knew that Notor was afraid of her, and indeed, if he had some news for her, she knew she wouldn't give him anything for it—no powers. Just a quick trip to Terra Demorte and then deposit him in the Keeping Room. Creed would miss his little spike but would have no idea as to his whereabouts. She smiled, watching the spike slowly advancing. "Ah," she said under her breath, "he'll bring a pretty price from the troll clan." The smile slowly turned into a hideous grin.

"I've got some news for you, witch."

"Yes, Notor. What is it?"

"Give me my killing powers and I'll tell you." Notor had to be cautious. If he overplayed his hand and tipped the old witch off, she would surely strike him down. He smiled curiously.

"What, spike? You want to bargain with me? We had a deal. Tell me the news, and if it's good enough, we'll see about your wants." Odium snapped at the frail little man. She knew he was afraid of her and had good reasons to be. "Or I can just take you to the trolls."

She snapped again at Notor. This time she pointed one of her fingers at him, and for an instant, the witch reminded Notor of his old master, Creed—his old master, who always pointed his finger at him. His mind went spinning out of control as the thought flooded his mind.

There, sitting in front of him was Creed, not Odium. It was Creed, sitting behind his dusty old desk, shouting at him and pointing his finger, threatening him, and the thought ran through his mind repeatedly.

"Well," shouted Odium. "Well, what is it you want to tell me?" Odium was getting impatient with Notor, and it was evident. "Don't just stand there. Speak."

Notor's mind came to a screeching halt; his thoughts of Creed vanished. He looked at the witch and softly spoke. His confidence was gone, and he was scared. "You promised me…" The rest of the words wouldn't come. He was blowing whatever plan he had, and nothing could be done about it.

"I promised you nothing, spike. Tell me or I'll dispatch you." Odium's eyes flashed, and as suddenly as she had spoken the words, her eyes glowed. They looked like a wolf's eyes, watching his every move. They were a deep yellow, and as he stared at them, the pupils dilated and became larger.

Notor had never seen anything like this; he panicked and fell to his knees. His mind was spinning. He opened his mouth to speak, but the words became a jumbled mess in his mind. They wouldn't come forth from his mouth. Only his mixed up thoughts flooded his mind. He looked at Odium, and in a frightened stare, spoke. "I was supposed to tell you something, but I forgot."

"Well, let me see if I can make you remember, spike." Odium mumbled a few words and flicked her hand toward Notor. "Speak, spike. Last chance before I dispatch you."

A strong force hit Notor. Still sitting on his knees, he looked up at the old witch. His mouth moved on its own, and the words that came forth were the wrong words.

"We're here to kill you."

"Well, why would you want to do that?" Odium looked at the door. She lifted her nose into the air as if trying to sniff some kind of smell. "Who's 'we'?"

Notor struggled. His mind was spinning out of control, and he tried to concentrate. The words that came next were a surprise to Notor. As usual, his mind rattled off the first thoughts that came into his mind. The names that came out of his mouth were the names that he had heard repeatedly since his death. "Creed and Olin."

"What? What did you say?"

Notor repeated it. "Creed and Olin." He had no sooner repeated the words when the front door of the old witch's house burst open. It was Roland, followed by Thor. Thor slammed the door, and it made a horrible sound. The bottles rattled on the wall, and the house shook.

Thor looked over his shoulder, ensuring no one was following him. Without saying a word, he hit Roland hard from behind. Roland's knees buckled, and he fell to the floor. Roland had managed to put his hands over his face while falling. The noise in his head sounded like a huge drum, vibrating out of control. He moved slightly and rolled onto his back. He was conscious, but barely.

His long cloak was tightly buttoned, and there was a red substance running down his face. Notor had seen this substance before, the day he had seen—it was so vivid in his mind—Wisteria and Katie falling down the stairs in Number 12…it was blood.

He flung his hands to his face and struggled to breath. He watched the substance drip from Roland's face to the floor. What was Thor doing? Why did he turn on Roland? This wasn't part of the plan. He looked at Thor and as he did, he realized that Thor had indeed turned on Roland and was double-crossing him, but why?

"Get up, witch," shouted Thor. "Quickly."

Odium had risen to her feet. She knew instantly that the man standing in front of her was an assassin from the dark side and would kill her without hesitating. "Are you here to kill me, assassin?" Odium made ready.

"No, witch. I'm here to save you. I need you alive."

"What do you mean assassin?" There were loud noises outside and voices. Odium could hear them. They were loud and there were many, many voices. "Who's out there?" she said. Odium looked worried. She stared at the assassin. She knew he wouldn't kill her. She was well aware of their code. She repeated her question. "Who's out there?"

"Creed, Olin, demon guardians, and—" Thor paused. He looked at the worried old witch. He could see the worry in her eyes and knew if she had time to think, she would be more powerful, so he snapped at her sharply. "And Master Umberto."

Odium's eyes opened widely; again, Thor could see her fear.

"They're here to kill you; witch, but I need you alive. I need you to help me. I can protect you, but you've got to listen to me and do exactly as I say. Do you understand?" They heard the voices once again, and this time they were louder. It was evident that whoever was out there was surrounding the house. "Do you understand me, Odium?" This time, the assassin put his hand on the old woman shoulder. She looked at him. "I need you alive," he said.

"Why do they want to kill me? We had a deal, a deal." She wobbled, and Thor kept a strong hand on the old woman.

"They know you are planning to steal The Secret of Life from Creed's house. You were there today, and Master Umberto—" Before Thor could finish his sentence, Odium spoke.

"Master Umberto knows I'm the one killing the little girls. Yesssssss, yessssss, he does, he does, and he tried to kill me before Master Olin locked him in the gold box, yessssss, yessssss." Odium was stuttering.

"No time to stutter, witch." Thor's voice raised as the voices outside became louder. "We've got to act now, and fast, if I'm to save you—and myself."

"What do you want me to do?" Odium pleaded, "Tell me, please, assassin. Please save me." Thor looked at the old witch, and at that very moment, he knew she wasn't as scared as he previously thought. He knew she was sorting things out in her head, and now only playing the part of a scared witch.

"We've got to fight them, witch, just you and I." Thor looked worried; he released the old witch and turned toward the door. "You will have to help me; there are too many for me to fight alone."

"What's he doing here?" Odium asked, staring down at Roland.

"He and Wisteria were on their way here to kill you, as well. Your little spike spy there told them you helped Master Olin kidnap their son. I killed Wisteria and brought him here. We need him." Notor was still sitting on his knees, babbling words about how they were coming to kill the witch.

Odium raised her hand and focused on Notor.

"Don't worry about that spike. We will deal with him later. Right now I need your strength, and all of it." Thor looked at the old witch and then cast a quick look at the door.

"How many?" Odium asked.

"Three warlocks, eight demon guardians, and four assassins," Thor responded.

"We can't defeat them all," Odium said.

"I know, and I don't intend to, but we can outsmart them." Thor turned toward the old woman. They heard footsteps on the front porch and loud sounds on either side of the house. "They're here. Do as I say or we both will die here tonight."

"What do we do?" Odium was clutching the assassin's arm. "What do you want me to do, assassin?"

"Simple. We will outsmart them." Thor grabbed Roland by the arm and pulled him up to his feet. "I thought we might be able to use you." He pulled one of his daggers from under his cloak and with a quick thrust, pushed it hard into Roland's stomach. Roland let out a loud moan.

"That will keep you manageable. Come over here, Odium." As Odium walked over to Roland, Thor threw Roland's arm around her neck. He mumbled a few words and softly said, "That will keep him quiet."

Odium stood there supporting Roland. "I don't see how this will help," she said.

"Do as I say, Odium, and do it now if you want to live. Shape-shift into Wisteria." Thor shouted the words at her, not hesitating. Death was coming in the front door, and they had to be ready for it. "Quickly, witch. Do it now."

The doorknob started to turn. Odium, not knowing what Thor had on his mind, realized she had no choice but to trust the assassin. She knew, on her best day, she and a lone assassin couldn't defeat three warlocks and that many demon guardians, let alone Olin.

"Why Wisteria?" she asked.

"'Cause me and this miserable human work for her. If they open the door and see Wisteria, they will know that we were here to kill you for housing Roland's son for Olin. Then we will kill them for kidnapping Roland's son. I hope they will flee because they know they have the upper hand, and, now, since we don't know where Roland's son is, we won't pursue them. They don't need to tangle with us right now, not until after Creed's transformation. If they run, we live. If they fight, we die."

Odium asked one more question as the doorknob turned and the door creaked. "Why do you need me alive?"

"I need you to help me kill Master Creed and his brother, Olin. If we make it through this tonight, and you help me kill those two later, you can have The Secret of Life as payment." Thor couldn't have said anything any sweeter to the old witch; the words struck Odium like a shock wave. "Do we have a deal, witch?"

The door started to open. "Hurry, witch. We don't have any time left. Shape-shift now or we die."

Without any more questions, Odium shook violently. And in an instant, there standing before Thor was Wisteria. She whispered, "I can't stay this way long. I'm too weak."

The door flung open with a mighty force. It struck the wall with a loud bang, and then bounced back. There, standing in front of Thor and Odium, was Creed. There were others behind him, waiting in the darkness, concealed by shadows, but the two evil warriors knew they were there.

There was more noise coming from the back and sides of the house, and it sounded like all of them were descending on the old woman's house.

"What the—" Creed stood still. The sight he saw was frightening. He'd expected to see Odium, but what he saw was Wisteria, Roland, and the assassin, Thor.

"What do you want, Creed?" Thor stepped in front of Odium and Roland. He turned slightly toward Odium and whispered softly to her so Creed and his band of thugs couldn't hear. "Turn Roland loose and step up here with me. Do it now and do it like you're ready to fight. Do it now." Odium did as Thor had instructed her to do. She pushed Roland behind her, and he stood there swaying slightly, from one side to the other. Her thoughts were that Roland might fall—he had been injured—but he stood there staring at Creed.

"What's the matter, Creed? Did you expect to find the witch, Odium? Now quickly, before I dispatch you, where is Mr. Roberts's son?"

Odium went along with Thor. She stood there, and every few seconds she would raise her hand as if ready to strike. No one but Thor knew she was weak, very weak.

Creed didn't move, but stood there in the doorway frozen with fear. The smell of it wreaked throughout the house. This wasn't what he'd expected to find, at all; he was leading the pack but now inched backward, joining the others in the shadows. His cloak covered him from head to foot, and nothing was showing, but Thor and Odium could hear his deep breathing. It sounded like air escaping from a huge set of bellows.

Everything was quiet, except for Creed's breathing, and then as suddenly as he had appeared in the doorway, his breathing stopped. Everything was deathly quiet, except one sound—a quick swoosh, then, something heavy hitting the floor.

The body of Odium slumped down to the floor, followed by her head. Standing behind her was Roland, both hands wrapped around the handle of a short sword, and the blade was now dripping with Odium's blood. Thor stooped to the ground and picked up Odium's head. He calmly placed his hand beneath his cloak and pulled out a sack. He looked at Roland and grinned, placing Odium's head in the sack.

# Twenty-Five

## The Babbling Fool

The trip back to Number 12 was uneventful; Roland and Thor had helped Notor to his feet. He was still spilling his gut about their plans to kill Odium, and he was shaking uncontrollably. Wisteria stepped out of the shadows and walked beside the trio.

"I see everything went as planned?" she said. She looked at Notor, and with a slight wave of her hand, he stopped shaking and babbling.

"What did you do to me?"

"I'm sorry, Notor. I had to cast a spell on you."

"Why kind of spell? That miserable witch could have dispatched me. I told her our plan! I couldn't help myself; it just came rolling out of my mouth. It wasn't me. It was that witch, Odium; she cast a spell on me." He was mad, not just upset, but furious and didn't mind showing it. "She—"

Before Notor could finish, Wisteria spoke softly to the brave warrior. "Notor, dear, I cast the spell on you. I knew that Odium would want to know why you showed up so late on her doorstep. I knew the first thing I needed to do was cast a truth spell on you and have you spill your guts.

"Remember the night you came to my house to kill me? The same spell." Wisteria stood erect, as if being able to cast a truth spell was something to brag about. "I'm sorry, dear, but I had to cast a different spell, one that would have you scared and babbling. It worked well, right into the plan." She smiled at Notor. You did well tonight Notor; your plan worked wonderfully."

Thor laughed. "Yes, Notor, a very good plan."

Yes, Notor's plan had worked, and had worked wonderfully, as Wisteria had stated. His plan was to have Wisteria's head, and yes, the only way Thor could return to Terra Demorte with dignity was to take Wisteria's head back with him. This would be the only way a rogue assassin could return to Terra Demorte and fall into the good graces of his evil home.

Good thinking, yes, but it took the masterminds of Wisteria and Thor to carry out the plan. The pretended clubbing of Roland and the fake blood caught Odium off guard. Before Odium had time to think, Wisteria had cast a spell to have multiple footsteps and voices sounding on the witch's porch and outside of her home.

Thor stabbing Roland was another brilliant plan as Thor was deadly with a dagger and knew exactly where to strike to hit the padding Roland had placed under his cloak. Then, of course, the surprise on Notor's face—as he wasn't aware of this double-cross—helped convince Odium that Thor was indeed trying to save her life.

The icing on the cake came when Wisteria had shape-shifted into a figure that resembled Creed, not actually Creed, but something resembling him. With the dark cloak and the night behind her, she was very convincing. It was only a small spell to talk like the demon, and Wisteria had pulled it off convincingly.

Odium had bought the idea, and when Thor mentioned The Secret of Life, she was all in. Wisteria knew of the conversation Odium had had with Creed earlier; she had learned it when she visited Creed's chambers.

Now the foursome had Odium's head in a sack, but the head didn't look like Odium. It looked exactly liked that of Wisteria. With this,

Thor could march into Terra Demorte with his head held high and, hope-fully, would be welcomed by Creed and Olin...after some explaining, of course.

They sat talking about how Notor's plan had worked. Notor was still upset about the spell Wisteria had cast upon him and sat mumbling to himself.

"Notor, your plan worked well, and thanks to you"—Wisteria paused—"we pulled it off to a tee." Wisteria looked at Notor and smiled. "Now isn't the time to be mad, Notor. You had a good plan and we carried it out. Now, let's move on.

When Notor visited Odium earlier that evening, the old witch shape-shifted into a monster to scare Notor. Realizing she could do this, it was his idea to trick Odium into shape shifting into Wisteria, and then removing her head. Wisteria's head was the only thing that could get Thor back into the good graces of Terra Demorte—that is, once there, if Thor could come up with a good explanation for his past actions. The problem Notor had was how to, actually carry it out, so Thor and Wisteria, filled in the blanks.

"We've got to move now if we are to do this. In a few days, Odium's spirit will realize what has happened and will go to Terra Demorte. Once she's there, this plan won't work. So, the way I have it figured, we have two days—maybe a little longer—to get Josh back, or we all fail." Wisteria shifted her weight on the sofa and continued. "We know we had a visitor here tonight, and we don't know how much he heard or who he was, so we need to get Thor out of here and on his way to Terra Demorte."

"I'm gone," said Thor.

"I'm going with you." Said Roland.

"No, you're not, Roland. Do you not understand what will happen if they catch you there? This I must do alone; you know that."

"It's my son. I'm going and there is nothing you can do about it, so let's get going." Roland had already stood up and was heading toward the door. "I'll get my stuff."

Thor shot him a nasty look. "Look, I'll be lucky if I make it out of there alive, let alone with, Josh. If you go it will be a distraction for me, and I can't have that right now. You aren't going and that's final."

Roland turned to face Thor. "I'm going."

"Yeah? How? How are you going, Roland?"

"What do you mean? I'm going with you."

"Where's your medallion, Roland, and where is the portal located? You can't go into the portal without a medallion, so you can't go even if I wanted you to, and *I don't.*"

"Where's Morto's medallion? I can use that. Thor, this is my son we are talking about. I have to go."

"No, Roland, you don't. Please trust me. I'll get your son back, I promise."

Roland paced the floor. Then, like a child, he sat back down on the sofa. Wisteria spoke softly. "Roland, Thor needs Morto's medallion, as well. If he is to gain the trust of Creed and the others, he'll need to have more than my head in that sack."

"OK, OK. I'll stay, I'll stay." Roland's mind was spinning. He knew he wouldn't stay in Johnston; he would go to Terra Demorte somehow. "I need to think; that's all."

"Think about what?" said Wisteria.

"Nothing. OK. Come on, Thor. I'll walk with you to the portal. Let me get you some things of mine." Roland played it down, but Thor wasn't the fool.

"I can find my way to the portal, Roland, and I can't show up in Terra Demorte with your guns. No, I must do this the assassin way." Thor grabbed the sack and looked at Wisteria. "Morto's medallion, Wisteria. I need it."

Wisteria stuck her hands in her pocket and produced the medallion. "Good luck. Thor. Do you need anything else from me?"

"No, just your head, witch." Thor laughed. "And I have that. Cross your fingers, guys. I should be back within a day, two at the most."

"Thor, may I see the medallion?" asked Roland.

"No, you may not, Roland, I know you, and I know if you get your hands on this, you won't give it back." Thor smiled, "sorry, but you can't have this."

"No, I don't want it, you hold it, I just want to see what it looks like," said Roland.

Thor look puzzled, but reluctantly held the medallion up so Roland could see it. "There, happy?"

Roland smiled, "yes, thanks, Thor."

Thor nodded his head, and Roland watched him head toward the door. "Good luck, Thor, and thank you, I won't forget this." He said.

Katie gave Thor a hug and smiled at the assassin. "Bring my son home, Thor, please." She said.

"I will, Katie, I promise." Thor knew his chances were, at most, promising—even with the head of Wisteria and Morto's medallion, but this was Terra Demorte, a place where lies were spoken every day, a place where no one trusted anyone except one's own clan.

The assassin headed down the street toward town; soon he would be out of sight, and vanishing with the only hope of getting Josh back.

"Notor, Horace, you guys want to get some air?" said Roland.

"No, I'm fine, Mr. Roberts," said Notor. He looked curiously at Roland. He knew Roland knew he didn't breath. Why would he need fresh air?

"Yeah, I'm fine too, Roland," Horace said.

"Come on, guys. Let's go into the backyard. I need some air and time to think, but I don't want to be alone." Roland shot a quick glance to Wisteria. She looked at him as if she knew something was up, but what, she didn't know.

"You men go with Roland. It's been a hard day, and I don't think Roland needs to be alone. So off you go. Fresh air will do—" Wisteria stopped. "Fresh air will do Roland some good."

The three men went down the hall, and Wisteria heard the back door open and then softly close. *What is Roland up to?* she thought. *He can't follow Thor to Terra Demorte. He doesn't know where the portal is and he has no medallion to enter.*

Once outside in the yard, Roland paced like a cat. He took a deep breath and exhaled it with a loud gasp. He spoke precisely to Notor. "Do you know where the portal is located, Notor?"

"Yes, sir, I do," said Notor. "Why do you ask, Mr. Roberts?"

"It's Roland, Notor. Call me Roland. Do you know how to open the portal?"

"Yes, sir, I do."

"How? How do I get in?" Roland looked at Notor. "Tell me how I enter the portal."

"You just—"

Before Notor finished his sentence, Horace spoke. "Stop, Notor. Don't tell Roland."

"It doesn't matter, Mr. Wheeler. He doesn't have a medallion, so he couldn't open the portal anyway." Notor was delighted with himself, since he knew so much about the portal. He, himself, had been to Terra Demorte many times with his master, and since he was a servant, his medallion wouldn't open the portal unless his master was with him.

"Quiet, Notor. Roland doesn't need to speak of these matters. You are staying right here with us, Roland, we all will wait until Thor returns with your son."

"I just wanted to know, Notor, that's all. I realize I need to stay but I want to know all I can about Creed and Terra Demorte. Information is the best tool a man can have these days." Roland's remarks swelled inside of Notor, and as usual, his mouth opened and out can the information Roland needed.

"You just walk over to that large mural on the old shipping warehouse and touch your medallion with one hand and place the other hand on the painted door. You will enter the portal. It's not hard at all, Mr. Roberts—I mean Roland—quite easy to do, I've done it many times with my master."

"Notor, for heaven's sake—and I mean heaven's sake—would you please not tell, Roland these things? Can't you see he's pumping information from you?"

"So what, Mr. Wheeler? He can't enter the portal 'cause he has no medallion, so knowing where the portal is doesn't help him, and besides, he's staying here with us. Isn't that right, Mr. Roberts?"

"No, that isn't right, Notor. I'm going to Terra Demorte, and I'm leaving in about fifteen minutes." Roland stood up and rubbed his chin. "Yes, in just about fifteen minutes. You guys stay here. I'll be right back. If anyone asks where I'm at or where I'm going, tell them I needed something to drink and I'll be back in a second."

"Roland, you can't be serious. You can't go to Terra Demorte. You don't have a medallion, and Notor's will only work if we have a master or someone who has a full-entry medallion." Horace spoke softly to Roland. "I've lost a daughter to this monster, Roland. I don't want you to lose a son."

"You have a medallion, Horace?"

"Yes, all spirits have them; the minute I came back, it appeared around my neck."

"Then help me, Horace. Help me before he does to Josh the same thing he did to Sarah. You know Creed and Olin aren't going to let Josh go."

"That's what I came back to do, Roland. I came back to help." Horace was pacing in the yard now, exactly like Roland had previously done.

"Then you, Notor, and I are going to Terra Demorte, and I mean tonight. You guys in for this?" Roland looked at the two spirits. "In or not? Either way, I'm going."

"I'm in," said Notor. "That's why I'm here; just tell me what to do."

"OK, Roland, you call the shots, and I'm in too. Like Notor, just tell me what to do." Horace continued to pace the yard. "We must be crazy to try this, but let's go." He stopped pacing for a second and spoke. "How are we going to get inside of the portal?"

"Leave that to me and be ready. I'll be back in fifteen minutes."

Roland slid into his car and headed down Calhoun Street. Five minutes later, he turned onto the crooked road that led down to Odium's house. He parked his car and walked the gravel road on foot.

The front door was ajar, and he used his flashlight to enter the old house. He saw the body of Wisteria laying on the floor in a large pool of blood. He stepped aside, and with his foot, pushed the sofa backward. As the sofa slid, it revealed three necklaces lying on the floor. Roland had seen them when Odium's head hit the floor, and while Thor was looking at Creed, he had slid them under the sofa with his foot, just in case.

The medallion wasn't like the one Thor had shown him, but it was something he had never seen before, and he assumed it was exactly what he needed, and he was right. He picked up the necklaces and stuffed them into his pockets, and as he turned toward the door, there stood... Odium.

She was bloody from head to foot, and in her hand was a vile of some kind. He let the beam from his flashlight drop down on Odium's hands.

"Blood," Roland said aloud. "That's blood."

"Yessssss, yessssss, it's blood, Mr. Roberts." Odium snapped a command, and the lights in her house put forth a brilliant glow. "Yessssss, yessssss, what do we have here? Yessssss, that looks like Wisteria's body, yessssss, yessssss. Did you kill her, Mr. Roberts, yessssss, yessssss, did you kill that meddling old witch, Wisteria?"

Roland was dumbfounded. What was he going to do now? He answered, "No, I don't know who killed her; I was just looking for my son, Josh."

"Yessssss, yessssss, yes, Mr. Roberts, yessssss, your son was here, but he's not here now. Olin took him to Terra Demorte. Yessssss, your son is in the most evil place, yessssss, yessssss. Yessssss, he is."

Roland looked at the witch; she wobbled a few times and then sank down into a large, soft chair. Roland stood there with nothing to defend himself; he didn't have his guns or crossbows. He hadn't expected to come face to face with Odium; she was supposed to be dead. He stood and stared at the witch. "What are you going to do with me?" he said. The witch's eyes closed and stayed closed for a few minutes before they opened again. She was weak and pale, as if she were dying.

"Yessssss, yesssssss," she said, "your son isn't here, Mr. Roberts, and it looks like you did all of us a favor by killing that witch there, so you can go, Mr. Roberts, but the next time I see you, I'll probably kill you. Do you understand me, Mr. Roberts?"

The witch didn't open her eyes. She had slipped the vile of blood into her pocket and sat as if asleep. "Yesssssss, yesssssss, you can go." Then, as if all of her energy had suddenly returned, she snapped at, Roland. "Get out of my house and don't ever come here again!"

Before he took a step, Wisteria's body vanished, leaving a pool of blood behind. Odium opened her eyes slightly, and then as if nothing had happened, closed them once again.

Roland, following Odium's command, headed toward the door.

"Lights out," snapped Odium. The house went dark. Roland fumbled for the switch on the flashlight but didn't find it before he managed to kick a side table. He heard some items hitting the floor. He didn't turn back but stepped hurriedly onto the front porch. He started off the porch when he heard a fierce growl and then snapping and gnawing of teeth.

Roland reaching his car, slid inside, and headed back down Calhoun Street within minutes. He turned into his drive and parked the car in the back. Horace and Notor were there to meet him.

"They wanted to know where you were but were satisfied with our explanation." Horace was the first to speak.

"Come on in the house," said Roland. "I've got bad news." They all raced down the hallway and turned into the den. Roland was the first to speak.

"Wisteria, Odium is alive. She's alive! I just saw her."

"What, Roland? Slow down. What are you saying?" Wisteria was sitting erect and Katie was, as well.

"Roland, what did you say? It sounded like—"

Roland interrupted his wife. "It sounded like I said, 'Odium is alive,' and that's because she is."

# Twenty-Six

## Thor's Return

Thor had made it through the portal and was standing across the street from Jake's Place. The laughter was heavy, and the pub was packed with people, as usual. He had missed this place, really missed it. He straightened himself and headed across the street, and walked straight through the door.

The laughter started dying slowly, and then as if someone had walked across their graves, everyone became quiet, deathly quiet.

It didn't take Creed and Olin long to look up to see what the disturbance was all about, why Jake's Place had become so quiet. There, standing in front of everyone, was the lone assassin, Thor, the assassin who had abandoned Terra Demorte—to make things worse, the same man who had betrayed his beloved assassin clan.

"You've got a lot of nerve coming in here," shouted another warlock.

Before anyone else spoke or said another word, Thor spoke, and spoke very loud. "Nerve, you say? Nerve to come to my home? You should welcome me here; I've just completed my contract on the surface and have come home to celebrate. Come home to drink and be merry. Since when is an assassin not welcome in Jake's Place?"

"You're a traitor, a traitor to Terra Demorte and to the assassin clan," said the warlock.

"A traitor? What do warlocks know about the assassins of Terra Demorte? Do we now have to inform you of our deeds? I had a contract on the surface, and I've completed it, so who is it that calls me a traitor?"

"I do," said the warlock. "Me and everyone else in this place, including your friends, the assassins."

"And, I do, as well," said Olin, standing up at his table. "You have betrayed me and my brother by taking up with that witch, Wisteria, and stealing from us. You tried to kill us, as well. I'm calling you a traitor, and we all know that you betrayed your clan, the infamous *assassin clan.*"

Olin emphases the words "assassin clan" as if making fun of the clan. "What's worse, you have betrayed Terra Demorte. You will die." Olin and more of the warlock clan darted toward Thor. He didn't resist, and within seconds, they had seized him and held him firmly against the bar.

"OK, OK, before you kill me, let me speak," Thor said. "First, if I had wanted to kill you, Olin, you would be dead."

"You are a traitor, and a traitor's death you shall have." Olin reached beneath the assassin's cloak and grabbed two of his daggers; he handed them to Roy and stepped aside. "Kill this miserable assassin. Kill him now, Roy."

Roy grinned at Thor and raised the daggers.

"Let me speak before you kill me, Olin. I should have the right to speak in my own defense." Thor struggled but the warlocks held him firmly, "warlocks have no right to kill an assassin in Terra Demorte."

"By all means, let him speak," said a kind voice. It was a woman's voice, and as she entered Jake's Place, a cold air filled the room. "Yes, let the assassin speak, Master Olin."

Another warlock spoke up. "I don't know who you are, witch, but we are going to kill this dirty traitor now." Before the warlock had gotten the last words of his sentence out of his mouth, the woman in the cloak waved her hand toward the warlocks, and they went spinning off in all directions, bumping into other warlocks and knocking over the tables and chairs.

They all lay on the floor, having been hit by a mighty force. Thor stood alone in the center of the pub. The hooded woman walked slowly over to him; she turned and faced the others in the room.

"The warlock clan is quick to want to kill an assassin of Terra Demorte. Is it not written in your laws of the land that you can't kill one another here...in Terra Demorte? Hear the assassin out, and if you still want his life, then you can bind him to this post and let the wood spirits have him, or if you wish, the council can handle his untimely death—but not the warlock clan."

She turned toward Thor and spoke once more. "OK, assassin, now's your chance. Speak now or I'll turn you over to this mob once more. Go ahead. Speak." She backed off, and there, standing alone in the middle of Jake's Place, was Thor.

Thor grabbed a spear off the wall. Assassins, warlocks, and demon guardians all snapped to their feet to defend themselves. All stood alert, ready to fight. With a mighty thrust, Thor drove the spear into the floor; he reached in the sack and pulled out Wisteria's head. He stuck it on the other end of the spear for all to see. "Yes, Master Creed and Master Olin, I do owe you an apology. Yes, I did betray you, but that is exactly what I wanted you to think.

"This witch, Wisteria, is very clever, and I needed her to trust me. No one and I repeat"—Thor raised his voice—"*no one* had ever beaten this witch. Morto gave her his head. And others have been struck down by this powerful witch, but not me. I had a contract on the surface, given to me in this very place, at that very table"—Thor pointed to the table where Creed sat—"a contract to kill the greatest good witch of all times, this witch, Wisteria."

Thor pointed to the head on the pole. Cheers and laughter filled the room. Thor held out his hands, silencing the mob. "My orders were, no matter what it took, or how long it took, to kill this meddling old witch and bring her head to Terra Demorte, and here it is, the head of the great surface witch, Wisteria…finally…dead."

No one said a word. All just sat or stood, staring at the assassin, then, just like a traveling salesman who was just about to sell his wares, Thor continued. "Master Creed and Master Olin, here is the witch that has interfered with your transformation. Here is the witch that killed the assassin Morto, the same assassin you sent to kill this witch. Yes, it appeared that I turned against my own kind, but I assure you gentlemen I did not. My contract is fulfilled, and here is my trophy and here, my good friend Morto, is your medallion." Thor pitched the medallion toward Morto.

All watched it float across the pub, as in slow motion, and then landed neatly in Morto's outstretched hand. "I have fulfilled my contract on the surface, and I have only to ask for forgiveness from Master Creed, Master Olin, the assassin clan, and others in Terra Demorte. I had to trick you, or I would never have gotten close enough to kill this witch. Sirs, I offer you my utmost, earnest apology."

The room remained silent, and then the woman in the cloak spoke to the crowd. "Well, is this not the proof you need that this assassin didn't betray you or Terra Demorte?" She brushed up against Thor, and with a slight movement of her hand, she dropped four gold nuggets into the assassin's hands. "I venture to say that the assassin would love to buy drinks for the house. What say you, assassin?"

Thor raised his voice. "Yes, my friends, drinks are on me. This is a great night, and we need to celebrate." He slapped the counter top, laying the gold nuggets on the bar. "Yes, Jake drinks all around."

Jake's Place went back to its normal panorama. It looked as if all was forgiven with Thor. At least the assassin clan was satisfied with his explanation, and it was time to get back to the drinking. They hailed him as a big hero, now that they knew he hadn't betrayed them. The assassins all sat in one corner of the pub, drinking and talking. They loved to tell tales, and since Thor was back, there would be tale after tale to expand upon.

Thor hadn't taken a seat with his friends; instead, he walked over to the table in the corner where Creed, Olin, and the demon guardians sat. Olin immediately jumped to his feet to meet the assassin.

He stared at the assassin, and Thor stared back directly into the eyes of Olin. Neither blinked. They stood staring the other down. Then something strange happened that no one noticed but Thor. Olin's eyes strayed for a quick second—in the blink of an eye—to the woman dressed in black. Then, as quickly as they had left, they refocused back on Thor.

"Well, assassin, I guess by brother and I owe you. You have done something for us that will keep us forever in your debt."

"No, Master Olin. I am in your debt. I deceived you and your brother, and for that, I do apologize. I needed to do that for the old witch to believe me. The wounds I gave you weren't life threatening, but nonetheless, I did give them to you. I beg that you and Master Creed will forgive me, and in time, I'll make it up to both of you."

Thor was as convincing as he could be, but at that very moment, what he really wanted to do was pull his daggers and kill the miserable warlock that stood in front of him.

"Well, Thor, I would like to thank you for killing Wisteria. You are right; she has been a thorn in our side for many months, and thanks to you, not any longer."

"Then we are square?" asked Thor.

"Not really assassin. You owe my brother and me some gold, the gold you stole from us. When might we expect that back?" Olin looked at Thor with intensity in his eyes, but before Olin or Thor spoke another word, the woman in black walked over and placed ten bags of gold on the table in front of Creed.

"This should more than pay the assassin's debt, should it not?"

Olin stared at the hooded figure; he squirmed a few times and replied, "Yes, this should do just fine."

"Then you and Master Creed are square with the assassin?" she said softly.

"Yes, of course. Thor, welcome back to Terra Demorte. We're square."

Thor excused himself and headed to the tables where the assassins had gathered to drink their ale. Before he left, he thanked the woman in black for her generosity.

Olin didn't sit down. He watched the assassin until he had seated himself at a table with the rest of his kind. "Sit with the dogs," he said softly.

The woman in black walked off. She pulled up a chair and sat down with the assassins. No one seemed to know her; she just appeared that very night in Jake's Place and now she was sitting with the assassin clan. They all wondered who she was.

"I saved your life, assassin," she said calmly to Thor.

"Yes, you did, and for that I'm very grateful," Thor said. The rest of the assassin clan all cheered and drank more ale.

"Is the assassin clan grateful that I saved the life of the great Thor?"

The assassins all cheered, raised their mugs of ale, and toasted the woman in black.

"Who are you?" asked Thor.

"It doesn't matter who I am," said the woman. "All that matters is I saved an assassin this night."

Thor looked at the woman.

"Yes, and thank you for doing that," said another assassin. "We kind of like having Thor around here." He raised his glass and toasted Thor. "A toast to the mighty Thor." Thor laughed and drank more ale.

The woman in black spoke once more. "Now for my payment, what shall it be?"

"What payment?" questioned Thor.

"The payment I shall receive for saving such a great assassin, of course."

Thor looked at the woman; the other assassins did the same. They all stared at the woman dressed in black. They set down their drinks and just stared at the strange woman who demanded payment. No one could see her face, but all could feel her evil.

"You are expecting a payment from me?" asked Thor.

"No, assassin. I'm expecting a payment from the entire assassin clan, a payment that will cost you no gold, but just a favor, when and where I need it. Deal?"

"That's not much of a payment, but if that is what you desire, I'll stand good for it," said Thor.

"Again, assassin, not you, the entire assassin clan," said the mysterious woman.

"Well, I'm afraid I can't hold the entire assassin clan responsible for something you have done for me. The payment will come from me." Thor raised a glass and drank some ale.

"Well, I assumed the entire assassin clan would be happy that I saved you. I guess I was wrong." The woman started to stand up when another assassin spoke.

"No, you are right. What say you, brothers? Are we willing to give this woman a favor for saving Thor? What say ye?" They all spoke up, and it was unanimous. Drinks went to their lips and they all swore by death or pain to give the woman in black a favor, a favor from the assassin clan.

"I'm the leader of the assassin clan. Your favor will be granted when you need it," said a rather cheery and slightly chubby assassin.

"Good," said the woman in black.

# Twenty-Seven

## The Portal to Terra Demorte

Roland stood in front of the large mural. He had seen this magnificent piece of art many, many times but never in a million years would have believed this was the doorway to all that was evil, or a place maybe even worse, if there was such a place. Standing there now, he knew that once he passed through the portal, there was no turning back. He knew he was endangering his and Katie's entire bloodline, and although none of their kin knew what he was doing, he felt they would support him.

He had told Wisteria and Katie about his return visit to Odium's house, how when he had turned to leave, there standing in the doorway was Odium. He also told them the witch was drenched in blood and described the vile of blood she carried in her hand. He told them how she let him escape without a fight.

"She's killed another girl. I'm sure of it," Wisteria had said. "But how? How is she alive?"

"Not only alive, but she, as well, believes that the body on the floor is you, Wisteria," he explained.

"Then we've been tricked, and she knows nothing of it. How? Why?" Wisteria thought and thought, but no answer came.

"Thor! What about Thor? Do you think she'll tell the clans in Terra Demorte that the head Thor brought there isn't yours?" Katie asked.

"No, dear. If Roland is right, then she doesn't know. She just might think that I'm dead, as well. If she shows up at Terra Demorte, all she can do is verify what they already know." Wisteria laughed slightly, and then her face turned to that of a confused old woman. "I do wonder why she let Roland leave without a fight, though."

"I can tell you that. I wondered that very thought and I know why now. She was worn out, so tired that she could barely keep her eyes open. She just said, 'Hello, Mr. Roberts' and sat down in a large chair. Then she told me to leave and not come back...ever," Roland said.

"Why did you go back to Odium's house, Roland?" questioned Wisteria. "Why did you go back there?"

"I went back to get this medallion," Roland said, holding up the medallion.

"Let me see that, Roland."

"No, Wisteria. I'm keeping it, and I intend to go to Terra Demorte. I know now that Thor might be in danger, and I intend to go there and find my son. If Thor needs any help, I'll be there for him, as well."

"You can't go there, Roland. If they catch you—"

"If I don't get my son back, then I have nothing to live for, Wisteria. I'm going there, and I'm going now. Thor told me that Terra Demorte was black except for the lights; I plan to stay in the dark until I find my son. They will never know I'm there."

The old witch tried her best to keep the man standing in front of her from going, but deep in her heart, she knew it was no use. Roland was going, and all she could do was stay there and try to protect Katie if his trip was discovered. She finally agreed with him, but not before Katie stood up beside Roland and spoke softly. "Sweetie, bring my baby back home."

"I will, or will die trying," he said.

Katie turned to Wisteria. She put her hand to her mouth, suddenly surprised. "Wisteria, I wonder who we killed tonight!"

***

Roland placed his hand on the medallion, and as scared as he was, he placed his other hand on the mural. Instantly, he was standing in some kind of room. Notor and Horace followed. There were no lights, and it was pitch black. He fumbled in his pack for his flashlight. A moment later, it put forth a brilliant light. He realized he wasn't standing in a room at all, but a tunnel of some sort.

"What all is in this backpack?" he said softly.

"What did you say, Mr. Roberts?" Notor asked.

"Oh, nothing, Notor, just that Wisteria put a lot of things in my backpack, things she said I might need. There's a cross and a wooden stake in here too."

"I hope, for your sake, there's not a gold snake's head dagger in there."

"No, not that I've seen, Notor, but then I haven't seen everything she put in here."

The tunnel was cold, dark, and damp, and the walls, which were made of stone, were moist and glistened as his light shone upon them. He took a small step, and as he did, a small torch on the wall emitted a single flame. A strange voice rang out, "Welcome, Deidre." Roland stopped. "Well, now we know whose medallion I'm wearing, but I wonder who Deidre is—or was?"

Notor and Horace followed Roland, and with each step, one torch would go out while yet another one would light. They walked for some time before a small light appeared yards in front of them. It stayed on, and all could see it was some sort of opening.

"Roland, that's the entrance to Terra Demorte. Let me go check everything out before you walk out of the tunnel," said Notor. "I've been here before; no one will care if they see me."

"Good thinking, Notor. Thanks," said Roland.

Notor walked to the edge of the tunnel and then disappeared from sight. Roland and Horace stood still in the cold, dark tunnel. "I wish that darn light would go out," said Roland. The minute the words came out of his mouth, the light went dark. "Horace, did you see that?"

"Yes."

"Let me try that again. Light on." The light flicked and put forth its small light, illuminating a small space. "Well, that might be useful."

Roland watched the entrance of the tunnel. "Horace, watch our backs. Let me know if you see anything coming this way. It won't be hard, just look for the lights to come on. Light off," he whispered. The small torch went dark.

"Sure, Mr. Roberts."

"Horace, until we get out of this place, call me Deidre. I don't want anyone here to know who I really am."

"Sure, Deidre it is."

Roland stood quietly and stared into the darkness at the small opening at the end of the tunnel. He wondered what Terra Demorte looked like, and he wondered who'd built a place for evil to dwell. *What kind of person or thing would—*

Roland's thoughts were interrupted. He saw what appeared to be Notor coming back into the darkness of the tunnel, but there was something wrong. There were two people coming, and as the first light came on, he realized it wasn't Notor, but someone else.

"Horace, quickly, hide. Find a place where we can hide. Go back up the tunnel, quickly. We've got to hide. Someone is coming." They started back up the tunnel and veered off into a small opening that led off into another direction. They watched the two figures approaching and could tell by the intense conversation that something was wrong.

"We've got to find the murderer, I tell you. The head of our clan thinks it's someone from Terra Demorte, maybe an assassin. You know we can't trust them."

"No, not the assassin clan. We have a treaty with them. I don't think they would break the treaty. No, not the assassins."

"Then who? That's six murders this week. Six deaths of our kind on the surface."

"Well, that's what we are going to find out; someone on the surface has found out about our race and knows how to identify us, but who, I have no idea."

The two men walked past where Roland and Horace hid. They continued their walk, and Roland and Horace watched the lights come on and go off as the men passed each one. Roland and Horace let out small sighs as the tunnel became dark and the figures disappeared around a bend. There were no more lights to be seen.

"Close," said Roland.

"Too close," said Horace.

The men saw another figure enter the tunnel. There was no doubt that it was Notor. He stopped at the entrance and waved for them to approach. "Hurry," he whispered.

"This way, Mr. Roberts, quickly. Come this way." Notor turned out of the tunnel and went down the street until they were standing in front of an alley. "In here, Mr. Roberts. No one will see us in here. Did you see the two vampires heading up the tunnel?"

"Those were vampires, real vampires?"

"Yeah, mean creatures they are. I heard them talking about someone or something that is killing vampires on the surface. Mean creatures I tell you. Real mean, Mr. Roberts."

"Notor, don't call me Mr. Roberts. Call me Deidre or D. That's whose medallion I'm wearing, so can you remember to call me that, just in case someone hears us?"

"Sure, Mr. Roberts—oops, sorry, Deidre." Notor grabbed his mouth, but as usual, the words had already escaped. He turned and pointed. "That place across the street there, that's Jake's Place. I'm sure Creed, Olin, and Thor are in there. I'll check it out shortly, but first you must stay here. Don't let anyone see you, OK, Deidre?"

"Yes, this is a great place to hide, Notor. Thanks." Roland backed into the darkness of the alley and pressed his back against the cool stones. He was standing in the exact alley of his dreams. "How?" he said. "How would I know of this place?" He studied the surroundings and then spoke softly to Notor. "Do you think you could go over to Jake's Place and peek in the window to see what's going on? Sounds like a party of some kind by all of the noise."

"Sure, I'll be back in a flash." Notor felt important now. He had been in Terra Demorte on more than one occasion. If seen, no one would pay him any attention. Most of the people who drank in Jake's Place knew he worked for Creed, and most of the time he sat outside on the street corner. On occasion, Creed would let him sit with him and Olin, but that was rare, very rare. So seeing him slipping around on the outside of the pub wouldn't raise curiosity or any cause for alarm.

"Vampires, Horace. Did you know they were down here?"

"Deidre, that's not all that's down here, I'm sure of it. I didn't know this place existed until I died and the dark side for years tried to lure me down here. This is a terrible place, and the faster we can get your son and get out of here, the better."

"I agree."

"I'm going down the alley to look around. I'll position myself in the next alley down. There I can watch your back and ensure no one comes up this way."

"Good idea, Horace. If all Hades breaks loose, save yourself and Notor. Don't worry about me, OK?"

"I didn't come to this place to save myself, Roland, so don't worry about Notor and me. Let's just all get out of here alive, and again, the sooner the better."

"Sounds good, Horace," said Roland. He smiled at the man, and with a slight nod, Horace vanished.

Roland sat quietly in the dark alley; he had pulled his cloak around his body and sat waiting for some kind of sign to let him know what his next move would be. It had been an hour since Notor had left, and he was starting to get worried. He felt his whole world closing in around him. He was so far from home and so far away from Katie, but he had promised her that he would find Josh and bring him home, and that's what he meant to do. He was sitting in a world where he was the alien, a place where no human being had ever seen or stepped foot, or at least not until Olin had brought his son there, a place deep in the belly of the earth.

He sat thinking about his son and about the conversation; he'd had with Thor concerning Terra Demorte and the evil beings that lived there. He pondered each word Thor had said as he sat in the darkness. "If they catch you there, Roland, the dark side will kill every living member of your family. They will wipe out your entire bloodline."

It felt like hours before he saw Notor coming back into the alley, and Notor was the first to speak. "They're all in there, Deidre—Creed, Olin, and Thor. Wisteria's head is on a stick in the middle of the floor, hanging there for all to see. Thor is drinking ale with the other assassins, and Creed and Olin are drinking in a corner with their demon guardians."

"Did you see any rooms?"

"Yeah, they're all up the stairs, hundreds of them, but Master Creed and Olin always take the same ones, head up the stairs and turn right, the last two on the left. I've been there many times delivering their luggage, but I had to sleep outside."

"Can I get to them, Notor? Can I get to the rooms without anyone seeing me?"

"No, Deidre, impossible."

Roland pushed his back against the cold wall; he slumped down in a sitting position and watched the windows that fronted the pub. "My son is in there, Notor, so close but yet so far way. I've heard that saying all my life, but this is the first time that it's had a true meaning to me."

"What do we do now, Deidre?"

"I wish I knew, Notor. Wait a while, I guess." About that time, a loud noise came echoing from the back of the alley. "Quiet, Notor." The men stopped talking; Roland slid his hands under his cloak and felt the two nine-millimeter pistols tucked neatly under his arms. He grasped the weapons of death and pulled them from their holsters. He continued to stay in a sitting position. "Less to see," he whispered.

Notor had turned invisible; Roland knew they wouldn't see him. "If only I could turn invisible," he whispered.

"Yeah, Deidre, that would be better, much better."

The men sat listening to the odd noise. It was a strange type of noise, and both men wondered what it could be. Then it became clearer. It sounded as if someone was dragging something. Suddenly they heard a man's voice. "Light." A small light hanging on a long metal pole illuminated, and Roland could see a large, rather fat man dragging two bags across the alley. Then, one at a time, he tossed them over a railing. He managed to throw the second bag over before the first one hit the ground, making a small thud noise. Then, what seemed to be many seconds later, the second bag hit the bottom of the pit, making the same soft thud.

*That's a very deep pit,* thought Roland. The man walked slowly back across the alley and out of sight. A few seconds later, a heavy door slammed shut. *This is just like my dreams,* he realized.

Horace materialized and looked worried. "Are you guys all right?"

"Yes, Horace. Yeah," said Roland.

"Wow, that was close. Scared me half to death, Deidre. I scouted the other side of the street from where I was hiding. There is an alley at the end of the pub, and the next building right across that alley is the Keeping Room.

"The alley—could you see down it, Horace?" Roland questioned.

"No, not really, why?"

"I want to know if there is a way I could get into Jake's Place without going through the front door." Roland looked at Horace. Horace could see the wear and tear this place had already put on him. The evil alone would take a toll on a good person. Evil hung in the air like a fog, drawing one's energy, trying to suck out any good that was in a being. The inhabitants of Terra Demorte didn't know Roland was there, but the evil did. And it sought to find him and devour him.

"Deidre, I've been in that alley. There is no back door, only two windows, but they're on the second floor," said Notor.

"Windows, Notor?"

"Yes, two of them. But they're high. You can't get up there without a ladder, Deidre." For a moment, Notor remembered his life when he was alive; he remembered how he used to help his father work from ladders. He remembered his life with Maude and how he, himself, was murdered by Creed. "I hate Creed."

"What did you say, Notor? Did you say you hated Creed?" Horace asked.

"Yes, he killed me, Mr. Wheeler, took me away from Maude. And I hate him for that." A tear ran down Notor's cheek, and he wiped it away with the sleeve of his shirt. "I hate that warlock."

"We all hate him, Notor," said Roland. Roland thought about the window. He didn't know of a way to get up that high without a ladder, but then another thought ran through his mind.

"If I can go up the stairs, I can get out with Josh through one of the windows. Horace, if I drop Joshua down to you, could you or Notor catch him?"

"Yes, I think so, Mr. Roberts—I mean, Deidre," said Horace.

"Good, Horace. Notor, can you turn invisible and go up the stairs, go to Creed's room, and see if Josh is there?"

"Ahaa sure, Deidre, sure, but I can't get into Creed's room. I can't pass through walls here. I can be invisible. That's how my master always wanted me to be unless he summoned me."

"We've got to know for sure which room Josh is in."

"I can try to steal the key; Jake has spares hanging behind the bar. When he delivers drinks, I could steal the keys, Deidre. I know which rooms they have."

"Good plan, Notor. We will wait here until we hear from you, and don't get caught."

Notor headed across the street. Roland whispered after him, "Notor, turn invisible."

Within a second, Notor vanished. He waited outside of the bar until a man walked out, and as the door opened and the man stepped outside, Notor stepped into Jake's Place.

Roland watched the man as he exited the pub; he watched every move he made. He glanced back down the alley, his mind spinning out of control. He had seen this place in his dreams; he had seen the man throwing those bags over the rail in his dreams. He wondered why he had had those dreams. Why had he seen these things in his dreams?

Then, as if a flash of lightning had struck him, he remembered something else he had seen in his dreams, something dark and evil, a monster with green eyes and a huge man. His thoughts quickly changed as he watched the man standing in front of the pub.

The man stood outside of the pub and lit a cigarette. He exhaled the smoke into a perfect ring, and it floated helplessly into the air and then finally vanished. He stood there puffing on the smoke. Then an odd thing happened. He started to walk down the street when he suddenly turned and faced the alley where Roland sat. From within his dark hiding place, Roland watched the man take another draw from the cigarette. He blew the smoke out in a long, straight line, until the smoke clouded up and floated upward in the dark night air. He crushed out the smoke and walked slowly toward the alley.

Roland placed his hands under his cloak; he pulled the pistols and held them down by his sides. The man continued his slow journey toward the alley. As he entered it, Roland was sure the man could see well enough to make out his profile. Moments later, Roland was proven right.

"Deidre?"

Roland didn't speak. His guns were ready, and he slowly pulled back the hammers on the death machines. Thoughts ran through his head. Silently he prayed for the man to turn and go back to the pub, but the man didn't.

"Deidre, what are you doing here? When did you get back? I didn't know you were coming back. You should have sent me word." The man continued until he was less than five feet from Roland; it was then he realized that the figure sitting in front of him wasn't Deidre.

"Who are you?" said the man. "What are you, and why do you have Deidre's medallion? Speak, man." The man took another step, and then as loud as he could scream, he let out the words, "You're a human!"

The man stared at Roland. He raised his hands as if to send some magic spell toward him, but Roland was faster, and within seconds, he was standing and the pistols, only making a soft noise, spit two lead slugs toward the man standing in front of them. The man fell to the ground like a sack of grain. He made no more sounds, and Roland was sure he was dead.

Roland's mind was spinning thoughts in every direction; he was shaking violently, and once again, slid down the cool rock wall to a sitting position. He placed the pistols back in their holsters, rubbed his face, and thought of what to do next.

"Mr. Roberts, are you all right?" It was Horace; he materialized in front of Roland. "Don't worry about him, Roland; he would have killed you in an instant. What are we going to do with him, Mr. Roberts?"

Roland didn't hesitate. He stood up and said, "We are going to drag him over to that rail and dump him into the pit. That's all we can do, Horace. We've got to get rid of the body so no one will find it." The men grabbed the corpse and, with little effort, dragged the dead man over to the rail. There was no need to pick him up. They pushed the man under the bottom rail, and it seemed like minutes, but finally there was a loud thud as the man's body landed in the bottom of the pit.

"That's done," said Roland.

As luck would have it, it wasn't done. At that very moment, the back door to one of the buildings flung open, and a heavy man came out dragging a rather large bag. He paid Roland and Horace no mind and continued dragging the large bag that seemed to enslave him.

Roland and Horace walked toward the entrance of the alley, heading back into the darkness, hoping that nothing looked suspicious and would appear as if the two men were leaving the alley. The large man continued his pace and dragged the bag toward the rail as Roland and Horace continued into the darkness.

"Hey, hey there," shouted the large man. Roland and Horace ignored the shouts and continued their steady pace toward the safety of the shadows. "Hey, you. I'm talking to you."

Horace stopped and turned to face the man. "Yeah, what do you want?" The man looked at Horace and then at Roland. Although he couldn't see Roland's face, he did something very unusual. He raised his head and sniffed the air.

"A human, a human in Terra Demorte." How it happened, Roland and Horace didn't know, but within a flash, the man had covered over thirty feet and was standing in front of Roland. He flashed a large smile, and it was evident that this wasn't an ordinary man, but another vampire. His four canine teeth were long and pointed. They were big, very big.

"Fresh meat," he said. He lunged at Roland, who went for his guns. The large man hit Roland with such a mighty force that the guns went spinning out of Roland's hands. They hit the ground and spun wildly as if performing some kind of ritual on the stone ground.

The large man's weight alone flung Roland backward. He lost his balance and fell to the ground with a mighty thump. He let out a small cry. The large man rolled off him but only because his large stomach made him do so. He quickly regained his composure and stood up, making ready to attack Roland once more. His fangs were longer now, and he made a loud hissing sound.

Roland rolled over. His shoulder was hurting, but now wasn't the time for that. He had to ignore the pain. He searched for the pistols, but the darkness of the alley had swallowed everything out of a three-foot range. He couldn't see his weapons on the dark stones. He rose and turned to face his attacker.

The vampire hissed once again and, without warning, stalked Roland. This time not quick and fast as before, but slowly, hissing with each step he took. "Fresh meat, fresh meat in Terra Demorte," he said.

Roland whispered for Horace, but Horace didn't answer. "Horace, do you see my guns?" Again, no answer came. The vampire walked ever so slowly toward Roland, and as he advanced, Roland slowly backed up until he struck something. "The wall," said Roland. "I'm trapped now."

The vampire was now five feet from Roland, closing the distance with each step. "How does it feel, human, to know you are about to die?"

Roland grabbed for his backpack, but it was lodged against something and wouldn't slide off his shoulder. He tried to step forward to release the grip on the backpack, but as he stepped closer to the vampire, the wall advanced, as well. Roland was confused, confused until he heard a voice whispering from behind him. "Roland, your guns." It was Horace; he was visible, but standing in the dark shadows behind Roland. Invisible to the vampire. He had found the pistols, and was pushing them forward under Roland's arms. Roland felt Horace's arms and slid his hand forward until he felt the two pistols. He grabbed them as Horace let go.

The vampire made one more loud hiss and started toward Roland, but his time, Roland was ready. There were four soft thuds, and the vampire fell to the ground. The death machines were true and belched out four brass casings. Each fell to the ground with a ting, and they spun around as if they were drunk, dancing out of control. Roland heard the large vampire hit the ground with a mighty thud, and he slowly put the pistols away.

He wasted no time, and like the other man he had just killed, he grabbed this man by the legs and started pulling him toward the pit. The man kicked several times, looked up at Roland, and hissed softly. He slowly rolled over and attempted to stand. Due to his large stomach, it took him several tries, but he did manage to stand. He once again stood in front of Roland hissing. He smelled the air once more and licked his lips.

"You can't kill me with those," he said, laughing at Roland. His hideous grin left his face, and he stared at the intruder standing in front of him. "I'm going to kill you; I'm going to suck all of the blood out of you until you are as white as I am." He laughed louder and then turned toward Horace. "I'll sell you to the trolls."

Roland had already begun to take action; he grabbed his pistols and once again called on their powers. He pulled the triggers four times each this time, and eight small rounds of lead headed toward the vampire. All eight hit him in the face, and the mighty vampire hit the ground again, but this time, Roland didn't hesitate. He quickly slipped the pistols back into their holsters and, without faltering, slung the backpack off his shoulder. He fished out the cross and pressed it hard to the vampire's face. Then, standing up and backing away, Roland watched the vampire catch fire and within seconds burned up. The ashes floated effortlessly in the alley, wanting to rise, but the moisture pushed down on the flightless dust, and the ashes fell to the ground.

"Glad you had that cross?" said Horace.

"Yeah, thanks to Wisteria. She gave me all kinds of weapons. For once, hers were better than mine were. Well, at least we don't have to worry about dragging him over to the pit and dumping him."

Horace looked serious. "If he hadn't been so fat, he would have killed you. Remember that, Roland. We just had a great deal of luck here. We have got to stay on our toes and be ready for anything."

Roland shook his head. "Thanks for the pistols, Horace. You saved my life."

Roland and Horace went back to the shadows. They were going to wait on Notor, but now that things were heating up, they needed to act, and act fast. Eventually, Notor would show up, and right now, sooner would be better than later.

# Twenty-Eight

## The Keys

Notor stood at the end of the bar. No one would notice him there although he had turned visible, and could be seen by all. Being in Jake's Place and being invisible would draw more attention to him than being visible. Jake had mounted scanners at the door to detect any invisible entity, and a huge sign on the wall that read, *NO INVISIBILITY*.

Jake wanted to know who was there at all times. Notor knew if someone did see him, it wouldn't matter, no one would care, except for Jake.

Everyone was having a good time drinking and talking to their friends. One would tell a story just to have someone else top it or expand upon it. The demon guardians were fast drinkers and had Jake and the two barmaids jumping and running pints of ale back and forth. It looked as if working the bar was as busy, if not busier, than the rest of the pub. The place was packed, and Creed and Olin were on the other side of the bar, so Notor assumed that no one would pay any attention to him—well, no one but Creed and Olin, of course. If they saw him, then there would certainly be a lot of explaining to do.

"More ale," said a demon guardian, "more ale." Jake patiently poured two more tankards of ale and headed toward a table. Notor saw his chance and slipped behind the bar. "Keys thirteen and fourteen," he said softly.

He grabbed the keys, stuck them under his shirt, and headed out from behind the bar.

"Whatcha doing there?" said a barmaid. "Whatcha doing behind the bar?" Notor turned around, and just his luck, there looking at him was a skuzzy old barmaid.

"Uh nothing, just looking around," said Notor.

"Oh just looking around, hey?"

"Yeah, just looking around a bit," said Notor.

"Well, we'll see what Jake has to say about that," said the barmaid. "Jake don't allow nobody behind the bar except me and Jess."

"Excuse me. This miserable spike belongs to me. Is he being nosy again? He can't help it, missy. He's just a nosy little spike. He can't hurt anything. Here, princess, let's just keep this between you and me. What do you say?" It was Thor. "Here's something for your troubles." Thor grabbed the woman's hand and slid a nugget of gold into it. "Something for you. If you keep quiet, I'll take care of my servant. Deal?"

The barmaid slid the gold nugget into her dress pocket. "Sure, governor. That will do just fine. I ain't seen nothing." She threw Thor a wink and went back to fetching more ale.

Thor looked at Notor. "Outside now." As they exited Jake's Place, Thor grabbed Notor by the arm. "What in the bloody blazes are you doing here, Notor? I thought you were with Roland. What the bloody blazes are you doing here? Do you want Creed and Olin to see you? Does Creed know you're back?"

"No, Thor, he does not. I came here to help Mr. Roberts, I mean Deidre, and Mr. Wheeler came here too. All of us are here, looking for Deidre's son."

"Who? Deidre? Who in the Hades is Deidre? What are you talking about, man? Quit your blabbering and speak so I can understand you. Who in the bloody blue blazes is Deidre?"

"Deidre is Roland, and we all are here to help get his son back." Notor spoke softly but firmly. "We are all in Terra Demorte now, here trying to find Mr. Roberts's son."

"You have got to be kidding me. Is Roland here?"

"Yes."

Thor rubbed his hair as he stared at Notor. "Where is Roland?"

"He's in that alley over there, probably looking at you right now," Notor said, pointing.

Thor shot across the street. His long strides were so quick; Notor had to run to keep up. Within seconds, he and Notor walked into the alley, and as if entering a monster's mouth, slowly disappeared into its shadows.

"Roland, what on earth are you doing here? Didn't I tell you what would happen if you were caught here in Terra Demorte?"

"Yeah, Thor, you told me, but my son is here, and I thought you might need my help."

"No, I don't need your help, and neither do I need the help of these two, either." Thor looked at Horace and Notor. "You guys have got to be kidding me. You have to be out of your minds coming here. How did you get through the portal, anyway?"

Roland held up the medallion. "With this," he said.

"Where did you get that? And what's more, whose is it?" Thor closed his eyes for a brief moment and then spoke. "It's Deidre's medallion, but how did you get it?"

"I got it at Odium's house. When we cut off her head, it fell to the floor and I pushed it under the couch then went back for it later. I thought it was Odium's, but it's not."

Thor ran his hands through this hair once again; he slid the band around his hair and rewrapped it. Obviously, he hadn't understood Roland completely. "No, it's not Odium's; it's Deidre's medallion. She's a friend of mine, Roland. Have you met her? Where is she?"

"She's dead, Thor, and we killed her."

"You killed her? Why?"

"No. I mean yes, I killed her, but—"

"Why would you kill Deidre? She's a nice person. You didn't even know her. Why would you kill her? Did you kill her for her medallion?"

"No, I killed her because I thought she was Odium. Thor, when we went to Odium's house, it wasn't Odium we killed; it was Deidre. It was Deidre I killed tonight."

"Not Odium's head?" said Thor. "How—why—why was Deidre at Odium's house? And why had she shape-shifted into Odium?" Thor was perplexed, confused. He rubbed his face and ran his fingers through his hair once again. "This changes things, Roland, and thanks for coming and telling me, but now you and these two hoodlums you are running with get the Hades out of Terra Demorte before anyone sees you."

"Who was Deidre?" questioned Roland.

"I knew her well, Roland." Thor rubbed his hands together and again looked perplexed. "She was a spy for the council and reported Creed and Olin's doings. If we cut off her head, she'll return to Terra Demorte, to the Keeping Room, and her clan will claim her body. Once they do that, her head will change. Since her head is here, she would be reincarnated, but where is she and why hasn't her clan came forward to claim her body?"

"Well, that's good I guess," said Notor. "Isn't it, Thor?"

"No, Notor. You see, the minute she returns here and her clan claims her body in the Keeping Room, the head I have on that stick in Jake's Place will turn into Deidre's head and not Wisteria's, and that, my friends, will cause me a lot of grief for me. We have to move. Someone or something is helping us, but who and why? Deidre's body has had plenty of time to return to the Keeping Room, her clan should have claimed her by now, but since they haven't, maybe their helping us, by giving us a little time, but why? Now, you three get out of here before someone sees you. Go back to the surface and don't ever come back here."

Roland looked at Thor. "Too late, Thor."

"Two men have already seen us, Thor; I killed them and pushed one into that pit over there." Roland pointed toward the pit. "The first man walked right up on me, and I had no choice but to shoot him. The second was a vampire. It took a little longer, but I managed to send him up in flames."

"You killed a vampire?" Thor asked.

"Yes."

"Not good. Someone or something has been killing vampires on the surface. The whole vampire clan is up in arms about it. They've called for a council meeting to discuss that very issue. They aren't very happy at the moment."

"I couldn't help it; he sniffed the air and attacked me."

"You shouldn't be here, Roland. That's the problem. Any one of the clans that live here could smell you out if they wanted to. The reason they don't is because no human has ever been here before so they don't concentrate on it. Anyway, it's good that you killed them. No witnesses." Thor's talents were coming to the surface; killing was second nature to him, and as an assassin, talking about death—no matter whose death it was—was good conversation to Thor.

"I need you to leave, Roland," said Thor. "Please, will you leave?"

"Not without Josh, Thor. Do you have a plan?"

"Thinking. The pub's so busy I can't make any moves, and I won't argue with you about leaving. OK, let's see if we can plan this thing out together." Thor was irritable, but nonetheless, he knew trying to convince Roland to leave was out of the question. "What was your plan?"

"We sent Notor over to the pub to steal the keys to Creed and Olin's rooms; we think Josh is in one of their rooms. Notor, did you get the keys?"

"Sure, Deidre," Notor said.

"What is this Deidre, stuff?" questioned Thor.

"Well, since people pick up on this medallion, and since it belonged to someone named Deidre, if anyone hears Notor or Horace call me that, they might not think anything about it," Roland said.

"Well, that's good thinking, but it doesn't work like that here, Roland," said Thor. "All right. We have the keys. Now what?"

"I'm going up the stairs and to the rooms. I'll find Joshua and then climb out of the window and run for it, hoping the jump isn't too high." Roland looked at Thor, hoping to see some kind of agreement, but Thor just stood there thinking.

"Might work, Roland, but Creed and Olin are watching the stairs and pretty much scan everything that goes up or down those things. I've been watching them. They have Morto using his scanners on each person that goes up the stairs. They're being careful, and I mean *careful*. They know what will happen to them if anyone finds your son in Terra Demorte. Morto will pick up on you the minute you take the first step on the stairs, and he'll know you're human."

"Then what do we do?" Roland asked. Notor and Horace were lost, as well, both had puzzled looks on their faces, and although they wanted to help, neither had a plan.

"Roland, do you trust me?" Thor asked. He looked directly into the eyes of Roland. "Do you trust me with your life and the life of your son?"

"Yes, of course, Thor. Yes, I do. Why?"

"If it came down to it, would you give your life for that of your son?" Thor moved closer to Roland. He spoke softly but clearly. "Would you sacrifice your life for that of your son?"

"Yes, in a heartbeat," Roland said. "Why? Why do you ask?"

"I have a plan; it's the only way we can get upstairs to get Josh. Again, do you trust me?"

"Yes," was all Roland said.

"Do you have plenty of ammunition?"

"Lots," said Roland.

"Good," said Thor. "That's good Roland, because you are going to need it. There is one problem, though."

"What's that?"

"If you get hurt or injured, or if you think you are going to be caught, you have to throw yourself into the pit over there, the same place you threw the man you killed earlier. You can't let anyone here catch you. Do you understand?"

"Yes, Thor. Don't worry about me. They won't catch me."

Thor looked at his friend. How did things get so messed up? He had never known the love of a father, and he had never felt love until he met Katie and Roland. He had felt something different when he met Deidre the first time, and whatever that feeling was, it grew each time he saw her. He was beginning to understand the feeling now.

His life was that of a simple assassin. Kill and fulfill your contract—that was it. That was his life. Now, standing in front of him was a human, a human that had managed to invade a place that had been a secret to humans since the fallen angel created it, and for the first time, a human was in Terra Demorte—not just one, but two.

What was he to do now, now that he was back in the good graces of Terra Demorte? Back with his beloved assassin clan. Should he turn on Roland, rat him out, and go back to the good life as an assassin? The longing for the dark place, he had called home for so many years, was overwhelming to Thor, drawing him in like an addiction. A dangerous thought for Roland, ran through the assassin's mind. "What to do, now?" he said softly.

"Guys, we have to act now. If Deidre's body comes to the Keeping Room, her head will change, and then everyone will know that I tricked them and my life will end, and then the chances of getting you son back, Roland, will be gone, all hope will be lost." Thor thought for a moment. Why should he risk his life? Why should he turn the only people he ever cared for against him? He softly spoke, only to himself. "No, I won't do it; I won't betray my clan."

But Roland heard the words.

# Twenty-Nine

## The Turncoat

Thor spoke clearly to Roland before walking away. "OK, I'll cause a distraction in the pub as soon as I see you walk in, Roland. Once you have entered the pub, head straight for the stairs and don't stop for anything. Don't look around. Don't be surprised at what you see. Just head up the stairs. Pretend you belong there, Roland." Thor looked at the man standing in the shadows. "Do you understand me? It's imperative that you do exactly as I tell you."

"Yes, Thor, I do understand."

"After I enter the pub, give me thirty seconds, and then make your move." Thor snapped at him. He was aggravated at the situation. He was there to save a little boy, or at least try; now, he had to worry about an outsider, another human in his beloved world—a world where humans didn't belong.

"What do we do, Roland?" asked Horace.

"I don't know. Watch my back, I guess. Let me know if anyone comes down this street, in either direction. Thor has reached the pub. Here we go. We're on." Roland walked slowly toward the pub. The closer he got, the more adrenalin pumped through his body.

Instantaneously, his body came alive with different types of emotions. His heart pumped massive amounts of adrenalin through his veins, forcing them to awaken his body. He was more alert, sharp, and ready to act. His eyes scanned even the most obscure shadows, searching every nook and cranny, probing for his enemies.

His senses kept telling him to draw his weapons; with the death machines in his hands, he would be ready to fight in a split second. The guns could answer his beck and call and smite his adversaries down instantly. He fought for his sanity; the urge to obey the mass amounts of messages in his mind was overwhelming, but he knew had to keep his head.

*No, stay cool. I have to be calm and act normal. I can't walk into this place with my guns blazing. I can't draw attention to myself. I've got to ignore everything and everybody, just walk in and go straight up the stairs. My son's life is at stake here. Be cool.* His thoughts fought his urges, and he kept the guns tucked neatly under his cloak.

"I'm going to do this, no matter what it takes; I'm getting my son and getting out of this place. Twenty eight, twenty nine, thirty," Roland counted.

Roland pushed the door of the pub open; the watering hole was full of smoke and many different kinds of creatures. His instincts were to stop and stare—the sight was unbelievable—but he knew in order to be incognito, he needed to keep moving.

There was a group of assassins sitting directly in front of him. They had grouped themselves at a large table, talking, smoking, and drinking. He heard one cursing as he spoke. "Well, no matter who's killing vampires on the surface, it's no business of the council. This is a matter for the vampire clan, and it's not our problem. Besides, I don't care who's killing them; I hate that bloody clan." He paused for a moment. "Get it? *Bloody* clan." They all laughed, smacked the table, and lifted their pints in agreement.

Roland's eyes quickly scanned the room. It was crowded with patrons who were very busy telling lies, drinking, laughing, and of course, swearing. He was sure no one would notice his presence. He saw Thor, standing at the bar sipping on a drink; the assassin was watching his every move.

Roland pulled the cloak tighter around his face. He left a narrow opening so he could see. Walking toward the stairs, he glanced once more at Thor and froze. The assassin's expression was different from what he had seen earlier in the alley. He had never observed this expression before; it wasn't one of friendship and concern, but one of hate and contempt. Thor stared at Roland and then turned slightly to his left and focused on Creed's table.

Roland, making his move, walked straight toward the huge, winding staircase. He pushed between men and brushed up against two demon guardians, and so far, no one had paid him any attention. He continued to serpentine through the crowd until he reached the staircase. *Nothing*, he thought. *So far, so good.*

Roland started up the stairs; he hadn't taken the second step out of the many that lay before him when he heard the distinct voice of Thor, the assassin.

"Halt, an intruder." One of Thor's hands dove under his cloak and, within seconds, a large dagger hit dead center in the post beside Roland's head. No one paid any attention to the dagger, as far as Roland could tell as he looked around—no one except the table where Creed and Olin were sitting.

Olin pushed his chair back and stood, staring at the man dressed in the black cloak, standing on the stairs. From under his hood, Roland returned the stare, and then started up the stairs. As loud as the pub was, he heard another sound that he recognized at once, it was the voice of Thor, shouting loudly.

"An intruder. Stop him. He's a human." The assassin at the bar was now pointing his finger toward Roland.

Roland stopped, turned, and stared at him. "Traitor!" he shouted at the assassin. He turned back down the stairs. There was a large demon guardian standing in his way, and Roland gave him a huge shove. The demon guardian fell into a table, and then he and the two demon guardians that were sitting at the table toppled to the floor like dominoes. They hadn't heard Thor's cry since the pub was so noisy, but the demon guardians, assassins, and other patrons on the side of the pub where Creed and Olin were sitting had heard. They were all heading straight toward Roland.

Roland pulled the two pistols. He didn't hesitate. If he were to get out of there, he would have to stay calm and make a hole through the crowd. There was no time to be polite. Roland didn't falter with the two pistols. He shot two demon guardians in front of him, and a large hole became visible. He heard another cry, which belonged to another familiar to voice. It was Olin.

"Stop her! Stop her!" Olin shouted.

Roland's mind questioned the remark. Why would, Olin shout, "Stop *her*"? then the answer came just as fast as the question. *He doesn't want anyone to know that a human is in Terra Demorte, especially a man.*

Roland had his hole. The patrons on the left side of the pub hadn't heard Thor or Olin's remarks as they sat drinking and cursing, but they saw demon guardians falling to the floor and had seen the other two demon guardians fall, as well. As they stared, they saw the large pools of blood spreading on the wooden floor. They started rising and wondering what was going on. They hadn't seen Roland shooting, and the pistols— still with their silencers—didn't make a noise except for the soft thuds.

All on the left were now confused and listening to the shouts from the right. They all turned toward the man in black standing at the door.

Roland heard Thor once more. "Stop that man. He's a human."

Roland pulled on the door, but before leaving, he turned toward Thor. The assassin was standing at the bar; he hadn't made any moves toward Roland. Why? "You want me, Thor, come and get me." He pointed the pistols at Thor, but Thor had expected that move. He knew Roland very well, and as quickly as Roland had lifted the pistols Thor, ducked behind the bar.

Roland saw Roy and Ray heading his way. They were pushing their way through the crowd, pushing others to the floor and knocking over tables. The biggest one tripped over a witch and fell forward. Trying to correct his clumsiness, he grabbed the back of a chair. Once he had his balance, he let go of the chair. All this he did while taking large strides toward Roland. Olin was in his wake, using the huge guardian as a shield. Roland, flashing the two pistols, aimed them at Roy and Ray.

Pistols were no surprise for these two demon guardians, and both grabbed two assassins, using them as shields. Roy kicked over a huge table, and he and Ray ducked behind it, falling on top of the two assassins. Roland opened fire, sending four slugs of lead in that direction.

"Get back and protect your, Master," screamed Olin. Ray was the first to act; he grabbed Olin and pushed him behind the table. Roy took two long strides and cleared the table where Creed was sitting. With a loud bang, Roy, pushed Creed to the floor and covered him with his body.

Morto stood up from his table, and pushing his chair back against the wall with his legs, fished out two daggers from under his long black cloak. He let them fly at the hooded figure causing the ruckus in the pub, but Roland was on his toes, his eyes scanning anything and everything that moved. And to him, everything in the pub that was alive was moving. He had seen the assassin and had anticipated that very move. He stepped to one side as the daggers struck the solid wooden door and dug deep into the grainy wood.

This was the last straw for Roland. He emptied his guns into the moving targets scattered throughout the bar. If it moved, he sent a cartridge in that direction. He let caution go to the wind, and his urge to shoot took full control. Demon guardians that had never felt the sting from a pistol squealed loudly. They had no idea what was happening, and they fell like dominoes.

Olin made a fist and flung a fireball at Roland. It just missed, as Roland stepped, once again, to the side. He pointed the pistols, although he knew they were empty, no one else did. Olin dove to the floor and rolled up against one of the dead demon guardians, keeping out of sight.

Roland exited the door; his strides across the cobblestone street were huge and quick. He ran into the alley where Horace and Notor were waiting. "Scatter, boys. They will be coming after me. Save yourselves."

"No," said Notor. For the second time that night, the spike came up with a great plan. "I'll go to the tunnel and make myself visible. Give me your cloak, Roland. Without hesitating, Roland slid out of his cloak and handed it to Notor. "You guys hide, and once they see me, they will come after me. If I can stay far enough ahead of them, they just might follow me all the way up the tunnel."

"Be careful, Notor, and don't let them catch you," said Roland.

# Thirty

## The Deal

Horace and Roland started down the dimly lit alley. Roland took one more look at the pub. Men, demon guardians, and other patrons were now pouring out onto the street. One shouted, "There he goes; he's heading for the tunnel." They had seen Notor. The deception was working. The creatures in the street headed toward the entrance of the tunnel.

Then a strange thing happened. Olin, was standing in the middle of the cobblestone street, yelling at anyone who would listen. "You there, and you, go that way, just in case he tries to double back. Roy, you and Ray search that alley." Olin pointed directly toward the alley where Roland and Horace were standing.

Roland pushed the small levers on the pistols, and the clips dropped onto the ground, making a clanking sound. He quickly reloaded. "Horace, we've got to get out of here."

The men ran down the backside of the alley. Horace, who didn't understand what was happening and could not stand the suspense any longer, posed a question. "Roland, what went wrong in there, what happened?"

"Thor, doubled crossed us, he ratted me out as soon as I took the first step on the stairs. I had no choice but to shoot my way out, and now everyone in that place is after us, or rather me. Horace, they don't know you are here, quickly, get away from me and no one will ever know you were with me."

"No, Roland, too late, I'm sticking with you, we need to run faster and just keep running."

Both men saw a door open ahead of them, and at that very moment, they thought the same thought, *a good place to duck in and hide.* To their dismay, two men stepped out and screamed at the two fugitives.

"Stop! Stop right there," the tall one shouted.

Roland didn't hesitate; he pulled the triggers on the two pistols and shot the men in the chest. They fell to the ground.

"Catch that door, Horace. Catch that door, and maybe we can hide in there." The door slammed long before Horace could reach it.

"Sorry, Roland. I missed it."

"Keep running, Horace."

Roland peered over his shoulder, right away he saw two demon guardians turn the corner and head down the alley. "Roy and Ray," he said. He quickly turned and, while running backward, fired off four rounds from each pistol. He knew his chances of hitting them were slim, but it might slow the guardians down a bit. Both were familiar with pistols and knew the damage they did, and although they couldn't hear the shots being fired, they certainly would hear them ricocheting off the stone buildings and walls.

He was right on both accounts; the slugs hit everything but the two huge demon guardians. As the bullets hit the walls, they ricocheted, and the eight rounds now sounded more like sixteen—striking the walls, buildings, and everything in their paths. Two lights suddenly burst, sending small shards of glass in all directions. They made a loud screaming sound, and at first Roland thought he had hit someone.

He and Horace stopped to watch and catch their breath. The small lights stopped their screaming and seconds later put forth their uncanny muted glow once more. Roy and Ray had ducked behind a large rock jutting out from a wall, and neither looked up until the last lead slugs struck their final targets and fell dead. One came to a rest, spinning and dancing, beside Ray's leg.

"Look, Roy. That one just miss me. Me going to kill whatever that is."

Roy looked at his partner. "Yeah, right after I kill him you can have your turn. We've got to catch this intruder and put him in the pit, Ray. That's Master Olin's orders. He doesn't want anyone to know what we do with the body."

***

By now, Notor was heading up the tunnel. He turned slightly, and looking over his shoulder, he counted six—no, seven figures chasing after him. The torches in the tunnel would light for him, and then go off. Moments later, they would light again for his pursuers. He laughed as he ran over the moist stones. *As soon as I reach the portal, I'll get rid of this cloak and make myself invisible. They will never know who I am or catch me.*

He laughed once more, and for once, Notor was using his brain instead of his mouth. He felt proud of himself. After all, this was his idea, and it was working. Looking over his shoulder, he knew he was keeping the right amount of distance between himself and his followers.

He took a few more steps, when something, out of the darkness, hit him. The force was so devastating that it sent him crumbling to the ground, and for a brief moment, he could feel the coolness of the moist stones on his face. Then all went dark.

***

Thor stood at the bar; the place was all but empty now, except for Creed and Morto. Roy had crawled off Creed. His huge body had protected his master, and the small lead slugs Roland had fired had missed both the warlock and his guardian. Roy had met Ray outside, and they joined the hunt for the man in black. Creed had clambered into his chair and was sitting with his back against the wall. Morto wanted to join the rest of the men in the massive manhunt for the intruder but stayed with Creed. He knew who the intruder was. After all, he was working for Creed now, and he knew darn well it was the human they called Roland.

Of course, he had also heard Master Olin tell Roy and Ray to kill the intruder and throw him in the pit. From inside the pub, they could still hear Olin, in the street shouting out orders. "If you catch him, bring him to me. Do you understand? I don't want anyone else to see the intruder," his voice called.

Morto knew about the small human boy upstairs. He knew why he was scanning the stairs when someone went up them. He was an assassin, Olin and Creed had given him a contract, and he was filling it by scanning the stairs. It was a sacred thing for him to keep his word; and he promised the two warlocks that he would never mention a word of what was happening in Terra Demorte.

Although he was one of the conspirators to bestow the magical gold box upon Olin, at that time he wasn't working for the pair. Therefore, to Morto, that was just another piece of business.

He had sworn an oath not to ever mention to anyone the small boy Master Olin had brought there to anyone. He was a proud warrior, and his word was true, but little did Morto know that Olin had plans to keep his and Creed's endeavors a secret, as well. As soon as Creed's transformation was completed, he had his own plans of what to do with the assassin, Morto. He would reward the assassin with a trip to the pit.

Morto looked at Creed. "Master, let me go out there. I'll find Mr. Roberts for you, and I'll kill him." Creed became furious. He slammed his hand down sharply on the table, looked at Morto, and then hissed softly.

"Don't say that name in here, Morto. Don't mention anything about him or even pretend you know what is going on. It will be the death of all of us if you do. Now get out there, kill that human, and dump him in the pit. Don't tell anyone. Just do it."

Creed let out a loud breath of air, which was as raspy as ever. He sucked in another breath and continued. "I've told Roy and Ray to do the same thing. If you see them, you might want to remind them. You pretend to be helping and know nothing about who that was, and whatever you do, don't tell anyone what you know."

"Yes, Master, I'll tell Roy and Ray. They will be glad to kill"—Morto hesitated for a moment—"*that thing* for you." He started to leave but wavered for a moment. He turned toward Creed once more. "Master Creed, who will watch over you?"

"I'll be fine. Olin is in the street. He'll protect me if need be. Now get out there and do what I pay you to do."

"I'll watch over Master Creed," said Thor, pulling up a chair and sitting down at the table. Morto looked at Thor and then at Creed.

"Master?" said Morto.

"It's all right, Morto. Thor, are you going to kill me?" Creed asked.

"No, Master Creed, I'm going to protect you, sir."

"Go, Morto, kill that human and dump him in the pit. No one else must know he's here. Do you hear me? Too many of them know now, but"—he paused for a moment—"they don't know exactly who that is, and they don't know we are involved."

"Yes, Master Creed. Yes, sir."

\*\*\*

Roland and Horace ducked into another alley; it was a side alley that ran out into the main street. It, as well, was dark and moist. There was a light fog creeping in, trying relentlessly to consume everything in its path, but it was thin and offered no additional cover. They could see the main street from this alley. They were ahead of the men but not by much, a couple of blocks down from Jake's Place. Roland pointed across the cobblestone street.

"Horace, go invisible and cross the street. See if we can get in that building. We've got to keep moving or they will catch us." Horace disappeared into the cool night air, and moments later, he materialized in front of Roland.

"Yes, the door is open; we can hide in there if they don't see you crossing the street."

"You go; I'll go down the back here and get some distance between me and these monsters. I'll cross a few blocks down. Go now. I'll be along shortly."

Horace left and Roland saw the door of the building across the street open and then shut. He turned and left the side alley. He wanted to go back down the large alley that ran down behind the buildings on his side of the street, and after a couple of blocks, cross the street. He had just started to turn down the back alley when two huge demon guardians came up the alley from the main street. He had just been in that alley, and had just missed being caught by the approaching guardians. He glanced at the two guardians and they, in turn, saw Roland.

"There he is; get him." Roland pulled his pistols, and once more, the death machines made their soft, muffled sounds. He shot the first guardian three times in the chest; it stopped him dead in his tracks and he fell with a loud thud. The second guardian stopped, as well. He stared at his friend and then at his own chest. Massive amounts of blood were running from the wounds of the fallen guardian, and pouring onto the cobblestone street. He stooped and rubbed his hands over the wounds and stared at the blood oozing from his friend's wounds.

The first demon guardian had let out a loud squeal before falling to the stones. The second guardian stood up. He let out a loud growl and charged Roland. He snorted as he took long strides; Roland could hear his feet hitting the cobblestones. The beast was furious, and Roland knew it.

He pointed his weapon and shot four times at the huge beast. The monster did exactly as the dead guardian had done; he let out a loud squeal and fell to the stones. He didn't make another move, so Roland continued down the backside of the alley.

\*\*\*

Horace sat inside the building alone. He wasn't frightened but worried. He wondered if they were going to get out of this place, and now that Terra Demorte knew or suspected there was a human there, what would happen to Roland if they caught him. He knew quite well what would happen if he or Notor were caught, and he wanted to ensure that didn't happen. Now that all Hades had broken loose, everything that moved would be sniffed, scanned, or checked. Even if invisible, he could still be caught.

He stared at the large room and took a step deeper into the darkness. As he did, a small light illuminated, sending muted beams in every direction. Then he heard a voice. "May I help you?"

Horace froze; he stared into the darkness but couldn't see anyone. "Who are you?" he said.

"I'm the keeper of the Keeping Room," said the voice.

"Are you a woman or man?" he asked.

"I'm a woman. I'm the keeper of the Keeping Room, and do you wish to make a deposit or a withdrawal?"

"Neither," said Horace. "I would just like to stand here a moment, if that is all right with you."

The woman's voice was soft, and she spoke once more. "That will be fine. Just let me know if I can help you."

"Sure thing," said Horace.

\*\*\*

Roland ran quickly down the backside of the alley. He could feel the cold air and see more of the fog in front of him. It was creeping ever so slowly toward him. He stopped for a moment and looked backed over his shoulder. He made no mistake in identifying who was chasing him; it was Roy and Ray.

"There he goes, Ray. We have him now," shouted Roy.

As fast as Roy and Ray were, Roland was much faster. He quickly slipped down another side alley, then onto the main street, being careful to stay in the shadows. He went down the street a block and turned back into another side alley, he ran into a vampire and two people who looked to be crippled. They dragged their steps, instead of taking normal strides.

Without faltering, Roland shot the vampire several times in the chest. The vampire fell to the ground but quickly scampered back to his feet. Roland shot him again, and as the vampire fell, Roland reached under his cloak and grabbed the cross; he placed it on the vampire's chest. The vampire burst into flames, lighting up the street. The flames sent small glowing embers upward but only to have them fall downward as they were heavier than the night air.

He could see the two crippled people clearly now. They were heading his way, groaning, trying to run with their arms open and outstretched.

"What are they?" he muttered. The words had no sooner left his lips when a terrible thought flooded his mind. "Zombies," he whispered.

The two zombies were closing in, and Roland stood up. He took several steps backward and shot the first in the head. The zombie dropped and didn't make another move. The second kept up the slow pace, relentlessly closing in on Roland. He pulled the triggers and fired twice. The small pieces of lead sped at an incredible speed toward the awkward zombie, hitting her in the face. She too fell dead. She moaned as she fell, then went silent.

"Well, so much for hiding," said Roland, watching the vampire's body burning. The fiery glow illuminated everything in its path, chasing shadows into hiding. He turned back onto the main street and ran down to the next alley. Most of the buildings had lights burning, and he knew that most had no idea of the chaos happening in the streets. *Mostly,* he thought. *Just those monsters that were in Jake's Place know I'm here. I guess that's better than everyone knowing I'm here.*

He ducked back into another side alley. He didn't want to take the chance of crossing the street now that there was a bright fire for all to see in the previous alley. "I'll have to create a diversion."

Roland dodged in and out of alleys, each time trying to remember where he was in respect to the main street and the building where Horace was waiting. Finally, after trying several doors, Roland found a small door that opened easily with his push. He entered the room. It was deathly cold.

"In here, human. I've been expecting you."

Roland stopped. He didn't see anything, but he could tell that the voice belonged to a woman. "Who are you?"

"It doesn't matter who I am. You need my help and I'm willing to help you. Do you want my help?"

"Yes, please, but why do you want to help me?" Roland paused and tried to catch his breath. His eyes tried to penetrate the darkness, but he couldn't see his own hands, let alone anything else in the room. The room was consumed by darkness. "Why would you want to help me?" he repeated.

He turned and pushed the heavy wooden door shut behind him. His hands held his pistols; he stood there, as a pawn would sit on a chessboard, waiting on the opponent to make the next move. His palms were sweaty, his breath short and quick. He didn't move. The coldness in the room began to overwhelm him.

"Who are you?" he said.

"It doesn't matter who I am, Roland. What matters is what I can do for you."

"What can you do for me? Can you—"

"Can I help you get your son to safety and get you out of Terra Demorte?" she said. Her voice was soft and welcoming, but Roland could feel something else in the room, something evil, so he tightened his grip on his pistols.

"Yes," said the woman. "I can help you if you promise to help me in return. I need a small favor from you."

"What kind of favor?" Roland questioned. "Can you turn on a light?"

"Sure, Roland," said the woman.

"How is it that you know my name?"

"I know all about you, and I know that your son, Josh, is here, in Terra Demorte."

He slightly adjusted the direction in which he was facing, toward the voice. "How do you know that?" Roland questioned, still holding his guns in his hands. "Can you please turn on a light? I can't see you."

"Light," whispered the woman. A light flickered and dimly lit the room. The woman was sitting at a large wooden table. She was dressed in a black cloak, and Roland couldn't see any of her features. Her voice was calming, and Roland stood, studying the figure.

"Are you a witch?" he asked.

"Does it matter what I am?"

"I just want to know what I'm talking to."

"I can help you, Roland. Do you want my help?"

Roland didn't answer; he stood silent and studied the woman sitting at the table. Everything in this evil place was some type of creature; he didn't know if he could trust this one.

"Well, do you want my help, Roland, or not? You might make it out of here without it, and then again, you might not. I can help you, and help you get your son out of here, if you wish."

"Yes, I do wish," said Roland.

"Then put your pistols away and come sit with me; you will be safe in here." The woman sat quietly at the table. Roland walked toward the chair. He pushed the levers on the pistols and loaded new clips. He placed the two death machines in their holsters and sat down at the table.

"Door, lock," she said. There was a heavy sound as two bolts slid securely into place.

\*\*\*

Notor slowly became conscious; he couldn't understand why his arms hurt and why he couldn't move his legs. His head pounded, and as soon as he came to his senses, he realized why his legs wouldn't work. Two large arms were under each of his armpits, they were clutching him tightly. He realized two large demon guardians were dragging him.

"Hold it right there, spike," one of them said. "Don't try to escape. We've got you, and we are taking you to Jake's Place."

"Please, turn me loose. I'm waiting on my master. I wasn't doing anything wrong." Notor tried to convince the two demon guardians that he was just an innocent bystander and had nothing to do with the ruckus that was going on. "Please, I'm waiting on my master."

"Well, who is your master, spike?"

"My master is Master Creed," said Notor. "Now turn me loose. I have some important news for him." He knew the two beasts wouldn't turn him loose; they were so simpleminded. It had always amazed him how something as powerful as a demon guardian could be so stupid. He pleaded once more to no avail. *At least,* he thought, *I tried to get loose.*

Then a terrible horrifying thought crossed Notor's mind. *If they take me to Jake's Place, I've got to come up with some kind of cockamamie story to tell Creed, and one pretty quick.*

"We will turn you loose just as soon as we get to Jake's Place. Your master is there, and we can see if he knows you." The large demon guardian laughed. "If he doesn't, well, we will sell you to the trolls, and you just might fetch a pretty penny." The guardian snorted loudly and then laughed, "Gold that is."

The two guardians walked into the pub, dragging poor Notor by the armpits. Stopping in front of Creed's table, they dropped Notor onto the floor face first. He stood up and pushed the demon guardian back. "How does that feel? You had no right to drop me."

The demon guardian snorted loudly at Notor and then ignored him. "Master Creed, we caught this spike sneaking around. He was heading out of the tunnel toward the portal when we caught him. Two other guardians was chasing him; he says he was on his way to see you. Do you know this, Spike, sir?"

"Notor," said Creed? Notor, stood erect and shook the dust off his clothes. He stared at the creature sitting in front of him. He wanted to run but knew he would not get far and nothing short of a miracle would save him, if he did. He stood erect and addressed his Master.

"Yes, Master, it's me sir, Notor."

"What are you doing here and where have you been?" Creed's voice was raspy but soft. "Where have you been?" Before Notor had time to speak, Creed snapped at the two demon guardians. "Here's a piece of gold. Now go fine the intruder and bring him to me. This is my servant; I'll take care of him."

Notor, for once, didn't open his mouth and start blabbing. He thought for a moment. He thought about the happenings of the day, where Creed had been, and what he and his brother had been doing. Then he answered Creed's question.

"I was spying on Mr. Roberts and Wisteria, and I went to report to you, Master, and you weren't at the mansion. I went back to Number 12 and I heard Mr. Roberts say he was coming to Terra Demorte, and that you were here with his son."

"Notor, how did Mr. Roberts get into Terra Demorte?" Creed leaned forward and rested his elbows on the table. "Well, answer me, man. How did Mr. Roberts get into Terra Demorte, and how did you get here?"

Notor was scared, but he focused on his mission and answered his master. "I came with Mr. Roberts. He didn't know it because I was invisible, and when he opened the portal, I came in with him. Creed looked at Notor; he slid back against the wall.

Notor continued. "I came to tell you about him, Master. I came to warn you."

"Warn me? Warn me about what?"

"Warn you, Master, that he was coming to kill you, sir." Notor was shaking and tried to hide it but wasn't doing a good job of it at all.

"So, Notor, how did Mr. Roberts get into Terra Demorte? I know he is here. What I need to know is how did he get through the portal? With whose medallion?" Creed was becoming irritable. "Speak, man; do you know whose medallion he has?"

Notor thought for a moment before answering Creed's question. "Yes, sir. He has a medallion that belonged to someone named Deidre." Creed sat and didn't say a word. He studied the little man standing in front of him and watched his every move. Then suddenly he exploded.

"Do you expect me to believe that? Do you think I'm an imbecile? Do I look stupid to you? Well I'm not, and I tell you what I think." Creed jerked forward again and rested his elbows on the table. "I think you're lying to me, I don't know why, but I think you know a lot more than you are telling me. Where have you been for the last month?"

Notor was shaking but continued to stand firm in front of his master. As he stood there, for once, he decided this horrible creature wouldn't terrify him. "Master, I was at Number 12. That nosy old witch had me locked up in the house and I couldn't escape. I couldn't escape until today when she took the spell off of the house. I escaped and followed Mr. Roberts here. I was on my way to tell you when the demon guardians caught me." He stood there staring at Creed.

Creed didn't know what to believe, but he certainly wasn't afraid of a spike. And he had more on his mind than the old news Notor had brought.

"Thor, take Notor down to the Keeping Room and lock him away until I figure out what I want to do with him. After we finish this mess we're in, I'll talk to Olin." Creed leaned back against the wall. "Take him away and lock him up."

Thor rose and grabbed Notor by the arm. "Come on, spike. To the Keeping Room, it is for you. Now come on, and make it snappy." Notor walked toward the door with Thor on his heels. Once outside, Thor spoke. "Look, Notor, I'm going to turn you loose. Do you still have the keys to the rooms upstairs?"

"Yes, Thor."

"Give them to me. Wait five minutes and then I want you to come in here and shout this." Thor released, Notor, and whispered into his ear. He stuffed the keys under his cloak, walked back into the pub, and sat down beside Creed.

\*\*\*

Roland sat down with the woman in black. He stared at her but couldn't see anything behind the hood that covered her face. The dark cloak also covered her hands, and as he gazed upon her, he couldn't make out any of her features. He felt something he had never felt before. He felt evil in its raw form, for the first time in his life. He had known evil things and had seen evil in its making by humans on the surface, but this was the first time he felt nothing but pure unadulterated evil and it scared him.

"Who are you?" he said softly. "I know if you are here, you are some kind of evil person or thing. Which one are you?"

"Well, like you, Roland, I don't live here. I'm an intruder myself, and nobody knows I'm here, which is more than I can say for you. To them, I'm just another witch passing through, but you and I know better, don't we?"

"I don't know what you are. I didn't know you were a witch, but I can feel the evil you possess. I know you are evil, and I don't know why you would want to help me."

"Well, you and I have something in common, Roland, something that you will learn more about in the very near future." The witch sat and stared at Roland. She wanted that part to set in before continuing. "I'll help you, Roland; I'll help you get out of here without anyone knowing who you are. You realize if you are identified, they will kill your entire bloodline, you know that don't you," she laughed. "Of course you do, but that did not stop you from coming here, now did it, Roland?"

"No, it didn't. This thing we have in common, what is it?"

"Oh, something you will find out later, something you have that I need, something I'll ask you for later. If I help you get out of here, and your son too, will you give me a simple little favor in the near future?"

Roland could once again feel the evil the woman possessed. He studied her and wanted to know more about her. She wanted a favor. What kind of favor? His mind was spinning off in all directions. The only thing he wanted now was to get himself and his son out of this terrible place. He heard voices and many footsteps in the alley outside the door.

One voice became quite loud. "You, there. Go down that alley and meet us in the front. He must be here somewhere, maybe down farther, down toward the water. Go now. Search every unlocked door and in every niche and in every corner. He is here and we will find him."

Roland turned and looked at the door. *The bolts are locked; we are safe,* he thought.

"Yes, Roland, you are safe. If you want to remain that way, make my deal or I'll hand you over to those demon guardians myself. You realize Master Creed doesn't want anyone to get you but him and Olin. They plan on throwing you in the pit." The witch paused. "And of course your son too."

"What kind of favor do you want from me? I have nothing to offer you, nothing valuable. Why won't you tell me what kind of favor you want? Do you want me to kill someone for you?"

"No, of course not. I could kill you or anyone here very easily; I have the power, you know. My favor is simply I'll ask you for something when the time is right, and all you have to do is give it to me. It doesn't require any stealing or that you take the life of anyone; just give me something you have, something small that I need. Now, at the moment, I'm not sure that I need anything you have, but in the future, if I do, all I require is a promise that you would give it to me. Do we have a deal? You must hurry. Your time is getting short."

The witch talked softly, as if she was a friend, a friend who wanted to help Roland. She asked once more. "Roland, let me help you out of this place, and all you will owe me is a small favor. Agreed?"

Roland knew he couldn't trust this creature, but now his resources were gone. It seemed that all of Terra Demorte was looking for him, Thor had turned on him, and all he had left were Horace and Notor.

"OK, but first I want to know your name."

"I have no name. I was never given one, even at birth, my mother never gave me a name, and if you must know, the favor I'll ask of you is something you have that will help me know who my mother was...or *is,* I should say."

"What do I have?" said Roland. "Tell me, and I'll give it to you as soon as I return home. Just tell me."

"Well, it's not that simple, Roland. You see, at the moment, you don't have what I need, but in time you will. Now, do we have a deal or not?"

"So, if you don't have a name, what do people call you?" Roland pushed the question once more; he had to know who he was about to make a deal with. He had to know.

"They call me the Great Dark Witch," said the woman.

"OK, then once I get this thing, I'll give it to you. So, OK, you have a deal. Can you get me and my son out of here?" Roland watched the Great Dark Witch.

"Yes," she said. "Here is what we will do. I'll need for you to stay put until you hear the demon guardians chasing me, then I want you to meet, Horace, at the Keeping Room. Yes, I know all about Horace and Notor, and by the way, your little Spike has been caught by Master Creed, he's on his way to be locked in the Keeping Room by, Thor."

"I'm going to kill, Thor," said Roland.

"No, all you are going to do is meet me in the Keeping Room after I give these dumb, simple, demon guardians the slip. Then we will pick up your son and you can go home, never to return to Terra Demorte. Agreed?"

"Yes, agreed."

"When you hear them chasing me, and you will, slip out the back door and down to the front street. The street lamps will come on if you do not say, 'Lights out.' Simple. Do you understand?"

"Yes, I understand."

"Cross the street, and as you make your way to the Keeping Room, keep repeating 'Lights out,' and you won't be seen. Now give me about twenty seconds."

Roland and the Great Dark Witch stood up; he looked again at the woman in the dark cloak. "Thank you," he said.

"Oh, thank you, Roland. You've made a great deal. Here, put this on." The witch handed Roland another cloak. She smiled beneath her hood. As she passed Roland, she whispered, "Keep those pistols quiet, Roland. Just slip back up the street to the Keeping Room."

The witch unlocked the door and was gone, and as if magic, the room suddenly heated back up. What kind of deal had he made, and with whom? What was—or *who* was the Great Dark Witch? He wasn't sure, but knew Wisteria would know, and now all he wanted to do was get out of this place with his son.

# Thirty-One

## The Meeting

—————————————————

Roland stood by the door until he heard what the Great Dark Witch had told him he would hear. "There he goes. Come on. He's heading down to the lake. Hurry. Get him. We can't let him get to the boats. Hurry now. He's heading toward the lake." Roland heard more loud noises, and could almost swear he heard gunshots—or at least something that sounded like gunshots. He opened the door and ducked down the side alley. As he reached the main street, he started whispering softly, "Lights out." The lights in front of the building went dark. He whispered the same phase again and ran quickly across the street.

"Lights out," he said, reaching the other side of the street. The lights went dark right before he entered into its mistrustful glow.

He had no sooner stepped up on the sidewalk when a voice cried, "Lights on." The lights came on, shining their brilliance downward. It wasn't just one, but multiple lights, and there stood Roland for everyone to see. He saw four demon guardians standing up the street with at least four assassins. They all looked at him, and for a moment, all were frozen like statues, and then one spoke, "after him." They all broke into a run and headed toward the human standing in the middle of the street at Terra Demorte.

Roland headed back across the street to the alley. He fired several bullets toward the pursuers, not caring if they hit anything or not. However, he did hope it would slow them down. He heard a loud squeal and knew instantly he had hit at least one demon guardian. Roland started up the alley and quickly recognized Ray and Roy standing at the other end. They as well, broke into a run and headed toward him, their feet pounding the cobblestones, and each step they took was followed by a loud grunt.

Roland had only one way to go. He headed toward the water. He remembered someone saying there were boats there, and with the fog closing in around things, he just might be able to row out into the water and lose his pursuers.

Roland ran straight down the center of the main street, lights turning on and then off again, just to turn back on, lighting the way for another chaser. He looked over his shoulder, and the distance between him and his pursuers wasn't closing. He now realized that Roy and Ray had joined the other men and saw two zombies coming out of another alley he had just passed.

*If the boats aren't there, I'm dead,* he thought.

Roland ran forward and saw a huge black void—the water. There were shiny glimmers of light flicking on and off as if controlled by an automatic switch. The overhead lights lining the shore cast their glow on the water, and their reflections danced on the liquid surface.

He spotted multiple boats, highly visible under the lights—not at all what he had experience in this otherwise dark and dreary place.

To his left, away from the lights, he saw a dock that housed a small pier. There was a tiny building perched slightly askew, near the end. It was darker there, and the dock was barely visible. The fog had all but consumed it and the tiny building. There were several rowboats tied to the pier, and the small light over the door made them visible. He needed less light than the boats on the shore offered, so he headed for the pier. With a little luck, he could hide there until the hunt for him was over.

He had just reached the building and started for a boat when he heard voices. He ducked into the old shack.

"You there, search all of the boats along the shore line; he may be hiding under one of them." It was an assassin taking charge. "You, Ray and Roy, come with me, and we will search the pier. You there, you two zombies, come with us." They all headed toward the shack.

Roland checked his backpack and reloaded his pistols then looked around the shack. "I've got to get out of here. Trapped like a rat in here," he whispered. He found a side door and decided his chances would be better on the pier than in the shack itself.

It was then that a figure dressed in a cloak jumped up from one of the boats and headed back toward town. The creatures on the pier spied the figure and shouted for the others to catch it. Everyone on the shoreline started chasing the mysterious figure in black.

"Let's go, Roy," said Ray. "There he goes." Roy started back down the pier with Ray in close pursuit.

"Hold on, boys," said the assassin. "That's not our man."

Ray and Roy stopped and stared at the assassin. The two zombies hadn't had much of a chance to move as they were so slow, and by the time they realized what was happening, it had already changed again.

A vampire joined them. He smiled at the assassin. "They're chasing a witch, nothing more. I agree; that's not our man. Our man is here; I can smell him." The vampire lifted his nose and sniffed the air. "Yes, he's here, and close."

Roland wasted no time. He picked up an oar and, stepping around the corner, swung it toward the vampire and the assassin. His aim was deadly and true, and the mighty blow sent the two evil beings straight into Ray and Roy. All four plunged into the dark-black water.

Roland grabbed the line of a boat, pushed off the pier, and started rowing as fast as he could. The fog was closing in, and within minutes, he was to the edge and slipping slowly into the water's gentle embrace. For the first time since he had arrived in Terra Demorte, he felt safe.

The assassin and the vampire climbed back onto the pier, and Roy soon followed. The two zombies stood there watching and waiting for directions as to what they should do next. The assassin cursed and shot a blast from his hand into the air. The sky, or what seemed to be a sky, lit up with a bright, reddish light. It chased the fog back and lit up a large area in and around the lake.

Roland was sitting at the edge of the light. They could barely see him, and he had stopped rowing. He had thought that if he rowed a few more times he would be lost in the thick fog. There, he might lose his sense of direction and might not be able to find his way back out of the dense soup. And he had used the light from the shack as a small beacon, but now that the assassin had furnished a bigger one, he knew he could disappear into the fog and still see the flaming reddish light. Now he knew he could find his way back to the main street where Horace was waiting.

Why didn't Roland row into the fog? Why was he just sitting there a hundred yards away from the shack, in plain view of his pursuers? The reason was simple: no one, not the assassin, the vampire, the two zombies, or Roy was paying any attention to the most wanted man in Terra Demorte. They all were watching Ray.

"Roy, save me. Save me, Roy. I can't swim. I drowning."

"Ray," screamed Roy. He paced the pier, screaming his partner's name.

"Roy, Roy, helps me. Helps me, I drowning."

Roy watched Ray go under for a second time; he was flinging his arms and legs like a huge alligator rolling repeatedly on its prey. He was squealing, snorting loudly, and large quantities of water were entering his mouth only to be choked and spewed out again by the drowning guardian. At one time, the huge beast looked like a whale spouting water out of its blowhole. He would curse, snort, and then squeal loudly. Then he would start the whole process all over again.

"Ray," shouted Roy. "Ray, can you hear me?"

"Help me, Roy. I can't—" Ray went under for a third time, only to return to the surface spitting water and snorting loudly.

Roy watched as the vampire looked at the assassin. The assassin shook his head and spoke in a whisper. "I'm not going back into the water." He cupped his hand to his mouth. "There are things in there."

The vampire agreed and both stood motionless, watching Ray drown. The two zombies looked at each other and shook their heads, as well, indicating they wouldn't be saving the demon guardian.

"Roy, Roy!" Ray's voice was getting weaker. His great commotion was now slowing down, and his heavy arms and legs were trying to slip down into the dark abyss. His legs would start to sink and he would pull them back toward the surface, and as they surfaced, his muscle-bound chest and head would dip beneath the water. Soon, both would fall in unison, and the huge demon guardian would surely sink.

Roland stared at the sight. For some reason, seeing Ray drown was worth the risk of someone continuing to chase him. He sat in the small rowboat and watched the activity at the shack. The large reddish light lit up everything, and from where he sat, he could tell that Ray was tiring and slowly giving into death's simple call.

"Ray, Ray, listen to me," shouted Roy.

"Roy, Roy, helps me. Please save me, Roy." Ray couldn't understand why his long-time partner was standing on the pier. Why was Roy not trying to save him? His large eyes focused on his enduring friend; he knew he wouldn't have the strength to fight the water much longer.

Ray's head went down for a fourth time. His arms and legs floated, which allowed him to lift his head for the much-needed air. He would fight to keep his arms and legs afloat, only to sink his head. He was tiring, and knew he was doomed; soon he would succumb to the dark water's calling.

"Roy," was the only sound that his voice managed to say as he choked on the water.

Roy responded, "Ray."

A few moments passed, and Ray's large eyes focused for the last time on Roy. He had stopped fighting the water now, and he felt his life sinking into the dark chasm. He was calmer now. As death approached, and for the first time since he had fallen into the water, he heard Roy's voice, loud and clear.

"Ray, can you hear me," Roy was shouting loudly. Actually, he was screaming.

"Yes, Roy. I hear you."

"Listen to me, Ray...Stand up. Put your legs down and stand up."

Ray heard his buddy. He was so tired that he complied and let his mighty legs drop to the bottom of the lake. Surprised and bewildered, he stood up. He was waist deep in the pitch-black, mucky water. He looked at the assassin, the vampire, and the two zombies, and then at Roy. "Me was drowning, Roy. Me was afraid."

"Get yourself out of the water, Ray, before I come in there and drown you myself," shouted Roy. He shook his head and said softly, "You simpleton."

Ray was wading out of the water when the assassin and the vampire turned their attention back toward the fleeing Roland. Roland, for the first time since he arrived in Terra Demorte, chuckled as he sat in the small boat.

The assassin shot a fireball toward Roland, but the shot fell short and fizzled out in the water. The vampire changed into an enormous bat and took flight, heading toward Roland. Roland grabbed his pistols and his cross. He watched the bat head his way, and he waited, waited, waited until the bat was upon him before he stretched out his arms and pulled the triggers eight times on each pistol.

The bullets silently went forth, and the bat knew nothing until the slugs hit him in the face. He nose-dived into Roland's boat. Roland had anticipated that and put the cross on the oversized creature; it burst into flames. He pushed it over the side of the boat with his oars.

The assassin watching, realized that the being he was after had just killed his friend; he cursed and shot another fireball toward the boat. It, like the first, fell short and drowned in the water.

"Well, at least something drowned tonight," Roland said with a small laugh. He rowed into the fog, keeping a sharp eye on the bright light.

"Me thought me was a goner, Roy, me can't swim," said Ray climbing onto the pier.

Roy looked in puzzlement at his soaked friend; he knew that Ray was a simple demon guardian. When it came to thinking, Ray was definitely impaired, but when it came to doing battle and killing, he knew he could have never picked a better partner.

Roland rowed a few yards into the fog and was out of sight. The fog surrounded him like a thick blanket, except this blanket was moist and damp. He thought he would row a few more yards and then turn left and follow the fog back toward the shoreline. Once he landed, he would slip up the main street to where Horace was waiting, in the Keeping Room.

He had turned toward the shoreline when he ran into something, something solid, and the small rowboat came to a sudden halt.

*I've hit land,* he thought. He knew he hadn't rowed long enough to be back on shore, so he figured it had to be a small island. Roland was right.

He could still faintly see the reddish light on his left, and knew which direction he would need to row, so he took his oar and pushed off the island. Then something happened that he didn't expect. From out of the darkness, something grabbed the boat. He saw at once what it was; it was the hand of a huge man.

"Get out of the boat," said the man.

Roland went for his guns, but before he could pull them, a large hand slapped him across the face. He fell backward into the boat and then jerked forward and was thrown onto the island.

"Well, what do we have here? A human."

"Let me go," was all Roland could muster up. "Please, I've got to save my son."

"Oh, I don't think so; I think you would make a good meal."

Roland was pulled to his feet, but finding solid ground was hard. It appeared that the island shore was lined with wet, round, rocks. He tried repeatedly to gain some steady footing but was unable to do so. He started to fall when a strong hand grabbed him by the throat.

"Hold on there. I've got you." With a mighty thrust, the huge man threw Roland upon solid ground. He turned and started for his pistols when another, smaller beast, one that looked like a gargoyle with wings, grabbed his arm with its teeth. Its teeth dug deep into Roland's forearm, and the animal growled softly as it drank his blood.

Yet another beast repeated the same actions on his other arm, biting and sucking the blood out of his muscle. Roland lay on the ground with two beasts pulling his arms in two different directions.

"Now, now, boys, I've got to eat first, and then you two can have the scraps."

Roland watched as the huge man pulled out a long, sharp knife.

There was a flash of light, and the huge man and his two small beasts vanished in a flurry of ash and fire. Roland jumped to his feet and grabbed for his weapons.

"No need for those, Roland," said a soft voice.

Out of the darkness stepped the Great Dark Witch. She looked at Roland, pointed at the small boat, and spoke. "I told you I would get you out of this place safely, Mr. Roberts. Get back into the boat, and it will take you to shore. Please try to stay invisible, if you can. Horace is waiting on you."

"Thank you. What was that thing, or those things?"

"That big thing was a Terra Demorte bounty hunter. Mean creatures, they are. And his two small beasts are glocks. Small vicious beasts. As far as I know, they only live on this island. They're the results of some serious crossbreeding between something and something else...but neither good."

Roland staggered off the solid ground and onto the round slippery rocks that lined the island. He was still rocked by the heavy slap to his head but fought back the pain. He had much to do and time was wasting away. He realized, by the fire that was burning brightly now, that the island wasn't lined with round rocks, as he had suspected, but with the skulls of human heads.

Roland made it back to the main street. He recognized it at once. This was the main street that ran down in front of Jake's Place. He had safely made it across the street, which was all he'd wanted to do in the first place. Now it was easy, maybe too easy. He gradually made his way up the dark, dreary street, crossing one side alley after another and making his way along the fronts of stores, or what appeared to be stores. Some were lit up and others dark, as dark as the streets when the lights were out.

"Lights out," he kept repeating long before he entered the eerie glow of the tall, possessed street lamps. Soon he found himself standing before a large building and saw, written on the window in large letters, "THE KEEPING ROOM."

"This is me," he said softly, entering the door and stepping into the dark room.

"Roland, is that you?" came a voice from the back of the building.

"Yes. Where are you, Horace?"

"Quick, back here. Look for a small light. Come on back here. We can hide here. How did you make it across the street?"

"I'll tell you later; you probably wouldn't believe it anyway."

Roland stood beside Horace and slid down the wall into a sitting position. "We have to stay here, Horace, until someone by the name of a Great Dark Witch comes to us. She's going to help us get Josh and get out of this miserable place."

"A Great Dark Witch? Why would she want to help us, Roland?"

"She needs a favor later on, something in the near future, something that I don't have now that I'll get. That's all I know, Horace, but anyway, we've got to wait on her. Quiet. Someone's coming in the door."

The two men heard the door open; Horace turned toward the light and whispered, "Light out." The light went dark.

They heard noises, and then a voice whispered, "Light on." Another small light near the front of the room flickered and put forth an uncanny glow. There was no mistaking who the figure was. It was Notor.

"Notor, back here," Horace whispered. Notor made his way back to where Horace and Roland stood.

"It's good to see you guys. I'm glad you haven't been caught. Creed has everyone looking for you, Roland."

"Who's in the pub, Notor?" Roland asked.

"Just Jake, Thor, and Creed," said Notor. "The rest are out looking for you, including Olin."

"Good, we will wait here until the witch gets back, and then we will get Josh," said Roland. "Oh, it's good to see you too, Notor."

"Thor told me to come back in a few minutes, back to the pub." Notor thought for a second and figured he had better not tell Roland what Thor had told him to say, so he just stood there, looking at Roland.

"OK, then when you have to go back, just do it. We have to wait on a witch; she's going to help us get Josh out of the pub," said Roland.

Notor didn't ask any more questions, nor did he tell Roland and Horace that he had been caught. For now, that seemed immaterial.

***

"The meeting of the Great Council will come to order," said the hooded figured standing at the head of the table. "As usual, we have many things to discuss, but tonight the vampire clan has business that the council needs to address. That is the reason for this special meeting. We don't have much time, so let's get started." There were voices of agreement and grunts, followed by a loud belch, from the head of the demon guardian clan.

"Yes," said the head of the vampire clan, "yes, we do have much business to discuss. Someone is killing surface vampires, and we need to know who."

"Quiet. The council will come to order. No more speaking unless I call upon you to do so. Is that clear?" The hooded figured spoke precisely and very clearly. "Now," he said, "we will come to order, and I'll call the roll. Is the warlock clan here?"

"Yes." The voice was very irritated.

"The creature clan?" said the hooded creature.

"Yes."

"The assassin clan?"

"Yes."

"The demon guardian clan?"

"Yes."

"The vampire clan?"

"Yes."

"The troll clan?"

The large troll made a grunt that sounded a bit like a yes.

"The goblin clan?"

"Yes."

"The zombie clan?"

"Yes."

"The human soul?"

"Yes."

"And finally, the dark witch clan?"

"Yes."

"Good," said the hooded figure. "Now, for the first order of business—" Hands went up from all of the clans. "The first order of business will be that of the vampire clan. The vampire clan has the floor."

"Someone is killing surface vampires," said the head of the vampire clan. we now have reports of seven that have been killed within the last week—seven powerful vampires. This is not the doing of a weak person; this is the doing of a very powerful person. It's hard to hunt and kill a vampire, let alone seven."

The head of the warlock clan spoke up. "Oh, just because someone or something killed seven of your type, does that means it was someone very powerful?"

"Vampires are very dangerous, and you might remember that, warlock. It might serve you well to remember that." The head of the vampire clan looked at the warlock and pointed his finger toward him. "My question to this council is, what we are going to do about it?"

"Well," said the hooded creature, "exactly what does the vampire clan want the council to do about this? We have no authority on the surface. What happens there is none of our concern."

"It seemed to be your concern when the warlock, Creed, was trying to complete his transformation. It appeared to be all of our concerns, but now that it's merely vampires, does the council have no concerns about that?"

"Yes, of course we do, but the warlock; Creed's transformation had consequences that spilled over into Terra Demorte. That was why we were concerned about him. I think the vampire clan should hire someone to investigate the killing of vampires on the surface. All agree?"

All of the other clans agreed. Some nodded their heads, and others said their ayes. "Then, it's agreed. The vampire clan will hire someone to check into this. It's not really a matter for this council." The head of the vampire clan sat down; he shook his head in disagreement, but agreed to hire someone to investigate the killings.

"All right. Now, is there any issue we need to discuss from the head of the assassin clan?" said the hooded creature.

"Yes," said the head of the assassin clan. He turned and stared at the head of the vampire clan. "Sirius, the assassin clan would like to help you. So we will volunteer to send one of our best assassins to the surface to see what he can find out about these killings."

The head of the Vampire Clan shook his head in accord, once more. "Thank you and I thank the entire Assassin Clan. It is very odd, but a witch came to us this very night and volunteered to find out who was killing the vampires on the surface, she said she would do this and all we would owe her would be a favor, a favor to be paid in the future. Maybe, you can assist her in her investigations?"

"Very well," said the head of the Assassin Clan, "other than that, I only have one more piece of business. Thor, returned tonight, and all who thought he was a turncoat or a traitor were wrong. I have told you that, and tonight, he has justified to the warlock clan and others his actions." The assassin turned slightly toward the head of the warlock clan and bowed ever so slightly.

"He brought the head of the great witch, Wisteria, back with him, and it's on display in Jake's Place, on the head of a spear, for all to see."

The head of the assassin clan smiled and took his seat. "I have no other business I would like to discuss," he said as he sat down.

"Yes," said the hooded figure. "I heard he was back and did indeed bring the head of the great witch, Wisteria. I think congratulations are in order."

"Hear, hear," was the cry of the other clans.

"Good news," said the hooded figure. "How about the warlock clan? Do you have any issues you would like to discuss?" The hooded creature turned toward the head of the warlock clan.

"Yes, as a matter of fact, I do have some issues. I would like to know where your spy is, you know, the one you have spying on Master Creed."

"Deidre is indisposed at the moment. She isn't well—"

Before the hooded creature could explain any further, the head of the warlock clan spoke up once more. "Indisposed? Don't you mean...dead?"

"Well, no, I wouldn't say that, not dead, exactly."

"Not dead? Her body is lying in the Keeping Room. I saw it myself. The only question is where is her head?" The warlock watched the hooded figure as he struggled for words. "Well? Do you know where your little spy's head is, or don't you?"

"Yes, as a matter of fact, I do, but we can't get to it at the moment. We will discuss this at a later time." The hooded figure's voice was shaky.

"No, I think we will discuss this now. Something is going on, and we all need to know what it is." The head of the warlock clan stood up. "Speak, man. What's going on with your surface spy?"

"Deidre is no concern of yours," said the head of the human soul clan in a fiery shout. "She is our clan, and if we want her to lie dormant for some time, then that's our decision and no concern of the warlock clan."

"So there is something going on," screamed the warlock. "No matter. You are right, but mark my word. I'll find out what's going on with this spy of yours."

"Thank you, Master Warlock. I'm sure you will."

"Well, I would still like to know who or what killed your Deidre."

"That's no concern of this council's as she was killed on the surface, doing errands for her clan, errands which I'm not at liberty to discuss with this council."

"Very well, sir. We will find out, sooner or later." The warlock sat down, and with a slight wave of his hand, gave the head of the human soul clan the brush off.

The hooded figure gave each clan a turn to discuss business, and more business was discussed, but nothing of great importance. Then the leader of the dark witch clan spoke.

"The dark witch clan has some new business, sir; we want to know what is going on at Jake's Place tonight. There are rumors of a human being in Terra Demorte. Is this true?" All of the clans started talking and swearing, making jesters with their fists shaking their heads. The head of the Demon Guardian Clan slammed his fist down on the table, grunted loudly, and then, as usual, top it off with a loud belched.

"Quiet, quiet please, yes I have heard these rumors and me and a few more of the Council members have investigated this rumor." The hooded figure laughed. "Yes, it's a rumor. There was a ruckus at Jake's Place and someone—" The hooded figure raised his hands and made pushing movements downward a few times trying to keep the council's noise at a minimum. "Yes, it was only a rumor, someone playing a trick. Too much ale tonight, I'll assure you. I personally checked into this; nothing but a rumor."

The room became noisy again, and most of the heads of the clans begin to laugh and talk loudly. "If there is no more business to discuss, then the council is adjourned. There are a few of you I need to speak with, will the heads of the people clan and the assassin clan, please stay for an extra minute?"

"I have one other piece of business," said the head of the dark witch clan.

"Yes, what would that be?" said the hooded figure. "The head of the dark witch clan has the floor."

"The head of the vampire clan said that a dark witch offered to investigate the surface killings. I'm not aware of any such agreement." The witch looked around the room. "I want to know who this witch is. She isn't of our clan. And if she isn't of our clan, how can she be in Terra Demorte and how did she get in here?"

The hooded figure stood motionless. The heads of the clans were quiet, and no one made a sound. Even the rude, belching demon guardian sat quietly.

"Again, the dark witch clan has made no agreement with the vampire Clan, so who is this witch? An agreement like this would have to come from me."

The head of the assassin clan was the first to speak. "There was a witch in Jake's Place tonight, and she went to Thor's rescue. And in return we gave her a favor, but we thought she was just another dark witch, one of your clan."

"She is not," said the clan leader. She stood up, and with a wave of her hand shot a fireball into the air. It burst into small flaming birds, and they all flew straight up for about ten feet and then did a nose dive into the huge stone table and disappeared. "What sort of favor did she want?"

"Well, we aren't sure; I assume she wanted us to kill someone on the surface."

"If not yours, then what is she? There is only one witch clan—excuse me, only one *dark* witch clan," said the head of the zombie clan. It was hard to understand his statement but all had dealt with him before and each knew very well what he had asked.

"There was a witch that bought a favor from us tonight, too," grunted the head of the demon guardian clan. "She gave us much gold for ale and my clan agreed to do her a favor. She did not tell us what it was that we were to do for her; she said she would tell us later, but she had plenty of gold, so we agreed. After all, what's one favor?" He grunted and slapped the table with both hands. He lifted his head, squealed several times into the air, and then snorted loudly. "She bought us our fill of ale."

"Again, this witch isn't of my clan. We need to know who she is—or what she is—and more importantly, why does she want favors from us?" said the head of the dark witch clan. "Do you think—"

Before the witch finished her statement, all of the heads of the other clans shouted no and shook their heads.

"No, it can't be; It's just a rogue witch. I'll leave it up to the dark witch clan to solve this issue. She's a rogue witch, nothing to worry about, nothing of any importance; I'm sure. Or it might be someone playing tricks on you—all of you." The hooded figure laughed, but deep in his thoughts, he wondered if it could indeed be the small child, they had ostracized so many years ago. He dismissed the thought and spoke. "If there is no more business, I move the meeting be adjourned."

All agreed and all left the great hall except for the hooded figure, the head of the people Clan, and the head of the Assassin Clan. When the room had cleared, the hooded figure spoke.

"We will forego the formalities, if you don't mind." Pete, the head of the human soul clan, agreed, and so did Billy, the head of the assassin clan.

"Both of your know there is a human in Terra Demorte. We must find him and discover who he is. As you know, Thor brought back the head of the great witch, Wisteria. I don't know how he did it, but the head on the spear is not the head of the great witch. It's the head of Deidre, my spy. I don't think Thor knows this, as Deidre is a friend of Thor's, a very dear friend. The only reason no one else knows this is that I, along with Pete, cast a spell on her body, and as long as I have that spell on Deidre's body, the head in Jake's Place will remain as is—Wisteria's head."

"That was a good idea. Lucky you thought of it in time," said Billy.

"Not luck. Deidre sent me a message that something or someone had found her out and that she might me in trouble. That was the last I heard from her. When her body came back, I went to Pete. He agreed to help me until we could meet with Thor and see what he was doing. Only we three know of the contract that Thor has on Creed and Olin, and we have to give Thor a chance to fulfill that contract. But we are running out of time."

Billy and Pete agreed by nodding. The assassin spoke up. "The witch everyone is talking about, she was the witch in Jake's Place tonight. She was an odd one, and there was something about her that didn't ring true. Do any of you know who she is?"

"No, just another witch I suppose," said the hooded figure. "We don't have time to worry about her at the moment; we've got to keep our heads. We have to find this human and kill him; we can't let anyone else know that he is here. He is using Deidre's medallion, so Billy can track him on his scanners. Find this intruder, kill him, and take Deidre's medallion, no matter what the cost. Find him, kill him, and dump him in the pit."

Pete and Billy agreed and started to leave, when the hooded figure spoke once more. "Release the hounds," he said.

"No, Syras. We can't do that," said Pete. "You know we can't do that. It's against our laws, and the entire council has to agree to that. As head of the council, you know that."

"Yes, I know that, but these are desperate times, and desperate decisions need to be made. Release the hounds of Terra Demorte," said the hooded figure.

"Syras, if we release the hounds, we also release the bounty hunter. What excuse would you give the council when they find out? And they will find out." Billy spoke loudly. He knew Syras and knew once the bounty hunter and the hounds were released, all of Terra Demorte would know.

The hounds were huge beasts, with large, bright-green eyes that sensed body heat and movement. They had a sense of smell that could track prey hours after it was gone, and once on the scent, they wouldn't give up, no matter what. They wouldn't stop the hunt. Hunger, pain, and thirst didn't stop these beasts; only death or the bounty hunter could stop them or control them. They were fierce beasts and usually ate what they killed, or at least gnawed upon it.

The bounty hunter was just as evil. He, himself, was an outcast from Terra Demorte. He belonged to the human soul clan but chose to stay isolated on a small island in the Black Lake of Terra Demorte. He would rather stay with the hounds than socialize with the other inhabitants of this evil place. How many bounty hunters there were, no one knew. They had assumed there were more, but no one ever went to their island, at least no one who ever returned. Those who ventured there had their heads join the others in lining the beaches of the small island.

When they needed to be summoned, a council member would leave a note on a post by the dock, and the bounty hunter would do their bidding.

"Syras, we can't do this. It would mean death to us all. We can't release the hounds in Terra Demorte." Billy spoke softly. "I won't be a part of this."

"You, assassin, are already a part of this. You, Pete, and I—we all are a part of this. If we don't find this human and kill Creed and Olin, there won't be a council and we won't have a world." Syras spun around and turned his back to the head of the assassin clan and the head of the human soul clan. "We've been friends for years; we have to act while there is time."

Pete spoke first. "What do we tell the rest of the heads of the clans?"

"We will tell them it was an emergency, and we had to act fast," said Syras.

"And if they don't believe that?" said Billy.

"They have no choice. The only one that will argue the point is the head of the warlock clan. He's thrown in with Creed and Olin and knows very well what Creed plans to do once he has had his transformation. We agreed to stop him—we do it now, tonight—or we let him and Olin rule us all." Syras turned back to his friends. "Well, are you with me or not?"

Billy looked at Pete; they shook their heads and agreed. They knew Syras was right, and their spy, Deidre, had told them of Creed's plans, and all would rather die than to be ruled by a warlock.

Syras stared at his friends. "We will kill Olin and Creed tonight, here in Terra Demorte, and blame it on the intruder. The bounty hunter will then kill the intruder and dump his body into the pit, never to be found. A perfect plan."

Pete and Billy looked at Syras. Billy was the first to speak. "You want *us* to kill Creed and Olin?"

"Yes, you and Pete. If we do this, no one will ever know. They will blame it on the intruder. Don't you see? The timing is perfect and no one will know the difference. We just need to kill Olin and Creed before the bounty hunter kills the intruder."

Pete and Billy smiled. They knew Syras was right, and it truly was the perfect plan.

"Release the hounds of Terra Demorte," said Syras.

"It will be done," said Billy. Pete agreed by nodding. "Stay off of the streets tonight, Syras. It won't be safe."

# Thirty-Two

## The Escape

Notor left the Keeping Room. He thought about what Thor had told him to say upon returning to Jake's Place; he didn't know why, and now that Roland had actually shown up in the Keeping Room, he was more confused than ever. But he barged into the pub and shouted loudly, "Roland's in the Keeping Room; he's coming to kill you, Master Creed."

Creed started to stand up. He gulped a large breath of air, and then, as if having an epiphany, he sat back down. Thor rose to his feet, as well; he turned toward the door, as if getting ready to defend the warlock sitting beside him.

"Come on, Master Creed. We've got to get you to safety," he said.

Creed didn't move. He sat there as if something had deflated him, and for once, no one could hear him breathe. The raspy breathing had stopped, replaced by clear and unlabored breathing. "I see," he said. "I see."

"Hurry, Master Creed," said Thor. "Hurry. Let' get you to safety." Creed pushed himself back against the wall, folded his arms, and sat there calmly.

"I see this little plot now. I don't have to worry about you killing me, assassin, because you have already told me you were here to protect me. And you, Notor—you have no killing powers, so I don't have to worry about you killing me...*either.*"

"I see what your plan is, and you have succeeded quite well. You have emptied out the pub, and now it's just you, Notor, Jake, and me. I can't and won't fight you, assassin, and you can't kill me. Your plan has worked quite well. You want the boy, and now there is no one to stop you." Creed paused. He took in another long breath, and this time, as before, the breath was clean and taken without any stress.

"Well, Master Creed, you are a smart one, and I won't kill you unless I have to. I'm getting the boy, and there is nothing you can do about it," said Thor. "If you get in my way, I'll strike you down, just like the dog you are."

Notor looked at Thor; he stood, still wondering what was going to happen next. His old master knew he had betrayed him, but he didn't know that he had crossed over and back again.

"Notor, attack Thor," Creed commanded.

Notor froze; he was surprised by his old master's outburst. He had no powers to fight an assassin. What was Creed thinking? He stood erect and spoke with a clear and confident voice, "and why should I do that?"

Creed didn't move, he spoke again to Notor, in a condescending voice. "I gave you an order, attack the assassin." He inhaled a large volume of air and once again, his lungs were clear and made no raspy sounds.

"I don't think so. I don't serve you anymore. I'm here for the boy, as well." Notor said. Looking at Thor he asked. "What do you want me to do, Thor?"

"So you have betrayed me and my brother, as well, Notor?"

"Yes, I have," said the thin man. "Yes, I have. I'm tired of you yelling at me and tired—so tired—of your insolent and condescending commands."

"You're my servant. You have to obey me. You have no choice," said Creed.

"Really?" said Notor. "Watch me. Thor, what do you want me to do?"

"Then both of you will die tonight," screamed Creed, but the voice that came out from under the hood wasn't the voice of Creed, but the voice of Olin. Olin sprang to his feet, and with a flick of his hand, he hit Thor in the chest with a large fireball. Thor, being so close to Olin, had no time to react, and fell backward, hitting two tables and knocking chairs in every direction. He wobbled a few times before his body fell to the floor. Thor, the assassin from Terra Demorte, was dead.

Notor started to run, but Olin was ready for him, as well. He quickly mumbled a spell, and Notor's feet stopped their retreat and he started speaking in a strange voice. He tried to move, but his body wouldn't budge.

"Sit, Notor," said Olin, "I'll deal with you later." Notor crossed the room and sat down as Olin instructed. He stared at Olin as if waiting on more instructions.

The front door opened and in came Creed, followed by Roy and Ray. He walked as if he were Olin. He didn't swagger, and his strides were long and crisp. He was lighter on his feet than he had been in months. He walked to the back of the room and sat down across from his brother. Olin spoke the magic words and both warlocks shape-shifted back into their own identities.

"You were right, Creed. Thor is a double-crosser, a traitor, and a disgrace to us all. We will kill him and dump him into the pit. Roy, cut the assassin's head off and put it in this sack." Olin threw a sack toward the huge demon guardian. "I'll cast a spell that will keep his body from returning to the Keeping Room. Take this measly little traitor"—he pointed to Notor—"to the trolls, and tell them it's a gift from Creed and me."

"Yes, sir, just as soon as I cut this assassin's head off and dump him into the pit, I'll be happy to, Master. Come on, Ray. Open the sack."

About that time, Roland burst into the pub. He had his pistols in his hands and pointed them at Creed and his brother.

"Hold it right there. I won't hesitate to kill both of you—and you too." Roland pointed at Jake, who was behind the counter.

Jake placed his hands on the counter and laughed. "I have no business with you, human. Just don't kill me. I'm just a barkeep."

Olin raised his hand, and before he could cast a spell or fire a fireball, Roland shot him several times in the chest. "I told you—all of you—not to move. Notor, get—"

Before Roland finished his sentence, Jake had fired a fireball that hit Roland squarely in the chest. He swaggered forward and tried to regain his balance. His eyes rolled back into his head, and he fell forward, dead.

Seriously wounded, Olin made his way back to his chair. Creed looked at his wounds; they were grave. Blood oozed out of the bullet holes, and Olin's shirt was quickly becoming soaked with blood. He mumbled a few words and the bleeding stopped, but Olin was dying and Creed knew that neither he nor his magic could save his brother, not there, not in Terra Demorte. He cursed and kicked the table.

Olin looked at his wounds. He remembered the same wounds—back over a hundred years ago, the day he had met the Great Dark Witch. *If only she were here*, he thought.

Thor moaned and turned over on his back. Everyone had thought the assassin was dead, but life had not left his body. Where clothes and flesh had been, there was now a gaping hole. He was dying, and without his assassin friends, there was no hope for him.

Roy grabbed the assassin and straddled him; he put his hands beneath Thor's cloak and fished out a long dagger. "This should do just fine," he snorted. He raised his head and grunted loudly, and then snorted even louder, bringing the knife down into the throat of the assassin. Again, he snorted loudly and ended it with a pig like squeal. "Ray, get the sack ready, and then we will drag this traitor to the pit." He snorted again and started to cut the head off the assassin.

The duo was just getting started when the front door to the pub swung open. In walked Billy and Pete. Pete spoke. "Hold on. No one make a move. We are with the council, and we will take over from here.

This is our business, and you, Master Creed, are under arrest and will be locked in the Keeping Room. Furthermore—"

Suddenly a lightning bolt struck Pete in the back; he fell without uttering another word. Billy turned quickly, but another bolt was already on its way. The bolt hit him with such a mighty force that it pushed him into the spear, and he and the head of Wisteria fell to the floor.

Wisteria's head rolled over repeatedly and came to a rest beside Thor. Pete fell to the floor, and like Billy, he was dead before he'd started falling.

Creed and Jake looked in the direction of the bolts, and there, standing alone, was the Great Dark Witch. She walked toward the center of the room, and in a soft voice, started giving directions. No one interrupted her, and all did exactly as they were told, all but Roy.

She looked at Roy and Ray, "you, demon guardian, bring those two men over here to me."

"My master told me to dump them into the pit," said Roy with some hesitancy, "and that's what I'm going to do."

Roy, didn't know who he was dealing with, and if he had known, he might have escaped the mighty force that hit him next. Without warning, the Great Dark Witch moved her hand, ever so slightly, and the big demon guardian went flying into the tables and chairs that Thor hadn't knocked over when he fell. The witch paid him little attention and went back to giving directions.

"Now that we have that settled, let's move on." She looked at Roy and Ray, Roy had just gotten to his feet and most of the stars he was seeing had vanished. "I'll say it once more. Bring those men over here and sit them in these chairs."

The witch walked over to Olin, who was still conscious. "My dear Olin, have you not learned anything that I taught you? But as always, it's good to see you."

Olin managed to speak. "Good to see you too."

The Great Dark Witch pushed open Olin's shirt; she spoke so softly that no one else could hear. Olin's wounds bled more, and then the bullets that had penetrated his chest, pushed out and fell onto his lap. Olin managed to move somewhat but was still very weak.

"Now, Master Creed, he'll be fine. We need to take both of you home, back to the surface, back to your mansion. Demon guardians, hurry. Go to your masters' rooms and get their belongings. Quickly, now. Do as I say."

Roy and Ray, seeing what the Great Dark Witch had done for their master—and Roy having felt the witch's wrath—hurried up the stairs, Ray tripping over Roy, trying to pass him on the stairs.

"Slow down, Ray," scolded Roy.

"Now, for you two," said the witch. She waved her hand over Thor and then pulled a vile holding a mysterious substance from under her cloak. She poured it on the assassin and then mumbled more of her magic words. Thor opened his eyes and stared at the witch. The wound in his throat slowly closed, and the blood stopped oozing out of the place where Roy had plunged the dagger. The chest wound performed the same action and started slowly closing. Thor blinked his eyes a few times and stared at the woman in black.

"Feeling better, assassin?"

"Much," said Thor, "and who do I thank for this?" Thor wasn't too worried about his old wounds. He was in Terra Demorte, and like all assassins, his clan would have resurrected him within hours of his death.

Of course, Thor didn't know he was about to be beheaded, and that would have made a significant difference. Since Olin would have had his head, the assassin's body would lay dormant in the Keeping Room for a long time, if not forever.

"Well, it doesn't matter. Whoever you are, thank you. That's twice tonight you've saved my life, so I'm indebted to you, very much so."

Thor looked at Roland. He knew he was dead and knew where his body would be thrown. He also saw the heads of two of the clans lying dead on the floor. Within the hour, the two bodies on the floor would return to the Keeping Room and be brought back to life by their clans.

What came next, however, was a shocker, even to an assassin from Terra Demorte.

The Great Dark Witch pulled a large knife from under her cloak and straddled the head of the people clan. With a smooth motion, she severed his head. "Do you have a sack, Jake?" she asked with a soft voice.

Jake responded with an answer and a question. "Yes I do, but are you sure you want to do that? If you separate their heads and put them into sacks, their clans won't be able to bring them back to life."

"The sack," said the witch sharply. "Give me two or I'll get three myself." Jake did as instructed and brought two sacks to the witch. The witch pushed Pete's head into the sack and tied it off; she performed the same ritual on Billy's body and tied the second sack off, as well. "That should do nicely," she said. Both bodies disappeared, along with their medallions.

Roy and Ray came downstairs, loaded down with Creed and Olin's belongings. They stared at Thor. "Why did you save him?" Roy asked.

"We need him, for the time being," said the witch. She looked at Thor. "Are you well enough to travel back to the surface?"

"Yes," said Thor. He looked at Roland once more.

"Then take that bag there and leave, before I change my mind." Said the witch pointing to the bag that held Josh.

"And, Roland?" said Thor.

"He's my concern," said the witch. "Leave and take the boy with you."

"No," shouted Creed. "We need him."

"No, Brother," said Olin. "We don't need him any longer. Since the great assassin, Thor, killed Wisteria, she is out of the way and no one will interfere with your transformation again. Once we are back in the mansion, we will complete this thing."

Ray looked at the witch. He picked up the two sacks and put them with his master's other belongings. "I'll carry these to the surface," he said. The witch gave him an inquisitive look and went back to watching Thor.

Thor picked up the bag that was placed before him; he placed it on the table and peered inside. To his relief, Josh was sleeping quietly in it. He touched the small boy's curly hair. It was ironic, he thought, on the night the small boy was allowed to leave the most evil place known, his father died in that same place. "Thanks," he said. "Will you answer me a question?"

"Yes," said the witch.

"Why are you killing these two?" Thor pointed to the two sacks Ray was carrying.

"They're the only witnesses that there was a human in Terra Demorte," she said. "Oh, don't worry about, Jake. His lips will stay silent, won't they, Jake?"

"Yes," was all Jake said as he went back to doing things that barkeeps do.

Thor walked out of the pub carrying what he had come to get. He only wished he could have left with Roland, as well. His heart was heavy. His best friend lay dead, and he knew Roland would never know that he hadn't betrayed him.

# Thirty-Three

## The Death of Roland

The witch looked at Roland's body lying on the floor. She stepped over him and walked over to where Olin sat. She stared at his wounds; the bullet holes were sealed tightly and had stopped bleeding. Olin looked up and stared into the witch's eyes.

"What are you doing here?" he asked. "You know what will happen if anyone realizes who you are?"

Underneath her cloak, the Great Dark Witch smiled. "No one will find me out, Olin. I made sure of that. I have a few more things to do before we leave. She turned toward Jake. "I need to make sure you are quiet, so I'll make you a deal—your life for a promise of silence. What do you say, Jake?"

Jake was no one's fool. He studied the witch and nodded. "I'll be silent; you have my word on it."

"Yes, Jake, you will be silent," she said. She waved her hand and a lightning bolt stuck the barkeep in the chest; he fell backward with a loud thud. "Quickly," she said, looking at Roy. "Grab him and drag him over here."

Roy did as instructed, and within minutes of the witch's demands, he stood in front of her, grasping Jake's legs. The witch straddled the barkeep and pulled the dagger again from under her cloak. With a smooth motion, she severed Jake's head from his body. She looked at Roy. "Put this in the sack with the head of the assassin clan." Roy did as instructed, and Jake's body disintegrated, along with his medallion.

There in the pub were Creed, Olin, the two demon guardians, Roland, and the Great Dark Witch. The place was quiet as all watched the Great Dark Witch separate Jake from his head.

Olin was the first to speak. "What are we going to do with the human's head?" he said. He spoke if he had never met the handsome man lying on the pub floor, the man who had fought him and his brother ever since he and his family had come to the small town of Johnston. Olin knew this man, and even in death, gave no respect to this worthy adversary.

The Great Dark Witch turned toward Olin, and then with ease, pushed Roland's body out of the chair in which the demon guardian had placed him. She looked down at the dead human. The blood had stopped oozing out of his wound; it had stopped the minute his heart was burned to a crisp. She bent down and turned Roland's body over so he lay on his back. She slowly straddled the dead human, and as with the assassin, she pulled the knife once more from under her cloak. This time, however, she paused to mumble more of her magic words over Roland's body. In a smooth motion, she severed Roland's head from his body and tossed it to Roy.

"Go behind the bar and get another sack. Hurry. We need to get out of this place before anyone returns. I don't like witnesses." Roy did as instructed, and while he was getting the sack, the witch whispered once more over the body of the human lying on the floor.

"Roy, you and Ray take this body and dump it in the pit. I'll bring this sack with the others to the surface with me. Go now. Do you understand me?"

"Yes," said Roy. "Ray, grab his feet and get him over to the pit." Ray grabbed Roland's body and started out the door.

"Ray, hurry back and gather up your master's belongings. Now go. Hurry." The witch watched the huge demon guardian drag the body out of the door. "Now," she said, "as soon as Ray gets back, we will get you all out of here and on the way to your mansion. Agreed?"

"That will be great," said Olin, "but we have one more witness." Olin paused.

"Yes?" said the Great Dark Witch.

"Morto," said Olin.

The Great Dark Witch moved toward the head lying on the pub's floor. "I have already taken care of the assassin, Morto," she said. She pulled out a medallion from her cloak. "This belonged to him, I believe?"

"Yes, it's his, but how? And how did you know?" asked Olin.

"I saw him sitting with you earlier, and I saw him scanning everyone that went up the stairs. Just another task I had to clean up after, but no problem. We won't hear anything from Morto for a long time." The witch smiled, and if listening to her words, one might have caught a little laughter in her voice.

The witch picked up Wisteria's head. "Things aren't as they seem, Olin." She spoke more words that were magic, and the head changed back into the witch, Odium.

"That's the dark witch, Odium," said Olin. "The assassin did trick us. He killed Odium." Olin turned toward Creed. "He killed Odium. Now we have more problems. She was the only one who knew where the spirits were we needed."

"Oh, not to worry, Olin. This isn't the dark witch, Odium." More words that were magic came from the witch's mouth, and the head turned again. This time the head turned into that of Deidre.

"Who is that?" asked Olin.

"This is a little spy I found in your mansion, listening and reporting back everything to the council, here, in Terra Demorte."

"A spy in our mansion?" questioned Creed.

"Yes, she told everyone she lived in the chair in front of your desk, but she didn't. She lived over the door in your chambers. I found her and used her to lure the assassin, Thor, here and the human, Roland. My plan has worked out quite well."

"You see, Olin, someone here in Terra Demorte. has placed a spell on the body of this little spy. That is why her head never changed, but I knew that all along. I wanted to know who she was spying for. I don't think it was all of the council members, just a few. And I wanted to know why."

Ray came back in and, clumsy as ever, tripped over one of the chairs. He grabbed it with one hand and sent it crashing into the walls. "Stupid chair," he said.

"No doubt," said the witch. She pointed to the two demon guardians. "Quickly, grab your masters' belongings, and all of you, go to the mansion. Leave the heads with me." Roy and Ray grabbed the luggage and headed toward the door. Creed helped his brother up, they walked passed the witch and headed out of Jake's Place too. Olin turned toward the witch.

"You are coming, aren't you?"

"Yes, I'll be along, Olin. I'll meet you at the mansion."

The Great Dark Witch sat alone in the pub. The same pub that earlier that night was full of patrons and laughing people and beasts. She sat there with the heads. She slowly opened the sacks, and the heads rolled out. She mumbled her magic words, and the bodies of the three men reappeared. She held out her hands. The heads reattached themselves to the bodies, and the men opened their eyes. They didn't move but lay there as if a comatose state.

She bent over Pete's body first. "Do you hear me?"

"Yes."

"You are over the people clan, correct?

Pete answered, "Yes."

"I'll let you live if you promise to serve me. Do you agree? If you don't agree, I'll sever you head again, and I'll take it to the surface where it will remain for all eternity. Do you understand me?"

"Yes."

"Well, what is your answer?"

"I'll serve you, if you let me live."

"Good," said the witch. "Good, but not only will you serve me; the entire People clan will serve me, as well. Do you understand?"

"Yes," said Pete. He slowly stood up. He staggered a little before finding a chair. He watched the witch.

The Great Dark Witch bent over the head of the assassin clan. She made Billy the same offer, and Billy agreed to serve the witch—not only him, but the entire assassin clan.

"Good, you two may leave," she said. Both men headed for the door.

"Don't think twice about double-crossing me. I have put a curse on you, and if you even think of crossing me, you will pay with your lives, but not without a great deal of pain before you die."

The two men stared at the witch.

"Who are you?" said the head of the people clan.

"It doesn't matter who I am. All that matters is the promise you made me. Now leave, before I change my mind." The two men headed out the door. They didn't look back at the woman dressed in black.

The witch sat alone once more in the quiet pub. She rolled another head out of the sack, and watched it as it came to rest at her feet. It was that of the barkeep, Jake. The same ritual took place, and Jake's body reappeared on the floor. With her knife, she pushed back his cloak, exposing his chest.

As she did, the Great Dark Witch froze. Many moments passed, and the Great Dark Witch sat frozen in her seat. This was the first time in the witch's existence that she was beside herself, fully aware of her surroundings, but totally spellbound. She stared at the chest of the dead barkeeper. One might have thought that her heart had suddenly quit beating and she had died while sitting in a crouching position, but this wasn't the case. She gazed upon the body of Jake and slowly pushed more of the cloak back with her knife, exposing more of Jake's chest.

Jake had a large scar, one shaped as if a serpent had coiled itself in the middle of his chest. This wasn't a tattoo, but a burn mark, a brand, leaving a horrific disfigurement. The scar was put there by magic and was of perfect design and color, with not a detail left out.

The serpent had three heads, and each carried some type of object in its mouth. She stared intently at the first head; she noticed that the object in the snake's mouth was a pyramid. The snake carried the pyramid as if protecting it, ensuring its teeth didn't penetrate the stone.

The second serpent's head looked the same, but this head had its teeth clamped down on a rock, and its venom was mixed with blood. It dripped off the rock and trickled onto the third head.

She pushed back more of the cloak so she could see the third head more clearly. It was holding a small baby. The snake's teeth penetrated the child's stomach, and the baby was crying red tears that flowed off its face and pooled beneath its body.

She softly touch Jake's chest with her finger. The snakeheads came to life and starting moving about on Jake's chest. The three heads turned upward and focused on the Great Dark Witch that sat crouch over the body of Jake, the barkeep. No matter where the witch moved her head, the heads of the snake continued to focus on her. The eyes of all three heads glowed a bright red, and the pupils would dilate and then shrink again. They were focused on the Great Dark Witch.

The witch spoke softly. "So, you are the one."

She covered Jake's chest, and as she spoke her magic, the head reattached itself to Jake's body and he opened his eyes.

"Do you hear me, Jake?" asked the witch.

"Yes."

"I know you can't move, and I feel you trying very hard to raise your hand against me." The witch taunted Jake. "That wouldn't be a smart move." She bent over the comatose man and rubbed his face with her hand. Jake jerked upward and fell back to the floor. His eyes opened wide, and fear spread across his face. He couldn't speak, but within his body, the witch heard his heart screaming in fear and excruciating pain. His mind went spinning out of control as old, forgotten memories began to flood his mind—memories that he had never wanted to remember again.

Jake had felt this feeling only once in this afterlife, a touch of pure evil. This wickedness and magic terrified Jake; after all, of these years, it was still most devastating and most impious—much different from the magic and evilness that the creatures in Terra Demorte possessed. This evil rocked his very being, and like some deadly virus, consumed his spirit from within, devouring his essence. The last time he'd felt it, that evil had belonged to a tiny baby that had been cast upon the surface of the earth to die, and now it had touched him again, for a second time.

Yes, he had felt that feeling—once, a long time ago when the council had called upon Jake to do a simple task. He had readily agreed to do the job, as doing tasks for the council was always rewarding, and most of the time, very profitable. Not knowing what it was, he vowed he would do it.

His task had been to carry a sack to the highest peak of the granite mountain, one that had a sheer cliff of over two thousand feet, straight down to the valley floor. Once there, he was to cast the sack upon the surface of the earth. There in the dead of winter, the ice and snow would be deep, and there would be no chance of survival for the sack's contents. Jake, had been warned repeatedly, not to open the sack or touch the contents, just discard the sack in the deep snow and ice and walk away.

Normally, this would not have been a problem for Jake; he couldn't have cared less what was in the sack. His payment was waiting for him when he returned to Terra Demorte, the one thing he had always wanted in his afterlife, his own pub...Jake's Place.

He didn't like the surface and only visited it on rare occasions. He thought of it as a nasty and wicked place. In his afterlife, he hated surface humans. He disliked the snow and ice even more, but the council insisted that he was their man.

Jake recalled the words the hooded figure had spoken. "I'm placing this package into your hands. It's wrapped tightly and you aren't to open this...ever. You must do as we instruct you to do. Do you understand?"

Of course, Jake had replied with a yes, so the hooded figure continued.

"Once you have gone to the surface, you will take this package high into the Granite Mountains, and there in the deep snow and ice, you will place this sack. In the dead of winter, there will be no chance of survival for the sack's contents. Again, you must not open the sack or touch what's inside. If you do, you will be scarred you for life, if not killed. You will leave it there, and you will never speak of this to anyone. Are we in agreement?"

Jake had agreed, and in return, he had been granted his pub, Jake's Place, a place where all inhabitants of Terra Demorte could come, socialize, and drink ale.

Over the years, the patrons had narrowed down to only a few of the clans. The warlock clan, the demon guardian, the human soul clan, the vampire clan, and the assassin clan made up most of the visitors. Occasionally, a zombie would venture in, or at times a troll or two, but most of the time they would stay on their side of the lake. However, it didn't matter. In Jake's Place, all were welcomed; that is, if they were spending gold and drinking ale.

Jake snapped back to reality as the Great Dark Witch rubbed his face once more. He shook violently, as he remembered that day. It was high in the mountains, and on that particular day, it was blistering cold, as a snowstorm was descending on the mountain. Jake had tried to dress for the cold weather but quickly found he wasn't.

He remembered walking into the valley floor and climbing as high as he could go, all the way to the top of the huge granite rock. Once there, Jake made a fatal mistake, one that would scar him for the rest of his life. He opened up the package and dumped its contents into the icy snow. There, lying on the ground was a small baby. As Jake's eyes looked upon this small infant, he felt the evil the child possessed. The baby was hideous—in his life and afterlife, he had never seen anything like it. He couldn't stand to look upon the face of the repugnant child.

Jake was from the human soul clan, or as some calls it, the people clan which consisted of humans who had died and whose spirits hadn't crossed over to the other side. One reason might have been that they were evil and stayed on the surface for some type of revenge. Some, however, weren't bad people in life, but for different reasons, they didn't crossover when they died. After a time, these spirits would succumb to the evil warlock that was stalking them.

Once captured, they would remain in servitude to that warlock. Some would be taken to a dark and dreary place, Terra Demorte, where they would be traded or sold to the other clans. At times, they might win their freedom or purchase it from their master, however; they would always belong to the dark side. The light had long vanished, and they would never be able to find it again. Jake was one of these spirits.

On the day Jake had dumped the baby into the cold snow, a small flame had ignited in his heart. No matter how hideous and evil this child was, Jake's heart wouldn't allow him to leave it in the freezing ice and snow. He couldn't walk away and leave it there to die.

After all, he'd thought, weren't all things in Terra Demorte evil? Yes, they were. Some hideous and ugly, especially a troll or goblin, who stunk, as well.

Nonetheless, on that frigid day, Jake had picked up the small child and no sooner had he touched the child than his chest caught fire. He rolled and screamed, but the flames grew. He tried to release the baby but could not; his skin had bonded with the baby's and it held tightly. He lost consciousness and fell into the subzero-degree snow.

The next morning, Jake had found himself inside a teepee, lying beside a warm fire. He had no idea how he'd gotten there or how he'd managed to find his way off the mountain in the snowstorm. As he woke up, he looked at his hands, and they were normal.

He lay there until an old man came in to stoke the fire, and as Jake watched him carefully placing wood on the fire, he could see the old man was blind. He'd asked him several questions, but there were no answers. As Jake started to leave, the old Indian muttered these words. "Evil has scarred you; you are scarred," he said.

Jake turned to face the man, but the man was gone, and Jake was alone in the teepee. That day, Jake left the valley floor and returned to Terra Demorte. He now bore the scar on his chest and vowed not to let anyone know he had it.

The witch touched Jake once more. He jerked violently before his body settled back to the floor. "So it was you," she said. "You remember me, don't you?"

Jake spoke. "Yes."

"So what will we do with you?" said the witch. Jake lay there. He couldn't make out any features of the hooded woman, but he could feel her evil, so he stared at her.

"I'll let you live," she said, "but you have to tell me everything you know about the council and the small baby that was abandoned by Terra Demorte." The witch paused. "And you will have to promise me your loyalty, or I'll kill you, now…agreed?"

Jake lay and listened to the witch. He answered her. "I'm sorry; it wasn't my doing."

"No matter. You will tell me everything you know, but first you have to promise to serve me, or you will die this night of a violent death…agreed?" The witch's voice became loud and irritable. "Do you agree?"

Of course, Jake agreed, and when he did, the witch released her magic and he stood up. He wouldn't speak again to the Great Dark Witch until she asked him to do so.

It was at this time that Roland burst into the pub. Jake had positioned himself behind the bar, and the witch sat waiting on Roland.

Roland had pulled his two pistols; he looked at the witch sitting at one of the tables that hadn't been overturned in the previous scuffles. She watched as the warrior entered the room. She had grown a small amount of respect for Roland; she knew he was way in over his head, yet was relentless. And a persistent warrior deserved to be respected. After all, that was what had drawn her to Olin over a hundred years ago.

"I'm here for my son. Where is he?" Roland came closer to the witch, his guns pulled but down by his sides. He shot the barkeep a quick glance. Jake made no moves and put both of his hands on the bar. He had already had enough troubles for one night; he'd had his head removed and then reattached. He had never seen this before. Usually when bodies disappeared, they went to the Keeping Room, but this witch had the power to make them disappear and then reappear at her command.

Roland walked toward the witch. "Where's my son?"

"Your son is safe. He's gone," said the witch.

Roland saw the head on the floor; he turned it over with his foot. "That's me! What is this? You promised me I would get my son." He looked once more at the head.

"I promised you that I would get you and your son out of here safely, and that is what I've done. Your son is on his way home with the assassin, Thor, and your two helpers—Horace, I think, was one and the spike, Notor."

Roland studied the witch. "You say Thor took Josh home?"

"Yes, Roland. Thor is on his way to your home now. I'll keep my promise to you, the promise that I would get you out of Terra Demorte safely. Now, go. Use the medallion and go the surface. Go now before anyone else comes in here and sees a human in Terra Demorte. I have held up my part of the deal. Now leave."

Roland stared at the witch and then at the head on the floor. He turned to leave. The witch made one more remark before Roland exited the door. "Mr. Roberts, we made a deal, a bargain. I expect you to live up to your end."

"I will. Just let me know what you need." Roland pulled the cloak that the Great Dark Witch had given him around his face and headed toward the tunnel and to the life, as he knew it, on the surface. He wondered what all had happened and where Olin and Creed had gone. What about the two demon guardians? Where had they disappeared to? He also wondered about the head on the pub's floor. One thing he knew: it wasn't his. So whose was it?

\*\*\*

The witch sat alone once more in the pub. The evil world was quiet now, at least in Jake's Place. She hated this place, hated being there, in

Terra Demorte, the land that abandoned her so long ago, but she had plans and work to do and making sure Master Creed completed his transformation was at the top of her list. She had watched Olin spread his evil in a distant land and, for once in her long life, had confided in another person. She was drawn to Olin, and now that he and his brother needed help, she was there for them and swore to herself nothing would stand in their way again. "It's just business," she said softly.

Jake made busy behind the bar. He wondered, as well, whose head was on the floor.

The witch looked down on the head; she nudged it lightly with her foot. Then she spun her magic once more, and a headless body appeared on the floor. It was dressed in a black cloak, and she studied it before she spoke her words.

The head shook and started changing shape. She watched as the head reattached itself to the body. She bent over it and stared at it.

"Do I need you, assassin?"

"Please, yes. I'll do anything you ask," came the reply.

"OK, I guess I could use you. Do you promise to serve me?" She laughed slightly. It wasn't in her nature to laugh, but the Great Dark Witch, who all of Terra Demorte had abandoned, was truly having fun tonight. "Well, assassin, do you promise to serve me? Quickly, give me your answer."

"Yes, always."

"So be it." The witch waved her hands and muttered some magic, and the body came to life. There, standing in front of Jake and the Great Dark Witch was the assassin, Morto.

# Thirty-Four

## The Bounty Hunter

Thor walked out of the portal with the sack in his hand; he waited a moment, and out stepped Notor and then Horace. Josh was sleeping quietly in the bag, but Thor picked him up and carried the precious boy in his arms.

Josh wrapped his arms around the assassin's neck, and fell back into a sleep. The spell he was under was working well and keeping Josh in a quiet sleeping state.

"This isn't going to be easy," said Thor. "It's not going to be easy telling Katie that we have her son but that her husband will never be coming home, that he's lying in a pit, deep in the belly of the earth."

The three men walked slowly toward Number 12. No one spoke. Somehow, it wasn't the same without Roland. Thor kicked a stone and watched it roll down the sidewalk and then skip into the grass. His friend thought him to be a traitor and had died believing that to be so.

"I had to do it, you know. I had to betray him. I had no other choice but to turn on him if I was to save Josh. The plan worked, but I thought Roland would escape. I guess I figured it wrong."

"It wasn't your fault, Thor; you did what you had to do. You saved the boy, and that was the only way you could have ever gone up those stairs. They were watching them too closely. No one knew about the Great Dark Witch." Notor tried to comfort the assassin. In their hearts, Thor, Horace, and Notor knew they would have sacrificed themselves to save Josh. If they had to do it all over again, any one of them, including Roland, would have readily sacrificed his life to rescue the small boy.

"Thor," said Horace, "don't be too hard on yourself; Roland knew the chances of making it out of there alive were slim. He would want you to do the same thing again, if it meant saving his son. You and I know that Creed and Olin would have killed the boy just as soon as Creed's transformation was complete. We both know that, and Roland did too."

"I know, I know," Thor said. "There was no other way, Horace. I didn't think there was any other way. Once Wisteria's head turned, they all would have figured out our plan. Creed and Olin would have known I was there for the boy. Time wasn't on our side this time, Horace."

The trio stopped in front of the walkway that led to the front porch of Number 12. Although they had Josh, no one turned to go up the walk. It seemed to go on forever, and the two giant trees that stood watch over the front porch didn't look as tall as they once had. Something was missing, and that something was Roland.

The night birds and crickets were singing, but their songs weren't happy and cheerful as they often appeared to be; tonight they sounded gloomy. Although the night air was moist and warm, it was stale and touched with a small chill of sadness as it gathered around the trio. The moon's glow seemed to be dimmer, allowing shadows to creep into being, and the darkness seemed to be devouring the light as it crept forward, casting the world into darkness. It felt as if everything they heard, felt, or saw mourned the death of Roland. Deep in Thor's heart, he felt a sadness and a loneliness that he, as an assassin, had never felt before. A tear ran down his cheek as he turned and took the first step toward the old house they called Number 12. As it fell to the sidewalk, everything became quiet, deathly quiet.

\*\*\*

Roland had just walked out of the pub and started toward the entrance of the tunnel when he heard a horrifyingly familiar sound. He had heard this sound before, but not in Terra Demorte. The sound sent chills up and down his spine, and the night air around him suddenly became colder. He had heard this same sound in his dreams—in his nightmares—long before he had come to Terra Demorte to rescue his son. He didn't turn to see what it was. If his dreams were right, he didn't want to face the evil behind him.

He heard the sound again, like someone dragging something heavy—like iron—on the cobblestones, which amplified the sound.

Roland wrapped his hands around the pistols and walked briskly up the street toward the tunnel. He heard the noise again, this time much closer. *If I hurry*, he thought, *I can make the tunnel and maybe, with a little luck, I can get out of this place before...*

Roland couldn't have been more mistaken. The noise behind him became louder, and now it was accompanied by a loud growl. Roland froze; he stood resembling a statue, hoping he could become invisible to the eye if still long enough. Seconds passed, and all was quiet, deadly quiet. It took all of the courage he could gather to turn and face the creature that was stalking him.

He pulled his pistols and turned around; there, standing in the shadows, was the silhouette of a huge man. Beside the large man stood a beast of some kind. The shadows hid both well. The beast's eyes were glowing; they flashed bright green as they stared at Roland. He could hear it breathing, taking in huge amounts of air, and a soft growl would accompany the air as the beast exhaled.

It was exactly as it had been in his dreams. *How can this be?* he thought. *How could I have known about this beforehand?*

"Lights on," shouted Roland. The streetlamps lit up, and Roland could see clearly the huge man and the monstrous animal. Once again, he didn't know what to do. Should he run for the tunnel or fight where he stood?

The beast was at least five feet tall; it had shaggy fur and a ferocious head that bore four large fangs, two on the bottom jaw and two on the top. They crisscrossed one another when the beast had his mouth shut. They were six or seven inches long, like that of a saber-toothed tiger. The beast had enormous paws, each with claws like a bear. It pawed at the ground and then shook its head from side to side, waiting to attack.

The man was tall and stood staring at Roland. He didn't speak nor move; he stood perfectly still and just stared at the man in front of him. Roland had seen a man like this earlier that night when his boat landed on the island. The Great Dark Witch make him disappear, he wished she were there now.

Then, as if taunting his prey, the man pulled on the thing that had made the noise. It was a hammer—not a small repairperson's hammer or even a sledgehammer. No, this was a huge hammer, something that a man like Roland couldn't lift, and Roland noticed it was stained with blood.

The man pulled on the hammer and the beast growled once more. The man, not taking his eyes off Roland, bent down slowly and un-snapped the chain around the beast's neck. The next thing Roland heard was terrifying.

"Kill."

The beast lunged forward. Roland raised his pistols and emptied both clips toward the charging beast. The death machines made their small sounds, and brass casing danced on the cobblestones with each pull on the triggers. The beast made a loud cry but didn't stop its charge. Roland reloaded. The clips slid out of the guns, and he quickly pushed two more in place. He raised the pistols and emptied them once more at the rushing beast. This time the beast turned to one side and let out a loud cry. It fell to the ground whimpering.

Roland reloaded and stared at the beast lying in front of him, then at the huge man. The man raised the enormous hammer and returned Roland's stare. Roland raised his pistols and repeated the same actions as he had taken toward the beast. The slugs were true and hit the bounty hunter in the chest. Roland didn't stop shooting until the guns refused to make their subdued sounds again. He knew he had shot all of his bullets, and once more, the guns were empty. He reloaded.

The man didn't make a sound but staggered and fell to his knees; Roland turned and headed toward the tunnel. He hadn't taken many steps when he heard the growls again. He glanced over his shoulder, and to his surprise, there were two more beasts standing beside the man. The man slowly rose to his feet and repeated a word that Roland had already heard that night.

"Kill."

Both beasts started toward Roland. He fired at the beasts and heard them yelp and whimper as he turned up the tunnel. He knew he had hit them, but how badly, he didn't know. He wasn't about to wait around to see. He knew the man had managed to get to his feet, so he assumed the slugs he had sent his way had not hit anything vital. He quickened his pace, running as fast as he could, up the tunnel.

The lights would light and then go back to their dark state as he ran. Roland glanced back toward the entrance of the tunnel, the lights came back on, and he could see the two beasts and the gigantic man enter the tunnel. The man didn't drag the hammer this time. Instead, he carried it with his hands as if ready to strike; that is if he could catch Roland. The hammer was huge. A blow from it would bring sudden crushing of bones and probably death, but Roland wasn't waiting around to find out.

Roland raced toward the end of the tunnel. The beasts were gaining on him, and he prayed as he raced toward the portal. He turned and emptied both guns down the tunnel toward the beasts and man. He didn't take aim and knew some of the bullets would miss their mark, but he was hoping that some would hit just enough to slow the pursuers down. He quickly reloaded as he ran toward the portal.

Roland was lucky. His bullets had hit their marks, hitting the first beast in the head, who fell fast, tripping up the other two. The man became entangled in the hounds, and he too fell with a might thud.

The huge hammer fell on one of the hound's tail, and it yelped loudly. Moments passed before Roland heard them moving about again.

"Kill," scolded the bounty hunter. "Kill that human."

Roland reached the portal; he exited without slowing his stride. He heard the concealed voice saying, "Exit, Deidre." He turned and headed across the street. There he would be safe. He knew that the beasts and the monstrous man wouldn't come out of the portal.

\*\*\*

Thor, Horace, and Notor stepped onto the porch of Number 12. Thor started to knock when the door opened and there stood Wisteria.

"Come in, dear." She stepped back and allowed them to enter.

"Where's, Katie?" asked Thor.

"She's in the den. Oh, thank God. You have Josh."

"Yes, we saved him. He's fine," Thor said as he walked into the den. Katie slept on the sofa and made no movement. The noise Thor, Horace, and Notor made entering the house hadn't disturbed the sleeping woman. Wisteria's sleeping spell was working as planned.

"Should we wake her?" asked Thor.

"Yes, dear. Give me a moment." Wisteria waved her hands, and Katie opened her eyes. She waved her hands once more and Josh opened his eyes, as well.

"My baby," she said, as she sat up on the sofa reaching for her son. She grabbed the little boy and hugged him. Tears rolled down her cheeks as she kissed her son softly. Josh hugged his mommy and held her tightly.

"Oh, thank you. Thank you so much." Katie hugged her son again, and for a moment, all was right once more at Number 12.

Suddenly, she noticed something missing. "Where's, Roland?"

Thor dropped his head; he didn't know what to say. These things weren't common for an assassin. *How do I do this?* he thought. As an assassin, Thor, answered the only way, he could.

"Roland didn't make it, Katie. I'm sorry."

"Roland," said Katie before fainting. Wisteria caught her, and Thor's quick reflexes allowed him to catch the small boy. Wisteria placed Katie on the sofa. "What happened, Thor? What happened to Roland?"

"We were running out of time. I had to use Roland as a decoy in order to save Josh." Thor placed Josh on the couch with Katie.

"How did he die?"

"Jake, the barkeeper, killed him with a fireball. Me too, but I was resurrected."

"You mean you came back to life in Terra Demorte?"

"No, something different. Wisteria, I was resurrected—dead but not dead. A witch brought me back to life."

"A witch?"

"Yes, she cut off my head, but I didn't wake up in the Keeping Room. When I was resurrected, I was still in the pub."

"Where's Roland's body?"

"In Terra Demorte. We couldn't get it; I was lucky to escape with my life and the boy."

"Why would a witch save you, Thor?"

"She wanted a favor from me. That's all I know, and at that particular time, I would have given her anything. Creed and Olin played a trick on me and caught me off guard. If it hadn't been for the witch, I might not have made it back either."

"We've got to go back and get Roland," Wisteria said as she sat down in the chair. We can't leave him there. We can't let them know who he is, and you know that. So get ready. We are going back to Terra Demorte."

"I'm ready, Wisteria. I was planning to go back for his body anyway. I just wanted to get the boy here first."

"I'll put a spell on Katie, and get several of the witches in my order to watch her. I don't think she'll be in any danger for now. Creed and Olin will be coming for the child again. I'm sure of that. It's just a matter of time. Right now, we must get Roland's body out of that evil place. I'll put Josh in his room and cast a spell on it. No one will be able to enter his room, and he won't be able to leave it. He'll be safe there. I'll cast a sleeping spell on him, as well. I'm sure he needs the rest."

"I agree."

Horace, you and Notor stay here with Katie. I'll put her in a deep sleep until we arrive back."

The men agreed and took seats while Wisteria gave orders.

"Wisteria," said Notor, "you don't have a medallion. How do you plan on getting through the portal?"

"Hogwash," scolded Wisteria. You let me worry about that. Don't think for one minute that I can't get in. I'm a witch, you know."

Thor cast her an inquisitive look. "You can pass through our portals?"

\*\*\*

Roland had just made it to the other side of the street when he heard the first beast exit the portal. "Dear God, no. This can't be happening," he said. He slumped down behind one of the riding mowers in front of the hardware store. He stared down the street. He knew that seven houses down this very street was his home, and there he would find safety. He wondered what he should do next, what his next move would be. Should he make a run for it or fight the beasts from this position? He didn't want the beast that had just exited the portal going into his house where Wisteria and Katie were. "What to do?" he said softly.

He had no sooner gotten those words out when out came two more of the massive animals, followed by the bounty hunter. He hid in the darkness, watching the beast as they lifted their heads and smelled the air. He noticed the bounty hunter had three large chains wrapped around his hand, and the other ends were securely fastened around the beasts' necks.

"Maybe he is just taking a look around before returning to Terra Demorte," he said softly. Both the bounty hunter and the three beasts looked in the direction where Roland was crouching. His mind was spinning. *Did they hear me?* he thought.

The bounty hunter snorted and spoke. "You can't hide, human. The hounds of Terra Demorte know where you are; they can smell you. Did you think I wouldn't come through the portal? I always get my man, and right now, you are my man. Why don't you come over here and I'll kill you quickly. Don't make me come after you. If you don't come over here and you decide to run, I'll kill every living thing I come in contact with while I'm chasing you. Do you hear me, human?"

Roland sat quietly. He hadn't come this far to give up now. He checked his pistols and then his pack for more ammunition. The adrenalin flowed as he realized he had no more clips in his backpack. All he had left were in the pistols, and he didn't know how many shots he had fired coming out of the tunnel.

He remembered emptying the guns in the tunnel and reloading, and then before exiting, firing off rounds in the direction of the beasts, but how many? He knew the guns weren't empty, the slides were still closed, but he had no idea how many bullets were in each pistol. He didn't know, and it would make too much noise to check his pistols now.

The hounds of Terra Demorte stared in the direction of the hardware store. Roland knew they had found him, but what were they waiting on? Why did they not attack? His thoughts were answered as the bounty hunter made the first move.

"Have it your way, human." He bent down slowly, and all Roland heard was a snap, and then another one. "Kill," was the next thing Roland heard. The hounds charged in the direction of the hardware store. The third hound pulled hard on the chain, but the bounty hunter didn't release him.

Roland made a dash across the side street and down Calhoun Street. He knew he couldn't outrun the hounds, and knew he had to find some way to slow them down. He glanced over his shoulder and saw the hounds heading straight for him. *One house, now two*, he thought. Five more to go.

The hounds were gaining, and now Roland could hear them taking in huge amounts of air and growling louder than before as they exhaled the stale air. He knew he had to fight, so he suddenly stopped, turned, and waited on the first hound to attack. He knew he couldn't let them catch him with his back toward them or he wouldn't have any chance of killing them.

He had actually made it to the third house on Calhoun Street. "Four more to go," he said softly. He turned slightly, and for a second, he saw the lights of Number 12. "So close," he whispered. "This is as good of a place as any to make my stand."

He was surprised with himself as he turned to face the two hounds. He hadn't known how close the hounds were, and they were closer than he had imagined.

The first hound was upon him, and Roland stood facing the first hound head-on. He calculated each stride and configured how much time he had before the hound would leap for him. The second hound was a few steps behind the first, and Roland figured his strides, as well. He had the pistols in his hands, with no idea of how many bullets he had left. "Please, God, please let there be enough."

He had just spoken those words when the first hound leaped toward the warrior. It was coming straight for him, speeding through the air like a freight train. Roland continued to calculate its speed and the amount of time it would take for the hound to reach him. One advantage for Roland was that the hounds were so large and heavy, they were slow enough for Roland to calculate their every move down to a nanosecond.

"Here is the first one, and with any luck, the second one will be the one I have to really deal with first." The ferocious beast came directly at Roland. It opened its mouth wide and its green eyes rolled back into its head. The animal was now operating on pure instinct, and Roland knew its intentions, which were to sink its teeth deep into his face.

Roland waited. The hound was in midair, and Roland's mind was calculating every inch. It was as if his mind had slowed down the whole process, and as in a movie, was watching the charging hound one frame at a time.

The hound opened its mouth wider and prepared to snap its four huge fangs down on the human standing in front of it.

Roland waited, and as the hound came within a foot of his head, he stepped quickly to the left. The hound was already in midair and had no braking system. What it saw next, right behind where Roland was standing, was an iron lamppost. The hound hit the post with its mouth wide open, and Roland saw two huge teeth go flying by his face and land on the sidewalk. For a moment, the huge hound folded up like an accordion. The noise was horrendous, and the light in the post went dark from the tremendous impact of the hound. The post stood its ground and didn't waver from the collision. The hound let out a loud scream.

"No need to worry about you. That's the one I need to deal with now," Roland said loudly. The second hound heard the scream of the first hound, but the noise didn't distract him at all. Roland had counted on that. As soon as he dodged the first hound, Roland's concentration had centered on the second attacking beast. He had made ready his guns and prayed that they would repeat their actions as they had done all night in Terra Demorte.

If he was to miss this beast with any bullets left in his guns, he was doomed and would die within seconds. He had raised both pistols and had them circumspectly on the second hound, calculating each step and moving the pistols accordingly. It was like a dance. The more the hound closed the distance on him, the more Roland adjusted his arms, his hands, and the pistols he was holding.

Finally, Roland couldn't wait any longer. He realized, although the slides were closed, he might have closed them in the tunnel; it would be something he would have done without the knowledge of doing it, just a reflex.

So what he thought now, was one or both guns might be empty. If the first pistol was empty, he had to have time to try the other one. He pulled the trigger on the first pistol. Nothing happened, and the adrenalin pumped through his veins as the gun clicked instead of firing. He quickly adjusted the second pistol one last time. This was his last chance, and if this pistol performed the same actions as the last, then it was over for Roland. The hound would certainly take off his head with one swift bite.

He wondered why the witch had lied to him. She said he could leave safely. And then he remembered. He was in Johnston. He had made it safely...out of Terra Demorte.

The hound charged directly at Roland, same as the first, and made a humongous leap toward Roland's head. Roland fired the pistol directly at the hound. The death machine performed perfectly as two speeding bullets struck the hound in the face. The first couldn't have been placed more perfectly; it hit the charging hound directly between the eyes, and the second bullet followed, slamming into the beast's head. The hound hit Roland in the chest, and the impact itself felt nothing less than a runaway train hitting him at an incredible speed. He was thrown backward with such a mighty force that he dropped the empty gun.

The hound fell to his side and didn't make a sound. Roland lay on his back; he opened his eyes and struggled to gain his composure. His head rang as if someone was banging a muffled bell. He shook it off and cleared his thoughts. Somewhere out there was a bounty hunter, and he had to prepare himself to fight him, as well.

He rose and knelt. The bell sound was still ringing but now at a tolerable level. He focused his eyes and looked down the street to where the beasts had started their attacks.

"Nothing, nothing," he said. He managed to stand and, although wobbly, managed not to fall. He stared down Calhoun Street. Still no bounty hunter.

"Looking for me?" said a voice. Roland squinted. He knew the bounty hunter was there but where. Somewhere up the street a bit, he figured, somewhere in the darkness.

"Good move, human. My hounds are fierce fighters and can rip a man's head from his shoulders with one bite, but they're no match for lampposts and that weapon you have there."

Roland knew now why the bounty hunter stayed in the shadows. His pursuer, must have come to respect his pistols, and was afraid to step into the light.

"You better not show yourself," said Roland, picking up the empty gun. He was now in a dilemma. He still didn't know how many bullets he had left, but then the bounty hunter didn't know that, either. For the first time, he felt that he had the upper hand on the man chasing him.

"Show yourself, and I'll do the same thing to you, the same as I have done to your hounds," Roland shouted.

"Oh, that's OK. I'll just wait for a minute until my hounds recover and we'll continue this fight."

Roland freaked. *What? What did he say? Until his hounds recovered? You mean these things aren't dead?* Then he realized that the bounty hunter didn't understand what kind of damage the guns did. Another advantage—he knew the hounds were dead, that they wouldn't be returning to life, but for the moment, the bounty hunter didn't know this.

"Time to move on," said Roland.

Hopefully, he thought, as soon as the bounty hunter realized his hounds weren't going to rise up from the dead and fight again, he himself would return to Terra Demorte and be out of Roland's life forever. Roland slid the two pistols into their holsters and slowly backed down the street toward Number 12.

The bounty hunter stepped into the light and watched his prey continued down the city street. His eyes stared at Roland, and Roland stared directly back at the bounty hunter. The exchange of hate was so thick that one could have cut it with a knife.

Roland could see the chains the bounty hunter used as leashes on the hounds. He saw the third hound pulling on the chain, but the bounty hunter held it tightly and didn't unleash the monstrous animal. The loose chains were wrapped around his shoulder and under his arms. They were enormous, but nonetheless, the bounty hunter had wrapped them around his body as if they weighed nothing at all. After some distance, Roland turned and walked briskly toward home.

He hadn't taken but a few more steps when he heard a familiar sound; he glanced back over his shoulder while he continued his pace toward Number 12.

"Jimmey Cricket," he said. The first hound, which had hit the lamppost, had risen to its feet and stood there shaking its coat vigorously. It let out a loud growl, and its green eyes stared directly at Roland. Roland didn't hesitate or slow his walk but kept his steady pace toward Number 12.

"Fifth house, and there is number six, and that one there is mine," he said. He turned up the steps, stopped, and glanced down the street once more. There, standing on the sidewalk, were all three of the hounds of Terra Demorte and the bounty hunter. Roland watched as all four monsters stared in his direction.

"Now what?" he said. "What do I do now?" All four of the monsters walked slowly toward Roland.

The front door of Number 12 burst open, and in walked Roland. He had pulled the pistols from under his cloak once more, wondering if he had any bullets left. His hands were holding the pistols, and Roland slammed the door using his foot.

"We've got problems," he said, locking the door. "I don't think this house will keep those beasts out of here. He didn't stopped to say hello or even acknowledge anyone. For Roland, there was still a war going on, and another battle brewing just outside.

Thor, Wisteria, Horace, and Notor all stood in awe as they stared at the dead man standing in the living room. Wisteria, who had no more than ten minutes ago been told that Roland hadn't made it out of Terra Demorte, was staring at the man they were just about to go back to that evil land to find. Standing in Number 12 at this very minute was none other than Roland Roberts.

# Thirty-Five

## Creed's Return

The Great Dark Witch sat alone in Jake's Place; she finally stood up and looked at the barkeeper. "Don't repeat what you have seen here tonight. If you do, you will suffer the most horrifying death." She turned her back toward Jake, and then whispered, "And I'll make sure you can't be resurrected."

"No, I won't. You have my word. I'll be silent," Jake said.

"Good," said the witch. She thought of the three-headed snake on Jake's chest. Her memories flooded her mind, of Jake's actions when she was a baby, and how he had dumped her out of the sack into the snow. "A baby," she said softly. She turned and faced the barkeep once more. "I'll be back for you, Jake. One day when you least expect me, I'll return and you will serve me, as promised."

"Yes," said Jake, "I'll serve you." Jake looked at the witch. He knew he would never serve her. He would never serve a witch; that was below his status.

The Great Dark Witch laughed under her breath. She knew she didn't need a lowly barkeep like Jake, but she also knew that one day she would return to Terra Demorte, and when she did, Jake would pay for what he had done to her when she was a helpless child.

***

Creed and Olin had returned to the mansion with the demon guardians, Roy and Ray, in tow. The guardians had ensured the house and grounds were safe and locked up tightly for the night. That, of course, was their job, and they were glad to be back doing it.

The Edgefield Police and the FBI had completed their investigation at the mansion. The pond was indeed filled with blood, but the body parts had turned out to be small pig remains. They assumed there was some kind of occult meeting in the old abandoned mansion and turned that investigation over to Johnston's own Officer Jim.

The demon guardians were glad to be back at the mansion. That too was simply because their pay would commence once more, and it was well known that gold was the biggest motivator for a demon guardian—although, at times, ale would substitute just fine for payment, except for Ray, of course. He loved his gold, but Ray—well, Ray loved killing. It was just a pleasant thing to him. It motivated him in such a way that Roy had to keep a constant check on him or things just might get out of hand when Ray was on the surface. Ray normally drank his gold away, but at times Roy had the familiar feeling that Ray would pay just to have someone to kill.

Roy would watch him at times, just sitting around killing ants with his big thumb, or stepping on insects crawling around on the floor. At times, he would chase butterflies in the garden just to pull their wings off and then squash them with his fist. He loved killing all kinds of things, but his favorite thing to kill were those meddling humans.

Roy would wake him in the mornings, and the first thing Ray would say was, "Me wants to kill something, Roy."

Creed sat at his desk, and Olin sat in the oversized chair in front of him. The mansion was as they had left it, or at least, it appeared to be the same. Olin's wounds had stopped bleeding, and he had regained some strength, although he was still weak. The Great Dark Witch had given him more potions to regain his strength, and he was feeling the effects.

"Sit still, Olin. I'll make you another potion. We will kill all who betrayed us. We will have our revenge." Creed stirred a strange mixture in a vile and handed it to Olin, who drank it immediately.

"Let me check your wounds," said Creed.

"No need to. They're healed. The Great Dark Witch seen to that. I'm just tired and weak, but your potion will remedy that soon." Olin slumped back into the chair; he didn't want his brother to know that the Great Dark Witch's potions were far better than Creed's. "Can you believe there was a spy here, here in our home, spying on us? Oh, yes, Brother, as soon as the Great Dark Witch gets here, we will finish your transformation, and together we will kill the traitors and rule Terra Demorte and all of the other warlocks. The spy had to have been working for the council."

"Yes, you shall," said the Great Dark Witch, appearing suddenly. "We shall complete your transformation, Master Creed, and once we have finished that, we will wreak havoc, death, and destruction on all of those who have stood in your way." She laughed loudly and strolled over to Olin. "And yes, the spy was working for the council, but not anymore."

Olin smiled. "You took care of that, didn't you?"

"No, not exactly," she said. "I was ready to kill her, but she gave me the slip. She was quite cunning, but that won't happen again. Regardless, she was found out, and now her head is in Terra Demorte." She changed the subject, "I see you are feeling better. Here, drink this." The witch gave Olin a small bottle, and he opened it. As soon as he pulled the cork out of the top of the bottle, it glowed in the dark. "Quickly, drink it."

Olin tossed his head back and emptied the bottle into his mouth; he swallowed the potion and handed the bottle back to the witch.

"What was that?" asked Creed.

"Oh, something special I make for Olin, something he needed." Olin laid his head back into the soft cushion of the chair and went into a deep sleep. His white-streaked hair turned back into a rich dark black. "I like that much better," said the witch.

\*\*\*

Thor was the first to speak as he stared at Roland. "How on Hades did you make it out of Terra Demorte? You were dead; I saw your body on the floor in Jake's Place, your head severed from your body."

"Not now, Thor. I have a huge man and three beasts on my tail, and the beasts won't die. I shot one of them. I thought I killed it, but it didn't stay dead. We've got big troubles, and by now, they should be right outside of this door."

"What are you talking about? Did you say something followed you out of Terra Demorte?" said Thor.

"Yes, a huge man with three monstrous dogs of some kind, the man was dragging a hammer." Roland rechecked the locked the door. "We've got to get ready, they will be here any minute, and they did followed me out of the portal. I fought them all the way here but no matter what I did, they would not die."

"Did you say a huge man dragging a hammer?" Thor tried to get Roland to slow down so he could make sense of what he was saying. "Roland, did you say a man dragging a hammer, a huge hammer?"

"Yeah, huge, but that's not the issue; it's the three beasts he has with him. Thor, they won't die. I'm telling you, I shot them, but they won't die."

"Roland, that's a bounty hunter, and he has the hounds of Terra Demorte with him. They will die, but you've got to be quick. Something is wrong; someone in Terra Demorte wants you dead, someone besides the heads of the clans. It takes all of the heads on the council to release the hounds of Terra Demorte, and they do release them, but it's very rare. The hounds will die, Roland; they are of meat and bones."

"No kidding I shot one of them, and it didn't die. So how do I kill them?"

"Your bullets should do the trick; you must have missed."

"I didn't miss, and one of them ran full bore into a steel lamppost and it didn't kill him either. I tell you, no matter what I did, I couldn't kill them."

"They're vicious, Roland, but you can kill them. Are you sure they followed you here?"

Thor had no sooner gotten the words out of his mouth than a loud crash hit the front door. The door stood its ground and didn't open. Roland slowly backed out of the living room into the edge of the den.

Wisteria made ready. She looked at Katie and mumbled something under her breath. Katie opened her eyes.

"I guess you better be awake, dear. We are going to need you."

"Need me for what?" said Katie. She looked up and saw Roland standing in the den. "Roland!" she said. She ran toward him and threw her arms around his neck. "They told me you were dead. Oh, Roland, I'm so happy to see you."

Roland hugged his wife and then gently pushed her away. "Katie, where's Josh?" He looked at Thor, then at his wife. "Where's my son?"

"He's upstairs, dear, in his bedroom. I have cast a spell on his room. No one can enter it, and he can't get out. I thought he needed the rest. He'll be safe there." Wisteria looked at Thor.

"What do we need to do to fight these things, Thor?" said Wisteria.

"Fight what?" said Katie.

"Three beasts and a huge man. They're coming to kill us," said Roland. "They followed me out of Terra Demorte."

"How did you make it out of there, Roland?" asked Thor.

"Not now, Thor. I'll tell you later. Katie, can you go into the butler's pantry and get me the duffel bag under the cabinet? I need my ammunition."

"Yes, of course." Katie left the room, and before long, she was back, carrying a small duffel bag. She handed it to Roland, and he sat it in the huge chair in the den. He quickly grabbed two clips and reloaded his pistols. He tucked one neatly under each arm and stuck more clips in each pocket.

"This will do nicely."

"What can I do?" asked Katie.

Thor was the first to answer. "Katie, you need to go to the back of the den. Don't let the bounty hunter see you. He'll try to kill one of the women first. He'll think it will disorient us, and if we're confused, he'll have the upper hand."

"Thor, can you kill those things?" said Roland.

"Sure," he pulled several daggers out from under his cloak. Then he pulled out a small bottle. He opened it and dipped each dagger into the mixture.

"Poison," he said. "This stuff is so powerful that it will kill anything it strikes." He laughed. "Even a bounty hunter."

Roland looked confused. "My bullets didn't kill the beast," he said.

"You missed, Roland. Your bullets will kill them and the bounty hunter too. I'm sure of it; they have no magic, just brute strength, and plenty of it." He laughed. "He probably doesn't know I'm here. Once he sees me, I'll send him packing back toward the nasty island he lives on. We don't have to be worried about him."

The door took another huge banging then fell forward and hit the floor with a loud crash. There was a large hole where the door used to hang. They all watched with anticipation. Thor stepped forward and took full control of the situation. "Katie, back against the wall. Wisteria, come up here with us. We can use your magic. Easy does it. As soon as we see him, I'll send him back to Terra Demorte."

The bounty hunter stepped into Number 12. He was bigger than the door, having to bend slightly to avoid hitting his head on the door's casing. The three huge beasts followed him. The bounty hunter held them securely with the chains, and the hounds stood in front of him, staring at their prey. The huge man didn't say a word; he just stood there scanning the room.

Thor stepped forward. "Your work on the surface is finished, bounty hunter. Go back to Terra Demorte and take those hounds with you."

"I don't think I should do that," said the bounty hunter. "I'm here to kill this miserable human and his family." He stood erect as if proud of what he was saying. "Then I'm going to kill you, assassin, and then that old witch."

Thor measured the bounty hunter up and down. "Aren't you forgetting something? You can't kill on the surface unless the heads of the clans give you a specific order. Have they given you such an order? If so, I want to see it. I, myself, work for the council. Well, come on, man; show me your orders." Thor snapped the words and took another step toward the bounty hunter. He stepped back, but the hounds met his advance and pulled harder on the chains.

"I have my orders, assassin, but not in writing. I have my orders to kill all of them, and you too"—he paused and laughed—"*assassin*. I used this human to bring me here; he did just as the council members said he would do, and now, I'm here."

Roland raised his guns. "You know what these can do?"

The bounty hunter laughed once more. "Oh, you think I don't know what pistols can do? You think I haven't seen weapons like that before?" He slowly pulled back his coat, and strapped to his hips, with a large belt, were two pistols. "I only wanted to make you think I didn't know what they were and that I was afraid of them. That way, you would escape and lead me right to your doorstep."

The bounty hunter laughed loudly. "It worked," he said. "Good job, human. You've made my work easy. My first hound wasn't attacking you. I told him to attack the lamppost. And the second—he's never been that slow." The bounty hunter laughed loudly once more.

Thor spoke once again to the huge man. "Go home, bounty hunter. I can kill you faster than you think—and those hounds, as well. You know that."

"Normally, you could, assassin, but I have special magic and so do my hounds."

"Bounty hunters have no magic, and the council members would never agree to give you any magic. You are an outcast, even in Terra Demorte. You have no home and no magic, so leave before this gets ugly."

Thor took another step toward the bounty hunter, and again the hounds met his advance. They pulled harder on their chains, wanting to charge. This time, Thor didn't retreat but pushed his hands beneath his cloak and grabbed two daggers.

"How in the Hades did the heads of the all the clans give you magic? Most hate your kind."

The bounty hunter snapped at Thor. "Watch your tongue, assassin, or I'll kill you first. Only two clan members gave me my magic; the rest don't know I'm here. Yes, only two, and guess what, assassin? One of the clan members was the head of the assassin clan." He laughed loudly and sneered at Thor. "Feeling betrayed, assassin?"

"You lie," snapped Thor. "You lie. It takes all of the clan members to release you and give you a contract. You sorry dog, you lie." Thor drew back one of the daggers. "Leave now, or I'll dispatch you where you stand."

Thor made ready. If it was a fight the bounty hunter wanted, he was ready to give him one. He knew this mangy dog and knew very well that it took all of the heads of the clans to release him on a contract. He also knew that the head of the assassin clan would never turn against another assassin.

Thor stared down the bounty hunter. "I gave you your chance; now you will die." Thor threw his dagger; it flew straight toward the bounty hunter and struck him squarely in the chest. The first one had just hit when Thor threw the second one. It hit within inches of the first, and the bounty hunter fell backward. He would have fallen out of the door if he hadn't grabbed the door's casing and straightened himself. He slumped to his knees and looked at Thor.

Thor returned the stare. "I warned you, bounty hunter; now you will die. Shoot his dogs, Roland."

Roland did exactly as Thor had instructed; he pointed his first pistol at the hound and pulled the trigger four times. The silencer kept the noise to a soft thud, and four rounds of lead hit the hound in the face. The hound let out a terrifying cry and fell to the floor. Roland didn't hesitate;

he quickly fired four more rounds at the second hound. It too screamed loudly as it fell to the floor, and so did the third hound.

"See, Roland? They aren't hard to kill; you just have to be faster than they are," Thor said. He then turned to the bounty hunter. "The daggers in your chest have poison on them; by now you should be feeling dizzy, and in a few minutes, you will die."

The bounty hunter wobbled a few times on his knees; then as Thor had described, he fell face first toward the floor. His face hit the hard oak floor, and he lay there without moving. The daggers in his chest were driven deeper into the thick muscles.

"In a few minutes, he'll vanish and go back to Terra Demorte. There the council members will resurrect him; that is if they want him back. If it were up to me, he would stay in the Keeping Room for years. We assassins don't like his kind, and neither does anyone else, as far as that goes."

Thor looked at the dead bounty hunter from across the living room. "Any moment now, we will be rid of him and his hounds."

There was a loud laugh from the bounty hunter; then slowly, he pushed himself up from the floor and back again onto his knees. Then slowly, he rose to his feet. He laughed and looked at Thor. He brushed himself with his large hand, as if dusting dirt from his coat.

"I told you, assassin, I have magic. Even you can't kill me. But guess what? I can kill you." The bounty hunter stepped farther into the living room and flung his hammer. As heavy as the hammer was, it flew through the air so fast that the human eye couldn't see it until it hit its target. The hammer hit Wisteria directly in the chest. The sheer force of the object was so powerful that it flung her back across the den and into the back wall. Pieces of plaster shot out around the huge witch and fell to the floor; she made a loud gasp and fell to the floor as well.

Katie screamed and knelt down to help Wisteria. "Wisteria, are you OK?"

Wisteria moaned. She was out cold, leaning against the plaster wall. Katie rubbed her face and continued talking to the fallen witch.

Thor took a step backward. What he was seeing wasn't normal, and as an assassin from Terra Demorte, he had seen many unnatural things in his life. The bounty hunter pulled one of the daggers from his chest, slowly raised the sharp instrument to his lips, and tasted the blood. He dropped the dagger, and as with the first, tugged slowly on the second dagger.

It slipped out of his huge chest, and blood dripped onto the oak floor. He dropped it and muttered a few words under his breath.

The hounds of Terra Demorte started stirring, and then all three stood up and, with a violent movement, shook all over. Their hair stood up as if some kind of magnetic force had attracted it. Then they stood still and growled loudly at Thor and Roland, their green eyes glowing.

"You see, assassin, my hounds are OK. You might want to watch this." The bounty hunter waved his hands, and the bullets fired from Roland's guns slowly backed out of the hounds' oozing wounds and fell to the floor. The wounds stopped bleeding, and Roland stood watching the bullets as they spun around lazily on the floor before coming to a stop.

The hounds pulled hard on the chains as they lunged toward Thor. The bounty hunter held them tight and slowly started pulling them closer to him.

Thor looked at Wisteria, who was still leaning against the wall. Katie had brought her around to a semiconscious state. Katie would ask Wisteria a question and the old witch would shake her head or answer with a simple yes or no. Katie looked at Thor and then at Roland. "She won't be of any use to you. She's hurt really bad; she's barely alive."

Thor flung two more daggers toward the bounty hunter, and as quickly as he had let the weapons fly, he went beneath his cloak, pulled out two more and sent them flying toward the hounds of Terra Demorte.

He watched them as they neared their target, but instead of striking hard, they stopped in midair and hung there, suspended by magic.

"What are you looking at, assassin? Do you think these little daggers are going to kill me?" The bounty hunter laughed and, with his pointer finger, flipped the two daggers in front of him to one side. Thor watched as the daggers hit the floor. Then with a small movement of the bounty hunter's hand, the two daggers in front of the hounds fell to the floor, as well.

Roland said, "I told you they wouldn't die."

Thor flashed his hand, and a mighty fireball raced toward the Bounty Hunter, it as well, stopped within inches of the huge man's head and like the daggers, was suspended in mid-air. The Bounty Hunter made a slight motion and sent the fireball off in a different direction, watching it as it struck the wall and died out. "You can't kill me Assassin."

The Bounty Hunter made another hand jester and the huge hammer shot back into his hand. He stood there looking at the two men.

Roland raised his guns and fired at the bounty hunter. He stopped firing when the guns didn't recoil but made a soft snapping noise. He quickly pushed the levers on the side, and both guns belched out their clips. Roland quickly pushed two more clips into the pistols.

He looked at the bounty hunter to ensure his bullets had hit their mark, and to his surprise, they had. The bounty hunter was forced backward a few steps, and then regained his composure and stepped forward, back to the same spot he had been standing before Roland had fired on him. This time, the bullets didn't suspend in midair. There were holes in the bounty hunter's shirt, and blood was oozing out. Roland had hit his target with his bullets and felt that he, Thor, and the rest had some kind of chance of beating this monster.

The bounty hunter flung his head back and let out a loud scream, but as horrifying as the scream was, what came next was more horrifying. The loud, excruciating scream turned into a loud laugh, and as he laughed, he lowered his head and looked straight at Roland. "I'm going to kill you last," he said.

To Roland and Thor's surprise, the bounty hunter stared at his chest and then under his breath, mumbled a few words. The bullets backed out of his chest and fell to the floor; the wounds closed, and Roland couldn't see any more blood oozing from the huge man's chest.

"Your guns can't kill me, human. I have magic, and now I'm going to kill all of you."

Roland and Thor backed farther into the den; no one said a word as they stood watching the bounty hunter pull the dogs closer to him. Thor knew what was to come next; he looked at Roland, and for the first time since he had met the assassin from Terra Demorte, Roland could sense the fear mounting in Thor.

"What do we do, Thor?" asked Roland.

"Nothing we can do, Roland. I can't kill him with my poison daggers, and your bullets don't hurt him either. I have no more tricks up my sleeve. It's up to Wisteria and her magic; that's the only thing that will stop this man."

Roland paused and turned slowly toward Wisteria; she was unable to return the stare. "She's not going to be much use to us, Thor." He sent her a thought: *Wisteria, can you hear me?* She didn't answer but Katie did: *She's no help, Roland, she's dying.*

"Oh, are you worried about your old witch?" said the bounty hunter. "The head of the assassin clan told me to take her out first. They say she is very powerful, and if I can bring back her head, they will triple my reward." He tossed his head back and laughed once more.

It was then that a small figure stood in the doorway of the den. The bounty hunter didn't see him until he stepped out of the stairwell and into the den.

Roland let out a loud gasp and said, "Josh."

Yes, the small figure was none other than Josh. How he had gotten out of his room with the spell Wisteria had cast on him and his room was a mystery.

"Oh, the boy, yes. That will make a nice, moist treat for my hounds," said the bounty hunter. He slowly let out some chain on one of the hounds. "Fetch, boy."

Roland screamed. "No! Josh, run to Mommy. Run, son. Run now." He fired his pistols at the hound heading toward Josh. The hound let out a loud howl and spun around as if trying to bite its tail. The bounty hunter muttered a few words. The hound straightened itself up and stared at its prey.

Josh had heard his father's command and searched for his mother. Katie, diverting her attention from Wisteria, shouted for Josh to come to her. Josh did exactly as commanded; shot across the room and jumped into his mother's hands.

"Nice job, Josh," said Roland.

"Katie," said Thor.

"Yes."

"Can Wisteria stand?"

"No, she conscious, but I don't think she can stand."

"If we can't get her on her feet or conscious enough to handle this, we are all dead. Get her on her feet or at least alert."

The bounty hunter heard Thor's words and laughed again. "Oh, I don't think she's going to be much help. Her chest is crushed, and in a few more minutes, her lungs will fill with blood and she'll suffocate, drowning on her own blood." He slowly pulled on the chains that held the hounds and pulled them closer until they were at his feet.

"Katie?" said Thor.

"No use, Thor. She delirious; she's not going to be any help." Katie brushed the old woman's face, and as she did, a tear rolled down her own cheek and fell onto Wisteria's face. Katie slowly took her thumb and wiped it away. "I know you can hear me, Wisteria. We need you now, more than any other time. Do you understand?"

The old witch moaned and opened her eyes; then she spoke only one word. "Thor."

"Thor, she's asking for you."

The bounty hunter smiled at Roland and watched as Thor stepped back toward Wisteria. He pulled the hounds close to his face and kissed them on their heads, one at a time.

"Wisteria, what is it? What can we do?" Thor was bending down beside the old witch. He had come to love this woman, and although he had never felt love before, he knew what it was now and knew there was no chance to beat the destruction that was facing all of them at this very minute. He took his hand and rubbed the old woman's face. "Rest now, Wisteria. You rest."

Wisteria raised her hand and put it on Thor's shoulder and then behind Thor's head. She slowly pulled his head toward her mouth, and when it was close enough, she whispered something into the assassin's ear.

Thor shot up like a rocket and turned toward the bounty hunter. He searched every pocket, patting them and running his fingers in the openings. Then as suddenly as he had started the ritual, he stopped. He stood erect and called to Roland.

"Roland, come on back here. Come and stand by me."

Roland's worst fears came flooding into his mind as he watched what the bounty hunter did next. He heard a snap, and then two more. Then, as before, Roland heard only one word.

"Kill."

Roland had backed to where Thor was standing and looked at the assassin, but something was different in Thor's eyes. The fear was gone, and for once, Roland had hope that he and his family might just survive the night.

Thor saw the approaching hounds and looked at the bounty hunter, who stood watching his hounds slowly stalking their prey. The hounds didn't rush in, but methodically stalked their quarry, one step at a time, closing the distance between them with each step. They snapped their jaws, showing the large canine teeth. The teeth that would soon, crush their bones.

The bounty hunter knew they had nowhere to run and no weapons to use on them, and their magic wouldn't hurt them now. It was all a show to the bounty hunter, a show the huge man had watched many times as his hounds attacked and tore into their victims, snapping limbs off and lapping up the blood until there was nothing left. This was the bounty hunter's zenith; this was what he lived for, watching his hounds do their dirty work. This was his high, and he was ready to reap its reward.

The bounty hunter spoke softly, "kill them boys, kill them."

Thor pitched a small object toward the approaching hounds. The bounty hunter watched as the item flipped repeatedly until it hit the floor in front of the hounds. The hounds stared at the small capsule as it came to a halt and spun on the hardwood floor. All watched until the insignificant capsule slowly stopped spinning.

Roland, as well, stood staring, waiting on some type of magic to strike down the approaching danger, but nothing happened. The hounds sniffed at the small item lying in front of them and still nothing happened. The bounty hunter watched in earnest; he stood there, ready with his magic to cancel out any weapons the assassin might use against him and his hounds, but still nothing happened.

"Roland, get against the wall with Katie and Wisteria. Now. Move."

"You got it. What is that thing?" Roland knelt down beside Katie; she grabbed his arm and cuddled Josh in her lap. All four of them sat huddled together as the hounds raised their heads and focused, once more, on the task, at hand.

"Oh, that?" said Thor. "That is a jungle."

The words were barely spoken when all around them was a big, beautiful jungle. Birds were flying around, and strange jungle sounds surrounded them. As Roland, Katie, and Josh looked up, they could see monkeys jumping in all directions and screaming at the intruders. They heard a large river with rapids rushing down toward some unknown destination. Other jungle noises didn't sound so friendly, as Roland, Katie, and Wisteria stood up.

"Quickly, get into this tree." It was Wisteria, barely alive and leaning against a huge old tree. "Quickly. Up you go. There are things down here that you don't want to see."

"How do we get up there?" asked Katie.

Then, as if magic—and it was magic—a large rope ladder fell from the top of the tree. "Quickly, climb the ladder."

"We need to carry Wisteria," said Roland. "Help me, Thor."

"No, you can't carry me. I'm too heavy, too much cheese cake. All of you go now. Leave me. I'll be all right."

"No, we won't leave you here. I'll stay with you," said Thor. Thor could have disappeared at any moment, but being an assassin, he would never leave a companion and run. No, Thorton, the assassin, would stay and fight, even if it meant giving his life.

"No, Thor. You are the only one that can remove the spell. All of you, go now, and climb to the top." Wisteria took a deep breath in and then slowly closed her eyes. As the air escaped, the old witch slumped down and didn't take another breath.

Thor, Roland, Josh, and Katie climbed the ladder into the heavy greenery of the tree. They climbed until, to their surprise, the ladder rope ended at a huge platform. It was made of wood and was very stable. Horace and Notor, who seemed mesmerized by the huge, thick jungle, met them all. Notor had lowered the rope ladder.

Then there were loud growls in the jungle. The monkeys and birds stopped screaming, and all was quiet. There were more growls and things snapping and breaking as the jungle echoed every movement from its floor. They all knew it was the hounds of Terra Demorte, who had been hunting them, but now, killing something else.

"Wisteria," said Katie.

"Where is she?" asked Notor. "Where is Wisteria?"

"At the base of this tree?" said Thor, "Notor, can you go check on her? I think she's dead."

"No!" screamed Notor. "She can't be dead. She's Wisteria, the most powerful witch on the surface. She's not dead." He dove off the platform and headed down to where the body of Wisteria lay.

As if the inhabitants of the platform had inhaled some magic drug, they all huddled together and fell into a deep sleep. Horace sat and watched as the spell took over; he would watch over them and would stay awake until they all woke up...but the intense jungle and the magic that was stirring took him, as well, into a deep, deep sleep.

There were strange growls in the jungle and screams as darkness approached. Then, as if nothing had happened, the night birds and jungle sounds came back to life, and the jungle echoed with beautiful sounds.

And if one had looked through the branches of the huge tree, one would have seen the most spectacular sight as the moon and stars shone their lights down and lit up the treetops in a magnificent way.

# Thirty-Six

## The Awakening

The morning sun showed through the treetops, lighting up everything in the jungle, its rays chasing the last bit of darkness into hiding as the whole jungle came to life once more.

Roland sat up and stretched. He rubbed his hands through his hair, and for a moment, he forgot where he was. And as the strange sights came into focus, he remembered. He shook Thor, who was already awake but enjoying the early morning air and the many smells. He too had forgotten about the battle with the bounty hunter and the hounds of Terra Demorte. It was if some concoction was wearing off as reality came crashing down.

Katie sat up, and breathed the morning air. She, as well, had forgotten why they were so high up in a tree, and why they were there in a thick, lavish wonderland. Josh snuggled close to his mother's side. Notor circled above them and landed on the platform.

"Wisteria, she's gone. She's not there."

"That was last night. Where have you been?" asked Horace.

"I fell asleep under the tree."

Thor rubbed his face and looked out into the jungle. "What will we do without Wisteria? I loved that old witch."

457

"You would do just fine, dear, and watch how you use the word *old*."

They all turned, and standing on the platform was a very healthy Wisteria. They all stared at her as if seeing a ghost.

"How did you—look at you. You are a perfect picture of health. How did—" Thor had a big smile, one might say it went from ear to ear.

"Oh shush. Do you want to discuss this here or at my café over breakfast? I'm hungry," said Wisteria.

"More cheesecake?" he said.

"No," replied Wisteria. "I see your memory hasn't failed you."

Thor smiled at the old woman. "Is it safe?" said Thor.

"Safe? Yes, my dear, it's safe. Do your thing, Thor." Wisteria crossed her arms, and Thor stepped closer to the edge of the platform. He spoke only three words.

"Jungle, be gone."

As soon as the words were spoken, the jungle, monkeys, and birds were gone; there they all stood, in the den at Number 12.

"Well, let's go the café and we'll get some breakfast," said Wisteria. "I'm as hungry as a rhino. How about you, Josh?"

"Me too, Miss Wisteria. Me too."

They all walked down the street toward town. The birds were singing, and the insects were flying around. A beautiful butterfly flew effortlessly by them, and Josh tried to catch it. "I liked the jungle, Miss Wisteria."

"Well, I should hope so, Josh. It was beautiful, wasn't it?"

"Yes, I liked the monkeys."

Just then, Josh pointed up into one of the trees and screamed loudly, "Look, there's a monkey in that tree." Sure enough, there was a monkey, and another one, as they jumped from branch to branch and then sat on a huge limb, making monkey calls toward the group walking down the sidewalk. Wisteria gave Josh a chance to admire the animals, and then, as they walked past the tree, with a slight wave of her hand, the monkeys were gone, vanishing into thin air.

"Hi, guys," said Patty. Your usual table is waiting on you, and I just poured each of you a steaming hot cup of coffee, just the way you like it."

She smiled and patted Josh on the head. "Well, all except for you, Josh. I have a nice glass of milk waiting for you."

"How did you know we were coming, Patty?" said Katie.

"Oh, when you work for Miss Wisteria, you just know these things." She laughed and headed back toward the kitchen.

Roland looked at Wisteria. "She's a witch too, isn't she?"

Wisteria smiled and simply replied. "Aren't we all?"

They all took a seat, and Horace and Notor sat at another table, invisible of course. They had refused to stay home; they too wanted to hear about the night and how a poor, crushed witched managed to be so healthy the next day.

Wisteria noticed the saltshaker moving freely on the table beside them. "Notor, stop that. Stop that now." She scolded the empty table. "That will be hard to explain if anyone sees you doing that." She straightened herself and shook her head. Her long hair, as usual, came to life and drifted effortlessly around her before coming to a stop.

"OK, Wisteria, care to explain how you died at the foot of the tree last night? And what was the deal with the jungle? Thor, I didn't know you had magic like that." Roland slapped Thor on the hand. "Great job. That sure did the trick."

Thor blushed a little. "Well, actually, I don't have that kind of magic. I used all the magic I had on the bounty hunter. That little piece of magic belongs to Wisteria." Thor pulled out the capsule and laid it on the table. "Nice, Wisteria. Very nice."

"Put that thing away, Thor. Do you want to turn this place into a—" Wisteria grabbed her hand and placed it over her mouth. "Please, put that in your pocket. I'm just glad you kept up with it. You know how you are!"

"No. How I am? I don't know how I am. Why don't you tell me exactly how I am, witch." Everyone could see that Thor was happy. Wisteria was sitting with him and alive. He laughed and patted the old woman's hand.

"Well," said Katie, "how did you do it, Wisteria? How did you die and then come back to life? How do you do the things you do and always come back?"

Wisteria patted Katie's hand; then softly she picked it up and held it. "I know about the bounty hunters of Terra Demorte. I've slain a few of them in my time, and a few of the hounds, as well. Once I saw their magic, I knew nothing we had would save us, so I kept quiet. I pretended just to be a silent witness, out of the way, so to speak. I know these brutes, and I knew he would come after me first, so I cast a simple blocking spell on myself, one that no one would know about. Then all I had to do was act out the part. "'Poor, old witch. She's no use.' You see, with me out of the way, the bounty hunter had no fears. So with me down, he turned all of his attentions toward you."

"You mean the hammer didn't hurt you?" said Thor.

"No, dear, the blocking spell caught all of the force; I merely acted out the rest. You see, I had to make him attack you, not me."

"Us?" said Katie. "You wanted him to attack us?"

"Oh yes, dear. That way we could control him, and we could drive and manage the attack. We could manipulate him, and not him manipulating us. Does that make sense?"

"Sure, clear as mud," said Thor.

Wisteria continued, "As soon as I saw the magic he possessed, I knew Roland's bullets and your poison daggers wouldn't stop him or his beasts. Therefore, *we* had to manage the situation."

"You could have let us know," said Thor. Roland and Katie sat and listened to the old woman. Oh, they had questions. They had seen this witch in action before, and knew, if she had a plan, she would only let the people know who needed to know. Apparently, none of them needed to know at the time.

"Well, dear, once the bounty hunter considered me out of the picture and not a threat, my plan started to work. You see, I gave Thor that little capsule, and knowing Thor as I do, I knew he would have it, so I figured that if I was to use my magic, I would use it in the jungle."

Wisteria continued. "You see, with me out of the picture, the bounty hunter knew he couldn't be beat. He became arrogant, cocky, and confident of his victory…this is what defeated him and his hounds."

Roland patted the top of Wisteria's hand, which was still holding Katie's hand. "And if Thor hadn't had the capsule?"

Wisteria's hand dropped into her lap. "Well, dear, I would have had to use this one." She laid a small capsule on the table and then placed it back into her dress pocket.

"I pretended to be dead so all of you would climb into the tree. Then I cast a spell on you to make you sleep. I thought all of you could use a peaceful night's rest. You know, most of the time, people have to pay for a view like that and a good night's rest. I guess that's why they call it a vacation. Anyway, with all of you asleep, I could do my magic and show the bounty hunter who was the most powerful."

"Why could you just not do that in the house? Why did you have to pretend to be near death and then die on us at the foot of the tree?" Katie asked.

Wisteria looked at Katie, then at Roland. "Well, dear, there are things—" She paused for a moment, and then continued. "There is magic that I can do that you don't need to witness. You see, I'm the most powerful witch on the surface of the earth. There are things I can do that would horrify you, and I didn't want you to see that." She smiled and pushed her bosoms out, as if to say, "I'm good."

"What did you do with the bounty hunter and the hounds of Terra Demorte?" asked Thor.

"Well, dear, let's just say that Terra Demorte will never see them again, not for a long, long time." Wisteria laughed, then patted Katie's hand and turned her attention toward Josh, who was coloring the place mat.

The old witch picked up Joshua's hand, patted it softly, and then gently kissed it. "I do have one question that only Josh can answer." She bent over, looked into the little boy's eyes, and spoke softly to the young boy. "Josh, can you tell Miss Wisteria how you got out of your room? I know you know I put a spell on you and your room, and this is twice you have gotten out. Can you tell me how you do it?"

Josh pulled on Wisteria's hand, and Wisteria bent over so Josh could whisper into her ear. She sat quietly and listened to Josh, and then she smiled, patted his hand, and said, "Why, you little stinker, you."

# About the Author

Larry L. Rhoton lives in a small rural town in Tennessee with his wife, Marsha. A paranormal investigator with ten years' experience, Rhoton corresponded regularly with Ed Warren before his passing.

*Katie and Roland Roberts and the Warlock's Revenge* is the second book in the trilogy begun in *Katie and Roland Roberts and the Ghost of Sarah Wheeler*. Many of Rhoton's paranormal experiences and sightings have been fic tionalized for the series.

Made in the USA
Monee, IL
07 July 2020